# The Curious Case of the Vintage Car

# The Curious Case of the Vintage Car

Part One and Two

Dan E. Blackstone

To order additional copies of this book, contact:
Bookwhip
1-855-339-3589
https://www.bookwhip.com

# List of Characters

| 18. | Roberto | aka Rolando Carstalino; courier and old family worker & confidant for priest |
| 19. | Harold | Cart driver |
| 20. | Ramona | Housekeeper with mysterious past |
| 21. | Church Ladies | At The Resort<br>Irene<br>Jacqueline |
| 22. | Rowie | Granddaughter of Ramona, engaged to one man, but is she certain |
| 23. | Alex DuPhont | Rowena's father and died in tragic car accident |
| 24. | Carl | Chauffeur for Ramona's family |
| 25. | Carlos Farrocco | V.P. of operations for Cartel resort |
| 26. | Juline | Aglaea's mother |
| 27. | Novices | Possible spies and transporters of car |
| 28. | Rowena Duphont | Daughter of Ramona |
| 29. | Tomas | Son of Penn/N.Y. crime syndicate treasurer; aka Tomas Dolekczak |
| 30. | Priests | Vatican representatives with their driver and secretary |
| 31. | Euphaosyne | Secret name Carl has for a girl he loves (means Good Cheer) |

# Dedication

*Most people dedicate their works to someone or something . . . I am no different. The person to whom I dedicate this has the following qualifications:*

- *one of the most intelligent persons I have ever met.*
- *one of the most compassionate persons I have ever met.*
- *puts up with idiosyncratic misbehaviors or ideas for years!*
- *the most honest persons with whom you would want to identify. (Good thing no one asked about any of my misdemeanors . . . I'd be in BIG TROUBLE!)*

*This person is easy to love; Oh sure, there are times when disagreements occur, but in the long run, no one could ask for a better companion. And besides, who is perfect?*

*This person philosophizes about the most mundane situations and expects complicated psychological retorts as to the possible outcomes or reasons for such behaviors.*

*This person I have loved for many, many years unconditionally!*

*This person seems to be in almost perfect harmony . . . a pianist, a choir director, and claims I sing off key!*

*If this person had married me when I first asked her after knowing her for only two weeks, we would have been married for three years longer . . . Needless to say her name is BARBARA MARY AIELLO, and I love her very much!*

# Acknowledgements

To Jeannie B. Olsen for her tireless efforts to correct my typing and make suggestions; to Dara, and Beth, for encouragement and inspiration. The list could go on and on. You know who you are: Thank you.

# Introduction

The Curious Case of the Vintage Car was originally published in 2013. As a first time writer, I had so much fun writing this story that I didn't want it to end. So I have created the rest of the story to entertain myself and you, the reader.

# PART ONE

# CHAPTER I

The car careened off the road, skidding for a short distance while the driver tried to negotiate a curve approaching an alpine meadow. Had the occupants been belted, there would not have been injuries; both occupants had blunt head trauma which was responsible for their demise. The car was only damaged on the front end, while the rest of the car appeared to be in very good condition. There was broken glass where the occupant's heads and faces had impacted the wind screen and framing. The internal damage to the engine would have to be assessed by examination. Perhaps the transmission would need to be disassembled. Other than that, the car was in good condition. It was an antique, but in its current state, it was useless.

Had the temperature not dropped suddenly following a light rain, the car would not have skidded. An unpredictable condition created an unsafe situation for anyone who was not familiar with the road. The car with its occupants had just finished the climb up the mountain and would have easily been in the alpine plateau town in a few minutes. The road was not a main highway but a secondary scenic road used in the summer months by hikers and travelers looking for natural beauty. Now it was late October, a time of quiet changes in the weather. Had the car lights not remained on, no one would have noticed the vehicle for hours. A teenage couple returning home saw the dim taillight.

Using flashlights, the young couple investigated and discovered both men in the front seat. The passenger was slumped partly under the dash, as though on his knees in prayer while the driver was squeezed between the steering wheel and the left front door against the dash, as though he had slid in and gotten caught there while reaching for something. Both had been bleeding from their heads, noses and ears; they were not breathing. Later it was estimated that they may have been there for an hour. The youths drove to a phone and reported the accident.

When the ambulance, police and tow truck were leaving, they still had no identification for the two men. Why were they driving a 1932 Buick in this area? It was a four-door antique with two flip seats or jump seats behind the passenger and driver seats. It was a car that would have brought a nice piece of change in mint condition. Now it was basically worthless. It was towed to the junk yard a few miles away and left to end its existence as a rusting hulk. The junkyard men covered it with a plastic tarpaulin.

Another mystery; the registration tag was stolen. The police thought that was suspicious. Why would such a car have stolen plates? The I.D. of the occupants was unknown. No match of prints anywhere, not even Interpol! Who were these men and where had they been? Why were they on this back road? It wasn't until the police examined a pocket in one of the pieces of luggage that they discovered the occupants had come from a distant ranch to the southeast. Only then (and it was by a stroke of luck) did this information surface. There was a photo of a landmark identified by an officer who recently had been vacationing in the area and recognized it immediately.

Tracing the photo, the police discovered that the men had briefly lived in a hacienda at the end of a dirt road opposite the landmark. It was isolated, but some locals recalled the two men and said they kept pretty much to themselves; the old building they rented was quite run down and the owner felt lucky to have had anyone rent it. Evidently the two men were delivering an old car to someone in the northwest, but why were they driving such an old car instead of transporting it by truck or trailer? The answer came when they notified the prospective owners and discovered that a condition of purchase was that it had to be delivered under its own power and via roads of the same vintage, hence, the back roads. The reason was to create intrigue and evidence that it had arrived under its own power. It was good advertisement.

The contents of the car were not out of the ordinary. The car was towed to one of the two local garages and left with the other vehicles on a slope of the lot near the fence. The acreage continued on up to a tree line of spruces, a lovely alpine setting, where the vehicle would end its existence as scrap.

After the accident, the car sat for two years in the back lot. Many people showed interest in the car, but when they examined it and estimated the front-end damage, it seemed that it was too severe to repair. One young man, Piearce, who showed the most interest, had no money to invest. He kept coming back to look at the wreck. The garage owner said he had no release from the owner so legally couldn't sell or dispose of it until the police or an attorney issued a signed release. The young man finally initiated a phone call to the declared owner's attorney and received permission to salvage the car. The towing charges and storage fee were paid to the garage owner and a deal was cut for delivery to a small farm a few miles down the valley near the next town.

Once in the two bay garage/workshop, Piearce started dismantling the front end. He estimated a year or two to rebuild the mangled parts, many of which he could straighten with torch by heating and straightening. Milling new parts would take someone more adept than he was. Searching for replacement fenders would take some time, although they didn't look as bad now that he had taken them off the car.

Obtaining a new engine would be next to impossible, but perhaps another type of engine could be altered to fit the engine mounts. The tranny might be salvageable. The steering wheel was bent a little, but probably salvageable. A slow job, but the end result would be a historical prize. From the windshield/firewall back it was in almost perfect condition. It was a good thing the junkyard men had encapsulated the vehicle from the windscreen back while it was in their lot. Amazingly there were no field mice or any nests in the upholstery as far as he could determine. There was some evidence of discoloration on the rear panels and also on the front panels. These could be addressed at a later date after the initial front-end work had been completed.

Each weekend after work, Piearce diligently spent time heating, bending, stretching and straightening, so that six months later the front end seemed to be in good shape. He had located spare parts for the steering box, the column, and the tie-rod assembly. The wheels and tires were okay, so he was ready to start reassembling, ready to replace the engine and check the tranny. The firewall was unscathed, so that meant the transmission was probably without damage. The clutch assembly might be useable. He had made a much better deal than he originally thought.

His friends both admired and teased him about his spare time activities; as they would say in Scouting, his S.T.A. (Spare Time Activity). When he was twenty two, he decided that to be successful he needed an education and he started night school. Now, four years later he was less than two semesters shy of his bachelor's degree and would attend full time to complete the studies as they were currently laid out. His financial status wasn't the best at the moment, however, it was doable and he could always borrow money if need be.

His excitement mounted as he looked at the car and thought that he could finish it in time for the fall auto show if he spent extra money on parts. It was his pride and joy. A search for a motor and clutch assembly had been made, but to no avail. The block looked cracked and one could see where the line ran along the block: a greenish, rusty affair, outlined slightly with whitish crystalline precipitates, indicative of water and radiator fluids. It had probably been cracked on impact. He had borrowed various tools to accomplish all the work: special jacks, pullers, tension springs, and anything from anyone who had equipment and know-how. Cornelius, the garage owner, was especially interested and helpful, even going online to search for available supplies, which were few and far between. Now he could return some of the tools and move on.

The farm was prospering and his parents were more than delighted to have him live at home. Also, they were grateful that he had decided to go to school and encouraged him to go full time, but he was indecisive because his job offered opportunities that he felt he could ill afford to lose. The school was near his work and it allowed him the advantage of going directly there for his study and research as soon as his shift was up at work. It was only fifteen miles up the valley to his parent's farm. He loved the area and wondered why he had left it to serve in the military.

In a flash-back he thought of his youth and the awkwardness he had experienced growing up. School was not important then, but not altogether a terrible experience. There had been a girl and perhaps if she had not moved to another state things might have been different. She was not beautiful, but attractive as far as he was concerned. He asked her to a dance once and it was a wonderful experience for him. But at age fifteen, expressions of a trivial nature and quantity are magnified by boys and lead to crushed hopes. When he discovered that girls also went to dances, church suppers, and other activities with other young men, his own hopes faded. They were just friends as far as she was concerned and he acquiesced to that status. She was fourteen when they first went out, and almost sixteen when she left. It was a tearful departure for both; a good friend was leaving. She didn't know her new address, but indicated that she would write as soon as she knew. She sent it, he answered and wrote a few letters, but she sent them back with corrected grammar. This did not bother him and he thought it humorous, but the return letters became less and less frequent and his last two were never answered at all. He wondered why and came to the conclusion that perhaps he was too simple for her or not as intelligent as she'd hoped. She, he realized, was better than average intellectually, while he considered himself somewhat below average. In reality they were both the same, but the mind plays games with you at less mature stages of life. He had learned in the service that he was capable and learned the value of keeping himself physically fit! And he did! Without fanfare but with determination. Once, when he felt inadequate, someone told him he was no better than anyone else, but he was just a good as anyone else. This gave him confidence.

Work was easy for Piearce, and it tied in with school. He had been a corpsman/medic in the service and had received the best of training and qualified as a paramedic. When he came home, he worked for a short time on the farm, then as a qualified paramedic. He obtained a job on the rescue squad, qualifying as a training officer. Now, while in school, he did training on Tuesdays and Thursdays and occasionally on Saturdays after his emergency squad stints. He did this once or twice a year. It kept him current. Most weekends he reserved to stay home to study and help on the farm. But now he shared that time with his car.

His mother, Isabelle, met him with a broad grin and open arms as he came home from work early Friday because he had no class that day. He looked at her, smiled and said, "Okay, what gives? You have that all knowing smile that says you've got a secret."

She laughed, took his hand, and led him to the end of the porch facing the barns and his workshop. There sat a crate two plus feet by three feet by six inches. She just smiled as he looked with disbelief! A radiator for his vintage car! He'd left a standing order and a price with the online dealers and they obviously had found one. He hugged his mother, smiled, lifted the radiator and proceeded to the old garage/workshop.

"Dinner at six, you have one half-hour." His mother called.

He placed the radiator on a low work table and removed the crating. There it was! Not exactly shining, but in almost perfect condition for an artifact that old. Some of the coring was dented, but other than that it looked very good. Looking over the car, he checked the interior once more. He had done this periodically hoping that the stains would be removed magically. No dice! Probably the best way to do that would be to remove the panels and seats, and even some of the lining in the overhead. But the upholsterer said it might not be necessary. First, the seats should come out. The driver's seat as well as the passenger seat had a few stains due to the leaks from the windshield area. They were probably water stains from the tarp not being as securely fastened as it should have been.

The engine block sat in a cradle and he looked at it again, running his fingers along that crack in the block with a rag. Odd! It looked as though it came off! He rubbed it harder! Sure enough, the whitish edge was coming off, along with the dirt. No crack? All this time he thought, as did Cornelius, the garage owner, that the block was cracked! He may not need a new engine!

First, he cleaned the crack and examined the engine block carefully. It looked as though the line came from the pulley, which means it might just be a leak of fluid from the radiator or the hoses that was ruptured. Now he cleaned up the inside and made a closer examination of the engine; maybe he could be finished in time for the fall roundup. It was best to dismantle the engine to be sure, but what a find! But it was suppertime!

With a thrill as great as anything he had ever had, he went to supper, thinking this would be a great weekend, a turning point for his project. School would be out and he'd have evenings free to work. With the limited money he could save when not going to school, he would definitely be able to have the car ready for the fall show.

Isabelle was not happy with his decision. If he took courses this summer and went full time in the fall, he'd be finished by spring of next year. In less than a year he could have a degree and qualify for hospital administration work or lab work, and even continue on for a Physician's Assistant, a field that he apparently loved. "You can go another year and qualify as the history teacher you have talked about or you can take over here on the farm and run the business," was his father's input.

At that moment they were interrupted by the foreman, Josephus, who knocked, entered and told his parents that the mare had come into foal, and as no one was around he might need some help. Piearce told his parents to sit and finish dinner and that he'd go and assist. Excusing himself from the table, he walked over, took his mother's hands in his, kissed her on the forehead and winked at her. He left his smiling parents. His father, Matt, said, "I'll be down to help when I finish my meal."

*  *  *  *  *  *
*  *  *  *  *  *

Early next morning Piearce was in the garage, carefully taking the seats out of his chariot. The car was up on blocks and he could easily roll under on a creeper to tend the bolts. While there he noticed that someone had put reinforcing sheathing under the car to protect the old original part from salt, weather, or road hazards. This meant he'd have to cut out or remove the weld from the original frame. It was well done and not noticeable until you got under there and looked closely for the bolts and nuts. A beading of caulking had been put under there between the spot welds and even the painting and undercoating was done to perfection. Why had this been done? All they needed to do was to spray the framing or undercoat to protect it. Extra work! Now what to do?

Sixteenth-inch sheet metal had been used. They had painted over it for protection. It was really a waste of time and energy as far as he was concerned. Well, he had to get to the bolts before he would be able to remove the front seats. He decided to try to remove them from the compartment, so he started on the driver's seat. The bolts turned, but they would not loosen beyond a certain point which meant the nuts were spinning and he'd have to remove the sheathing. Getting under the car again, he estimated the distance to where the nuts and bolts might be and figured he'd get a cutting torch to cut out a small section. On closer examination he saw that the sheet metal was only tacked every foot or so between the bead of caulking. Well, maybe it would be better to take out the entire underside and then replace it later. It shouldn't take more than an hour if he was careful. It would be better if he had the car up another foot for ease of working, so that became a priority. He had two floor jacks, so he proceeded to jack up the front end a foot, place cement blocks and planks under it, release it and repeat the procedure on the rear. Then he reinforced the edges and the middle just to be safe. It was slow, but soon he was ready to get his fire extinguisher and torch to remove the undercover. Even though he could work on his knees now, he was going to slide under with his equipment on the creeper. His mother appeared as he was preparing to slide under. She said she had coffee and a scone for him because she noticed he had left before breakfast. That was a wonderful and welcomed surprise. He drank the coffee quickly and explained he could finish this before the day was out. Then he'd check the engine, and, finally, attend to the cleaning of the interior.

His mother left with the empty coffee cup and said she'd rather have him playing with her grandchildren than a 1932 Buick.

Smiling he said, "Don't give up, I'm still young and foolish, so no one knows what silly person might come along and sweep me off my feet." For the first time in years he daydreamed about when he was fifteen and had a romance, and wondered what became of that girl. Probably she was married and enjoying a great relationship. He wondered if there were any other young women of her caliber floating around anywhere, but that was enough daydreaming.

Now he had to get the sheathing removed. He decided to start just behind the transmission area, where the drive shaft connected. Funny, when he removed the engine he never thought of the covering because it looked normal there. It was a good job and not very noticeable unless you looked closely. Maybe this wasn't a good idea, but then it should be removed in order to check the drive shaft and the integrity of the undercarriage. With goggles and lights blazing, he started. A quick zap and with a small wrecking bar he pried the edge and bent the corner down a little then hit the second tack and popped out more of the sheathing with a little pressure. *This might be easier than I expected.* He had blocks of wood upon which to rest the sheathing so it wouldn't fall on him. In twenty minutes, the entire sheathing was resting on the blocks and all he needed to do was clear out all the lights and equipment and lower the metal to the floor. Five minutes later he had the sheet out from under the car and leaning against the wall of the adjacent stall. *Wow! Now just to get those bolts loosened and remove the seat.* The extension lamp was pushed under the car with his foot and he dropped to his knees on the padded creeper, slid under the car to find the nuts and lock washers.

They had been sealed with gunk and that was the reason they would spin. A few minutes and a few quick turns and they were free. He slid to the other side and repeated the operation. Now he could remove the bench seat and start the rear jump seats. They would be easier, and the rear seat would just need to be popped out.

He struggled with the front seat being careful not to mark the wood finish, then placed the seat in the spare bay area. Now, the jump seats. He slid back under, moved the light and froze! There was a plastic liner all along the area between the front seat and the rear. It was held in place by wire straps running longitudinally and laterally at about four inch intervals, holding the plastic in place. He just stared at it wondering what this meant. Someone had obviously and intentionally installed this very carefully.

His first thought was drugs. *Perhaps that's why they took the back roads to their destination. And what better way of transporting drugs than to steal a stored antique vehicle having a bill of sale and the destination of the recipient?* The internet is marvelous that way. But this? It took time and careful planning to accomplish this! Stolen car, stolen plates, and stolen drugs? Now this dilemma! If he called the authorities, there would be adverse publicity. Now what? Could this be rigged to detonate somewhere? There was a slight bristling of the hair on the back of his neck. He rolled around under the car scrutinizing the area. And what about the rest of the car? The door panels? The overhead? He lay there wondering which way he should attack the problem. Probably using wire cutters to clip the edges and the vertical wires that were periodically attached every couple of feet to avoid or prevent slumping or sagging. A very thorough job and well planned! He wondered if the two delivery men knew of this or if they were the ones who had put it together.

*Okay, start with cutting the edges and freeing the ends, then the middle connectors. But perhaps they went through the floor and could be seen under the rugs.* A quick slide out on the creeper, opened the rear door where he reached in and pulled back the rugs and felt padding. *No, nothing there! Must have been fashioned and attached in another manner. Maybe five connectors across and three rows, that's fifteen connectors.* Replacing the blocking so the section wouldn't fall on him, he started to snip the hangers. In five minutes the entire section was resting on the blocks. His concentration was broken by his father coming in and asking if he wanted lunch. Actually he didn't, but for once he'd rather his father wasn't here, so he scooted out, turned out the lights and went with his father to lunch.

Discussions at lunch ranged from his school intentions to his job activities, to any nice girls he was seeing. This pitch was the second time today his mother brought up the subject of possible marriage intentions.

"Mom, right now I don't have time or the desire to go looking for a bride. Someday one will come along and I'll know, just as you knew when you fell in love." His father smiled and shook his head. Rising, Piearce excused himself and walked over, took her hands and kissed her forehead and said, "You'll be the first to know, unless you have some ulterior motive and plans about which I know nothing." She looked up and said she wished she had.

*　　　*　　　*　　　*　　　*　　　*

　*　　　*　　　*　　　*　　　*　　　*

Lowering the section from the car proved to be as easy as taking down the metal sheathing. There appeared to be about fifteen packages individually wrapped in more plastic. Cutting a section out he unwrapped it and thought it didn't look like drugs. Inside, a wrapping of heavy waxed brown paper, about 12"x12"x3.5" and taped, was exposed. A water-proof block. Carefully he slit the taped area and started unfolding the paper.

All he could do was stare at the pictures of Grant! Ten of them! That meant a considerable amount of cash! All the packages appeared to be the same; so he took one bundle of Grants and counted; four hundred eighty. Why the odd number? Times fifty equals twenty-four thousand dollars, times ten equals two hundred forty thousand dollars! Could this be correct? He looked at the packages and wondered if they all were the same. Most likely, but he'd check later. Right now there was concern as to what should be done. Perhaps he should check each package! Not right now! He picked up the packages and stored them all in the metal cabinet; then cleaned up the wire mesh, storing it with the sheet metal against the wall in the adjacent bay.

Now what to do with the interior of the car! He did the math in his head while he started to remove the jump seats. If there was two hundred forty thousand dollars in each package and there are fifteen packages, that would be over a million dollars. Why would anyone go through such elaborate and sophisticated arrangements to transport money in this manner unless it was counterfeit, stolen, or part of a payoff for something illegal? What to do? Contact the original owners, or the perspective buyers of the car? Evidently neither of them knew of this situation or else they would have come for the car. This must have been concocted by the two men who were killed in the accident. But were they working for someone else who knew nothing of the mishap? Were they just delivering it or were they part of a conspiracy? How should one go about finding out? In the meanwhile, refinishing the car should continue as planned to avert suspicion.

Next he removed the door panels. In the midst of removing the window crank handles, and the door handles, he suddenly wondered if any further surprises existed in the panels. Carefully he popped open the driver's side door panel and was relieved not to find anything. The passenger side panel results were the same. He breathed a sigh of relief and started the rear door panels. There in the right rear were two packages wired to the framing. Walking to the left rear and removing that panel revealed the same results; two packages of the same dimensions as the ones found under the car. Carefully he opened one package and there he saw the picture of Franklin! Ten of them! Now he wondered if all the door packages were the same, and if the first packages were all Grants. He slit each package just enough to exposé one corner . . . another Franklin in each. That's four thousand eight hundred dollars per bundle, and ten per package, that is four hundred eighty thousand dollars per package, times four is almost two million. That brings the total to over three million! Are they counterfeit?

Storing all the money in the cabinet and locking it gave him a little satisfaction. It was three o'clock. The car was ready to be cleaned, but he decided to finish studying and after dinner he'd decide what to do. He had a lab report due on Monday, and really he should start studying for exams that were coming. Too many confusing issues were now facing him. Perhaps he could 'borrow' money from the package and use it to locate the owners or trace it to see that it got to its rightful owners. It was possible to 'borrow' some to finish his car and go to school full time, but with this new dilemma, that might have to be postponed till this riddle was solved. Where to start? What would the reward be if it was returned? Ten percent? That's three hundred thousand dollars! Even one percent is thirty thousand! No time to think about this now . . . hit the books! This type of thinking was interfering. At eleven he finished and turned out the light. He was tired and ready for sleep.

It was Sunday morning, and his folks were finished with breakfast as he came down for coffee. They were surprised that he had slept so late, until seven thirty! He had his coffee as they asked if he was coming to church with them or going on his own. He smiled and said he had several projects that needed his attention at the moment, and one item he was thinking about was that of taking off from work and going to school full time. His mom thought it was great and beamed, asking if he finally made up his mind as to what he was going to do when he finished. History? Science? He mentioned that the medical field was interesting, as well as forensic science. He could switch majors and add only another six months or so to the current program. Maybe even add a pathology lab. Isabelle wrinkled her nose at that, but was delighted that he had finally taken the bull by the horns and was thinking of more schooling. His father said it was an admirable endeavor. If he needed money they would be more than willing to help. Smiling, he said he thought he had a benefactor from whom he would be able to borrow the cash.

"What's the name of this benefactor?" his parents asked.

Thinking quickly he said that he shouldn't give out that information but that a Mr. Grant and a Mr. Franklin came to mind at the moment.

"Do we know them?"

"Probably not intimately, but they have been around for some time."

"Are these people you met in your travels?"

"You could say that," was his comment. Did he lie? Not really, was his rationale.

"In any event, I could continue to do the EMS work, but I don't think I want to do that forever. I'll decide soon."

"You mean that car has your undivided attention," His father said laughingly.

"Kinda, I'm close. Maybe a month and it'll be ready if I can work on it uninterrupted."

"When did you decide to do all this?"

"Last night and this morning. I had a flash thought when I finished studying."

He walked to the garage, unlocked the cabinet, took a few of the Grants and a few Franklins and put them into his pocket; it was imperative to find out if they were real or counterfeit. He then started to check the cleanliness of the upholstery. Most of the stains didn't seem bad, but a few needed more work than he would be able to do here. He decided to take the seats and panels to town for a professional clean up. One stain on the car overhead could be removed when he drove the car into town after the reassembly. No sense making a mess, as they said to bring it in when you get it finished. He loaded everything into his pickup, put a tarpaulin over the load and made ready to drop it off after work or during lunch if he had time; he'd need to call them and make arrangements.

It was time for church and his parents were about to leave when he entered the house. His mother said she noticed he was putting the seats and panels into the truck.

"Good idea to get them taken care of by a professional. It'll save you time so you can get the essentials done."

He decided to make a list to follow:

- Job future

    1. Lab tech?
    2. Teach History?
    3. Geology/Archeology?

- Time Frame: June, July, Aug, Sept?
- Search for origin of car

    1. Check police record
    2. Return to owners
    3. Return to living area of men

        a) Examine farm (after so many years)?
        b) Why?

4. contact perspective buyers for more info

    a) Repeat above
    b) Who declared or dictated the mode or avenue of delivery?

• Locate origin of men; history

1. Why was there no record or evidence of their past?
2. Illegals? Aliens?

    a) Smugglers of illegals?
    b) Smugglers of money? Laundering?
    c) Thieves of international set? A gang?

3. Out of country then no claim of bodies
4. DNA available?

# Chapter II

It had been a fast three weeks! The garage had picked up, the engine, disassembled and reassembled it, claiming it to be tip top condition! They had found fan belts, and looked at the front end pronouncing that Piearce had done a great job with his reassembly. The fenders and lights were sent to a body shop to be refurbished, and they gave him a price on repainting the entire car which was satisfactory with his budget. He'd have it completed by the Fourth of July parade! He decided to take some of the money as a loan and hire a private agency to see if they could trace the unknown men so that he could determine if the activities in which they were involved were legal or maybe some sort of investment that had gone awry. The best part was that he had discovered that the money was legal tender when he changed it to smaller bills at the bank!

Exams were over. Enrollment for summer school should be completed by next week, and he could go to school or work for the summer and sign-up full time in the fall. He had an opportunity to take on a minor hospital administrator's position part time in addition to his EMS duties. The new job didn't pay much, but it would open up an avenue to a more critical care type of employment in the future.

There were two doctors being added to the staff, one in the ER and one as a full time director of the newly formed Dietary department. The Physical Therapy department was also looking for additional help. It was rumored that one of the doctors was looking for a part time assistant. He entertained the idea of learning physical therapy skills, but that would mean extending his schooling for another two years. In any case, the staff was growing, as were the EMS squads. They were not as shorthanded as they were in the R-1s (First Responder) area, thanks to his own and other instructors' diligence in training programs.

It had been an intense period these last few weeks and Piearce needed a rest. Time off for good behavior he thought, so he decided to go for an overnight jaunt to the lower valley that neighbored his parent's farm. He always loved the area, and hoped to purchase it someday and perhaps build his own cabin or house. His father had occasionally leased the property, which was the status at the present time. There were two peaks with a saddle area between and a small body of water fed by a small stream that began as a waterfall. It meandered to the pond, exited, and continued to follow the valley along an old logging road for about a mile to the highway that led to town. The highway actually went for six to seven miles along the valley from his parent's home, arching around in a 'U shape' to where the logging road entered the highway. The western part of the 'U" had an 'S' that led through the shallow pass to town. Thank goodness very few people knew the existence of the old logging road. It was a saving of four miles if one could improve the road and use it. It was a pleasant relaxing area and he looked forward to giving himself this mini vacation in reward for the completion of another school year. With the money he was 'borrowing,' he felt at ease, but continued to speculate about what to do with all the rest of it. This little jaunt and some time alone would give him the opportunity to clear his mind and make definite, realistic plans.

After loading his knapsack, he picked it up and told his mother where he would be.

"As if I didn't know your hide-out-valley. Your sanctuary! Is that rock cave still fit as a shelter?"

"Mom, you know it has been there forever and very few people know of its existence. I don't even think the owners know of it. I still think that if I cleaned up that area that looks like a pile of rocks, I'd maybe find a continuance of the current area and a larger cavern behind. It might make a nice underground house! You know very well that it can comfortably accommodate ten or more people as is, so it is large enough to be a shelter. I'm only going for a day or two, or three."

"You must have some major thinking to do if you're leaving your car for so long. Each time you go, you come back refreshed, so go to it! If you are needed, I know where to drive and pick you up."

He hummed as he left, picked up his hiking stick, and headed out to his valley, about three miles away. Even though it was out of the way, he loved it and felt at home there. Over the years he had left tables and chairs he had made and some other equipment in the cavern. Right now he was thinking of getting there, perhaps taking a swim in the pond, and just roaming around.

One portion of the pond was very shallow so it would be warmer. As he climbed toward the saddle, he kept admiring the abundance of flowers. The leaves were almost full, the dogwood trees were starting to bud, and the few redbuds were just a little past their peak, but a magnificent display.

The path he was taking was overgrown, but passable. Some of the shrub buds were ready to bloom. The lupine were in full swing, some blue bells bloomed here and there, and he saw a lady slipper patch in the small pine and scrub-oak grove. Buttercups were adjacent to a small open meadow near the brook. And here was a wild geranium, and there, columbine! If nothing else it was worth the trip just to walk amidst such beauty in the spirit of spring with Mother Nature's grand displays. *How often we miss the 'Soul of Life' by not taking 'The Road Less Traveled.'* A splash of red spotted off there! Painted cups or Shooting Stars were low in the short grass, a violet welcome mat. In the low wooded area were some Solomon Seals and not much further along were Adder's Tongue. A most enjoyable walk but, ahh, there's the plateau and pond. First, a jaunt through the spring flower filled field, and on to the slab cave.

It looked like a sheer rock cliff to the casual observer, and unless you climbed the pediment-like talus slope at the base and looked carefully, you would not see it. He had found the cave years ago while climbing alone. Shrubs at the base stood near the slab and hid the opening, blending with a ragged Juniper that also helped conceal the gap. Even then, one had to maneuver around the slab to actually see it. Looking back there was an aspen stand near the small knoll. A beautiful sight!

As he approached the opening, he again turned to gaze at the meadow and pond from his elevated position, tracing the meandering stream up the small valley where he knew there was a small waterfall, the streams origin. He smiled thinking he'd stash his gear and hike up to the falls. They were not high; a pleasant display of Nature's artistry. He pulled back the old crudely made wooden door that he'd placed there years ago and entered the hidden shelter. The door didn't seem to be hooked the way he'd left it, but probably the wind and weather had dislodged it which wouldn't be unusual. He walked in and looked up to see the slit overhead that allowed light in. Very little rain entered, even during the most torrential deluge; due to the slight over-hang of the cliff above. Also the shrubs growing out above reduced the direct rainfall. There was a spot or two that allowed one to see the stars at night as you looked up from your position on the floor or bed. He had made the crude bed from saplings and rope, and had placed a double folded canvas padding over the ropes. Placing his backpack and sleeping bag on the table, he moved the bed and picked up the canvas to shake it and spread it over the ropes. He must have folded this the last time he was here and moved the bed as he left. He didn't recall doing it, but that is a minor matter. After repositioning the bed, he then laid out the sleeping bag. It had been awhile since he'd been here, much too long ago.

He had brought a pint of kerosene for the lamp and lantern. He checked them both, and both needed oil, so he divided the oil between them, trimmed the wicks, and cleaned the chimneys to be ready for evening reading. He was surprised at how little oil was left, but that could have been due to evaporation. The fireplace was in good condition and the grate was clean, as was the coffee pot and other utensils. The water bucket had a half inch of water it, which surprised him. Did he leave a bucket of water the last time? Was there slow evaporation, or was there a leak from rain? Possibly that was the case. Anyway, he'd need spring water, so he better get that first. He arranged his supplies and went to get a bucket of water, remembering the first time he'd gotten the stainless steel bucket from his father. He had to pay for it on a 'time period' program, and his father had insisted on stainless steel rather than the galvanized one in the original plan. Sure it was more expensive, but it was easier to clean and did not rust or oxidize.

The spring was halfway to the stream and looked clean. There were not many leaves in it and although it was not large, it was adequate: about three feet around, coming from under a large tree and stone. There were several springs, but this one was the best. Rinsing the bucket, he filled it and looked at the stream in the valley and decided that the water should be put up in the shelter. Then he'd hike up the valley to the falls. It was only another mile or so and the lupine would be blooming as well as the Indian Paintbrush amidst the aspen and it would be a lovely walk.

Piearce placed the bucket on the small table next to the wash rack and glanced at the drying rack where he hung the utensils; did he leave them that way? They were almost opposite his usual alignment. He must have been in a rush when he last left. After rearranging the spoons, spatula, long fork and knife, he turned to the pile of rocks at the back of the shelter, and wondered if there had been a cave in or was it just the natural rock formation. Someday he was determined that he'd find out. But now, to the falls.

Taking a small knapsack he'd left there, he transferred a few snacks, a notebook, water and the usual survival stuff, picked up his walking stick and headed upstream along the logging road till the stream branched off to the small valley toward the waterfall. The walk was worth every step. The late spring flowers were quite evident and the white cumulus clouds and blue sky along with mixed forests on the slopes, made the hills beautiful. The ridges converged as he neared the falls. It looked as though the falls were the origin of the hills and ridges.

There! There is the waterfall and its small pool! Another bathing area. The falls were only twelve to fifteen feet high coming off stratified flat sandstone with a shale cap. The stream above went back to an upland meadow-like basin that acted as a collection and drainage area for the region. He sat on the edge of a large slab of stone that was adjacent to the pool, about fifteen feet from the falls. At times the falls were only a thin veil of water a foot wide, but today it was six feet wide and a thin film of water, like a cellophane window shimmering in the sunlight. The sky and clouds above the falls gave an illusion of a dancing girl holding a chemise and peeking over the top of the falls. It was as though it were alive: as if Nature was sending messages to the surroundings, giving life to the needy, giving hope to the environment and the future, so that they could merge and bond and share. It was a message that said we are mutually dependent, one upon another. The Master of Life springs forth and serves all equally. Each one gets a share, takes what he needs, and moves on to new acceptable habitats.

Looking back down the very shallow valley and the small meandering stream was one of the most refreshing sights he'd ever witnessed. Blue sky, fluffy white clouds, flowers, birds, a soaring hawk, the warmth of sunshine, odors of the forest and the music of the falls and stream, made one want to dance and sing and yell and jump with joy. It was most pastoral. It was interesting how the small streamlets and springs all added to the flow, so that by the time it got to the large plateau and pond area it was a substantial brook or rivulet. Sitting on a rock in the serenity of the pool area was an almost indescribable feeling of solitude. Calming sounds in the lushness of the fern valley subdued extraneous thoughts.

But all at once, Piearce became concerned about the 1932 Buick, and what he could do. Taking his notebook, he began listing priorities for solving the dilemma and choices facing him.

1. Finish the Buick
2. Check investigator he'd hired.

    a. Get report
    b. Find owners?

        1) How much was the insurance claim?
        2) Why did no one come to claim car?
        3) Who reconditioned the car?

            a) How long ago?
            b) What was the cost?

  c. Buyers?

    1) Actual location?
    2) How involved?
    3) How contacted?
    4) If they wanted car, why not come and get it?

3. Why was money concealed?

  a. What was the origin of money?
  b. Was it a robbery?

    1) Any media reports of large ones in that time frame?
    2) Why Franklins and Grants?

      a) Large secret business transaction?
      b) Was it illegal money?

        1) Were there smugglers?
        2) Was drugs or dope involved?
        3) Was there theft from a private home or bank?
        4) Laundering?
        5) Merely transporting money somewhere?
        6) Church?

4. The two men?

  a. Who?
  b. Innocent of $?
  c. Owners of $?
  d. Earned $

    1) Legally?
    2) Illegally?

      a) Why concealed?
      b) Safe keeping in transport? Why? Expect a holdup?

5. How to release the money to the correct authorities? Who are they?

6. Should I donate anonymously?

Piearce looked down the valley, smiled and lay back on the rock with his hands behind his head, then looked toward the falls, the sky, the clouds, the trees. How does one get rid of three million dollars, less his finder's fee? The mystery is its origin! He kept mulling over reasons for the money being in the car; then reasons for his borrowing. That was easy to justify. He was just borrowing it, and he felt that if he had intentions of returning it, then it was justifiable. The sounds of the water and the occasional lapping on the rocks startled him back into consciousness. He checked his watch and the sun. Both read the same! He had slept for over an hour. He reached for a snack, a package of peanut butter and cheese crackers, and an apple and had a picnic.

As he ate, he gazed down into the valley with the falls making melodious sounds as did the lapping of the water along the edges of the pool. The running of the stream blended in and all sounded as though music suddenly resounded from everywhere. It was a symphonic performance that reminded him of a pastoral symphony: Beethoven's sixth symphony. He could mentally blend it in with Beethoven's ninth! Also, if he were a musician, this is where he could come to compose a sonata, or a symphony, or write a poem of some sort. He had tried poetry once or twice but came to the conclusion that wasn't his forte. That didn't mean he couldn't appreciate good literature; however, it is odd how your mind wanders and recalls various events.

Looking toward the falls he recalled how he had often envisioned a cavern behind them, and had gone behind the falls on numerous occasions but his investigations under the overhanging rocks only got him wet, because the projecting rock was only a foot or so out from the wall. At the height of the season water seeped from various fissures, but at low water periods, it was reasonably dry. However, the footing was not stable, certainly not like in the movies when there was a flat ledge or platform on which to stand.

But back to the problem of the money! Who was it that once said "Look beyond the problem, look beyond and see what you see?" Needless to say it was the correct approach, look beyond the problem. What were the choices of action that needed to be addressed? Who were the owners of the money? How to find backgrounds of the two men to determine their origin? What was the history of the car?

He finished the apple and tossed the core into the shrubs, wondering if any seeds would germinate, or if insects would enjoy a meal. *If a seed should grow, would it survive? If it survived, would it produce apples? Where did apples come from originally? Certainly not from the Adam and Eve story, for that story was proven false long ago. No one knows what the forbidden fruit was supposed to be, but they are sure it was not the apple! Apples were first introduced to America by an early settler in the Boston area in the 1620's. But this thought process was not going to solve the current dilemma!*

A splash drew his gaze to the pool edge where the water exited and flowed into the small discharge stream. Again, in the reeds or the tall grass he saw ripples as though something had jumped. A frog? A fish? Concentrating, he watched as there was another movement that looked like a brownish partially submerged body. Maybe it was a weasel, muskrat or even the back of a large fish, but certainly too small for a beaver or otter. He rose and walked to the outflow and stared into the depths of the water. Whatever it was may have gone down stream, and could be any distance along the bank with its many hiding places.

Shouldering his knapsack and taking his walking stick, he took a few quick steps and leaped across the five foot expanse. It was a slightly soggy landing on a reasonably firm grassy area. This trail, or rather the remnants of a trail, had not been used much and was less defined. He anticipated that when he arrived at the junction of the streams and pond area, he'd have to wade or swim to the other side.

The return trip had just as many feeder streams and springs and was equally beautiful, with flowers and shrubs in bloom. He looked to the ridge above and decided to climb, follow the ridge to the meadow area, then down to the pond. He hadn't done that for years. It was only a couple of hundred yards to the top and a gentle pediment. He had plenty of time and the view would be worth it.

Climbing, he saw the new growth and flowers; he had made the correct choice. Wild geraniums, snow drops, and in one small clearing wild strawberries were blooming and would be ready for harvest in a few weeks. At the top the path led into a mixed forest.

He walked the ridge trail looking down into the widening valley with its meandering stream and its changing colors as it reflected the sunlight and sky from different angles. Gazing below he saw the pond and the exit stream turning to flow adjacent to the old logging road with the bridge in the distance that gave the illusion of disappearing. It wasn't much of a bridge and it was made of logs, but it reduced the need to cross in the two feet of water and the possibility of getting into the mire. Someone had placed stone and gravel in the stream originally, where it acted as a dam, but it was decided to build the bridge for crossing. At least, that was the story he had heard. Trudging down the slope he arrived at the crossing point of the streams and pond. He removed his clothes, rolled and placed them in the pack, then proceeded to walk across to the other side. The water was cold and waist deep, not conducive for swimming as far as he was concerned. He had spent a great deal of time on the ridge and the sun was lower and not warm. Also, a cloud drifted across the sun to blocking the remaining radiant heat, making one quite cognizant that it was not yet summer. Sitting on a rock to don his socks and shoes, he realized how warm the rocks had gotten and appreciated the heat. During dressing, he glanced toward the shelter about two thirds of a mile away and thought he saw movement. Was it his Mother? He looked again with greater intensity and concentration, but there was nothing! Maybe it was a deer and was probably his imagination.

Piearce finished dressing and started back to the shelter. He proceeded slowly, looking at the different flowers and types of grasses. The sun was at the setting stage. No one was there when he arrived and he didn't expect that there would be. He had dismissed the idea that his mother would have come out.

After looking more closely, it was obvious that someone had been there! Someone one had eaten some of the canned fruit, and had left a note saying, "Thanks, sorry. I couldn't stay to see who is sharing this mutual sanctuary. Maybe next time!"

Who had done this? Who knew of this location? It certainly wasn't his parents! Then he began thinking of the arrangement of the utensils and the bed, the folded canvass, and everything else. There was no question in his mind that someone else had been using this place recently, and now a note of thanks for the can of fruit. Why didn't he leave his name? Had the person seen him? Probably not because he came from the ridge through the trees and shrubs from an area that was not easily seen from this location. He wondered, which way had the stranger gone?

He decided he'd look for signs of a hiker or the sign of some other mode of transportation; possibly a horse? There was an old trail that went up on the opposite ridge that crossed the stream that fed the falls and then went down to the old logging road. It was shorter, but more rugged. If a person had traveled that route, he never would have seen them. It was getting dark so there was no sense looking for indications of an intruder. No, not an intruder, an interloper, an unknown friend or companion. At least they left a note on a scrap of paper. He lit the lamp and lantern, made supper, ate and sat down to check what he had written at the falls.

What to do about the windfall? Should he advertise the 'find' somehow? If so, what kind of advertisement would be recognized by the correct people without jeopardizing the need for secrecy? You just can't say, "Hey, I just found a ton of money" or anything along that line! The wording would have to be such that one would recognize the true meaning without spilling the beans. 'Without spilling the beans' . . . *I wonder where that saying originated?*

Then he thought about school! What direction should be taken? Borrow enough money to finish school and then seek his benefactors? Should he take the summer to trace the clues that the investigator might find? Perhaps it was best to simplify the options, have two or three priorities and let the rest fall into place. His eyes left the paper and strayed to the empty fruit can bringing him back to the present reality and a new thought of who shared his Shangri-La, his sanctuary? Obviously, someone had known about it for some time and did not just happen to just find it. Or like him, maybe he did not frequent it as much as he'd done in the past. It was amazing that they had never seen each other.

Piearce looked through the slit above him and saw the sky and thought he could make out a star, so he went outside for a better view. Even though his eyes hadn't adjusted to the darkness, he could see that the sky was a blaze of sparkling points and that the hazy Milky Way streaked across the sky. It was an awesome sight, an astronomer's delight. He remembered what his mother had told him years ago, that it was the same sky that the Three Wise Men had witnessed. He questioned that when she first told him, because every night was different, each night brought a different intensity when the sky was visible. On the horizon there was a faint glow, a halo, or hint of one. He smiled and wondered if that was the same view that the shepherds had seen. That was long ago and now he understood what his mother had meant and tried to tell him. That light takes years to reach us, and that the miniscule changes are not discernable to the average person. Now, hundreds and hundreds of years later, even the North Star is in a different location than when all that transpired, due to something called perturbation or the procession of the poles. Too bad he couldn't recall the details of his astronomy course. Looking at the sky he leaned against the rock wall, folded his arms and just stared at one constellation, then another that he recognized. Perhaps another class in astronomy would be fun. He was interested in many areas, but science seemed to be at the center of all, although he liked some history also.

He spent an hour looking and then there was a diminishing of the brightness of the stars due to the increased illumination by the moonrise. The meadow below and the stream reflected the moon just above the horizon. It was very restful and quiet; so quiet. There was movement on the flats, probably deer, which was not unusual. At first he toyed with the idea that it had been his supper guest, but it would have been most unusual for a person to be out hiking around at this hour of the night Although, here he was! It was time to go in; there was a slight chill and a slight breeze. Better go in and read his lists and iron out a course of action.

# Chapter III



Something woke him at 4am. There was someone in the shelter with him! He sensed it before he heard it. An almost imperceptible movement; he heard it again. With his eyes looking through opened slits, he tried to locate the exact position. The sound was over by the crude table! He slipped his hand to his flashlight; the moonlight illuminated the outside but did little to enhance one's vision inside. Piearce pointed his light in the direction of the noise and switched it on! The brightness almost blinded him! There was no one there! He lowered the beam toward the floor and there in eloquent tones of black and white was a skunk. How did it get in? What was the best procedure? The skunk did not seem disturbed by the light, but just stared, then sniffed the air and in a swagger, stagger-like hustle, went off toward a small opening that it had evidently used before. How lucky! No spray and not an odor that was noticeable. Perhaps a stone might block the entrance to deter any future visitations. The smell of food was the apparent reason for its foray.

Extinguishing the light, he lay back down and looked up to what little sky he could see through the slit. There was enough light coming in to highlight the upper part of the cavern in general, but not in detail. He wasn't tired now, so why not rise and shine with the moon. Actually, the sun was making itself known, so there was no sense lying there waiting. He got up to see the morning with all its glorious dew laden grass, and the early sunlight reflecting off the dewdrops.

*Get up! Light the lantern, start your coffee, dress while the coffee perked.* Propane gas bottles are marvelous, but this one was almost empty, only enough remained to supply this weekend's needs. There was nothing like the smell of perking coffee! Drip-o-lators were okay, but there is never the aroma like that of perked coffee. He dressed and headed for his makeshift latrine. The corolla of the sun in the east was causing a pale blue on the horizon, blending into the darker blue above. Some of the brighter stars were still visible even though the moon and sun just about nullified anything spectacular. He returned from the latrine and washed, dumped the waste water and looked down the valley at a lone deer. The perking coffee was at its peak, and the smell was divine, so he lowered the flame and regulated the perking till it was slow and steady. Another four or five minutes and it would be ready.

After cleaning up, he decided to hike the old trail he supposed was used by his visitor. Not the skunk: the other one! Locating the trail was not difficult and there was ample evidence that a horse had been tethered near a birch at the trail entrance. Footprints were not evident, but following hoof prints was not difficult. He ambled along, noticing where the rider had apparently stopped to view and study the scenery. At the falls area, he was able to look down from the opposite side of the valley. The falls looked just as inviting from this position.

Horse prints lead across the meadow over the feeder stream to the falls and down another ravine toward the old logging road. It was a leisurely walk, rugged, but quite pleasant. A casual observer would hardly notice the trail he had just traveled. This was another reason this had to have been someone familiar with the area. The logging road looked as if it had been improved, with less grass growing. Someone had evidently added light gravel to improve the roadbed. He decided that on the return trip he'd follow it back to the bridge to see how far the improvements reached. Evidently someone else had been logging or mowing the more distant lots that his father didn't lease. He finally arrived at the battered gate near the highway. Culverts had been placed there to allow drainage and though he traveled the highway frequently he did not notice any improvements on the side roads. That was probably because the shrubbery and trees hid the entrance. Also, it was usually dark when he passed this area.

It had taken him over two hours to reach the gate due to his meandering and leaving the trail. He took another hour of traipsing the improved road, occasionally wandering off to view a plant or shrub but all the time looking for the horse prints. Just inside the gate there was an area where someone had parked a vehicle. Now he knew how they may have traveled to this point. He had been prepared to cross the highway and look on the opposite side at the old logging trail that also led to an old farm. He recalled an early childhood friend who had lived on one part of the farm: a rental property. That house was closer to the other road nearer the town. It was a huge farm, originally staffed with tenant farmers. But that was years ago, a forgotten era. He would ask his parents about the road improvements when he returned home.

Had he not worn his hiking boots, he would have been 'dewly' soaked. Several cars had gone past him while he was at the road and had tooted, and someone waved. One slowed, tooted, and signaled if he wanted a ride. He waved and indicated 'no', so they tooted again and continued toward town. There was an entirely different view on the return. People say they've been down a road before, but that is only one way! The other direction whets your appetite for new visions, new horizons, with different lighting, different shadows.

To gain the true blessing and beauty, one would need to stand at a strategic location for an entire day, to observe hour by hour or minute by minute, the minute changes that occur. There, a butterfly flitting past, bees buzzing, birds singing, and all passing through a location, giving that extra feeling of glory to life.

Someday, when he had time to spend, he would sit and record the changing light and how it altered a view, the visitations of animals, the sounds, the winds, the interdependency of the environment and the interaction of various forms of life for one another. But then, nothing just sits and watches: each gives something of itself to compliment the harmony of life and love, the giving of self to sustain life. Nature does this!

Energy for life is just changing form; it goes on forever. He considered the relationship between the wildebeest in Africa and the dung beetle. The wildebeest eats the grass, drops the dung, the dung beetle rolls it up, buries it and the dung breaks down and supplies nitrogen to the soil so that grass will grow more plentifully, supplying food for the wildebeest.

Grasses grow to keep the soil in place, to retard runoff to reduce erosion. It absorbs nutrients and changes light energy into chemical energy and then in turn is eaten by many animals (but not destroyed), for the roots regenerate the plants, and so it continues to produce or yield fruit.

Piearce considered how all of nature was interdependent; even animals. When they die, they are simply transformed into a different type of energy, acting as fertilizer to encourage hardy growth or maturation. Man is no different! He usually doesn't return to the soil to be reclaimed. Instead, others plant mortal remains in a marble orchard! What a waste! It is a great point for cremation for then the ashes can be returned to help complete the cycle.

At the edge of the trees before the bridge, the improved road ended. There were a couple of well-traveled logging roads going off into the small valleys and dales where someone had evidently been carting something. He crossed the old log bridge and was on the other side of the stream which was a longer walk unless he wanted to cross at the old ford and get wet. It wasn't a problem as it was only knee deep with a gravel and cobble base once used to insure that wagons and oxen wouldn't get stuck in the mire. During the dry periods it had only about six to eight inches of water flowing, but now, the water was about two feet deep. The safer drier crossing was about a half mile upstream. Piearce could see the rise and the shelter area and wondered if anyone had visited today. He hoped the visitor had come again. He removed his shoes and socks, rolled his pants above his knees, and waded across. During the crossing, the water was about knee deep, but the water rode up his leg on the upstream side and soaked his pants. He should have taken them off. An old, bleached, fallen tree on the edge of the bank served as a seat while he put on his socks and shoes and rolled down his pants. At least his shoes were dry and also his pants from the thighs up.

But disappointment! No one was there at his shelter. Maybe next time.

Now it was Sunday morning again! He had read and finally gotten to sleep around midnight, after wrestling with the difficult decisions to be made; but once resolved, he relaxed and slept till the night marauder tried to push the rock out of the hole. He smiled and thought tough luck, rolled over and went back to sleep.

His intention was to take away the nearly empty propane container for refilling after he had his coffee so that he could accompany his parents to church, but he woke late, seven thirty. He could still make it if he rushed off without breakfast or coffee or the propane container! He wrote a note in response to the thank you note, saying that his guest was welcome to enjoy. He also left his poncho and a pair of socks he had rinsed out but were still damp.

There was an elevated area about a mile or mile and a half from which he could see the trail leading down from the meadow area that looked down on the falls. He stopped and turned for one last view then looked again and thought he saw something. It was a flash of some sort, so he took out his bird watching binoculars and scanned the area. Sure enough, a rider was descending toward the shelter! He entertained a thought of retracing his steps, but he was less than half an hour from home. He smiled and was glad he had left the note. At least he had a secret friend with whom he could possibly commiserate in absentia. He wondered who it was?

His mother was delighted to see him and his father said he had halfway expected him. Did he have breakfast? No. He showered, dressed and accompanied his parents to church. They usually went to the alpine church above the valley and farm, but today they were heading to the city in the low valley where Piearce worked and attended school. There was a district meeting they were to attend.

He thought that while in town he could easily check with the detective agency for any information they might have obtained, plus stop by the EMS facility for his check and any updating. After church, while his parents attended that special district association meeting, then supper, he had enough time to do his errands, and return to take part in the supper. Several members were bringing their single daughters! Well! You can guess who added that last tidbit! Mom never missed a chance. *Okay Mom!*

# CHAPTER IV

The duty agent at the investigation office was getting ready to leave, but indicated that they had received some leads on the former owners and possibly the origin of the car. The prospective buyers had moved, but had left a forwarding address. An agent had contacted them at their new address, an updated resort in an isolated location, hours from their old address. Furthermore, one of the men delivering the car apparently worked as a mechanic adjacent to the storage area for old cars, and he had evidently made the arrangements to sell old cars to couples who answered his advertisement. That was the supposition.

The amazing thing is that other collectors did not respond to the ad, although it was in an obscure magazine. Was this ad targeted? Who was responsible for the ad? The one who placed the ad was not the man killed! A very complex arrangement, a circuitous set-up. Had someone planned this from the beginning? Were the two men duped into thinking they were just delivering a car? No, the investigation at the ranch from which the men with Buick left indicated that they had welding equipment there. But then, many ranches have such equipment. Why the Buick? There were hundreds of ways to transport money to another location. Was the delivery to some place in between? That was a strong possibility! Perhaps none of the individuals involved knew about the money except the two men, who obviously must have known of it and its possible destination. If they welded it in, they may have done it without ever opening the packages!

It was likely that the delivery was to be made to a destination between the alpine meadow village and the buyers' residence. The agents learned that delivery of the car was to have been made two days after the accident occurred. It had only taken Piearce an hour or so to dismantle the undercarriage and the rear panels, so a stop for removal, sanding off the weld spots and spraying the undercarriage could well have been accomplished in an hour and a half or less and they could have been on their way. This hypothesizing created a new twist, and it may have been a means to distribute the money and get rid of two men whom no one knew. Or maybe they had been paid to do a job and never accomplished it. Or, they had already accomplished the job and were somehow establishing an alibi! What a mystery!

Piearce decided to visit the buyers anonymously and listen to their story. The McCracken Detective Agency gave him the data and the drive would only take a day. He could easily extend his vacation, but then wondered if he should stop and see where they had lived when the car was supposed to be delivered, prior to their current address. It might give him some insight about what the status might have been had the car been delivered without incident. What might have happened if the men had not been killed in the accident? Would they have transported the car via a flatbed? And if anyone knew of the accident, wouldn't they have come to the area to retrieve the vehicle? He decided to go and see the original destination of the car, just for background information.

*    *    *    *    *    *

*    *    *    *    *    *

A few days ago, he had brought a fall victim into the E.R. properly splinted and back-boarded with an IV started. He turned the patient over to the staff and attending physician, one of the new doctors whom he hadn't met. She was a trim, mousey haired woman, short, who moved with athletic determination. His report said, "The patient had no allergies, no meds, was not diabetic, and had no past history of illness. It was a ground level fall. The patient fell about four feet and as she fell she reached out for the nearest thing which was a full garbage can on a platform. She fell on her 'fanny' and she claimed she did not hit her head nor lose consciousness, but the heavily loaded can fell and landed on her legs. She has a suspected fracture of the left tibia plus a possible partial dislocation of the left knee which has been immobilized, and iced."

He handed the doctor the preliminary log he had completed. "Nice job," she said. There was a tingling, electrifying feeling at the sound of her voice! There was something familiar, yet she was a stranger, and he had no recognition or recollection of her identity. Her mask and cap hid her face and her name tag was hidden by the lapel of her coat. He took the copy back, finished the report and left with the ambulance to change his clothes and go off duty. He did a few errands and headed home. He was leaving early to tend to some finishing touches to the Buick, but he had a tingling sensation as he looked toward the treatment room at her back as she continued her examination and prepped the patient for x-rays.

The other techs were all gathered at the station when he changed clothes and were seemingly intrigued with the new doctors, dietitian, and P.T. All wanted to know if they were married or had significant others. Although the new doctors had been there a while, their shifts had never coincided with his. He smiled and told the crew to be realistic! What doctor would go out with uneducated morons? They threw paper clips, crumpled paper napkins and balled up paper at him, jeering and claiming he should be so lucky as to find anyone, least of all a doctor, especially one of those dolls!

He left, thinking of how familiar the doctor had seemed to him. He remembered her laugh when the patient asked if Piearce was her husband, and her comment of 'Oh, no, not this week.' It took him back to his youth and his one and only romance. He wished he could have gotten a good look at the doctor's face, but she was behind a bright light so that he only got a hint of her features. Wearing the mask and cap also didn't help.

At EMS headquarters, he obtained his check and looked over the schedule. The crew asked if he was coming in that week or finishing his vacation. They also indicated that they had seen the new doctors doing duty in the ER and commented on how young they looked. However, he wasn't really listening, but was trying to decide whether to delay his vacation or finish it now.

The conversation among the others dwelt on the new doctors looking for a small farm or home near town. The new home could be further out if it was near enough to allow them to get to the hospital in a reasonable time. The only reason they knew of the decision was that one of the cute MDs was talking about it during duty last weekend. All three are 'kinda cute' one of the Paramedics said, and he speculated that if Piearce had not gone into the service, he might have been an MD himself, providing he had the money!

No! If he had not gone into the service, he wouldn't have chosen this type of life; he'd have been a farmer or maybe a teacher if he could have gone to school. The service gave him superior training, confidence and discipline, and when he received his degree he even was considering reenlistment to show his gratitude for all it had given him. No, the service was one of the best things that had ever happened to him. And no one tried to sway his feelings. He was too respected for his experience.

When he arrived at the church supper, he found that his ticket had been paid for and he was assigned to a numbered table, which was not unusual. Looking for it and finding it was not difficult. It was the only table with five young ladies and a vacant chair! *I wonder how this happened* was his amused question to himself. The young ladies were delighted to see him and laughed and teased him about various activities. He knew them all and took their good natured razzing in stride. It was then one of the girls said, "Of course, you know this table just happened to have five girls and a vacant chair, and you just happened to get assigned to that chair . . ." Everyone laughed! They all knew the facts! These young ladies were not fooled about the set-up by his mother! Each claimed they went along with it to protect him from wayward girls at the church! It turned out that each had a boyfriend, but if they hadn't, they'd have been calling him long ago. It was nice to hear and a good way to catch up on all the activities of his old friends and their whereabouts. They also knew how hard he had been working and admired him for his efforts and dedication, especially going to college. They encouraged him to continue and go on to grad school.

Jeannie inquired if he had gotten college credits for his service schools, as she was working on her Master's degree in counseling while employed at the V.A.

He said, "No, I don't think so," whereupon she suggested that he might get as much as a year's worth of credits for some advanced schools.

"Gosh, that means I could graduate now," was his reply.

"Stop by to see me tomorrow with your service papers and we'll check it out," she said. "You were always a bright guy, just too shy."

He had an enjoyable evening and later had to explain to his mother about all the laughter and joy originating at his table. A parting comment was, "Thank your mother, but mention that we are all spoken for at present!"

Needless to say, on the way home he played a game, saying that he had a date tomorrow with one of the girls, to which his mother responded with a sigh, an all-knowing smile and a grin at her husband. He then wondered if he should tell her it was to check his accreditation and possibly early graduation. No! It would be more fun to surprise them later.

*　　　*　　　*　　　*　　　*　　　*

　*　　　*　　　*　　　*　　　*　　　*

The first thing he did was pull out his service file and discharge papers; he was still in the inactive reserves until he finished school. He mentioned to his parents that he might go on a trip for a week just to look into other areas of the region after he had met with the girl for lunch. He needed to finish up some odds and ends.

When he arrived at the V.A., Jeannie took his file, went through it and converted the course credits. After finishing, she handed him several sheets of paper and told him that he only needed to take these to the administration at the school to see if they would accept the courses. It was all in order.

"They may not take them all, but it certainly will save you at least a semester, if not more," she said. "I'd say that you have over two semesters worth of credits! Didn't they tell you that your advanced medical training would count if you went to college? I spoke with my supervisor and she'll fax a letter to the administration, probably the Dean, and will include a copy of these files I have just given to you. If you leave now, they might even get there before you do. If not, you can have these copies."

"How about lunch?" Piearce asked.

"Only if you don't mind if my boyfriend comes along."

"Done!"

They left together for lunch, which he was going to buy for all of them. Holy Mackerel! He could have graduated this month had he known. Wow! Well, that is if they accept the credits here.

Later, he met with the Dean who saw no reason why Piearce couldn't transfer the credits and receive his degree! Processing and confirmation would take three weeks, so technically he would have his B.S in science! Should he tell the family now? Better wait and surprise them with a 'sheepskin' or diploma.

After stopping by the school, he went to the McCracken Detective Agency to confirm the addresses they had given him and indicate that he was going to see the old buyers.

Mr. McCracken, the owner of the agency said that he should remain alert because they had knowledge that there might be more to this ownership story than meets the eye. They were to start a branch hotel, but these people, the recipients of the car, were recalled to the new address, a classic period hotel, where only the 'elite meet to eat'. These buyers were part of a private resort conglomerate that caters to period living conditions that replicate the 1920's and mid 1930's, from prior to the depression to post depression recovery. In construction it was based on that time frame, complete with a uniformed staff! Only the very wealthy were catered to at this establishment, so that's why they wanted a 1932 Buick.

They had been trying to buy old period cars to let guests drive around on their private roads to picnics, swimming, and golf, for an extra fee, of course. A great idea.

"So if you go, just be prepared. I suspect that the couple who bought the car were trying to make extra money, but that is just supposition! An agent is still there nosing around for the next few days. I'll notify him that you are coming, and he'll contact you if need be. Good luck!"

That explained why they wanted a car of that vintage, but not how they were contacted. Perhaps the agent would have some additional information. If Piearce left now, he could be there by tomorrow morning, but maybe that wasn't too smart. He thought he'd drive until he got tired and then get a room or maybe sleep in the back of the truck. No! He had better wait until next week and stay on schedule!

By the time he got home, it was later than he expected. He worked till ten on the car and then went into the house where his mother had prepared a snack for him. He smiled and thought that if he ate everything that she prepared, he'd gain fifty pounds! Most of the time he'd put it into the fridge and have it for breakfast, but this evening he was hungry, so he sat down and started to eat. Isabelle came in and said, "If you had a wife, I'd be able to be free of this chore," to which he replied, "Mom, I've told you dozens of times not to have a snack for me; I can get my own if I'm hungry."

"What do they look like?" she queried.

"Who?" he asked.

"The new hospital dietitian, and the doctors, of course!"

"Mom, I don't know. I only saw one the other day for the first time. She has blondish hair, light complexion, about five feet tall, and wore a mask. Why?"

"A mask? Just thought I'd ask; thought I've seen them myself and wondered. A few new people came to church late and left before the service was over so I never got the chance to speak to them, and I wanted confirmation. A mask, you say?"

"Surgical. And you are testing the waters to see if they are appealing enough for you to introduce them to me."

She smiled and said there was plenty of room for grandchildren here. She then continued saying that she had been riding over near his retreat just before dinner and thought she saw a horse and rider coming over the rise above his secluded hideaway.

"Guess that intruder must be sharing your cubbyhole. Ever find out who it is?"

"No, he always cleans up and leaves notes of thanks and an occasional replacement can of something to restock what he has used. He apparently is a loner and he is appreciative of Nature in all its glory. In the last note, he mentioned the view at night looking over the valley saying it must be great with a full moon."

"Hey . . . maybe he's there now waiting for the moonrise! Let's see, it's ten fifteen, you can be there in ten to fifteen minutes by truck or horse, and half hour to forty-five minutes if you jog," said his mother. "Just don't get shot!"

Piearce filled his knapsack with a few items he'd need and proceeded to the barn and his horse with an obvious thirst for adventure. It had been several weeks since his first encounter with the visitor and they kept missing each other, except through notes.

The moon was rising, illuminating the trail and though it dimmed the stars, diminishing their numbers, it was absolutely beautiful! As he approached his, well, not his anymore, their retreat, he could see a tethered horse and it sent a sort of shudder of anticipation through him. He'd finally meet this stranger, yet a friend, who shared his secret Shangri-La. A person who evidently loved Nature and didn't mind being alone, and perhaps would rather be alone. Would this be an intrusion into the privacy sought by this newcomer, a newcomer only because it had only been a few weeks since they made their initial contact?

A horse whinnied and his horse answered, there-by giving warning that there was an approaching party. He wondered how the person would act to this intrusion; Welcoming?

Cautious? Openly friendly? He reign up next to the mare and dismounted.

"Hello the camp!"

The voice that came from above on the outcrop that overlooked the valley shocked him,

"Is that you, Piearce? Watched you ride up the valley from the direction of your house and thought it might be you!"

Well, it definitely wasn't a male voice! It sounded familiar, yet strange! Where had he heard it before? His mind raced to make an identification. It was a recent yet distant memory! He walked over and up the rise to where a woman was standing, viewing the valley, stream and moon. He was shocked! He stared at her haloed, by the moon, hiding her features, like the light in the E.R.!

"Aren't you going to greet an old friend? We just gotta stop meeting this way," she said.

"Or start," he heard himself say. "Aglaea, is it really you? This is a riot! I didn't recognize you in the E.R., but thought, I know that voice! The light blinded me, and the mask didn't help, but even then I wouldn't have recognized you out of context. My God!" He hugged her, and she responded, holding him and nuzzling into his shoulder with laughter.

"I was going to say something in the E.R. when I first saw you, but felt it would be better if our previous relationship was not known. You look well, Piearce."

"Oh, I don't believe this!" he said; laughing louder. He let her go and raising his arms spun around and looking back at her laughing startled face.

"Gotta explain," he said. "It's my mother!" He then proceeded to explain about how she always wanted to him to meet someone, and of her inquiries about the new staffers, and of her church incident, plus seeing someone ride in the late afternoon, hence this trip.

"By the way, how did you know about this oasis?"

She said, "I spied on you once long ago, just before my family left, while I was out riding. I was too far away at that time and got here just as you were going out of sight, on the very trail you just took here. I nosed around and found this cavern and thought how nice. Periodically, I'd come in but never stayed, especially at that age! But it always intrigued me, and when I returned four months ago, I decided it was the first thing I wanted to see. I knew who was writing the notes and kept the mystery going until I was more established. Congratulations on going to school! Do you intend to go to med school? You really should. You have already established yourself as having the ability."

He reached out and took her hand and started walking down toward the stream. "Are you tired?"

She said, "No, not now."

"As to school, I doubt I'll try for med school. I have a few things to iron out that are pressing at the moment, but after that I'll finish school and perhaps pursue art history or something like that. I know I have the med background, but it is trying and although I love the field, I am more interested in nature and art, so I thought the art history program might be a possibility. I came to that conclusion in the past month; perhaps teaching at a junior college or be a museum curator. I don't really know at this point."

She held his hand tightly and said both sounded like admirable goals. "By the way, I owe you an apology," she continued.

"For what?" he said.

"For not answering all your letters. We, my family, just got so busy that there never seemed to be enough time and all my good intentions went out the window."

He smiled and said she was forgiven, and that he had wondered about her for years. It was a teen-age infatuation that he had finally let go, but mentioned that his mother had asked about her not too long ago,

"Whatever happened to Aggie?" was the question she asked right after I returned from the service and again recently. So you see she never forgot you. She thought I should take a job as a Hospital Administrator, which is another alternative after I get my degree. Also, I'm still in the reserves and could qualify for OCS if I so desired. Another option!"

They talked for the next two hours until she stifled a yawn; he smiled and said, "Sleeping bag time. I assume you have one with you?" She said yes and they trudged up the slope to the sanctuary.

"Who gets the cot?" she asked.

He smiled and gallantly said she could have it; he'd sleep out under the Juniper.

"Oh no! We can share the cavern. You know, talking to you this way makes it seem as though we've never been separated and I feel like a kid on a first date."

He slept on the ground and she on the cot, and the rustling of the skunk didn't bother them at all.

The next morning he sneaked out while she seemingly still slumbered, to get water for coffee and to use the latrine. He washed below the spring outlet, then looked up to see her in the early morning sunlight, smiling as she approached. As she washed, using his towel to dry off, Aglaea said, "What a glorious morning, you look even better in daylight!"

His comment was that she was dazzling in either moonlight or sunlight, "Nothing could dim your glow."

"Oh you flatterer! Keep it up!"

They both chuckled and he said, "Coffee in about ten minutes."

"Any gas left?" she asked. "Do you think your mother will come searching for her night marauder?"

"If she does, she's going to be in for one gigantic surprise! I never asked you, where are you living? I know it has to be within so many minutes of the hospital, so it must be within the town limits somewhere."

"Not necessarily," she responded. "I managed to buy the old farm and am starting to fix it up."

"What?" he exclaimed! "Right across from the logging road?"

"Yup!" she said raising her eyebrows and smirking in great pleasure. "Seems they'll give anybody a loan if they have a fairly good job, even if they can't pay other bills!"

Coffee was better than usual according to Aglaea, "I never was a good cook," she said.

They fed the horses and decided to ride the old trails for a few hours, then return to the farm and reintroduce her to his parents.

"Mother will be ecstatic! But we really must keep our meetings under wraps for a while," he suggested. "Mostly to keep the crew dangling and because there are certain things brewing about which you know nothing and I am not in the position to mention because it might jeopardize the future. Would you mind? As soon as we reacquaint ourselves, would you mind if I dated you occasionally?"

He then explained how he'd felt when she had dated others after their first and only date; how awful he'd felt in the service without knowing what had happened to her; and only recently how he'd thought about her, thinking she must be married by this time and put her out of his mind. But yesterday, after hearing her voice in the E.R., there was a thrill to the sound, and he didn't realize the reason till last night.

She laughed and indicated that she would go along with his proposal for a while, but there was really no reason why they shouldn't date. After all, she had thought about him in the same manner for the last few years. She had made inquiries and that was one of the reasons she had chosen this hospital, because she had done the research and found that he was still here and doing the Paramedic program, so she knew he would be at least sympathetic to her type of work and odd hours. No, this was not a spur of the moment decision. She had not forgotten their early date and always wondered why he had not pursued her more aggressively, but recalled their decision to be very good friends and nothing more. It was the correct decision for the time, but now, "let's see where it takes us."

It was almost noon when they rode into the yard. His mother came out of the house to see who was riding with her son, already assuming it was the other 'cave dweller.'

Piearce said, "Mom, here is my new old friend and buddy."

Aglaea swung down from the horse and approached Isabelle with a smile.

Isabelle said, "Oh, didn't I see you in church the other day?"

Aglaea said, "Yes!"

Then, his mother shaking her hand, held it while studying the face, suddenly looked with amazement at the recognition saying, "Aggi? Aggi? Aggi, is it you?"

Aglaea nodded her head and his mother pulled her into her arms and hugged her saying, "I don't believe it! I don't believe it! It is you! How did this happen?"

Slipping her arm under Aggi's she marched her to the house, calling over her shoulder to her son to take care of the horses.

Another dilemma to solve but a more pleasant one this time, thought Piearce. When should I tell Aggie of my problem? As soon as he saw her and recognized her, he knew his search for a life partner was over. Now the only concern was, does she feel the same way? First indications seemed to support the idea that she has this pheromone reaction also. Unsaddling the horses, he turned them loose in the paddock where they could drink and graze. He thought that this might be as good a time as any to tell her his secret so he could appreciate her advice.

He showed her the car and explained about the trip he was going make to locate the car's true owners. She had heard of the palatial resort and wondered what it would be like; she envied him his adventure. He shook her hand then hugged her when he left her at the gate. When he turned to go she pulled him back and kissed him, saying, "I never liked aggressive unwanted advances by boys, but you are still too reserved. I am a woman now, not a child any longer."

"I didn't want to seem too forward, too daring to spoil any possible chances of renewing something I thought I lost." He kissed her, assisted her onto her saddle, and said, "I still think I should escort you to your house."

"No. I want to ride and think. Have a good trip. Call me when you return."

She galloped down the old wagon trail that led to her old new home.

# CHAPTER V

 **B**efore driving he reviewed the information the investigator had given him about why the 1932 Buick was purchased. It explained the reason for the car of this vintage, but not how they were contacted. How was the connection made? Perhaps the agent would have additional information by the time he arrived. If he kept driving he'd be there by tomorrow morning, but that isn't too smart. He'd drive till he got tired and then get a room, or sleep in his truck.

The "Midnight Motel!" How appropriate! It was almost midnight. He wished he had a few M&M's right now with a cup of something hot. He was about a half days drive from his destination and it would be best to see it for the first time in daylight. Besides, he was tired and sleep was a great rejuvenator. A continental breakfast was included at the motel, probably weak coffee, juice and a doughnut. The room was clean and neat. Even the shower was immaculate! And no drip stains from faucets! By twelve fifteen he had showered and climbed into bed, shut off the light and dozed off.

At 05:45 AM, he awoke wondering where he was for a few seconds, then smiled and wondered what the people were like whom he had come to see. Now that he knew they were part of a large corporation, he wasn't as concerned about getting their money back to them as rapidly, although it would be a marvelous way to gain their confidence, offering them the price they had paid and thought they had lost. Okay, up to stay, no time in bed to lay; start the day in a positive way. After his wakeup shower, he finished packing, dressing and was ready to take on the world, after a cup of coffee, of course.

Surprisingly the coffee was strong, and a bright eyed elderly person was offering a cheese Danish as he sipped. What an unexpected pleasure! Taking a second cup for the road, he left and drove toward his primary destination.

It was ten thirty and his stomach was complaining of neglect. A Danish doesn't sufficiently supply the body's needs even though he wasn't exercising. After all, he 'was still a growing boy' as his mother would say. Just before a small town, there was a drive-in-restaurant, so he treated his stomach to an energy surge. The waiter, cook, and probable owner was loquacious and full of information.

The town had not grown much after they had constructed The Resort, a themed destination hotel that represented the best of the 1920's and 1930's. They hired summer help from colleges, and some locals worked there. A few had even moved into the area and built houses, but except for the resort part, there hadn't been much of an increase in population. Not like some other areas; it was still a rural community.

The big lake on this end was almost entirely owned by The Resort, except for a small waterfront area owned by the town, with docking facilities for boaters. There were rigorous boating regulations as to speed and horsepower for motors. Except for rescue boats, the horsepower was limited to five horsepower or less.

Most boaters and fishermen rowed or sailed, a forgotten art. Canoes and kayaks were plentiful here, whereas in other lakes this size, they were outnumbered by speedboats and larger craft. A pity about them, but this town and the surrounding villages were proud of the ban on larger motors and boats. The Resort especially responded positively to this with the exception of their two or three old 1930's Christ-Crafts, and the rescue boats. Even the excursion boats with their canopies were only 'one-lungers' with speeds up to six knots. "Real nice easy livin'."

The Resort location was not well marked for obvious reasons: the driveway was a plush entrance as though to a private home.

No 'Keep Out,' no 'Solicitors,' no 'Private,' or 'Do Not Trespass' signs were visible. The drive curved to the right and disappeared behind the shrub and tree lined borders. It continued through a wooded area bordered by edged lawns, except in a tunneled pine grove covered with needles. The road then opened into brilliant sunlight coming out of the darker pine grove.

The building was huge, with a circular drive, the center of which had an ornate fountain. A step back into time! Definitely well done to depict an era of 'bygone-days of yesteryear!' One parking lot was partially hidden by shrubs, but evidently was one for the guests to park their vehicles. In front of the entrance several vintage cars were parked, where the 1932 Buick would probably have been had it continued on its voyage.

A great deal of money must have been spent on this place; and a great deal of money to locate, recondition and prepare cars for guests to use. This was a serious hotel or vacation location if you did the full venue. The least expensive room for a week was $3,000.00 with meals and golf, tennis, swimming, and boating included, plus an escorted hike to the peaks, a one day round trip. The cost was just another investment for Piearce if he was to locate the owners of the money he wanted to disperse.

He paid cash, hoping his agent would contact him before the end of the week. No need to waste time sitting around; he'd check the personnel records or work schedule of employees to ascertain whose names were there. A time clock, or some other method of job assignment was probably posted in a laundry area or within a manager's office. But the agency had said not to contact them until their agent approached! Was this a mistake?

His room had 1930's decor. No TV was visible. A Majestic radio stood prominently on a Queen Ann reproduction table next to a Tiffany style lamp. There was a grand view of the hills and the grounds, but, of course, the lake was on the other side of the hotel. What do you expect for the lower price! Dress of the time period was optional, except for dinner. That was formal or semi-formal in the dining room. The café was casual, as was the cocktail lounge; no bathing suits or shorts, possibly tennis shorts of the proper time frame or period were allowed.

There were also private cabins somewhere on the grounds, and the grounds were enormous. Acres and acres of flowering shrubs, walking trails, dirt horse trails, and even dirt roads for cars! Every contingency or amenity was carefully planned for living it up in the past! It was odd to see swimmers at the pool in full body bathing suits with tutu-like skirts and bathing caps. Of course there were the occasional non-conformists in their two-piece suits; quite a contrast! It would be supposed that wearing a 'speedo' was probably not considered appropriate by some, but then, the old 'Union Suit' style swimwear wasn't much different. Piearce sat at a table at the opposite end of the pool one row back from the poolside with coffee and a snack watching the activity

A pair of 1930 'swimmers' giggling, stammering, acting as though they had really just stepped out of an old magazine ad, made their way past his table and proceeded toward the other end of the pool. The only thing missing was a cigarette between their index and middle fingers as they sauntered to the diving board area. Unusual; diving boards were declared a hazard in most pools, but then, this is the 1930's! They giggled and walked to the board, one wiggled her fingers in a silly way, like a person going on a great adventure. But that was the last of the foolishness. She turned, squared her shoulders, chin up, arms and hands at her sides, lifted both her arms measuring the distance as swimmers used to do, parallel to the board, dropped her arms in a swinging downward motion to behind her back, took two steps sprang up, landed on the end of the board and did a perfect one and a half, cutting the water with minimum splash! This was no ordinary, silly, giggly girl, but an accomplished diver! The second one was on the board and with equal determination walked to the end of the board and executed a back jackknife cutting the water with even less splash. With their bathing caps, it was difficult to determine if they were blonde or brunette. Evidently they were playing the part and were probably from the same swim team or part of the staff to induce activities encouraging the guests to participate in adventures. The giggling continued as they swam to the ladders, climbed out and headed for the board again. They spent about fifteen minutes doing various dives, then swam a few laps. Observers ventured onto the board and tried to duplicate what they had witnessed with mostly disastrous results, especially the men in their 'Union Suits'. It was all done with laughter and good sportsmanship.

The girls left the pool, retrieved their terry-cloth robes and approached the hostess. They were seated near his table. Without their caps he saw that one had dark auburn hair, the other light sandy hair so he would have been incorrect judging hair color. They ordered drinks, smiled at him and nodded. He nodded in return and lifted his cup as a salute of acknowledgement. He poured another cup, added cream, a little sugar, stirred and sipped. He looked at the schedule of events that were available that he thought he might attend. As he read, one of the girls stood and moved to a position opposite her friend, closer to his side of the table and almost adjacent to his chair with the normal giggling and small talk and occasional laughter. He glanced at them, smiled and continued reading noting those activities in which he thought he'd participate.

The ladies had finished their drinks and were starting to leave when he glanced at the girl closest to him. Looking into his eyes, she said, "You must not like swimming since you have no suit."

He replied, saying, "No, just arrived and getting acclimated."

"Oh! Then perhaps we could show you around after we change."

That was a shock! "Fine! I'll be here."

Ten minutes later, a record as far as he was concerned, the two young ladies appeared with their period dress of the late 1920's. They were in the swing of things even doing a couple of swirls and spins as a model would do in showing their merchandise. They put their arms through his and escorted him toward the rear exit of the massive room to walk one of the trails, all the while talking and giggling, and plying him with questions as to his business. He said he was in the medical field.

"What kind of doctor are you?" was their question. He had formulated the idea that they might be a couple of hustlers who were out to get whatever they could, gold diggers, or maybe hired by the hotel to solicit or entice investors to part with their money. These ideas are not beyond reason, even in a high-class resort; actually, larger stakes here and more profitable! The walk proceeded along the shore and close to several homes or rental houses, and there they stopped as did the giggling and they faced him.

"That is the home of the people who bought the 1932 Buick. Be careful!" one said as she adjusted his lapel. The other girl giggled again and winked. What a slick scheme! They had him completely fooled! They continued walking and smiling.

"You are both agents?"

"Not really; we do special assignments and this happened to work out for us; we are really here on another aspect of the same case as you. Your agent had to leave suddenly and fed us the info to enhance our case. Apparently you have a fairly high security clearance from their investigations, so we merely exchanged favors. We are not Feds or anything like that; we investigate insurance frauds and foreign money investments that have ties to unsavory origins. Some people are very clever at bringing in money and somehow use it to support subversive groups. The people who bought the 1932 Buick were legitimately looking for a vehicle and thought they had found it until the accident. They really don't have interest in the Buick at the moment. Recently they looked at a 'Cord' convertible, or was it a Whippet, and are waiting for delivery. The couple are a team who may have some interest in the hotel. Seemingly they work for the hotel and solicit various needs. Her husband apparently is in control of the fleet of cars and supervises the outdoor staff. Her tasks are less defined. She definitely has something to do with their business department, whether it's the computers or as a business manager of some sort, we haven't determined. Each morning they leave the house at eight; certain mornings they take breakfast in the cafeteria. Then, she goes to the hotel office suite and he to the maintenance garage and docks. She luncheons in the cafeteria, then goes home, changes and does her exercise routine; occasionally he'll join her, but he usually is out on a trail or at the boathouse or maintenance building. She acts the dutiful wife, but has a fair amount of independent time and must get paid well to maintain her life-style. Once a month they go on a trip for a long weekend for four or five days at a clip, and not always in the same time frame."

"You girls are very well informed! How do you manage to afford this?"

"Oh, we also work here. This is our day free and as long as we entertain the guests to some degree, we have pretty free reign during our off time as hostesses; as directors of activities we get to all the functions, parties, and shows, and lecture the new arrivals as to how one would act in the late 1920's and early 1930's if you still had money." Period History Classics in college was not wasted on these girls!

They left him at the boathouse where he was able to observe the superintendent in action. How was he going to find out about the Buick and how much money they actually paid for the car, plus where the delivery was to be made? Not here! Probably at the old estate they rented a few years ago; a routing area till The Resort was finished. It is possible that this couple had legitimate jobs and knew nothing. It is also possible they know the hierarchy of the conglomerate and about the channels for the money laundering that the girls mentioned might be going on. Why burden him with all that knowledge, when he only wanted to know who ordered the car and where the car was to be delivered and why the specific route? Were they baiting him or setting him up? Not likely. However, the justification for actually knowing the route would be interesting, to say the least. Proof of the car being in running condition was a stipulation, and what better way to prove it than by driving it from its origin to the site of delivery via the highways. Okay, that is understandable . . . but what of the elaborate method of concealing the money? Granted, the unforeseen accident altered the delivery of the car, and, interestingly enough, no one ever inquired about the money so it apparently was not meant to be delivered to the people who purchased the car. Then to whom?

The waterfront was scenic, a step back into time. An antique show of boats and people strolling with parasols and straw hats! He started a leisurely walk to the west where the land, sparsely treed, jutted out a hundred yards, with a boardwalk path ending half way to the point, continuing as a gravel trail. Painted stones lined the path along the water's edge.

At the point there was a small spit of sand that continued for another hundred feet on the other side. The spit hooked along the promontory. There, flowing into the cove, was a thirty foot wide stream that was the source of the sand and mud deposition.

A path continued on back toward the mainland and the mouth of the stream, then upstream a few hundred feet to a footbridge. There was a rocky outcropping fifty feet higher where a footbridge crossed. The trail continued along the stream toward the headwaters. It was not a fast moving stream, so canoeing up stream would not be difficult, relatively easy, possibly something he'd try later. Another two hundred feet was another bridge, for cars. Probably it was the same dirt road he was on with the two young ladies.

The footpath continued under the bridge with a foot of overhead clearance. The construction was a wooden trestle type structure but as you passed under and looked up you could see the steel girders that really carried the weight. The wood was a clever façade. He climbed the stone steps that led to the road. It was a one lane bridge with planking going crosswise, but with two longitudinal plank strips running lengthwise to reduce the rumbling of tires or wagons over the cross planks.

He looked up stream and could see where it curved between rising peaks. A sign said 'Falls One Mile.' Another worthwhile adventure for the future. Deciding against the exploration he returned via the road to the boat house and maintenance building to inquire about the canoes and a trip up to the falls. The superintendent was there next to the boat dock so he asked how far up stream could one go in a canoe.

The man smiled and said, "Alone or with help"?

Piearce answered, "Alone at the moment; the stream doesn't look that swift from the bridge."

"It isn't, but if you want to get to the pool at the falls, there is a two foot drop in about three hundred yards and the walking sign of one mile cuts off a couple meanders, so it is longer by canoe. You can always portage and float down, or drag the canoe the three hundred yards; there is a path along the stream to the pool."

"Well, do you want some exercise?" he questioned the super. It seemed like the ideal way to make his acquaintance.

"Can't right now, but it is possible I'll be available later or perhaps tomorrow if you need ballast," he said jokingly.

"Really, you wouldn't mind?" was Piearce's response.

"Do it several times a season; we all do. A lot of the guys bring their girlfriends and they could care less about canoeing, so we often go with them."

A great opportunity, so he immediately reserved a time the next morning, or afternoon, depending on the superintendent's other appointments. Leaving his room number, he departed.

# Chapter VI

It had been a long time since she had had that feeling, that excitement, that desire! He had ridden back with her along the old road to the highway, across from the back entrance road to her home. During the ride he mentioned he was going on a business trip that could affect his future decisions. He'd be gone at least a week, perhaps two and three at the most. What kind of business? It must remain classified, but it could be lucrative in the long run.

His parents were quite elated over her visit and invited her back anytime, "Just come over, borrow a cup of sugar, flour, coffee, anything at all." His mother was trolling and it was cute and obvious.

Aggie sat in her kitchen thinking of him and wondering, just what was this mysterious girlish interest? Love? Reuniting or igniting sparks from long ago, an unfinished affair? Or sincere re-association based on genuine desire for companionship from someone she admired in her youth, one whom she respected, one who was intelligent and understood her work, was equally enthused about helping others; one whose medical background was at least familiar to hers in the E.R., one who could easily go to med school, but also one who had a great interest in the Arts and History. Each person must choose for themselves in order achieve happiness, but he didn't seem to include making money as a must. An interesting outlook: could be an interesting companion or life partner! Was she being foolish thinking this way? He has only been gone two days and she was already wondering.

05:30 AM. She was almost to the E.R. She had promised the staff that she'd relieve the duty doctor so he could get away with his family. She parked, went in and changed into scrubs and checked the computers. The duty doctor had just finished an admission so she reviewed what he had done, asked if the patient's doctor had been notified. The radio crackled; an incoming call:

"Hospital E.R. this is Y330, do you read?"

"Affirmative"

"We are on route to your facility with twenty year old male MVA, blocked, c-spine, boarded, E.T.A seven minutes. Vitals are . . ."

She listened and readied herself for their arrival. The nurses readied room two: this crew was organized!

The ambulance crew arrived, entered with the Stryker stretcher, pushed it into Room Two, handed the computer nurse a slip of paper with the name, SS#, address, vitals which she took and entered into the system.

The EMS orally gave info quickly, efficiently; standard procedures followed with duplicating the CMS and ready for x-ray. While waiting for the results, the doctor told the paramedic he'd done a good job.

A second ambulance arrived . . . Two more patients. The already busy ER became a beehive of activity as a third ambulance pulled in with another patient. Twenty-five minutes later one patient remained in her care. She became aware of how capable these crews were, how decisive the paramedics were and how accurate their analysis. Going past the Write-Up rooms, she popped her head in while they wrote up their run forms and said what great job they did.

"Thanks, Doc."

"Okay, Doc."

"Not bad considering we're short-handed",

"How's that? Someone sick?"

"One sick, one on vacation, the annual picnic."

"Who is ill and who is on vacation?'

"Actually two on vacation, Piearce is taking a leave of absence, so that makes us short this weekend. You going to the picnic later, Doc?"

They were jovial, yet attentive to their respective jobs. Bantering was the code of the day, she thought as she left for her computer. She reflected on Piearce. She smiled and thought of how quaint his mother was and how obvious! She wanted grandchildren! Back to work!

# CHAPTER VII

A ringing phone woke him. He had overslept. His canoe ride was scheduled for 09:30am. A not so early trip upstream, a portage to the upper stream, pool and waterfall. Perhaps a climb to view the valley and survey the lake from that height.

Breakfast was extraordinary. He had never eaten such a variety so superbly prepared and extravagantly served.

Super was waiting with an Old Town canoe plus a box lunch should they overstay their exploration.

"Ready to pull your weight and paddle against the current?" he asked.

"A beautiful morning; the lake is like glass. I think I can get up enough energy to try it."

"It isn't always this calm. If the wind is generated from the other end of the lake, the waves can crash over the breakwater. A few of the smaller cap-stones were moved a few inches during the storm last month."

"Just so long as it doesn't happen today."

The canoe cut the water as though it were self-propelled, so smoothly and efficiently did the two paddlers work together.

"I see you've handled a canoe before. It's nice to have someone who knows how to balance and stroke without rocking the boat," said the Super.

"Boy Scouts," was the comment. "Never made Eagle but enjoyed the camping and canoeing and hiking. Especially White Stag training in scouting"

"So many guests are 'dead wood' I almost dread taking them sometimes."

The canoe rounded the point of the peninsula and headed toward the stream mouth, then up stream. A slight current was causing a ripple as it entered the larger body of water. Quite picturesque. An entirely different effect than from the hiking trail. The conversation varied from youthful activities to jobs to travel to cars. That's when the super perked up and started a detailed description of the cars they had and how he enjoyed working on them and driving them.

"We have a fleet of twelve at the moment. A Cord will be delivered during the next few days."

"How do you determine whether they are good enough to accept? Do you inspect them first?"

"Originally no. But now we go and inspect them. We had a bad experience with one a few years ago, so now we check them over beforehand and map out the route to be taken."

"What happened? What was the bad experience? They ship a lemon, or what?"

"The car had an accident in route. Killed a couple of guys. Actually it belonged to a priest and he was having it delivered by two men he commissioned, but no one knew they were connected to the church at that time."

"What kind of car?"

"A 1932 Buick. They apparently were conned and thought they were doing a legitimate thing but as it turned out the plates were stolen. Quite an unfortunate mess."

"Did the insurance company pay for your loss or hadn't you paid for it yet?"

"Look, there's a fawn! The mother can't be far off."

They had paddled slowly. Rounding each meander brought a new patch of sun, highlighting blossoms of laurel, white birch clusters, now this small field with the fawn.

"There she is near the large pine. I don't recall the entire episode. The legalities are part of the upper echelon's business. I thought it was a donation and any money that transpired was probably for transport and updating. The priest came from an extremely wealthy family. It is my understanding that he disappointed his father by going into the priesthood."

"So the car came from his family? Did you know this priest?"

"Not really."

They reached the rapids, headed for shore, pulled the canoe, lifted it and portaged to a launch area above the rapids. During that time they discussed the rapids and the trails.

"The rapids are easy to run going down; as you can see there are only three boulders to dodge."

"Must be fairly easy to do it alone."

"It is. If you have any experience there is no problem. Even without it you can drift down and make it, but you'd be surprised how many get dunked."

They traveled another half mile in reasonably calm water. The sound of the falls reached them before they rounded a curve and saw the half acre pool with the falls on the far side. The water fell about a hundred feet from a hanging valley of sheer rock. Breathtaking with clouds and sunlight and blue sky. There was no breeze yet. The reflection on part of the pool emphasized the beauty. It was going to be a warm climb if they decided to go to the upper rock overlook.

"There is a horse trail that is much easier but it's about an hour and a half longer. There is an easy hiking trail, takes about an hour plus, or the more rugged climb for the more fit about forty-five minutes, but involves some climbing. You look like you could take the climbing route and judging from your canoeing and portage you can do the forty-five minute trek with ease."

"Okay, let's give it a try."

It was rugged. Both men were too stubborn to slow down and admit fatigue. They communicated between deep breathing and gasping about their youths and travels. The topic came back to the car between grunts, of how the super had located the car through the ex-priest who was coming out this way to live.

"He'd been in the priesthood many years, but tired of it or became disillusioned. The priest always said he had made a mistake and was too worldly. When he saw the ad for the Buick car he called and made arrangements but was saying that the delivery would be a challenge. Called himself 'Father Tom' at one time. It seems he was connected to a large church in east Europe. We contracted and paid for the vehicle and the transportation by bank draft, made out to an L.L.B. firm. Unusual in some respects, especially for an ex-priest. Then again, how long had he been out of the priesthood? One year? Five years? Twenty years?"

Gasping, they had reached the top in thirty-two minutes. The view was spectacular! The stream origin was from an upland meadow that drained from the surrounding hills and into a series of ponds and a lake. So similar to his own home hideaway area. This caused him to reflect and day-dream for a few seconds about Aglaea. No matter where he looked, he saw a reminder. As he was dreaming the Superintendent asked, "What kind of business are you in? Investments? The cartel is always looking for investors. You almost can't go wrong. Before you answer or say anything, I'm not paid to solicit. Just thought if you're so inclined, this is a first-rate operation. Very sophisticated. My wife and I are both investing."

*Was this a casual remark or was it a planned and calculated manner of duping investors, or a legitimate invitation to invest?* Still in reverie, Piearce said, "Right now I'm just looking and enjoying. A splurge, with my eyes and ears wide open. I came into some money unexpectedly and may want to invest. Time will tell. Where does this trail lead?"

"To the cavern area. Bunch of slab caves and some possible archeological sites they plan to develop. Early American sites, Oh, Oh! Phone!"

He answered and listened for a few moments, and then said, "I'll have to get back, sorry."

"You go. Take the canoe if you want or I'll take it if it is faster for you to jog."

"You don't mind? I know you're capable and it would be faster to get picked up by car."

"No, go ahead. I have food. Think I'll nose around up here and leisurely get back by two or three."

"Okay, Thanks."

He was off.

Looking at the trail to the cave area, he strolled in that direction. The trail was reasonably clear and evidenced very little use. He saw an opening on the way down to the caves, so naturally went off the trail to investigate. The opening was just large enough to allow him to squeeze in. His eyes became adjusted to the dim light and he maneuvered to a very narrow ledge that looked down into an abyss. He reached into his bag and got out his flashlight. Not too many had travelled this route. The abyss turned out to be about ten feet to a lower passage floor of talus rocks about six feet wide. Not large; he climbed down and continue for about fifteen feet, looked back to check his bearings only to see that he had turned slightly and there was practically no light illuminating the passage he had just left. Looking ahead the passage disappeared; actually it had narrowed and made a right turn. He squeezed along for another fifteen feet and the passage turned again. He looked back. Absolutely no light was visible. Not good, at least the floor was not rock strewn. He'd better get back; not good to be here alone. Ahead it looked as though the passage went left. He thought he'd advance to that location and then return.

As he approached the turn he thought he heard a noise. Someone talking? He cupped his light and shone the light on his feet and the cave floor as he proceeded. Someone was definitely talking in hushed voices. He advanced cautiously. The voices were louder. He peered around the corner and thought he saw something ahead. The slabs of rock opened and a dim light shone. The passage ended about six feet away to a drop-off. He was about to un-cup his light and call to them when the higher pitched voice said,

"No! You've got to deliver this sooner than that!"

"Why? We've waited this long, what's another week going to do?" said a lower toned voice.

"The key must be delivered sooner. They need the papers from these boxes to consummate the deal. Listen, I've jeopardized my life by delivering this and I can't be seen with anyone or they'll get suspicious. I've got to go. Good luck. Wait thirty minutes till I'm clear."

During this time Piearce had moved cautiously to the edge and looked down and left to where they were standing.

"Okay. Good luck. I'll leave for my contact as soon as I can do so without arousing suspicion. Why didn't you mail the key and number?"

"Because they'd have intercepted the mail either here or there. Got to go!"

Piearce waited with the light off, hearing odd sounds as the person left; scraping? Piearce decided not to move until the second person left, standing quietly for thirty-five minutes; then heard the other person move. He looked out and saw the man moving about a hundred feet away into the sunlight. He decided to retrace his steps so as not to be seen in this area.

On top he took the other trail and viewed the path down. There were four trails on the top: the cavern trail, the one he and Super climbed, the horse trail and the hiking trail. A man was walking up the trail from the caverns; his clothes matched the ones on the man in the cavern and when Piearce waved and called a greeting, he recognized the answering voice.

Piearce decided to get back to the waterfall trail and twenty minutes later was in the canoe gliding across the pool and then to the stream. He wondered about the two in the cavern and their hush-hush meeting; and what the key was for? And what papers were so valuable that they needed immediate attention? And who was the person who had jeopardized his life to hand off a key? Who was so closely watched that they had to plan going to a hiding place to pass off this information?

Just before starting down the rapids, Piearce was thinking he'd get back to the hotel and watch for the hiker, to see if he could get his name. Then he experienced a quick adrenalin rush as he maneuvered the stream. It was fast and exciting, but not difficult. The trip around the peninsula was easy and fun.

He moored the canoe, took the empty box-lunch remains, and deposited them in a wooden barrel. He went into the main lobby to the adjacent cafeteria, ordered a coffee, and waited. An hour and twenty minutes passed before the hiker came in and ordered a cocktail. The hiker appeared to be in deep concentration: preoccupied, signing for the drink without looking at the check. Piearce wished he could have seen the face of the other person in the cavern, but the back lighting was not conducive. The man ordered another drink, probably needing false courage. Now, how to get to see the check to view the name? At that moment one of the girls came by with her note book cradled in her arm. He made eye-contact with her, casually put his finger to his lips in a Shhh! motion so she wouldn't talk to him and then from his lips he bent his finger in the direction of the man. She frowned, and then smiled, walking on with determination. She got the message. What a bright woman! He'd know by dinner the name of the individual.

The activities director was making an announcement in the formal dining room as he passed to take dinner in the semi-formal area. He momentarily stopped to listen to her invitation to the group. The hotel was sponsoring a 1929 speakeasy dance and entertainment program in the ballroom. He smiled and moved on to take his meal. He thought he had passed the stage of being interested in 'flapper bunny-hops'.

His seating was at a table for four. Apparently most patrons had eaten earlier or had decided on the formal dining. Then, there was also the cafeteria. Roast beef sounded pretty good, with all the trimmings. His dinner came with a complimentary glass of wine. The hostess, dressed in a black and white uniform complete with apron and lace tiara, brought his meal and asked if he desired company. Noting that he was looking at her quizzically, she responded with, "Oh No, Monsieur, nes moi! We always ask to assure that the patrons do not mind if we seat another person at the table, in case they do or do not want to eat alone."

"In that case, should you get a sudden rush, I'll be delighted to have company."

He finished eating, enjoying the rinky-dinky piano of the twenties era. Another glass of wine arrived. He was going to refuse it, but noticed a small envelope under the glass; so he lifted the glass to sniff the aroma, taking a sip while slipping the envelope to his lap, and replacing the glass while opening the envelope. He glanced at the name and replaced the card then slipped the small envelope into his pocket. 'Roberto Carstalino'. Now he knew who had sent the wine and the name of the caveman. That's funny. Caveman. But who was the second person? The voice was too hushed except for the first sharp report of, "No!" It was a little higher pitch voice than Roberto's.

He wondered if he'd recognize it if he heard it again; obviously another guest at the complex, but with hundreds from which to choose! Just stay alert.

An announcement of a movie about the 'Keystone Cops' with Charlie Chaplin was made by the pianist with directions to the theater. The information was delivered as though the movie had just been released, a talkie! The pianist then went into a rendition of 'The Charleston' so several couples got up and danced.

Piearce called the McCracken Detective Agency and asked them to check on a Roberto Carstalino to get as much information as possible. Yes, Interpol if necessary. Then he stopped by the activities director's office, more of a cubby hole, to thank them for their assistance. One was with a customer. The other said, "You are most welcome. Will you be here for the week or the month?"

"Just for the week this time," was his answer. "I may have to leave on a moment's notice in order to follow up on some unfinished business."

"Oh. Please keep us informed and we'll make ourselves available to assist you in your needs."

"Thank you. You have been ever so kind." With the patron still there, he started toward his room thinking that they had indeed gotten his message. He was overtaken by the sandy-haired agent just as they reached the lobby and she said in passing, "9:45pm, canoe dock," continuing toward the theater. He took a leisurely stroll and saw the super and his wife heading toward the hotel in formal attire. She had a familiar look, like all well-dressed people: a movie star? Which one did she resemble?

At the dock he secluded himself and waited. Suddenly out of nowhere the auburn-haired one appeared.

"What? Are you able to materialize out of the night at will?"

"Of course. It's a special course we take. Actually, there is a path that is concealed for the staff to get places without interfering with the mood of the customers. Now, what have you got to tell us?"

He immediately relayed his experiences in as much detail as possible and still kept it short, up until dinner, that is.

"Wowzo! That's the vernacular of the thirties for . . ."

"I know what it means. I have grandparents that still converse in that tongue. I suspect there is a mole here somewhere."

"Could the other person have been a woman?"

"My quick glance was not good. Roberto had his back to me and the other person was in front of him, plus the sunlight gave a haloed backlighting. The hair was a little long I think, but the voice sounded like a man's, higher pitched than Roberto's, but hushed. I don't know," he replied.

"Eat breakfast in the morning room tomorrow at eight o'clock."

"If Roberto leaves, I want to know where he goes. I don't think he is involved with the Buick, but I'm curious, especially if it is a life or death situation."

"He came by shuttle from the airport and so far no scheduled flights are on for tomorrow, except incoming."

A voice in the darkness behind him startled him, "You two have to stop meeting like this."

It was her sandy-haired partner.

"Get back to the game room on the double! Sorry, we have to go."

They just melted away into the semi-darkness.

# CHAPTER VIII

U p early, he showered, shaved, dressed and went down to look around. He decided he could get used to this sort of living. The sun was low, reflecting off the lake. Another calm, picturesque morning with some mist escaping from the lake surface, as though escaping from an entrapment. In half an hour the smoky parts would disappear. So lovely. He wondered if they had any places for a hundred dollars a week. Two hundred? Three? No! This at three thousand certainly wouldn't allow that kind of discount.

At eight, he was seated near a window looking out across the cove to the peninsula, with its slight wispy curling smoke-like vapor disappearing one to two feet above the water surface. The breakfast nook was comfortable and not crowded amid the tantalizing aromas of bacon, coffee and fresh pastries. Auburn and Sandy, as he had dubbed them, picked up their trays and sat at an adjoining table, with acknowledging nods. He rose and they spoke saying, "Sit." The table was close enough so that one could communicate in a normal voice without disturbing anyone.

He was taking a drink of coffee during the lull when suddenly his whole body tensed. A voice said "Oh No!" in reference to a serving and continued to ask for sausage instead.

Was it the voice of the other caveman? He froze momentarily, looked over his cup's brim at the girls, then slowly lowered the cup, lifted his napkin to pat his lips, turned to the server and signaled for more coffee. At the same time he focused on the source of the voices. It was the Super and his wife getting breakfast. She had a deep throaty voice! Could he have made a mistake? He glanced at the girls. Both were watching him. He just stared, then made an almost imperceptible nod. He said, as the server left passing between him and Super, "I'm not positive, but very, very close." They got the message.

Super strolled over and introduced him to his wife.

"Super has mentioned that for once he had an accomplished outdoorsman whom he could trust. Marla is what my friends call me."

He had risen and invited them to sit with him, but they indicated that they had notes to go over this morning and were going to rush through breakfast and pick up a large contingent from Indonesia at the airport. They went to a corner table where Marla spread a note book and while sipping coffee started showing her husband different lists.

"What do you say? Are you sure or not?" Auburn asked him.

"I'm fairly sure. What have I stumbled into? How did you know?"

"Listen. We didn't know. Just guessed. We're grateful. It gives us something to work on. An entirely new slant. Write down as much detail as you can remember. Their exact dialogue. This could be part of what we are looking for."

As he was writing of the cave experience, he included his thirty-five minute wait, recalling the strange muffled noise after the person exited the cave. He knew now it was Marla. The sound outside the cave was too distant, but familiar. He finished writing, placed the sheets into an envelope and watched several people going for sailing lessons. He discreetly left the envelope for the agents, glanced toward the cottage of super and Marla and wondered what he might find in there. Leave it alone, Piearce!

He decided on a scenic horse and wagon ride to mingle with the other guests. There were five other people signed up.

"Good," said an elderly man in fashionable dress of the period. His wife dressed in the 1929/30's well-to-do woman's attire, and their daughter, plus another couple: an older woman and a young man with side-burns. *Perhaps he was her husband?* The daughter carried a parasol, was blonde and vivacious.

"We need another gentleman to be our daughter's escort. We are going to re-enact a day's travel by wagon to the upper valley. You game?" continued the man.

"Sorry I'm not dressed for the occasion, but yes, I'm game."

The team started prancing in readiness as the crew climbed into the open wagon.

"This doesn't look very comfortable," his wife commented.

"Well, it was your desire to duplicate what early settlers experienced, so here we are."

Dora, the daughter, just looked at him and smiled. In her prim attire, she was dazzling. Dora and he sat in the third seat, she on his right; Side-Burns sat on the second seat and the woman he escorted on his right; while Dora's parents sat in the seat behind the driver, with the same seating arrangement: men on the left, women on the right. He thought, *does that mean that women are always right?*

"My name is Paul," said Side-Burns as he turned and offered his hand. He offered his hand to Dora and noticeably held it longer than necessary. Everyone had introduced themselves and while Paul was holding Dora's hand, Piearce noticed that her father, Mr. Hornben, did not have a pleased look on his face. His wife, Madeline, was talking to Jeremiah, the drover, and didn't witness the exchange.

The horses headed up a dirt road that switch-backed to the upper valley. Suddenly Piearce froze! The horses were clomping over a lightly dirt covered slab of rock that reminded him of the sounds he had heard at the cave when Marla left. She must have been on horseback! That would account for her being able to get rapidly from place to place without seeming to be missing or out of place.

The wagon reached the meadow above the falls and stopped. Madeline, Dora's mother, said, "With all this bouncing and pushing for the past two hours, plus an extra cup of coffee, I need a rest room."

Jeremiah said, "There is no formal rest room, Ma'am, but I did bring along a small shovel and some toilet paper. Just pick your spot."

"WHAT?"

At that Hornben laughed, saying, "Well, that's how the primitives managed, without paper or shovel either!"

She sat there looking at him with a genuinely startled look, then turned to look at Dora, as if to say, 'will you go with me', inducing Dora to utter, "Me too, mother."

"Hornben, what are you laughing at?" as she took the shovel and paper. "What did they do years ago?"

"Leaves and grass," was the answer.

"What kind of leaves?"

"Anything except poison ivy or poison oak."

"How did they know the difference in all the types of oak, which was poison?"

"It only took one mistake, then you'd never forget."

They trailed off for some shielding shrubs. Harriet, the woman Paul had been escorting, went with them also, chuckling and mentioning some early experiences when she was young.

Jeremiah had done a very good job of explaining how travelers had made their way following trail signs left by scouts. They got out of the wagon to help push at one particularly steep grade to ease the load on the horses. It was strenuous work, dirty, hot, and demeaning for ladies of leisure. That happened four times before they reached the top. Now, with the "Pit-Stop," all had a chance to walk to the pool and wash their face and hands. Jeremiah produced one towel that he handed to them.

"Where are the other towels?" asked Hornben.

"Just one. That's about all they'd have out. Everything else would be packed away."

The ladies used the towel, each a different corner. Piearce just wiped his hands on his shirt. He was going to put them under his armpits, but they were wet with perspiration.

"We'll head up to the upper area near to the caldera and have lunch."

Getting into the wagon was a brief relief. Good thing someone had put some quilting on the board seat. It wasn't much but it was better than nothing. Dora proved to be quite talkative about her studies in college. She was in graduate school preparing for a possible career in writing.

"Ever thought of teaching?"

"A little, a fleeting thought. I did some work last summer at a newspaper and that interested me more."

Paul turned and looked at her, but spoke to Piearce, "She really is good at everything. She's too modest."

"What do you do, Paul?"

"I'm finishing my MS in finance, probably banking or investments. And you, Piearce?"

He was ready for this and noticed that everyone was listening, especially Hornben and Madeline. Harriet was looking off to the slopes.

"I just finished my BS after going to school part-time. While I was in school, I worked as an EMS staff member and will go back to that until I decide what I really want to do. I unexpectedly came into a great deal of money, so this is my reward to myself."

Harriet turned and looked at him, studying him with a slight and approving smile. She was again looking at the hillside.

There was no doubt about Paul admiring Dora, and Dora didn't discourage him in any way. They talked about everything along the way. The conversation had varied, especially about how tough the early settlers must have been.

Jeremiah took care of the horses and left everyone to fend for themselves for ten minutes, trying to cook up a meal. Harriet had an idea about the uncooked meat that was there and the potatoes. They had no utensils, so cutting or peeling was out of the question. Inventory consisted of three loaves of unsliced bread, seven pieces of steak, raw; five potatoes, tomatoes, and onions in the supply box. At least they had packed it in ice. Harriet said when she was a little girl, they had baked potatoes and roasted meat. Obviously they were all city folk. Piearce finally stepped in and said, "Okay, I'll cook. Get some fire wood and I'll make a fire ring with rocks. Someone get some water. If I recall, during the noon-day meal they would not have stopped to cook a big meal. That would have been done the night before."

In a matter of minutes he had a fire going and gazed over at Jeremiah, who smiled and gave a thumbs up. He evidently was waiting for someone to jump in. Had they not, he would have taken over. Piearce got the message. While the group waited for the food, they went looking for strawberries. Needless to say, Dora and Paul paired up. The potatoes were put into the fire wrapped in aluminum foil that mysteriously appeared after Jeremiah walked past Piearce. Piearce just smiled and knew that had he not been there, Jeremiah was ready to take over. He wrapped the entire lunch together, meat, tomatoes, potatoes, onions, into the foil and put them into the fire. In forty minutes, they would probably be done, especially with the small size of the potatoes. He checked his watch, looked at Jeremiah, nodded and both went off. As Jeremiah passed the rear, he tapped the box and looked at Piearce. Piearce smiled and thought, more food or supplies.

An hour later everyone was gathered around picking the foil apart to exposé their lunches. Miraculously, paper plates appeared as well as eating utensils.

"Are you part of this set-up, Piearce?" asked Harriet

"No, just a fellow sojourner."

"You in the service?"

"Yes, Harriet, I was."

"Learn this there?"

"Yes and no. Also a Boy Scout."

"That's what I hope for Paul. He's led a life of the very wealthy and is a little spoiled, but while in college he began to learn there are other ways. Didn't go to a prestigious school for college, thank goodness. I hoped to talk to him on this adventure. The only reason he's interested in finances is because of his potential inheritance."

"Is that a bad thing?"

"No, but it isn't what he really wants."

"How do you know?"

"I've watched him for years. It's more what his parents want."

"Well, if he's finished his master's, then he probably didn't go into the service."

"I wish he had. It would have given him a great experience and exposure to the real world. Until college, he had been in private schools or tutored. The best thing he's done is to go to the college of his choice. I think there is a girl involved, but he's very hush-hush about that."

"I see he and Dora are a little enamored of each other. Think that's a plus?"

"She is quite vivacious and educated. I don't think her parents seem very interested in the arrangement."

"They picked quite a few berries for dessert in record time. Not a bad sign."

"I'd like to invite you to dinner this evening. Not the formal dining room. Interested?"

"That would be my honor."

"Seven-thirty, if we get back in time?"

"Oh, I'm sure Jeremiah has this well planned to get us back on time."

"Here come the contingent from the heather on the hill. Looks like they are going to learn how to hitch the team. You interested?"

"Not really. I'd rather watch, but I see that Paul and Dora are into it."

"Good. Looks as though her father and mother are also bonding with the kids. Hornben is a very domineering man. Madeline is not precisely what she appears."

"What do you see that I do not?"

"That will be a good dinner discussion, if time permits. Give me a hand?" She nodded toward the wagon and he escorted her there and assisted her to her seat, but she climbed over and took the one that Dora had occupied on the trip up. Did she approve of Dora that much?

 

*　　　　　*　　　　　*　　　　　*　　　　　*　　　　　*
　　　*　　　　　*　　　　　*　　　　　*　　　　　*　　　　　*

 

When going down the steep inclines, everyone got out and attended to knotted ropes to hold the wagon back to relieve the horses and give the brake a chance to work. Hands and feet suffered: hands from the abrasive rope, feet from sliding to hold back the wagon. A well-planned trip to give maximum experience. The home-bound trip took less than half of the time going up. It was an interesting outing, not one he had expected to take, but was glad that he did. People would sleep well tonight after this strenuous outing.

"Seven-thirty?" said Harriet when he helped her down. Why did she really want to see him? Why was he suspicious? Time would tell.

The activities were in full swing. The airport bus was back and the new introductory program was being held, or rather was just ending. He stopped at the desk and there was a message for him to call Mr. McCracken, from the investigating agency. He checked his cell phone for a signal and went outside to call.

"Can you talk?"

"I'm outside."

"This could be an international concern and it looks as though The Resort is very well connected."

"What should be my pursuit?"

"See if you can get a postal address."

"I'll check."

"Stand by. We are also checking that paper work. This could be expensive."

"That's okay. Be frugal."

"Tell your contacts to be alert to sudden changes and to stay healthy."

"I'll relay that. Anything else? That all?"

"Yup. See ya, bye."

A play on words. This just might be connected to what the two girls were onto. Especially since he says they should be careful, and apparently McCracken is tracing the check copy that was found on the two bodies. Who were these people?

Piearce went to look over the evening programs as a ruse to really see if the girls were around for two reasons. One, the warning; and two, the sounds of the horse's hooves as Marla left. They weren't there, so he wrote a quick note asking if it was possible to go horseback riding in the morning. Music filtered up the hall, at least two types; a piano in rag-time, and a banjo/ukulele doing a rendition of 'Oh Susanna.'

After a shower and a change of clothes he proceeded to the dining room, grateful that they did not follow the construction plans to the identical format of the twenties and thirties for this complex. This one has air conditioning!

He was escorted to Harriet's table. She was listening to a trio playing dinner music.

"Good evening, Madam," he said with a formal clicking of his heels and slight bow while taking her hand and raising it to his lips, but never really quite touching his lips to her hand, at which she smiled and said, "You know, that is one thing about that period of time that should be carried on. I miss manners even though I'm not that old!"

"That is quite evident from your youthful appearance."

"I knew I made the right choice in asking you to dinner."

"Are we dining alone, or is the contingency arriving soon?"

"You are ten minutes early. Care for a drink?"

"A smidgen of what you are having, as long as it is not too strong."

"I ordered champagne."

"Fine. I don't usually drink, so one glass will suffice."

"A man after my own heart. Madeline and Hornben invited themselves and they'll join us at eight. My nephew, Paul, is supposed to be here at seven-thirty. He was exhausted and was going to take a nap. Dora I suspect will come with her parents. I invited Jeremiah but he wasn't sure if the management would allow such an arrangement."

"You are worthy of being the matriarch." She laughed, held out her glass; he took the bottle from the ice stand and poured, then poured half a glass for himself and sat. They clinked their glasses and raised them to each other.

"To follow up on what we were discussing this afternoon, Madeline is not the doting mother or dutiful wife she seems to be. She plays a good game, but is too quick on the uptake and doesn't really answer questions. She avoids answers by talking to someone adjacent to her or makes any comment on trivial things, rings, or any number of items."

"What about her husband? You think he is who he says?"

"Oh yes. And then some. He has a lot of money and knows it. He is shrewd and calculating. No one with whom to mess around."

"What about me?"

"You appear to be who you say you are. Honest and to the point. As a medical person you have the welfare of others in mind; your knowledge is beyond the normal. You have a varied background and do not need to prove yourself. That is why I wanted to talk to you. Tell me about your service time."

He explained his training and various areas of assignments, and moved on to his current paramedic involvement and his home life. He left out key periods though, but included enough to give her what she needed to know. Why was she so interested?

"So you have a chance to go to medical school?"

"Yes, but I think I'll hold off on that decision for a short time."

"Why?"

"My turn. Why are you so interested in me?"

"Because you are honest and have worked your way into a respectable position. I wasn't always a wealthy woman. Very early on I was lucky; from an average to way above average financially. My husband came from very wealthy people. I learned to be the Lady he was supposed to marry. I'm very successful at what I do. Now, I'd like to proposition you."

He looked at her quickly, a little suspiciously and started to answer, but she intervened and continued,

"No, not that kind of proposition, but thanks for the indirect compliment. My nephew needs someone to travel with who is learned and experienced and trusting. I think he has a girl-friend. I want to know who she is without hiring a private detective. I'd like to see if he would consider military service or work in other areas beside finance. His parents are too wealthy and very protective. All through school they have secretly hired students to protect him without his knowing. He indicated an interest in archeology and paleontology. I helped cover for him when he signed up for minors in both areas; his parents know nothing of this. Now with his MS in finance he is undecided as to what he should do. I don't want to decide for him, so I thought you, with your science background, might talk to him over the next few days. Befriend him and help him make his own decision even if it is contrary to his parent's demands."

"That, Madam, is one tall order. Where is this girl you think he has?"

"At college."

"How do you know?"

"He never came home for vacations or weekends unless his parents had a gathering. They threw several soirees for him to meet young ladies, but he just leaves them."

"Could he be gay?"

"No! Never!"

"How do you know?"

"He just couldn't be!"

"Here he comes now with Dora. That's in your favor. Would you accept her?"

"At first glance, probably. What time do you rise? Breakfast?"

"Yes. I usually rise early." He knew the conversation was over but also knew she wanted to continue this discussion.

"Good evening, Aunt Harriet. Good evening, Piearce."

"Good evening to you both," said Harriet.

Piearce nodded as he rose.

Dinner was ordered. Dora ordered for her parents, who she said would be along momentarily.

The reunion was full of recalls of their adventures. Dora finally stifled a few yawns, whereupon her father suggested she get some sleep. Paul said he would see her to her room and be right back. He was back in five minutes and there appeared to be a look of relief on Hornben's face and Madeline's as well.

After dinner aperitifs came and Piearce declined his. Paul toyed with his after a sip. Then Piearce rose and excused himself to take a brief after-dinner walk to the lake before he retired. Surprisingly Paul asked if he'd mind company.

"Not at all. Please join me," Piearce remarked as he looked at Harriet. She raised her glass as they left.

While strolling to the dock and lake, Paul said, "My aunt was particularly taken with your presence and abilities on the outing. What kind of work are you planning to do when you return home?"

"I'm a paramedic, so most likely I'll pursue that for a while. My plans for the future are indefinite. I'm thinking of continuing in school and perhaps teaching in a community college, or perhaps research. I have an interest in museums, especially art history, so it is possible I may change completely; change and not continue in the medical field."

"You'd actually do that? Go into a field in which you have limited training?"

"I'd go back to school or obtain a position so I could learn on the job, an internship of some sort. Another reason I'm here. It's decision time. What about you?"

"I'm pretty well expected to go into the family business of financial investments."

"Is that what you really want to do, or is it a parental decision?"

Paul stopped and looked at him. "I've studied for some time to prepare for running the family enterprises. It's too late now. I don't think of it as a parental dictate."

"What other interests do you have? Do you have a minor in an area other than business?"

"Odd you should ask. I love archeology and also took courses in paleontology. Those were to fill out my requirements. I spent a little time at Göbekli Tepe. Fascinating just being there!"

"Have you ever gone on any other digs or any rock-climbing adventures looking for fossils?"

"Several. Took coursework during my month or so of summer vacations from the family business; it was better than vacations," he said smiling.

"That's the feeling I have about teaching or being a curator. I could also go to med school, but my interest is really in art history. So you see, we have similar problems. You have a girl friend or significant other? I see you and Dora have an interest in each other. Nice girl."

"My parents have tried for years to set me up with their type of female. Matchmakers. That is one reason I refused to go to their choice of schools. I went one year to a prestigious university but rebelled a little; and with the promise I wouldn't get involved or embarrass the family, they let me go to the school of my choice."

"I think you evaded my question quite well. I didn't have anyone until recently, so I know how you feel."

"What do you mean?"

"Do you have a girlfriend or significant other? After all the years at school you must have met someone as a friend."

"Yeah, kinda. There is one who is more special than all the rest."

"Does she know you feel she is special?

"I . . ." he hesitated, "I think so."

"Is she like Dora?" He took a stab in the dark.

"Yes, very much so."

"Did you know Dora before coming here?"

Paul just stood and looked at him in the dim light. Not fear, but with a concerned and troubled look. He smiled and shook his head, looked down at his feet and kicked a pebble off the dock and looked back with a smile and said, "You are very observant. Please! Please keep it to yourself. No one knows. Not her parents, not Aunt Harriet, no one!'

"They'll never hear it from me, Paul. Congratulations on a good choice."

"Yes, we planned this excursion last year. We had to make it seem that it was their idea. Her parents are not very receptive to her choices. My parents want to choose for me, as they would in the old country. Aunt Harriet may be my only ally. I don't know. She has been quizzing me on all sorts of topics. Do you think she would approve of Dora?"

"Preliminary knowledge leads me to believe she would. If I were you, I'd take your aunt for a walk, stop, hold her hand and tell her you love her, then ask her to believe in you and tell her she must keep a secret. Tell her about you and Dora and if you feel inclined, tell her about your interest in archeology and paleontology, that you like it better than finance. And the sooner the better."

"Boy! You don't waste any time. My parents might disown me, but I'll give it some thought. Thanks, Piearce. Aunt Harriet is certainly quite a judge of character."

"I'm going to hit the rack," said Piearce. "I'm getting tired and breakfast is one of my favorite meals. Good night, Paul."

"Good night, Piearce, my friend," and shook his hand with both hands clasping Piearce's.

Piearce was amazed at this discussion. He had unwittingly accomplished in fifteen minutes what Harriet had asked him to do only a couple of hours ago. Phenomenal. Just phenomenal.

Now if he could only accomplish his own objective as easily and to everyone's satisfaction.

*          *          *          *          *          *
      *          *          *          *          *          *


Breakfast was a little later than usual because he slept until seven-thirty. At eight he was leaving his room. On the way to the breakfast area he met Dora.

"My, you are certainly up early. Going on another excursion?"

"Good morning, Piearce. No, not at the moment. I don't know what Daddy has planned yet. He and mother were just waking as I left for breakfast. They'll order in."

"Well, if you'd like, you may join me."

"Thank you. That would be pleasant. I don't know anyone, but I feel as though I've known you a long time. I enjoy buffets because you get such a variety of foods; I never got used to eating alone, even in college."

As they carried their trays, he spotted Harriet at a table for four.

"Look who else is an early riser," he said.

"Oh, let's see if she'd like company. She is such a delight."

Also, you want her to like you, he thought. Good politics. Harriet motioned for them to come over with a smile.

"I see you brought a friend," she said smilingly to Piearce.

They chatted and exchanged banter on how well they had slept. Finally Harriet said, "I had a visitor after I retired and he indicated that he had a good talk with you, Piearce. You rendered a service for which there is no way I can repay you"

Piearce quickly glanced at Harriet, then to Dora and back to Harriet. Dora was ignorant of the message and looked at each of her companions quizzically.

Piearce looked Aunt Harriet and asked, "Everything?"

"Every detail and then some."

"Wow! Good memory. Do you mind if I excuse myself? I signed up for a trail ride and I think you two may need to talk." He rose, bowed almost formally, took Harriet's hand and made a gesture as to kiss it. She squeezed very hard and he smiled, nodded to Dora and left. No doubt she was going to address

Dora in an entirely new manner. Secrets would be kept. Harriet said, "I WILL see you later."

Auburn was coming for coffee as Piearce was leaving. He nodded to her and said he was on his way to the stables.

"Oh, that's right. Let me see if I reserved a horse for you. Let me get a coffee and I'll check the schedule."

On the way she mentioned in low tones, "Marla doesn't like horses. She's afraid of horses. Something doesn't jibe."

"Does she go for walks? Could she be faking her fear of horses?"

"Also, Roberto is scheduled for a flight tomorrow."

"Do you have a post office address for any of these people? Roberto's destination? The detective was asking. He also emphasized, Auburn, that you two should be very careful!"

"Your horse is reserved for ten. Where are you going?"

"I was going to explore, but now I think I'll go to the cave and look around. I'm sure that was a horse sound I heard."

"She could be faking, or there could be another person lurking around as an accomplice."

"I was toying with the same idea. Someone who took the horse to her and brought it back, where would the exchange have taken place? Why the charade? Can we get a list of horseback riders that day and the time frame?"

"Gotta go."

Walking to the stables, he glanced at the breakfast nook. Sitting outside on the patio, huddled at a table were Dora and Harriet seemingly in deep conversation. He suspected deep secrets, confessions, and promises were the topic.

He took a lower trail, over the bridge, circled around and followed the directions of the sign 'TO THE UPPER MEADOW' with the times posted, thirty five minutes by horseback at a fast walk or cantor. He hoped it would lead to the cavern.

It did. Along the way he saw bicycle tracks amid the horse prints. A short trail led off to the caverns, where he found evidence of a horse having been tethered. This confirmed his suspicions, but was it her horse? He saw foot prints. Small feet, possibly a woman's. He had planned to go up and over and down by the falls on his return, but thought he should follow the hoof prints instead.

Retracing his path, he followed the prints to the main trail. Here they were not distinguishable due to the traffic. The bicycle tire tracks were there again, leading to a path off to the right; his horse started to turn in there but he nudged it on with his knees to the main trail and bridge. He stopped on the bridge and mentally cruised the stream in the canoe again. Two bicyclists came charging toward him laughing and calling hello. One advantage of horseback riding is that you have a great view.

He was about to continue but turned to watch the cyclists. Could she have ridden a bike and switched? If so, who was her accomplice? And why? He checked the time, wheeled his horse and galloped to see the area where the bike went off on the path. Dismounting, he hitched his horse to a tree and slowly walked the path. Sure enough, there was a grassy area where a bike had been parked or stashed. Also horse prints in the grassy area off the path. It was getting warm; he retrieved his horse and followed the path for a quarter mile ending at a gravel road.

Piearce assumed it was connected to the lake road that crossed the bridge. He headed in that direction at a cantor. In about a mile he came in sight of the side trail he had taken at the bridge. He thought that if the trail to the cavern hadn't been so steep, the bike would have been a good choice, but the horse made it easier for a person who wanted to stay reasonably fresh, especially if time was important. At the bridge he walked the horse to the stables. It was just a few minutes before noon. The handlers took his horse to the tack shop, unsaddled it and released it into a corral.

A cart pulled up as he started walking and offered him a lift.

"Thanks"

"Name's Harold."

"You just drive around picking up guests, Harold?"

"Yes Sir, we have four carriages. Three around the complex and one on the hiking trails. We take turns covering the different areas. Any place in particular, sir?"

"Call me Piearce."

Any place in particular, Piearce?"

"Let's see, it's twelve ten. Let me off at the cafeteria, I'll grab a quick sandwich and head to the boat basin."

"Going sailing?"

"No, probably a canoe ride or just walk around."

Lunch consisted of a Tuna Melt, small salad and water. Most people took their lunch in the dining room, living their roles of the thirties. He wasn't into that and preferred the small cafeteria. As he was getting ready to leave, a voice said, "Piearce, how can I ever thank you?" He turned in his chair, rose and greeted Harriet.

She gave him a hug, looked up at him and continued while holding his arms.

"Now I have a reason for being here. I'm having lunch with the Hornben's. My mission? To encourage the idea of what a nice couple my nephew and their daughter make. Those two did a marvelous job of keeping their secret these past few years. I was completely in the dark, and so thankful I met her and drew some positive conclusions before they revealed their relationship. If I can help you in any way, I am yours to command. And, if there is a wedding, I'll need your address in order to send an invitation! She is intelligent and well mannered: delightful! More than I had hoped for."

"You flatter me. By all means, if you want a commoner to attend, I'd be delighted. Thank you."

"I'm going to have lunch. Dinner tonight? Same time and place?"

"Of course, unless I'm called away."

"This is your vacation; you really do not need to respond, do you?" She asked searchingly.

"See you at seven-thirty."

He walked to the boathouse. The sun was hot. A light refreshing breeze was coming off the lake. A number of sail boats were racing, with canoers getting in the way. He looked toward the point, thinking of walking over there again, when a voice said, "Canoeing again?"

"Hi, Super. No. Was considering a walk to The Point unless, of course, you force me into a canoe."

"Have you considered making an investment?"

"Truthfully, no. Tell me something. You peaked my interest about that Buick the other day. Who did you pay the money to, if you can recall? Did you ever find out where the car was abandoned?"

"As I mentioned, the vehicle may have been stolen. That's maybe. It was once owned by or traced to a priest. He was supposedly to meet with us, but due to the unfortunate circumstances, we never met him. They did find out that he had retired. They say his family is gone, long gone. He alone was left of the family. It seems the family was part of a crime syndicate and he was the only one above suspicion because he was a priest."

"Boy, that's interesting."

"He bought a retreat in which to retire; he even made arrangements for a housekeeper to come with him. It isn't too far from here. Someone said the housekeeper had children but no one knows for sure."

"Is she there now?"

"I believe so. The house is located about twenty to thirty miles northwest further into the interior. There are several small lakes in that area and he purchased a home on one of them. Of course this is mostly hearsay. Stuff the insurance company dug up when they wanted to settle. He died unexpectedly just before the accident."

"What was the name of the insurance company?"

"Benefactor or Benevolent Life. Out of California. By the way, that housekeeper pays a visit here periodically with a group of new-found cronies from a church or religious group. They come for the show and dinner. There seems to be some connection to certain religious organizations and the management allows them to visit without registering ahead of time."

"How the heck was a priest able to purchase a home on a lake and afford a housekeeper on his kind of retirement? I thought they went to a hermitage or church home somewhere.

"That's old fashioned; some of them have benefactors, some have wealthy supporters or come from wealthy families. Besides, this isn't an expensive area to live in except for The Resort. Plus, recall what I said about his apparent dissatisfaction with the priesthood and inheritance."

"Maybe that explains the Buick; did he report it stolen? How did he get mixed up in this affair? Sounds unusual, or did he sell the car to the people and they had it stolen from them? It's very confusing."

"Shit! Look out there. I've got to take a boat out to rescue a sailboat that just flipped. Wanna come and we can continue this discussion? Do you know how to sail?"

"Yes."

"Good. You can sail it back."

The sailboat was half a mile out. It was righted, bailed, then Super left with the couple, who shouldn't have been allowed to take a sailboat in the first place. Super was waiting at the dock when Piearce brought the boat in.

"Thanks, that was a big help. I owe you."

"No problem. I enjoyed it; brought back fond memories."

*          *          *          *          *          *
    *          *          *          *          *          *

The rescued couple were nowhere in sight, but Harriet was walking back from the point with Dora and hailed him, so he excused himself from the Super saying, "We'll talk again," as he responded to Harriet's call. He wondered how she made out with the Hornben's.

"You have been part of the subject of our conversation this afternoon. Dora says she has a cousin she'd like to introduce you to; that you and her cousin would make a perfect pair," she said smiling.

"Harriet! How could you? He's probably married." Dora blushed.

He laughed and saw the twinkle in Harriet's eyes. She was a tease and outspoken.

"Dora, I'm single and my mother has been after me for years to marry and produce grandchildren; it seems to be a problem eligible bachelors have with their mothers. When I'm ready, I'll meet the right woman. But! She'll probably be married or engaged or not interested in me. Thanks for the thought and I know the concern was for your cousin's welfare, and I am flattered that you thought me a good candidate. What about your marriage? Speak for yourself, said 'Priscilla' to 'John Alden'."

They chuckled at that and began some serious talk about Paul's parent's concerns, especially his possible pursuit of archaeology or history of ancient civilizations. Dora continued to describe how Paul really gets so caught up in his discussions that they almost become a lecture.

"I'm just as bad sometimes when I'm with him. We go to libraries and I question him about details; that causes him to want to fly off and visit some site just to see it and read the findings first hand."

"So don't ask him any questions about that at dinner tonight," was Harriet's smirking statement. "I'd like to have an early dinner this evening if you don't mind; say seven?"

Harriet slipped her arm through his left arm and Dora took the right as they walked the path to the hotel, both talking at the same time about how well things had turned out and all the fears that never materialized.

"Now if we can only get my parents to really accept Paul."

"I did my best at lunch, and they had to agree that he was above average compared to past candidates," remarked Harriet.

"Well, I see you have monopolized both my girls in one afternoon," came Paul's voice from the patio.

"I knew I'd never get away with it. I told both of them they'd have to be more discreet, but no! Now look at the trouble I'm in."

Dora went to Paul, gave a quick kiss, took his hand and turned back toward Harriet and Piearce saying,

"Your aunt is marvelous and most intelligent about everything. All that secrecy and anguish we went through for naught. Silly how we magnify our fears, thinking we are alone when in reality we are surrounded with love and support. I hope my parents are impressed and accepting. And what have you been up to, Paul, while your aunt and I walked and talked?"

"Played golf with a foursome, with clubs that were made before I was born."

"I'm going to freshen up before dinner. See you youngsters later," said Harriet as she proceeded to the elevator.

Auburn caught Piearce's eye so he excused himself and walked to the corridor while the love birds busily headed toward a 'speak-easy'.

"Roberto is going to leave tomorrow. His ticket eventually is to Egypt."

"Egypt! Why there?"

"After Cairo he's eventually going to some other place called Nog Komody, or something like that, where ever that is," she said, looking at her notes. "Also, something called or sounds like Nagharmundy. Also, Super has an interesting background. He's traveled extensively in the service of the Canadian diplomatic corps as a secretary to one of the ambassadors, or ministers, but had a little trouble so was discharged about five or six years ago. Marla married him about five years ago. She is a world traveler and speaks three languages fluently besides English.

"That explains Super's speech pattern. His intonation is very good so it's possible he speaks another language. Most likely French if he was with the diplomatic service."

"Here is a flight schedule and possible connections should you want to travel."

"I may not need to; I received info today that leads me to believe a possible answer may be in this area. I'll let you know."

Super had mentioned that the housekeeper was in the general dining room with her cronies so he thought he'd venture in for a cup of coffee and a snack of some sort and a possible glimpse of the housekeeper. Just by chance they were seating him next to a table of fashionably dressed elderly ladies who looked to be in the midst of their luncheon or finishing it.

"Good afternoon," he said to the women sitting at the table as they were seating him. Although not young, they were attractive and joyfully smiling. He bowed slightly as he issued his greeting. They acknowledged his salutation with the nodding of heads and smiles and casual scrutiny. A woman never does a casual appraisal! In one glance she checks the clothes, shoeshine, tie, shirt ironed, hair do, cleanliness and whether he is wearing a wedding ring and married.

He ordered a coffee and a muffin and was sitting to observe the group. The priest's housekeeper was among the ladies and he wondered which one when the Super appeared and stopped by their table and spoke with one of the ladies. She smiled and patted him on the arm as he left and she held eye contact with Piearce for a fraction of a second. To the casual observer, there would have been no notice. Piearce felt an electric charge in that instant. A contact had been made, as fleeting as it was. There was an introductory connection.

When their dessert orders were taken, he couldn't help but smile as they debated whether the caloric intake was worth the consumption.

"Not me," one of the ladies announced. "I just took off three pounds after two months of continuous effort. It angers me that a delicacy weighing a few ounces can quadruple in weight as it goes through the digestive tract."

"It wouldn't be so bad if it just passed through but it acts like a virus and infects every cell in the body to retain their waist products, that's W-A-I-S-T products, advertising their presence."

"I wish they hadn't stopped making girdles; at least I felt as though it didn't show when I put one on."

"Yeah! But it caused circulation constriction and breathing problems."

"The heck! Let it hang out!"

They all ordered dessert.

One of the ladies asked, "Young man, how about helping me out and eating half my dessert? That way I won't feel guilty about not eating it; hate to see it tossed out."

He smiled and said, "Just eat half and take the rest to your room."

He was getting ready to leave and wished them all a pleasant day and stay.

"Where are you from? And why is such a dashing young man eating alone?"

One thing that comes with advanced years is the ability to ask personal questions of someone without a feeling of committing an offense. He mentioned his home area and that he was here on holiday to think out some future plans. The housekeeper perked up at the mention of his home area.

"Come, have a coffee with us and entertain some old ladies who may have eligible daughters, or grand-daughters."

"Speak for yourself, Irene. Jacqueline here is close to his age." At that everyone laughed and Jacqueline cowered. There was apparently much hidden humor, more than he first suspected.

The housekeeper, Ramona by name, spoke to him saying, "I understand you have a keen interest in old cars."

To which he replied, "Yes. And that is another reason I am here. I came to see some of the relics."

"The cars, you mean," laughed a bluish haired dessert lover.

These women may be old in body, but their spirits were young and their laughter echoed from their youth as though spirits from a by-gone era possessed the bodies periodically reminiscent of a care-free existence. Their aura captivated him. He felt welcomed, not at all what he had expected.

"Join us for a second cup of coffee." At that, several chairs were shifted to make room for him. He sat next to Ramona, thanking them all for the invitation, stating that he could only stay for a few moments.

They inquired about his work and he gave a brief background history, the same as he had to everyone he'd met. During the chatting and congratulations on his degree and recent financial acquisition, Ramona dropped her fork; while attempting to catch it, it pierced her hand. He immediately took a napkin and some ice from the pitcher doing his first-aid routine; then he took a Band-Aid from his pocket, tore it open and applied it. It was too small, so he put the napkin back on, placed the soiled Band-Aid and wrap back in his pocket, then accompanied her to the aid station.

"You should have them check it out just for safety reasons. I don't think it will need much more than a compress and tape."

While walking with her to the Infirmary, she asked about the 1932 Buick. The Super had mentioned it to her when he came in.

"That is a long story. I liked the car style and tried to buy one several times. There was one that had been in an accident in my area that I tried to buy for a long time. It was coincidental that the Super and I discovered that mutual interest and now you have mentioned it. There do not seem to be any secrets around here."

"Not so. I just happened to know who the owner was."

Piearce played it cool and said, "This isn't coincidence, it's Providence working. Here is the infirmary. May I see you later to talk about this?"

"Of course. Here is my card. We are in Room 227 till the evening performance, then about an hour's drive home. If we don't see you today, feel free to call on me at my home." He left thinking, *What a nice woman. She seemed too educated and too well-mannered to be a housekeeper.*

He headed for the postal exchange, where he wrapped everything he had in his pocket: the napkin, the Band-Aid, its wrapper, and her card. And after copying everything, wrote a letter to McCracken explaining the package's contents. He asked for ID and possible DNA results, then express mailed the package.

The prints should come back in several days. The express mail would be on the four o'clock run to the airport. With the detective's connections with the police and FBI, he may have the results as early as tomorrow evening.

Piearce passed Sandy on his return to his room and filled her in on his recent experiences and contacts, emphasizing the need for extra care in the presence of any of these women. He indicated that he was going to call on Ramona within the hour so as to check her comfort level. Sandy commented, "Piearce, you are in the wrong business. Consider this as your vocation. I would never have thought of doing that so quickly. By the way, here are our cell phone numbers . . . code them or memorize them. Use them only in an emergency." She left.

*       *       *       *       *       *

*       *       *       *       *       *

After showering, he visited Ramona. It was five thirty. The show started at seven and his dinner was scheduled for the same time. Room 227 was a suite; a large living room and adjoining bedrooms. Apparently they all shared bedrooms. He had been admitted by a maid, white lace cap, white apron, black tunic, skirt, stockings and shoes. She curtsied and questioned,

"You are Piearce?"

"Yes. Piearce is my given name."

She curtsied again, closed the door and led him in from the foyer to the living room where Ramona was seated. She invited him to sit, asking if he desired a beverage, wine, cocktail, anything? He assured her his only interest was her welfare. Whereupon she said, "The nurse insisted on this bandage/sling and a tetanus shot," holding up the bandaged hand. "Explain this Buick you have so much interest in. What is it that you are trying to discover?"

"I live in a town where a 1932 Buick met with an untimely accident, in which two men were killed. It was a sad state of affairs. Stolen plates and, I suspect, a possibly stolen car. The police were never able to find the answers. Eventually I was able to buy the car wreck and now after two years in a junk yard, have recently been able to refurbish the car and get it road-ready."

He spent several minutes explaining all the details and repeating that the car should be in perfect condition by the time he returned home. She was quite attentive and said,

"You say the police never found the owners?"

"Not really. I know that the Super was in contact with a supplier but I don't know if these suppliers were the owners. It had stolen plates and they declared that the car had been stolen. I haven't given the Super all these facts that I bought and repaired the car, just that I had an interest in it. It is my plan to do so if necessary. Most of it is curiosity about the delivery and why they chose that route; why they didn't trailer the car, why they insisted on transporting it under its own power. This car has become an obsession with me. As I said, it has been restored and should be perfect condition when I return home. And you said you know the owner?"

"Yes, I know the owners. It belonged to my hu-, uh, employer. He had a passion for certain things and the Buick was one. Would you consider selling the car?"

He looked at her for a long moment and asked, "Does it mean that much to you?"

"Until you started going into the details you just mentioned, I had decided it was gone. But if it's working and restored, it would be a nice memento of Father Tom."

"I'll consider it. What kind of man was he?"

"Are you a strong church person, Roman Catholic?"

"Not really strong. I attend periodically mostly because of my parents and no, not R.C. Not casting any aspersions, but I have a difficult time with certain beliefs."

"You are not alone in that view. I've delved into this sort of debate all my life but haven't really had an opportunity to voice my opinions because of my position. Please, continue, what else bothers you?"

"The virgin birth, life after death, a physical raising of the dead. The facts that the Bible, Koran, Veda, Taoism, Buddha, Confucius were all recorded at different times, by so many different people, so long after the events happened, has proven to be a factor in the errors and questions about these events. Modern interpretations and translations indicate a completely different viewpoint from today's meanings as compared to what the word meant at the time it was written.

"That's very interesting. I certainly won't disagree with you, but can you give me an example?"

"Several, but we can start with the word 'virgin'. The translation was incorrect or in doubt to start with. The word they translated as 'virgin' actually referred to a 'young woman' or 'maiden': that set the errors in motion for Christianity. There are similar misconceptions; and if you consider the time frame of the writing or recording, seventy to two hundred fifty years after J.C.'s death, words often changed their meanings. There are a phenomenal number of words that have lost their meanings, or changed their meanings even in the past fifty to sixty years. Gay was once a perfectly viable word with great connotations. Today it has an entirely different reference. Look into the Bible and check the different names applied to God for instance."

"I see where you are going with this. Father Tom had similar ideas and thoughts about the accuracy of the Bible. I personally never had much faith in any biblical literature after the age of eight or ten, when I reached the age of reason. By fourteen, I had fallen in love and remained in love, but not with the Bible. Living within the church environ out of necessity required me to delve into philosophy and theology

"Father Tom really had one biblical term that got him started in defining life. It was 'Goodness and Mercy shall follow you all the days of your life . . .' He started analyzing. Have you heard of Aristotle? Yes, of course you have."

"I've heard of him, but I can't say I'm a student of him or his works."

"Have you heard of Rhodian Scholars?"

"Yes, but that's as far as it goes."

"They were a select few that studied the classics and everything else under the sun, when some thought the sun was the center of the universe. Aristotle had a student who became very famous. You are probably wondering what this has to do with the quotation, but bear with me. Back to the quote. What is 'Goodness' as mentioned here? This gave Tomas some agony. Are we born good and learn evil? Then if we never come in contact with evil motives, ideas, deeds and the like, would we be eternally good by natural means? Then, what is the difference between good and evil? When did evil creep in? It seemed as though someone devised a method of distinguishing good from evil and therefore introduced evil into the Natural Realm, complicating the lives of all. This gave Tomas much anguish. He then determined that maybe it wasn't natural. What is the definition of 'Natural?' Sometimes definitions are impossible. Take the word 'life'. Can you define it?"

"Any living organism that can reproduce itself or sustain itself, for starters."

"That's fine but you used the word 'living' to define life and life is living so you are really using the word life to define life. Life can't be defined. It can be described, but it can't be defined."

Piearce sat a moment, thought, and nodded his head in affirmation saying, "Touché."

"Back to 'Natural'. It's a sense of right and wrong. A good dictionary, not the two-inch abbreviated kind, but the eight-inch Webster type, will give you detailed features and connections and classifications: occurring in conformity with the ordinary course, not the supernatural, developed by human reason or definition. Also, living in, or, as if in a state of nature, untouched by influences of civilization. Another source entertains the idea that nature or the orderliness of nature, or goodness of natural surroundings, integrity and ethical nature, controls the morality of nature. Our founding fathers would have understood the morality of nature; at least they would have known the term 'morality'. Nature is what they faced each day, unequivocally, without a second thought or regret.

"Sounds as though Nature is the answer to any dilemma."

"Are we getting the picture? Nature is the answer that repetitiously surfaces indicating that Goodness is Nature and that the interpretations vary according to mankind and its society. Aristotle knew this but it was a Rhodian scholar who brought it to mind, a disciple of Aristotle, His name was Eudemus. From his name comes a multitude of new words, which help define the aforementioned statement. First, Eudaemon meaning a good or benevolent spirit. Has a nice ring to it. Second, pertaining to a good demon. And lastly, the eleventh celestial house, that of friends.

"Tomas questioned whether this could be the origin of heavenly spirits."

"A complete state of well-being according to Aristotle. Additionally, the ethical theory which makes well-being, or pursuit, enjoyment and production of happiness, the supreme end in moral conduct. This regards the happiness of all mankind. An elation. No wonder most individuals are elated while hiking, trying to commune with nature. It's nature reaching out drawing one home, and when this is accomplished then 'Goodness and Mercy *will* follow you all the days of your life."

"It seems to correspond to a state of happiness within a person's life. Is there a belief based on faith in this natural habitat?" asked Piearce.

"Now what is faith? Are faith and belief the same? If one climbs from a valley and stands on a peak viewing the grandeur and returns, is the view the same after they have left? One might say they believe it is the same, while another may point out that the changing clouds, the changing seasons, the changing light of day or night will alter the vista, thereby redefining the scene at that moment. Has this revised the definition of faith or belief? One might say 'I believe the basic scene is unaltered' and have faith that the moments of time help to point to various details of change for that moment, but the basic belief of the overall vista is the same,"

"You have impressed me with your philosophy and knowledge. I may have to read a few more books to fully understand you."

"No. I was going to delve into Tomas's background and eventually get back to the car."

"Listening to you put the car into the background. Please continue," urged Piearce.

"You are an interesting person. Not many would be that interested in a relic, never mind the history behind it. The car belonged to my, uh, to a priest. It was the kind of car in which he had always been infatuated."

She continued to explain the priest's involvement with traveling from parish to parish and keeping the car as a memento of an important date in his life. She indicated that when her husband died she became the priest's housekeeper. Her husband had died at an early age and she and her two children had been fortunate to get this job and traveled where ever the priest was sent. Her children actually thought of him as a father more than a priest. They talked for over an hour quite congenially. A bond was established, laughter, confessions with cautious trust, a trust that wants to go beyond, a needed trust that comes and grows as though they'd known each other a lifetime.

"If I'd known you many, many, years ago, you'd have been my soul-mate."

"That would have been before I was born."

"How old are you?"

"Twenty seven."

"Over fifty years too late."

He was flabbergasted! This woman was over seventy seven years old?

"You can't be that old!"

"And then some."

At that moment the girls, Jacqueline and Irene, emerged from their rests, readying themselves for the evening performance. They looked the part.

He turned to Ramona and asked if he might call on her in the future, to hear more of the history of the vehicle. The ladies picked up on this and invited him to church Sunday.

"It's only an hour plus trip. Mass starts at eleven or you can come to the eight o'clock if you are an early riser. Jacqueline goes to the early mass as well as Ramona" they laughed. Still making fun; Ramona smiled, knowing some of his religious background.

"Perhaps," he answered.

He left thinking that this woman had more to tell than meets the eye. She was in need of serious talk, a confidant. He wished Aglaea or his mother were here, especially Aglaea. He took out his cell phone and called her. No answer. Did he punch in the correct number? She must have an answering service. Finally after a dozen rings she answered.

"Hi. Just thought of you because I wished you were here."

"Just got in. Long day. What are you up to?"

"Getting ready to go to dinner. I have met a group of people who invited me."

"They must have a daughter who is eligible," she said in an all-knowing voice.

"Yes, they do, but she is very much interested in a very nice young man that her parents seem reluctant to accept. I thought of you several times in the past few days, and after speaking with a woman a few minutes ago I wished you or my mother had been here to give a woman's point of view. So I said to myself, self, call her and say hello. So hello"

"What time is your dinner?"

"In a few minutes. I'm approaching the less formal dining room now. When we get a chance we'll have to come here for dinner some time."

"Yeah. Sure. A day and a half travel for dinner."

"Okay, gotta go. Have a nice evening. I'm at the dining area."

"Thanks for calling . . . let me know as soon as you get back."

"Will do, bye."

# Chapter IX

**D**inner was a jovial affair. The table arrangement was with alternate seating of Harriet, Piearce, Dora, Paul, Madeline and Hornben, with Harriet plying Hornben, calling his attention to how well-spoken Paul was and how she had hoped he'd meet a worthwhile woman sometime. Throughout the evening various topics were touched upon and each time Harriet managed to positively involve Hornben on a subject that Paul supported. She was a clever woman. Piearce eventually got onto the subject of paleontology with Hornben, saying that there was little evidence to support some of the finds. Hornben didn't agree, saying that there was considerable evidence that the earth was older than supposed. At the same time Paul caught Piearce's eye with a questionable look and Piearce suppressed a smile indicating that he was referring to evidence that indicated written history wasn't really supported by paleontology or archeology. Hornben said he disagreed asserting some scrolls that were found somewhere indicated earlier writing than was previously thought. Paul chimed in with, "Which set of scrolls are you thinking about? The Dead Sea Scrolls or the Nag Hammadi codices?"

"I think it was the Dead Sea Scrolls. What are these others, the Nag, what? Where were these found?"

"In Egypt two years before the Dead Sea Scrolls. But these writings are not the oldest. That would go back to the Sumerians and possibly before. The Nag Hammadi manuscripts, thirteen in number, comprising over forty books but not the kind of writings you would think of as books. It was here they found the book of Thomas and book of Mary Magdalene. I spent a summer in Nag Hammadi. Fascinating work! Sorry, Piearce, I have to agree with Mr. Hornben on this one. As a matter of fact, I'd consider changing my work and getting certified to do that sort of work or teach."

"Why don't you?" asked Hornben.

Paul had been waiting for this opportunity to speak out and silently thanked Piearce for the setup.

"Well, would you let your daughter marry a man who quit a lucrative paying job to pursue that sort of life?"

"It is an honorable profession. If she loved such a man and was happy with him, I don't see why not. What do you young people say? Go for it! Be happy."

Dora smiled mischievously, as did Harriet and Piearce. A beautiful job of entrapment. Madeline chimed in to support her husband and indicated that he should do what he wanted and not to pursue what his parents wanted.

"Don't let your life and happiness be thwarted by your parents. Strike out on your own and choose the girl of your dreams."

Paul had great support and he knew it.

"You say that now, but just suppose I made that choice and I was in that field. Now let's suppose I asked your daughter right now to marry me. How would you react to that? Think about it."

A silence ensued, and the smiles on the faces of all faded; after a few seconds, a slight smile appeared on Madeline's face while her husband's expression was one of concern,

"Yes, that is a hypothesis, and we can say that if she loved you then it wouldn't make any difference, would it Horn?"

"I suppose, it is, as I mentioned, an honorable job and as Mad indicated, if she loved the person, why not."

With that Paul turned to Dora, took her hand, and asked,

"Will you marry me?"

Dora smiled and looked at her parents for a long moment then turned to Paul and said, "I have loved you for a long time Paul, and never thought I'd have the chance to say yes before such a gathering of LOVE, so the answer is an emphatic yes! Because my parents said they approve."

With that they kissed and he produced a ring before the tongue-tied parents and the cheers of Harriet and Piearce clapping and standing. The adjoining tables did the same as the couple stood and he put the ring on her finger. Madeline had both hands over her mouth and Hornben just stood wide-eyed with bewilderment.

"Okay, let's stop the joking around. Enough is enough!"

After another kiss, Dora went around to her mother and hugged her, then to her father and did the same, thanking them profusely for their approval. Madeline had tears in her eyes. When the realization of what happened began to dawn on Hornben, a bit of anger seemed to set in.

"Dora, this is not funny so stop joking around."

Piearce shook hands with Paul then went to Hornben and shook his hand saying, "You have a wonderful daughter and now you have a better than average son. Congratulations to you both," and he then went and hugged Madeline. Both parents stood dumbfounded; overwhelmed!

Madeline turned to Hornben and said, "It isn't a joke, Horn, so get over it." She hugged Paul and started to smile; then the realization that this was not a chance meeting or spur-of-the-moment occurrence and asked her daughter, "How long?"

"About three years. I wanted to tell you but was fearful of your responses, especially Dad's."

At that point Horn began to get the implication, saying, "Did you really think I was too controlling about this, that you feared my reaction?"

"Oh, Daddy," she said as she hugged him and put her head on his shoulder.

Madeline continued saying, "Well, you could have saved me a lot of anguish if you'd told me sooner. I was beginning to think you weren't interested in men!"

She took Paul's hand and said, "Now let's sit and really talk. I'm in a very confused state, and I need a drink."

At this point Piearce excused himself and said a goodnight to them all. Dora hugged him and Paul shook his hand and hugged him as though he were a brother.

Piearce said, "I'd like to talk to you about Nag Hammadi sometime."

"Anytime, and thanks for the lead-ins."

Piearce headed to his room and felt aglow thinking about Aglaea, and the possibility of creating a similar situation should things work out for them. *It felt good to have money.*

When he entered his room, there was a strange aura as he reached for the light to flip the switch. "No light." A voice said, "It would be better to close the door before turning on a light." He recognized the voice and closed the door as a small light was lit. The girls were lying down, one on the bed, and the other on the sofa. He smiled and sat in the armchair stating, "You girls must be very desperate to hide-a-way in this pad. Need a place of refuge?"

"You could be in greater danger than us. Do you know who that woman is with whom you were dining?"

"I'm thinking it is the housekeeper for a priest that once owned the car I repaired and came to inquire about."

"That priest quit the order quite some time ago, but kept the housekeeper on. She appears to have come into some money years ago and really doesn't need to act as a housekeeper. The priest was part of a family that had connections to the underworld. He left the priesthood for a very lucrative career but never married. We wondered if he and the housekeeper had a relationship going on at one time and wondered if she was involved with the Family Business that he on occasion may have promoted while he was alive. His investment business was well run and there was nothing illegal while he was alive, but suspicion was strong when he was actively hearing confessions. That seems to be the collected data to which we have been privy. This woman could very possibly be a shrewd momma."

"I'll know more about her by tomorrow or the next day. I think that there is someone else involved. I had a long talk with her in her apartment this afternoon. She is articulate and very knowledgeable in many areas. We hit it off quite well and I was invited to go to church with them on Sunday."

"Them?"

Piearce then gave them a briefing on the events of the afternoon and the other women, one with whom they were trying to fix him up, mostly in jest. He inquired what they had found out about Roberto. They mentioned that the flight was on schedule so far as they knew. They also disclosed that they received a request for any information about the location of possible papers involving the Cartel in some church scandal. The information Piearce had given was dispatched about Roberto, and he would be discreetly tailed so it was not necessary that Piearce be concerned about his whereabouts.

"We told the administration we were going on a trip with a customer; this is a pullout bed. Do you mind? We are exhausted."

"Be my guest. You two take the bed, I'll take the pullout. It's really too small for two."

*      *      *      *      *      *<br>*      *      *      *      *      *

He woke to a shower running and hushed voices, rolled over and tried to get back to sleep. It didn't work.

They were trying to sneak out when he said in a whispered voice, "Don't wake the guy sleeping on the couch."

"Sorry Piearce. See you at breakfast?"

"What time is it?"

"Five Thirty."

"Am or pm?"

"Funny, funny, see ya." The door clicked. He didn't get back to sleep.

# CHAPTER X

$A$t breakfast he was greeted by none other than Harriet. She and Dora were locked in deep conversation that only women can understand. Men don't have the slightest idea of what goes on, and even if they knew, wouldn't understand in the same manner. Women seem to be heavily influenced by social and emotional factors.

"Piearce, come join us. What are you up to today? Golfing? Sailing? Canoeing? Hiking? Give us a rundown now that you are out of contention for this woman's hand."

"Wasn't that an evening to remember? Did you two plan that or did Paul just pick up and improvise?" asked Piearce.

"Complete improvisation that couldn't have been accomplished without your lead-in statements. Paul didn't get your drift at the first discussion with Dad, but he said he saw a slight twinkle in your eyes and knew you were familiar with the scrolls, so picked up on putting you down and the rest is history. Thanks again. And really, I do have a friend and cousin I haven't seen in a couple of years I'd love to introduce you should you ever get into our neck of the woods."

"No, thank you for the vote of confidence, but I have someone in whom I'm very much interested at the moment. And I think my parents approve, so I don't have that problem."

He went riding again, mostly to reexamine the cavern and the trails, trying to figure out who might have helped Marla or covered for her. It was perplexing. By noon he had returned and discovered that his intimate group had taken a trip on one of the old lake launches to cruise around the small islands and enjoy the era of the thirties on a vintage boat.

He stopped to see The Super, who was asked if he enjoyed the company of the girls. Piearce indicated that he really did enjoy the housekeeper's company and was taken by the fact that the women were such good fun, but was surprised that the housekeeper was so along in years.

"Yeah, she holds her age well. I was equally shocked when I first found out how old she is. Lived a good and pure life as a housekeeper, I guess. Too bad the priest died when he did. Apparently had some sort of connection with the cartel that owns this place, so allows her the opportunity to have a room here once or twice a month as you witnessed. Never met the priest though; too bad. I should say ex-priest. Very confusing. They always refer to him as the priest. Oops, another call. See ya, Piearce."

And just when he was getting ready to possibly divulge some tidbits of useful information. Piearce took the back path to the hotel to avoid other guests. He decided to call Aglaea. He got her answering service and concluded she was on duty or had turned off her phone for a rest. After all, it was Saturday. He couldn't remember if he had eaten lunch, so went to have a cup of coffee and a snack. Several people stopped by his table and commented on last night's wonderful engagement set-up. One of the ladies wanted to know if he'd do the same for her daughter. He was a celebrity now. They all were crediting him with last night's dinner activities as though he had been responsible and planned it all. He wondered what price they would pay to have such a plan evolve; how much time would be spent developing such a course of action and have it turn out so successful. New thoughts, new ideas.

His phone buzzed. It was McCracken.

"Can you talk?"

"No."

"Call me when you can."

"Within ten minutes."

"Bye."

He finished his lunch and went out where he could talk without anyone eavesdropping. Detective McCracken answered.

"What have you gotten yourself into? Those prints that you gave me belonged to a woman who died years ago. A Rowena Dolekeczak. Died in an automobile accident with her husband over fifty-five to sixty years ago. They had one child that survived at home with a Brother Tomas, the recipient of child-care and money. He was a priest. We don't know the blood type; that won't be available for a couple more days. There were no inquiries from the data bank, just the ID information and burial information. I checked the newspapers from that town and got the old obit. This person was killed with her husband in a fiery crash sixty years ago!"

"Don't jest with me. The prints are of a dead woman? Sixty years ago?"

"I ran a prelim on her, and her brother was a priest. They belonged to a crime syndicate family."

"Wow! Do you think there was foul play here? Someone killed in her place?"

"Don't know all the facts. Husband's name was Alex DuPhont. He had a minor connection I think. Whatever it is, has been a secret for over sixty years. The automobile accident was investigated, but I haven't got results yet. I don't know if it was a setup or not. The paper indicated that there was money missing and never located. They felt that Rowena and her husband may have absconded and relocated the money in a numbered account somewhere."

"This is flabbergasting. You are telling me that this woman who acts as a housekeeper is in reality someone else from a crime family syndicate, or family, who was supposedly killed sixty years ago in a 'supposed' accident? This is uncanny." Piearce wondered if this was the source of the money coming out of hiding.

"I'll email what I find later today or tomorrow. The news clippings, the FBI print ID and the location of her parent's home and his. It appears she was only married a short time. Watch yourself. There may be a syndicate connection that could hasten one's demise."

"Do you think I should tell Sandy and Auburn about this?"

"You might want to inform them that she has early connections through her family and see what develops."

"Okay. I'll call you later about the emails. Maybe the girls have a secure address. I'll check and let you know. I may go to visit her early tomorrow. I'll tell Sandy and Auburn. Bye."

"One other thing. One of my operatives recognized the name and said that it had been changed. That he thought the family originally came from Egypt, and being of a dark complexion they passed for Italian. Interesting? See ya."

That might answer the question of why Roberto was heading for Egypt. Just what is going on here? Now he would have to question Paul about the Nag Hammadi area. Was there a connection between those papers or papyrus? Is that what was meant about the papers and the key?

He saw Auburn and got her secure email address after telling her of his conversation with McCracken. He was invited to dinner again by Harriet. Everyone seemed to have accepted the engagement and was looking forward to a long planning date when Dora said, "You know, we have known each other for a number of years and we don't need a big pretentious wedding. Really. Please. Give the money to a cancer fund or other charity. We only want a small wedding with our closest friends and relatives. No more."

This didn't faze Harriet, but it brought an astonished look to Madeline and Horn. "Please Mom. Dad. I know how much you probably planned a lavish affair for years, but you'll get great newspaper coverage from making a donation on our behalf. It may even start a precedent and become known as the Hornben Movement."

Everyone smiled at that and Harriet said she thought it was a great idea. She asked just how long it would be before they tied the knot.

"We have to get Paul's parents to acquiesce, but not more than a few months. Paul?"

Paul said, "The sooner the better. With Aunt Harriet on my side and your presence we will overcome any obstacle. Piearce, are you going to be available?"

"Give me a date when you decide and I'll make arrangements."

It was another night to remember.

# Chapter XI

The next day Piearce was up at five-thirty and was ready to leave by six, with coffee for the road. The drive was picturesque and worth the early rise just to see the beauty. During the winter it may not have been so wondrous, but this morning it was remarkable. It was hard to realize that he was travelling to visit a person who had the answers or possible knowledge about an even worse situation than just the money trail. Would Ramona be at the eight o'clock mass? Auburn had left sealed copies of emails of the obits and news report in his box. He glanced at them just as he got into his vehicle.

Ramona took him to her side of the church; all ladies and a couple of husbands present. She asked if he wanted instructions on genuflection to fit in. He indicated that it didn't bother him. He faked it and clumsily followed the routine.

They had brunch at a local restaurant and then they went to Ramona/Rowena's waterfront home. Beautiful. Absolutely gorgeous.

"We've actually owned this for a number of years, but the paperwork wasn't completed until a few years ago before Tomas died, because of official reasons. Never had the opportunity to really enjoy it. Tom did investments after the priesthood and did exceedingly well. There was an inheritance in trust for him and his sister after his father died. Tomas died right after the car was lost in the accident before he could recover from periodic medical problems, possibly also the beginning of dementia."

"How did the Buick get to be donated or sold?"

"The Buick was originally his father's and the source of many good memories, all good with that particular car."

They sat and talked for two hours. He had compiled a lot of information that needed to be analyzed. A lunch was offered at twelve thirty. It was easy talking to her.

"You are uncommonly cooperative with your historical information. Most people would be reticent to divulge so much information to a total stranger."

"And some people are judges of character. You are someone I trust. It would surprise you, all the burdens I've carried over the years."

"I suppose working for a priest would put you into a position where secrets must be kept regardless."

"Plus personal secrets."

"You mean of the priest?"

"Yes, and some of mine."

"I have a very, very personal question to ask. I value your trust and I value your honesty with me. Please do not get angry and please continue to be understanding. I came here to find someone entirely different. The Super and the owner of the car. I've done both. I wanted to find out why the car was sent in the manner it was sent. During that luncheon when I first met you, I had myself seated beside you and your friends to meet you. When you cut yourself, I took your blood sample along with papers, with your prints, and sent them to be analyzed. The print ID came back last night, along with a newspaper article about the death of a man and his wife." Her eyes widened! Silence. She stared, looked down thoughtfully, then lifted her head, and looking directly at him and smiled.

"Thank you. That was a lot less painful than I imagined it might be. You have lifted a burden that we've carried for many years."

"You are Rowena?"

"Yes."

"Do your children know?"

"No, not really. I don't know. I don't think so."

"The priest?"

"My brother. No. He was more than a brother. Let me have them start lunch for us. We'll eat here on the patio. Tom loved this view and what better place to start the story that could have destroyed us if it had ever been revealed fifty or sixty years ago."

She left, tended her duties and came back with several albums. A maid followed with a coffee tray. She started while he sipped.

"Are you going to pursue the blood tests?"

"Only to the extent to prove ownership of the Buick and other items I haven't mentioned."

"It was really my fault for a major aspect in my not seeking to understand his perspective in our relationship, but let me start by saying these albums represent a history unto itself. I also have some of Tom's diaries, most of the facts in them I already knew about. You know who I am and what background I have so how do you know I won't have you annihilated when you leave here?"

"You wouldn't deny a man marrying and raising a family, would you?"

"Do you have a person in mind?"

"Yes, actually, a childhood crush with whom I've recently become reacquainted. Back then I was too shy and hesitant to approach her. I think she feels the same way about me."

"Good! I won't try to introduce you to my granddaughter. It's confession time. You seem to have an outlook on life and people that is not condescending. What I am going to say should have been said years ago. Will you promise never to divulge this until after I'm laid to rest, or only to those who absolutely need to know to save a life?"

"Only to save a life or do an honorable thing if it endangers anyone."

She continued her monologue, "The man killed in the accident was my husband, but not the father of the child we had. Our marriage was never consummated. The woman's family was compensated after the accident for not divulging that I was not in the car. Only five or six people knew. At the time, it was best that no one knew I was alive. It alleviated what could have been a devastating family and syndicate disaster. While my brother was in seminary, I had my first child, I have two. He really didn't want to be a priest but that will be disclosed as we progress. There are complications that would still create terrible consequences should they become known."

"My brother's secret diaries disclose a lot of what I'm going to tell you but this is my version of what I observed. Tomas was a very precocious child. Father was a treasurer for the MOB, or Brotherhood, or Mafia, Syndicate, and enormous amounts of cash were delivered, counted and some stored in our house or distributed for investment or payoffs all over the world."

"Tomas had often seen an open door to a room with stacks of money neatly stored on shelves. It didn't look real. The door was of thick metal, recessed behind a paneled door that concealed the location. To the casual observer the paneled room was his father's study. He didn't know what his father did, but he knew there were always people coming and going with briefcases or satchels. The cars varied but always expensive looking. It wasn't until he was a teen that he realized his father may have been involved in nefarious activities. On several occasions in his early teen years when he had need of cash, he 'borrowed' a few dollars but never put it back or replaced it. Sometimes there would be a pile of money on a small table waiting to be counted and that is the pile from which he 'borrowed'. Once he tried to estimate the total value of the supply stored on the shelves. The different denominations were separated and carefully packaged in stacks of one hundred bills per stack. It was the first time he had seen one thousand or five thousand dollar bills! Five hundred, one hundred, fifties he had seen, but five thousand dollar bills? Never till that day."

"In the room there were three sides plus the door. The room dimensions were roughly five feet by seven feet in the working area, not including the shelf space, and a small two foot by three foot table with barely enough room to get past the chair. Good thing they were not fastened down."

"The vault had been specially constructed: money was constantly coming in and going out. Coming home from boarding school, the stacks of money presented a temptation he could not resists, even as a youngster. In time Tomas became more observant and on occasion saw a photo of one of the visitors in a newspaper being depicted as a 'MOB' boss or a wanted criminal. At first he thought it coincidence; but then it became apparent that our father's business was not one that focused on honesty or legitimacy. He decided that taking a few fifties or hundreds from the table would not be missed. He knew he wasn't supposed to enter the room but periodically he'd come in and the study would be empty and the door open. He started wondering if there was an accurate count of the money and if he systematically 'borrowed' some to squirrel away for a rainy day, would it be noticed?"

"It became an obsession with him. At first he used shoe boxes in his closet for storage. Then boxes for the shoe boxes as years passed. By college he had systematically drained off millions and there was no evidence of his crime! He figured it was dishonest money, so it wasn't really a crime. Clever as a youth, clever as an adult. He had no idea how much he had made off with. The smartest thing he had done was to move it all to a secret hideaway before his father had to give up the business at home. He liked Pennsylvania; the home was huge, a mansion, and was eventually taken over by his father's replacement. Often, later on, he envisioned entering the home and visiting the person acting in place of his father and helping himself."

"Illegal money being taken illegally couldn't very well be reported to the police, so it would constitute a perfect crime. How much had been trafficked through that room? Hundreds of millions, perhaps billions from its early inception until now. He never took the largest bills; fifty's, one hundred's, perhaps an occasional five hundred and very few one thousand dollar bills if they were scattered on the table. He was clever enough to know he couldn't go out and freely spend the largest denominations; that would only draw attention to him. He was wealthy and needed only to maintain a job and lifestyle commensurate with his salary or a little more from investments. When suspicion arose he decided on the priesthood vocation to cover his misdeeds. Even as a priest he was able to take advantage of his connections to use the knowledge gained to hide his wealth."

"As you can see, I was intrigued with it all and, unknown to my brother, witnessed some of his acts in the beginning, and later became his housekeeper wherever he was sent until after father died. You'll have to bear with me. I may repeat myself or get things out of sequence."

"Early in our lives we were 'nannied.' He was four years older and I adored him. We went to private schools at first, then public but there was always a bodyguard somewhere close by. Our lives were almost normal. Often we were alone in our play area. There was always a stream of cars in and out. Mom entertained us and kept us in line. We had relatives visiting, like any family, but were kept out of father's way. He was the head of the family. My brother found a listening area above father's study adjacent to the vault, a ceiling register. I caught him listening when I was four. If we needed anything, even money, all we had to do was ask. But Tom had other ideas. He realized when he was refused money for a trivial item, that he could 'borrow' some from the vault. Father never knew, but that started Tom's obsession with cash."

"After witnessing his pilfering periodically, I began wondering about father's activities. My mother always shielded us from his work, calling it very secretive, and made it seem as though it was a covert but honorable operation. Suffice to say, I accepted everything then. As far as Tom is concerned, I always loved and admired him. He was super-intelligent, extremely attentive to me and my naive ways. I was crushed when he went to college, but that's getting ahead. In college he excelled. Father wanted him to assist in the family business affairs, go to law school, and expand, as he called it. I was a snoop and listened in on most of the talk via the register ventilator. I literally was in love with my brother and was jealous of his relationships."

"When I was sixteen, he graduated from college and there was an investigation by the cartel concerning a missing amount of money in the coffers. Tom had gone out with a female friend and came in about two. I waited up and told him of the visitations and accusations. He hugged me and kissed me on the forehead and said he'd had a frustrating evening with his friend and was going to shower. I kissed back on the lips, and left. I had been just as frustrated and while he was in the shower, I walked in on him and entered the shower stall, nude. He told me to go, asking, "What's wrong with you?" I seduced him. I had planned it many times over the years, but this was the opening I had been waiting for."

"During the next week we talked and decided that the priesthood would be a good cover. It took the suspicion off Tomas. Mom was ecstatic over the decision. Dad wasn't, but accepted it. Maybe with relief, I don't know. I lived for the time when he would be home. I always came home from college when he was home from seminary. Father wasn't too enthused about me being in college; being of the old school that thought women should stay home and have babies. I always countered with, what about mom? She went to college."

"I became pregnant, and to tell you the truth, I didn't even realize it for three months. I wasn't ill or had any of the usual symptoms. I had a friend who had been to the house a number of times and he became the target. I literally bought him, as I did his girlfriend and then her family after the accident. We wed. I had the child. I never slept with him."

"My love was always Tomas and only Tomas. Mom was so happy to be a grandmother. Father was equally as joyful, but about that time he was being replaced by another family member as the treasurer, or money launderer. Mom died very suddenly of a massive heart attack. I think the stress of being the wife of a cartel treasurer and having a multitude of threatening characters parading in and out at all hours and from all over the world must have been a terrible strain. Newsmen lurking around also took a toll."

"Tom's ordination gave father much pride and satisfaction. I personally always had reservations about religion since the age of fourteen. Sin didn't make sense to me in the manner described by the priest and all the do-gooders. So much happened via the family activities that I deemed sinful, but which the family described as business, that I started to question and have serious doubts. We were well indoctrinated into the need for keeping secrets, so that the outside world would never know, other than what they read in the newspapers. By the time I had seduced my brother, I had read philosophies; and through private tutors I'd had a background in early interpretations of the Bibles, not those the Christian church or Muslin mosque advocated, but to truer renditions, especially early Egyptian histories. That's why I believed marriage to a brother was not sinful. Look at the spousal ties of Pharaohs, early Roman Emperors, in The Bible and Chinese literature; none were declared sinful until the Christian church intervened. So I made a choice and never regretted it; nor did Tomas after we discussed it. He had also felt the same desire for me since I was about eight but had always put it out of his mind until that night of decision. When Father died, Tom came home for a month and as sad a time as it was, we were happy to spend the time together and have our intimate moments in the house my parents had moved to, another large house."

"One day Tomas mentioned he had been assigned to a small parish in another country. I was crushed and told him I would go with him as his housekeeper. Although I had enough money of my own to live near him without having to work, that would arouse suspicion."

"The next day, my husband and his girlfriend were killed in an automobile accident. I didn't wish for it to happen to either one, but it was a fortuitous opportunity for us. In any event, we decided that under an assumed name and as a housekeeper, I could travel and be with him without arousing suspicion."

"Getting a passport was difficult but accomplished by using the social security number of a child who had died in infancy. We benefited from family ties that had experience in setting up immigration ID's. Once done, the rest is history. I was pregnant with my second child and was passed off as a widowed woman in need of a job, so became the housekeeper. We eventually married but by a JP in a small town where it is recorded but not publicized, so few knew."

"One of the Family Dons did keep track of Tom and kept him informed of activities at home. Once or twice he was asked to act as a broker or go-between for the cartel or a family member, doing a favor for 'old time's sake'. As a priest he also heard confessions from many members who considered him above reproach in his position. Tomas acted this way only to keep the record clean. He didn't hate the priesthood but really wanted out of it. With the monies we inherited plus what Tom had acquired with his investment and storage, and I have no idea how much (we still haven't gotten that all straightened out yet), we could have retired and disappeared."

"Currently my securities advisors take care of all financial matters. I miss Tomas so much. This was our retirement home. This was our escape; in private we acted as husband and wife and no one knew. Normal. The kids all called him 'dad' and loved him.

"His diaries indicate possibly a couple to five million that he hid in investments and some stored in cash somewhere. Even at this stage, it would be dangerous if it were ever found that he had taken mob monies; even though he started at a young age, which might have been excusable. But in later life, a calamity for us. It is my intention to destroy the diaries."

"My daughter knows some of this and plans to write a novel based on it, without divulging names, of course. She has read the diaries through several times and although she hasn't said anything, I suspect she may possibly be suspicious of Tom after he married me, but I don't think she knows I am his sister. Tom wrote that his sister and her husband were reported to have been killed. A clever way of putting it. He wrote about attending the funeral of the husband and wife killed in an accident, which was true. He never said it was his sister. I wanted to tell Rowena several times. I'll do it when she returns. She and her brother were devastated by Tom's death, but accepted it due to age. My role as housekeeper was more as an overseer. I hired the help to do the jobs so I was able to look after the children and tutor them. Moving was never a problem; for me it was more an acting job in a real-life movie. I played the part with archbishops, bishops, monsignors, all."

"Finally Tom had had enough and resigned and went into finance. He loved it. We did another JP with the kids only, just for show and began living as husband and wife. We bought this hideaway but never told anyone about it. He had the car redone, doing some of it himself. We both experienced some wonderful times in the back seat as a safe meeting place. The kids were ecstatic over our marriage. Then we decided to come here and sell the car to The Resort people; the Buick would be close, almost like being in the family."

"His remains are in that garden you see there. Yes, he was dishonest, but I like to think we made up for it over the years. He provided well for the children. I know there were activities he continued supervising in Egypt and other countries; however, I don't know what they are or were. Periodically someone will appear asking for certain information, about which I have no knowledge. Tomas always told me that if I knew nothing of certain activities, then I could always pass a lie detector test. Several times since his death, casual inquiries have been made, very subtle, but definitely inquiries about books or documentations or records recalling certain events of the past, especially in places where he had acted as a priest. It is my belief that there are two safety deposit boxes of interest to the Family that may hold sensitive documents better to remain concealed, documentation disclosing financial holdings that may go back to the times when our father was treasurer. My daughter has the diaries and is looking them over as I mentioned; I saw nothing when I read them through, but I didn't look for anything along that line in that time frame."

"Are you spending the night? You have me doing all the confessing, revealing to you secrets that could be dangerous to your well-being. I suspect you may be able to help me unwind and relieve a considerable amount of pent-up stress. I had a flash of anger when you first identified me; fear; it had to come out; my children deserve to know. Perhaps, with you, I'll be able to practice and relieve myself of the burden and rehearse what I'll say to them."

"You've been quite cooperative and revealing. How did you manage to stay with the church so long with your questionable belief?" Piearce asked, "I consider your overnight invitation an honor. Besides, I haven't finished my story about the Buick."

"You are spending the night?"

He smiled and cocked his head as though he had to think about it. She continued saying, "I'll consider that a yes. There is a guest room with a shower next to Rowie's room. She's supposed to stop by later; if she arrives late she may make a little noise, but I'll be up or leave her a note that we have a guest. She'll probably see your vehicle anyway."

He stood and stretched asking, "Why would people want to know about your brother's, uh, husband's activities so long ago? And why during so long a period after his demise?"

"I don't know, Piearce. I suspect it has something to do with the church or cartel activities, or secrets that could possibly exposé a horrendous plot to control or takeover certain investments. The air is electric, they tell me, with charges of who is in control of real estate, banks, etc. That could have reverberations felt round the world. The church is involved somehow I think, but that is just a supposition or speculation."

"Is there cash involved?"

"Not really, as far as I know. But who knows; there are so many possibilities. No. No cash, but documents that would be dangerous in the wrong hands, so I've been led to believe."

"I found a couple of packages in the Buick while I was refinishing it. It probably should be returned to you. I'm using some now on this excursion."

"Good for you. Cash I don't need. If it was cartel money I'd be concerned; I don't recall Tomas mentioning anything. He did indicate he was transferring money, but that is what my agents are handling. If you found money, it isn't really traceable to Tomas. Keep it. How much?"

"I don't really know, I never really counted it. There were several packages of two hundred forty thousand dollars. I wanted to return it to the rightful owner. I could have kept it all but my early training took over. Do you think a finder's fee of ten to twenty percent would be asking too much? Unreasonable?"

"I said just keep it. I'm too old and rich to worry about money I never knew existed."

"My estimation is there is a considerable amount of cash. I haven't opened all the packages yet."

"Tell you what. After you've opened then all, then we'll talk about it. In either case you'll have to come back with it or the information."

"You have a deal."

A maid appeared and removed the dishes while Ramona spoke about her children and grandchildren.

"What time would you like dinner, Miss Ramona?"

"Would seven-thirty suit you, Piearce?"

"Fine."

"Miss Rowena said she'd be in by eight."

Then we'll wait 'til eight."

"Yes, Ma'am."

"How far back do Tomas's diaries go?"

"From the time he was fifteen or sixteen. He kept two sets. When I was reading it was marvelous to relive some of the events."

Ramona continued her monologue. "Tomas used abbreviations and code when he visited the vault. He also detailed descriptions of his convictions, especially concerning philosophies and critical reports on religion after a dispute with a tutor on the subject of God and other ideas about the propositions of other religious sects versus Catholicism. He wasn't as vehement as I, but he had similar questions about the truth of the matter. We talked about this later in our lives and had more questions than answers. Much of this came to a head while we were at Nag Hammadi in Egypt. Gnostic versus Agnostic, the Essenes and their viewpoints especially the thoughts of Aristotle and one of his students, Eudemus, who excited Tomas' outlook on life and changed his reason for living, I think. He invoked Aristotle's idea that goodness is Nature, living in a state of Nature untouched by influences of civilization and society. The orderliness of Nature, or goodness of natural surroundings, integrity and ethical nature controls the morality. A good and benevolent spirit. A state of complex well-being.

"At that time, Tomas began feeling depressed about listening to confessions of the dishonest and despicable activities that were widespread. Sin didn't exist until Catholicism declared it so. Marriage is a good example. There wasn't much of a marriage ceremony originally and adultery was unheard of until the church declared it sinful. You declared yourselves to one another, just as the Egyptians did. Especially in the families of Pharaohs in order to keep power. The more we discussed our position the more details began to unravel leading us into *the* or *our* evolution of religious development. Tomas was writing a very controversial report on how Jesus learned so much and why historic beliefs tied in with the region of China, India and Egypt, prior to Jesus' declaration that he was the Son of God. Actually, he never really indicated he was the son of God. That was placed there by authors much later. Tomas actually secreted documents for someone that he said would revolutionize the way the Church operates but he never elaborated on it and I found nothing in his diaries to support his statement.

"But I know that in the short time he spent in the Nag Hammadi region, he was inundated with confessionals from cartel workers who were visiting the archaeological dig. Two of the men had accidents that Tomas suspected were deliberately caused. We left, but he kept in contact with various businesses there. Not all the jars and contents went to the church."

Ramona continued until eight o'clock when her granddaughter arrived; about the same age as Marla. She was attractive and looked tired.

"Well G.M., didn't expect you to have male company and a handsome one at that."

"Rowena, this is Piearce, with an unusual background and who has let me unwind, since you are always off abandoning me," she answered while hugging her. "You are just in time for dinner. What have you been up to lately?"

"I brought back the diaries that mother borrowed; she still has a couple but decided you may want to read them again."

"We were discussing them this afternoon. Good timing."

Rowena turned to Piearce, "Call me Rowie. What employment are you in, Piearce?"

"Just finished college and planning my next adventure."

"Ph.D.?"

"No, B.S., a slow learner."

"Plus military time and a paramedic," added Ramona.

"I see he has tended you. What happened?"

"Did it at The Resort. Piearce helped me there so I invited him to church this morning and, of course, the ladies were there so they coveted him at church."

"And Piearce, I'll bet they invited you to visit with them and their unwed daughters and granddaughters."

"That is an understatement," he answered with a laugh.

Dinner was cordial and searching.

"Rowie, I have told him about my early life and that Tomas was at one time a priest and that I was his housekeeper, so you do not have to pussyfoot around. How did it go?"

"Should have some information by tomorrow, so they say, according to mother."

"Rowie is named after her mother, hence the name Rowie."

"Apparently they have sent someone to the source to see what's available. G.M., I'm sure there is more to this than we ever suspected."

At that moment there was a commotion and in came an athletic woman who Piearce estimated to be about forty plus.

"This is my daughter Rowena. Rowena, Piearce."

"Wow! Where were you when I was available?"

"Mother!"

"He looks like a better catch than many. Anything left?"

She acted the part of a forty plus year old.

"Rowena, act your age; after sixty you're supposed to slow down."

"You didn't. Well, Piearce, what do you think of the government?"

"I'm afraid I've been rather limited in my civic duties for the past few years. I don't even know the name of the president."

"Really?"

"No, but I'm amazed as to your youthfulness and your daughter and your mother! I don't do politics and have reservations about religion."

"I'm afraid in this household religion usually rules."

"Mother, we have to talk. There are several things in Dad's diaries that cause me to wonder. Will you excuse us, Piearce?"

"Piearce probably knows more than you about the diaries and our early life."

"And Rowie?"

"She'll need to know eventually."

"How long before Dad, or Tomas' resignation had you two been intimate? To put it bluntly."

"That's a very blunt way of putting it."

Ramona looked at Piearce as though she'd been hit by a truck, or a blow to the solar plexus. She looked to the floor, tears welled in her eyes, and she again gazed at Piearce.

He rose, walked over to her, took her hands, looked at her with a smile and said, "Whatever your decision I'm here for you."

"Give me a moment. I need to organize my thoughts. Thanks for the support."

She indicated that he should sit next to her and held his hand. She looked at him and said, "This is where God should intervene." Searchingly, she continued looking at him while she mouthed the word "Help."

He looked at the ladies, who were very quiet and startled by the reaction. Piearce said, "Sit quietly, don't say anything but just listen. This is very difficult for your mother and grandmother. At this moment she has only one ally who understands where she is coming from. She has wanted to enlighten you about a phase of her life that has never before, except to one individual, been disclosed. You each have fallen in love, just as Ramona had fallen in love. Please do not make any hasty decisions when you hear her story. Do you need a little more time or should I continue?"

"Oh Piearce, thank you; please, a moment."

Piearce looked at the ladies and back to Ramona, who had stopped weeping and was still dabbing her eyes. Piearce continued, "Ramona has only loved one man in her life. She loved him unconditionally and sacrificed her entire life to him and for him. This is not an easy task and I'm going to ask you both to never disclose what you hear tonight,"

Rowena said, "I have had some thoughts over the years and wondered but never mentioned anything, so I guess I can continue in that vein."

Rowie said, "I don't know what's going on, but I'm of the same set,"

Ramona sat holding Piearce's hand, in a white-knuckle grip. Looking at the girls, saying, "This goes back to my early childhood. My real name is Rowena."

Rowena gasped and put her hands over her mouth, lowered them and said,

"The accident? You, Tomas' sister?"

"Yes. Please, please don't be angry, Rowena."

"What do you mean, Mother?" asked Rowie.

"Does my brother know?"

"No. I had planned this differently. Not like this."

"Who died with your husband? And was he the only man you ever loved? What about dad, or Tomas?"

"One and the same."

"Your brother?"

"Yes. It was all my doing. I'm to blame for it all."

"MY GOD! Tomas was my real father! MY GOD!"

"Tomas was my actual grandfather? Wow! I always loved him, but now I love him more!"

"Mother! Who else knows?"

"Piearce."

Both women looked at him, then back to Ramona with wrinkled brows and a questioning expression.

"It's very complicated, don't ask. I'll get to it in my own time and way."

She continued explaining her life, repeating what she had told Piearce and more, including Rowena's search of Tomas' diaries and Rowie's inclusion. She indicated to them that no update or information from Egypt was expected this soon. The Cartel will trust Roberto. It was ten thirty. They decided to retire.

*　　　　*　　　　*　　　　*　　　　*　　　　*<br>　　*　　　　*　　　　*　　　　*　　　　*　　　　*

He was awakened by a cell phone's tone and loud murmuring at five a.m. He listened and heard Rowie's, "Oh No!" It was very distinct. She was apparently walking down the hall toward Ramona's room. After a few minutes quiet prevailed; he dozed again. At six-thirty he woke to a tapping on his door. He slipped into his trousers and shirt and opened the door. It was Ramona.

"Piearce, Roberto said the safety deposit boxes were empty except for a note to me that hadn't been opened. I had him open it. It mentioned that the papers and manuscripts had been moved, but didn't say where or how. It was dated a few years after we left. Did you say you had not opened all the packages?"

"No. Just a corner on them to verify what was in them."

"Do you think that possibly there are papers inside with the bills? I don't care about the money, I'd like to know if there are manuscripts or records in any of the packages."

"I'll check out today and head home. No one else knows and I don't want anyone else involved."

"I understand. It isn't imperative that we do this immediately, but as soon as you can without arousing suspicion."

He left after breakfast and drove to The Resort knowing that Rowena had made a rendezvous with Marla and Roberto. He cautioned Ramona about Marla. She apparently knew of Marla's involvement and reconnection with the Vatican somehow, and that there was some governmental and political issues; a very controversial affair.

*      *      *      *      *      *<br>*      *      *      *      *      *

At The Resort he filled Sandy and Auburn in on his meeting, as much as he dared without revealing details. He did mention that Roberto went to Egypt to retrieve some papers that were not there and it caused some consternation. The girls indicated that there was a conference planned within a month. Very hush-hush, but several suites had been reserved for people arriving from all over the world.

Paul was at lunch with Dora.

"Hi, lovebirds. How goes it?"

"Hi, Piearce. How are you doing? Missed you at dinner. How was your visit?"

"Very advantageous. A nice addition to my trip. Paul, you said you were at the Nag Hammadi site. The subject came up and I was wondering about it. I know they found some books that weren't immediately published, kept for years before releasing the information. What else was found there? Was the church responsible?"

"That is a forbidden topic. No one knows the complete truth. It was supposed that all the jars and leather books were impounded and interpreted by the Vatican. However, that is a supposition. I heard that all the codices were given except for a parchment or book that was destroyed inadvertently. So the church didn't get them all. Very controversial, especially where the religious faction is concerned."

Paul then spent the next hour explaining the Nag Hammadi, the political unrest, especially the trust he had developed with a few workers who knew the discoverers of the parchments and jars. "They indicated that there was another book, possibly two; that would be fifteen, but when he asked, one of the Bedouin leaders said it was just talk, that they were burned. After his interruption, I always felt cut off from asking about the possibility that there were other books available."

"I pursued the men later but they didn't want to talk or contradict the elder and said it was merely hearsay. I never had time to do any more. Besides, at that time it was a course of study I wasn't supposed to have been in. I often wondered what would have been the outcome if they had continued with their discussion and if the Elder had not interjected his opinion. When they finally released the books in about 1977, it changed many people's outlook on the Bible, the New Testament. If, and I say if, there was another jar or two of parchments or books, then they may have been put into a protector's or collector's vault; or the details may have been too revealing to be allowed into the hands of the public. Somebody in France had something to do with it.

"Look into the literature and you'll see vague references to special translators who were secreted away where only one or two knew their location or identity. There are various reports along that line of reasoning, hinting to possible clandestine sales of the originals, but that's all speculation as far as I am concerned. Why do you have such a keen interest in that area? You thinking of going into archaeology or paleontology?"

"No. Someone mentioned the Dead Sea Scrolls, and the Hammadi Books and I recalled you had some experience with them or that area."

"Are you leaving today?"

"Yes, but I may return to visit Ramona, the woman who injured her hand."

"Oh yeah, bet she can tell some stories. By the way, we may be setting the wedding date for two months from the day of the wagon trip. Dora wants it in her hometown area, so it'll mean a trip for you. Will you come? Dora has a plus one for you if you can make it and don't have a date, but one thing is certain!

She made her mother promise to let her plan a small wedding; otherwise we'd elope."

"She still thinks I'll match up with her friend? It's uncanny the way people think when they have a good friend and wish to share their happiness. I'll be better prepared to answer that in a few days to a week."

# Chapter XII

He called Aglaea, leaving a message of his arrival the next day around noon and a possible luncheon date if she was available. Also that he was still in pursuit of his project and would be leaving again shortly.

The drive home was now along a fairly familiar route and coffee stops. His questions never ceased. What was the reason for the bank? Why was the money included? Were there documents in those packages? He reviewed his activities at The Resort. He had met people of extraordinary wealth. He felt at home with them but not able to really fathom wealth. His financial income was a false wealth, one that would not allow him to continue along the lines of the past few days. He wondered about what illegal operations were going on there. How much danger was there for Sandy and Auburn? What was the reason for the conference next month? Who was attending?

He pulled into the yard and before he could open the car door his mother was on the porch and coming towards him. He hugged her and she asked, "Did you enjoy your foray? What did you learn? Lunch is ready."

"Mom, lunch is always ready around here."

"Oh I didn't prepare anything, Aglaea did it all."

He stopped, "Aglaea?"

"Yes. You told her you wanted to go to lunch, didn't you?"

"Is there nothing sacred or secret with you women?"

At that moment Aglaea appeared on the porch wiping her hands on a towel as he was walking towards her with his mother. He put his bags down and gave her a hug and a kiss.

"Day off? This is a very pleasant surprise."

"Worked every day since you left, so I took a few off. Did you complete your quest?"

"Not quite. But I'm in a better position to make some decisive plans. One thing I have decided. I will go back to school and prepare for a teaching career or position in Art History, including courses in paleontology and archeology affiliated with history."

"Great! What happened to cause you to be so positive about this?"

"A long story that may take several hours."

"I've got two days off."

"She's been here since yesterday. She's having her house painted and refinished."

"What? On such short notice?"

"Not really. Had already made arrangements to have a complete makeover inside and the painters and carpenters were available earlier than expected. Your mom insisted on me using the guest room while repairs were made."

"When did this happen?"

"In church Sunday. Aglaea mentioned what she was doing so I insisted she stay here and give them absolute freedom," his mother interjected. "Wash up and we'll have lunch. Here comes Dad."

Apparently Aglaea and his mother conversed once a day during his venture. Now he needed to get to the packages. He had mentioned to Ramona that he should know by Thursday. Should he tell Aggie? Lunch was pleasant and filling. Aggie fit in so well! It was as though she always belonged there. He excused himself and started to go examine the packages. Aggie suddenly appeared beside him.

"Is the Buick so important that you need to look at it before we take a ride to our site?"

They entered the workshop. The Buick was shining and ready to roll. Aglaea walked over and got into the driver's side.

"This is comfortable. Cute. Just my height. Afraid I know nothing about a standard shift. A big wheel."

He had gotten in on the passenger side. He looked at her. She leaned over, cupped his face in her hands and kissed him.

"Now I see the practicality of a bench seat."

"Aggie," he said a little sternly. She immediately looked at him and her expression changed to one of doubt and serious concern. "Aggie, I haven't been honest with you. I mentioned that there were some things about which I needed answers and to trust me and give me time. Remember?"

"Sounds serious. Have I misinterpreted and overstepped my bounds?"

"No! No! Not at all!"

The look of relief and reduced tension showed in her face.

"Aggie I've decided I need help and someone I can trust. First, let me say one thing. I've never been in love. Well, not true. I think I love you, but what is love? I don't know."

"This is serious. What have you gotten yourself into? If it makes any difference, I feel the same way. Since I was fourteen."

They hugged and laughed.

"Look. We have to be serious for a few minutes," he said.

"I *am* serious."

"No . . . Listen to me, please!"

He proceeded to tell her about the Buick and finding the packages. The money. The reason for the trip. Meeting the various people.

"Dora? You met Dora?"

"Yes! Do you know her?

"Is she still going with Paul? She's a cousin of mine and was one of my best friends. My side of the family was ostracized because we were the poor ones. Dora and I didn't know that so we stayed friends. Then we met in college but didn't tell her parents about it. Roomed together for two semesters."

"They are going to get married. Let me finish."

He continued giving a brief outline and mentioned why he was here, including the possible dangers and international connections. Then he went to the locked cabinets and began opening the packages. Finally he found one with money around the edges but in the middle only a few bills covered by plastic wrapping also covering an ancient looking book. Another packet had notebooks and another had formal documents neatly done up in waterproof containers. Five such packages.

"These are the documents that Ramona needed and indicated that there could be some dire consequences if placed into the wrong hands. Aggie, I'm sorry I told you about this. It could be dangerous."

"Don't be. That's what trust is all about. What are you going to do?"

"Take this back to her as soon as possible."

"Fly?"

"Good thought. I was considering copying some of it."

"That might take a day or so to complete."

"But it might be safer to have a copy just in case."

"True, but some look so delicate."

"Probably part of the Nag Hammadi books."

"What? Don't jest!"

"I'm not!"

"This *is* serious."

"I'm going to get a couple of suitcases and pack this stuff into them. Some of this looks too delicate to unwrap."

"We'll just do the books that are newer and the documents."

"Where?"

"I have copiers and printers with sorting capabilities."

"Leave the money as before. Ramona indicated finders are keepers, but I don't know. It's tempting. I'll take what I need to get back and play the part and see what happens."

They packed everything and left for Aggie's house. Her office was very well equipped. During the copying they discussed Dora and Paul and came up with a plan to play should they both get invited. They would not admit knowing each other.

At midnight they were tired and decided to return home. He had forgotten to call Ramona. He woke at six thirty, dressed and arrived at the kitchen with its coffee, bacon and biscuit smells and Aggie sitting at the table with Matt and Isabelle.

"Don't you ever sleep, Aggie?"

"You should know by this time that people in the medical field have different hours from the rest of the world. Are you ready to resume your copying? I told Isabelle that we had quite a bit of paper work to accomplish today, so she's making a lunch,"

"I've got to make one phone call before we go."

"Okay."

At eight he called Ramona.

"I think I have what you are looking for, in part at least."

"Oh good. When will you be back? Don't go to The Resort. Come directly here."

"Some of it looks very delicate. Very old."

"Those are not the documents in which the people are interested. Just the new ones. When will you arrive?"

"I'm not certain. I plan to leave by Saturday." Actually he planned to leave sooner but felt safer to say this.

"Driving or flying?"

"Don't know yet. I'll call."

They finished copying the documents that afternoon, except for the delicate book and parchments. They photographed them, and wearing gloves, also made a few copies of them. They returned to his house before dinner with the smell of paint and the sound of the printer clicking in their ears. They wanted to make more copies of the book and parchments but decided it was too risky, not wanting to chance destroying or damaging them. Someone had apparently made a typed copy or translation but neither could understand the script. During this intense working session, they planned what would happen when Dora called or wrote. It was more fun than they had had in years and during this period they grew closer as if they had always been together.

"Piearce, I'm so glad you didn't go the route of so many guys and I'm so glad I kept my nose to the grindstone and returned here. I have to admit, I was prepared to move on after a while if you weren't available."

"Thanks. We have the time to reestablish our relationship. Let's wait and keep the rest of them guessing for a while."

"Deal."

"Have you told your parents yet?"

"Mom has been on the phone every day since I first told her I'd met you. She is skeptical and very protective. I'm having fun kind of teasing her. I think she wants the FBI to do a background check on anyone I mention to her. They are planning to come here for a visit as soon as the house is finished. Oh. And I need a photo of you to send her. I took several while we were copying, but I want a better one."

At supper he indicated to his parents that he had to return to The Resort for more business, possibly to conclude it. He called the airport and made arrangements for a flight and a car rental. He called the detective agency with a limited update and asked the detective to contact Sandy and Auburn.

Friday morning after breakfast he and Aglaea said their good-byes at his vehicle while mother stood on the porch

"I go on duty today for the weekend, so you know where I'll be. Be careful, please?"

"I will. You take care. If you need cash to finish your home, help yourself."

"No way. Nice idea but I'll wait till it's all over. Say hi to your girlfriends. What are they? International detectives?"

"I really don't know their titles, but that is close enough."

# Chapter XIII

The plane landed with a jolt and taxied to the tower complex. His rental car was ready. He retrieved his two medium-sized bags that the porters had trouble lifting at first try. They put them in the trunk while he placed his knapsack on the back seat. He was off toward The Resort and the connecting road to Ramona's. He called Auburn indicating that he would go straight through. Auburn said, "There are a couple of letters here for you. The detective called. Apparently you indicated that you might be back, so we'll talk, I'll register you now." In a voice a little louder she said, "Yes sir, I'll see to getting your room ready immediately. Would the same one be satisfactory?"

Piearce caught the change in tone, apparently someone was near or standing at the desk. He said, "Okay. I'll stop by after I deliver the merchandise."

He arrived at Ramona's, drove cautiously to the garage, unloaded his suitcases into Ramona's car, took the keys from the car, locked it and then drove to the house, stopping and parking behind a large limousine. Carrying his knapsack he walked to the door and rang the bell. The maid opened the door, recognized him and led him to the library saying, "Miss Ramona and Miss Rowena are on the patio. I'll announce you." She left him while he looked at the book stacks and wondered if they were for display or if they had been read by Tomas and Ramona. He heard the two women coming accompanied by two men. He wasn't prepared for that. He had noticed the limousine in the drive but hoped it was a family car.

"Oh, Piearce. So good to see you. Rowena, you remember Piearce. Piearce is the paramedic who tended to me at The Resort. I thought you had left and returned home."

"I got to thinking about you and I so enjoyed my stay I thought I'd take another long weekend to relax and check on my patient. Am I intruding?"

"No, not at all. Gentlemen, this is Piearce. These gentlemen are from the church, checking on me and looking for old records that Father Tom may have had."

The men shook hands with Piearce and were almost obsequious in their demeanor. One motioned to the maid and said, "Would you go to the kitchen and tell the driver and secretary we are about to leave? Thank you."

"But you must stay for dinner," said Ramona.

"No, thank you. We are on a mission and we've looked over all you have shown us but this is not what we were looking for. "At that moment two other men arrived. The cleric closest spoke, and the two started to leave. The cleric added, "In about ten minutes."

They spoke in admiration of Piearce and his wonderful dedication working to help people. "God loves and blesses people like you for the marvelous service you perform. You say you were at The Resort. It must have put a dent in your savings to stay there."

"It did and it didn't. I was the recipient of a goodly amount of money, a windfall bestowed upon me, so I accepted the treat. It doesn't happen often, but I'm glad I did it."

"Ooh. Congratulations! Another disguised gift from our Lord."

One of the men returned and Piearce noticed an almost imperceptible negative head movement. They must have checked his car.

"Well, Ramona, we'll leave and bless you all. Thank you."

They left with Ramona and Rowena seeing them to the door. As the car drove away both ladies rushed back.

"You know they searched your car, don't you."

"Maybe they should have searched the car that these open," he said as he handed Ramona the keys to her car.

"You clever man. Let's wait and retrieve the stash as discreetly as possible; they may still be watching."

"Who are they, really?"

"They are from the Vatican. Special envoys, claiming there are documents here that prove the transfer of oil holdings to the Vatican years ago, inadvertently given to Tomas to hold. The cartel has also inquired about them and that's why these documents may be so important. Apparently several heads of states were in Egypt and exchanged favors and legally gave away what was supposedly wasteland but now are possibly productive oil fields. I know Tomas was unscrupulous in his early life and even later for a while, and I also, but studying and time changes one. Tomas was really an agnostic leaning toward atheist ideals. We'll save that discussion for later. Right now we need to plan our next move."

"Mom, the garage, or guest house, connects to the workshop, to the greenhouse, then there is the hedgerow from the greenhouse to the patio. We can gain access to the car right now without ever being seen."

"That's right! Good reasoning."

"Not my doing.

"My daughter saw her daughter go out to meet the gardener's son that way." They chuckled when Rowena said,

"She takes after her grandmother."

Immediately they exited to the patio door, to the hedgerow, through the greenhouse, the workshop, to the guest house, keeping low, aware they might possibly be seen. They returned with the bags. Piearce with the heavier, the women with one saying, "My God! So heavy! This much?"

"Only the documents, Ramona, nothing else," responded Piearce without disclosing he'd copied them and stored them or rather, Aglaea did. He was glad he'd given her a few thousand to get bank boxes or a vault for storage.

"We'll take them upstairs to the office. It has a security system separate from the rest of the house." The office opened onto a ten-by-twenty recessed raised patio overlooking the garden patio. A marvelous view. Off the office was a conference room where they placed the suitcases on the table, then carefully unpacked, Piearce undid the waterproof wrappings and said, "These are probably the scriptures that were found in Nag Hammadi area of Egypt, with possible translations or at least a copy of the original book."

"Piearce, do you realize what you have just implied?"

"Just a possible confirmation of what has been suggested previously."

"Look! This packet has what looks like title transfers of lands in various countries from the Church to some company in exchange for . . . I can't make it out. They switched to Latin or something else . . . It starts in English . . . Oh look, another almost identical in what looks like, I don't know, Arabic?" Rowena was carefully shifting through the stack continuing to mumble and talk to herself, finally saying, "Mom, this is going to have to be studied by someone who knows. This is evidently evidence for the cartel or someone who knows much more than we do. I don't condone the Godfathers of the family, but this could have serious implications."

"This is far more serious than I first realized. Oh God. Who do we go to? And we only have just looked at this assortment and already we see international subversive activities as a possible outcome. Piearce, any suggestions?"

"We don't know that this material is what it seems, but we could go to the government, the FBI or similar group . . ." He hesitated, then proceeded with, "I know a couple of international agents that I could show one or two documents to and see what their interpretation might be. They work for a private investigation concern that may even specialize in this sort of thing."

At that moment the phone rang three times, stopped, and rang three times again. Ramona said it was for her. She went to the desk, answered, spoke, listened, spoke again and said, "They have already been here," a pause, "About half hour ago," pause, "Be very careful."

She returned to the conference room and said,

"That was Rolando. He's on his way here now. There was a second key he didn't mention. He has a packet for me that was left in another safety deposit box. He's going to keep an eye out for the limo. He may stop and mail the packet express to me just in case. He'll be here by tonight. Rowena, how did we get so involved with this? It's time we got some of our attorneys here and the sooner the better. Piearce, your idea of the government is good, but this will risk the safety of all concerned. This could be huge. I'm sorry you are involved. Actually no one knows of your involvement, and about your friends who are agents, I'll let you know soon. What language do you think this translation, or copy, is in?"

"I'll defer to the linguist on that one. Maybe Hebrew or Arabic but if that is what I suspect it is, I'd keep it far away from the other documents until you know its content. If it is like the other books, it may not be very complimentary toward the churches."

"We really want you to stay overnight, Piearce, but in considering our recent visitors, The Resort would be better in keeping with the charade we've created. I'll phone . . ."

He interrupted her saying, "That won't be necessary. I have made tentative plans for a room."

"Piearce, these agents you know. How reliable are they? How trustworthy? Do you think they would know anything about this sort of activity?"

"I believe they deal in international money laundering, so this just might come under that heading. Just for argument's sake, how safe is your money should this come crashing down?"

"It's all taken care of. You are, of course, thinking of the Family and their reprisals. We have nothing to fear. Besides, I'm not long for this world now anyway. Why don't you present a hypothetical situation to your agent friends and feel them out? If you can do that conveniently without arousing too much suspicion, get back to me or Rowena. I'd appreciate it."

"Rowie! Rowie may have tipped a hand somehow. She and Marla!" said Rowena.

It was the first time that a definite connection had been made between Marla and someone else and it alerted Piearce to that moment in the cavern. He had forgotten that complex arrangement. So, family involvement may possibly exist.

"No. I don't think that is a problem. Rolando reported back to the Cartel that the boxes were empty, and the church and the family are satisfied that we have no information. They are pretty thorough and probably have been going over this for quite some time. If Marla is involved, it may be something of a different nature. Piearce, when you get there, go and see Super, and tell him thanks from me. Rolando was very loyal to Tomas."

"I'd like to hear more about you and your life sometime in the future. The library downstairs has a lot of philosophical books in it; did you read them or Tomas? Or are they for reference?"

"Tomas read just about all of them. I have read a goodly number, especially the ones that Tomas wanted to discuss. We kept them for referrals when I couldn't remember a point to argue with him. I miss him so much. If you see any you would like, help yourself. Take a couple of good ones and then you can have an excuse to return them and come and visit. One of our favorites was dealing with gnosis or agnostic situations."

Piearce left with a few books and made a call to Auburn to confirm that he had a room and to update her on the limousine. She had taken care of the room and had put his letters in his room for him, also mentioning the new arrivals.

He arrived at eight, went to his room, took a shower, and read the letters: one from Paul and Dora, and one from Harriet. They were both complimentary and wanted him to be sure to attend the wedding. Dora said that when she got home she was going to look up her cousin's number and invite her to the wedding, hoping he'd come alone but assuring him that his girlfriend was also invited should he feel he couldn't come without her. Piearce smiled and thought '*You are in for a very unique and shocking surprise.*' Harriet's note was deeply philosophical and full of admiration, hope, and looking forward to seeing him next month.

There was a card with a note that said 'Boat House- ten p.m.?'

He reviewed the recent activities and his delivery of the papers and books. The more he thought about the papers, the more he became convinced that there might be billions in real estate. No wonder secrecy was so important. And what of the papers that may be of as much value to the church as to some religious cult? And were Marla and the Super acting as brokers? Who were these people? Why was he involved? He thought after the delivery he'd be free of everything, but the search of his car by the church group caused him to be even more vigilant. Was the coming conference all part of this? Did Tomas plan this or suspect this years ago? Did someone here suspect and reveal that there was a possibility of a delivery? How? Who?

At eight thirty he was in the informal dining room enjoying a pot roast-dinner, a popular nineteen thirty's dish. He ate it all except for dessert; that he rejected. As he was finishing, he noticed the priests walking and chatting with officials, passing by the main entrance with a contingency in tow.

The girls were waiting as he walked the back path to their rendezvous.

"Welcome home," they said.

"Funny, funny," he replied.

They exchanged facts, gave updates. Piearce enlightened them about the possible real-estate fiasco that could have far-reaching repercussions. The only thing he didn't tell them about was the books and parchment or the copies. He referred to them as '*two other bits of interesting artifacts*' that he'd explain later.

"Such as?" they asked.

"Later. Right now it seems the church is trying to exploit the sale of massive oil rights that were signed over to private enterprises like the Cartel. It's also possible that there may be a laundering activity channeled in several countries to or by the cartel."

"Yes. And this resort may be one of the centers for that activity."

"Those two churchmen have been here before. We feel there could be a calamity in the making. The income here versus the amounts banked couldn't possibly be justified. They are depositing ten to twenty times their income as far as we can see. That doesn't count the stock or other investments that are being made."

"Boy, you two have been busy. How much oil has been purchased? That could tie in with the ownership of these documents. I didn't read them all, but there are a goodly number in a variety of countries."

"Which ones, can you recall?"

"Seems like Sudan was mentioned, plus several properties in Russia, Mongolia, Arabia, New York, and Iceland."

"New York? OIL?"

"No. Not all the documents were for oil; the New York reference was real estate, I think, that was once owned by the church and sold to private corporations many years ago. Apparently these papers prove the transfer from the church. It was probably a hush-hush situation and the church may be trying to reclaim it as theirs because no registration exists as to deeds that would have been recorded. I don't know, I didn't read them. The evidence will probably counter the churches demands and incriminate some top-ranking politicians and clergy."

"This may be why the meeting is scheduled at this resort. To avoid a scandal and avoid identification of persons who might have corrupted the church or someone close to the financial leaders."

"Who is the devil's advocate for all this? Did any of the papers indicate anyone?"

"The papers are from years ago, and I didn't read them. If they were from the Nag Hammadi era, it is possible that someone tried to squelch or control the find there at first, but that is an entirely different set of circumstances. Paul mentioned the Göbekli Tepe and Nag Hammadi visits he made when he spoke to me about his travels and I wonder if these papers had anything to do with that. It was mentioned that a settlement was established 11,000 years ago at Göbekli Tepe! I'll help, ladies, but I'm not in this field nor do I enjoy being a possible target in a foreign intrigue arena."

His phone vibrated. It was McCracken. "You're on speaker with the agents present but the volume at a minimum."

"What have you gotten yourself into? I just received a call from someone from the Internal Affairs at the federal level. Apparently they are very concerned about an international exposure with far-reaching consequences. They picked up on my inquiries and now I've been ordered to cease and desist. I have not revealed my clients name, but that will only be a matter of time before they show up here. You two ladies be extra careful."

"We will."

"Ladies, are you feds? Don't be candid, just yes or no."

"Not directly."

"Okay. Just wanted you all to know the score so far."

"I'll make a phone call, perhaps Ramona may have clued someone in. She wanted these girls to check out some of this for her and give her some assistance. I haven't gotten to that phase yet, but, ladies, I'll fill you in shortly. Anything else, Mac?"

"No. Keep in touch."

Piearce then revealed the entire episode to the two agents. Their response was that one of them would go and talk to Ramona and the other would remain at The Resort and contact their boss. Secrecy was of the utmost importance. Auburn was off duty and said she'd go. Her GPS would get her there with no problem especially if Piearce phoned ahead. They parted. He called Ramona and gave her a phone number.

Piearce started to call Aglaea, then realized the time and texted her instead. *your cuz dora left invite to wed. Harriet also*

Almost instantly a reply of: *mom left msg dora called her house.*

Two seconds later he hit the speed dial for Aglaea.

"Hi, just leaving the ER to get some rest. Looks like a busy weekend. Does your mother always pack a lunch for you? I found a picnic basket on the seat of the car with enough food for the weekend!"

"Yes, but I convinced her not to continue or I'd need new clothes."

"She is also convinced we were destined for each other. She also mentioned that she thought you planned to use the Buick as the honeymoon car. I mentioned that we were just very good friends. She took my hand and said, 'No, you are more than good friends. He looks at you with more admiration and adoration than his Buick, and that, Aggie, is a fact!' so now I know how I am compared, or measured. How did you do? No details, I need some sleep."

He gave a quick synopsis of his activities and his expectations for the next few days. He was quite sure Marla and Rowie were the co-conspirators with Roberto in trying to recover the cherished evidence, but how did they learn of the key? "Who initiated the recovery after the discovery of the meaning of the key to the forgotten safety deposit box? How did they determine what was in the storage boxes? Who was the recipient of the bills and bank notices for the box rentals? Someone in the Church? The Government? The Cartel?"

"Whoa! Stop! As much as I want to talk and listen, I'm too tired. How much of the relics were donated? No, never mind. I don't think I really want to know at this time."

"I'm going to let the family be concerned. I've turned over the data and if it weren't for doing a couple of favors for Ramona, I'd leave for home now"

"Wish you were here. No. I'm too tired to entertain."

"Sleep well. I'll call or text tomorrow. Sweet dreams."

"Nite."

Showering again, he reviewed the day's events while soaping up, wondering why Tomas had been chosen to be so highly regarded by the people who gave him the documents for safe keeping and why hadn't someone claimed the documents sooner. The Nag Hammadi books he could understand no one asking about, but the titles and deeds? Where did they come from? What about the money? Was it Tomas's that he had originally squirreled away, or hidden assets from investments? Should he keep it? Or donate it to a worthy cause, or return it to Ramona? She said to keep it, but . . . ! To bed. Tomorrow he'd face that problem. He started to skim-read the books he had borrowed.

# Chapter XIV

*At breakfast the news headlines were blatant and impressive. Controversy over ownership of oil wells in three separate countries. The headlines would have meant nothing to him ordinarily, but he quickly read the article of disputing property lines and ownership of newly developed oil discoveries. There were entanglements of missing improperly-recorded sales, thereby disputing the complex legal matters handled by a forty-year old warranty title transfer claimed by three separate (entities) claimants. The names were confluent, hidden in sub-companies that had false fronts to hide tax payments. The reporter didn't seem to be accusing any one group in particular but said that political implications of fraud were evident. Apparently a paramedic had inadvertently uncovered a plot to steal billions from prominent . . .*

*Piearce immediately stood, overturning the table. He was stunned! He turned to leave and the four 'Church' men from Ramona's were there with guns drawn . . . They fired!*

*　*　　*　*　　*　*　　*　*　　*　*　　*　*

He woke with a start! A dream? No, a nightmare!

At breakfast he sat with a sleep-deprived Sandy.

"Good morning, Sandy."

To which she replied, "My name is Ursula. Lavinia left a few minutes ago. Someone called her last night late from Ramona's house and left a message. Then we got an early six-thirty follow-up call. We have an unexpected flight from Bangkok today. The other three directors are doing a training program so it falls on my shoulders. Should be interesting. Hope wardrobe has oriental attire of that time frame. A busy, busy day. Your friends in the limo have a meeting at ten AM. Gotta go. Bye."

He looked around at the breakfast group. Amazing how much money was being spent to go back in time. And this was just the non-conformists. The formal group was seldom seen in here. Tomorrow he'd frequent the formal dining room, at least to look in. He was enjoying a second cup of coffee when Marla came in, said hello and asked if he minded her company. He rose and held her chair, while she tried to decline his assistance.

"This is unusual for you, being up this early and without a proper chaperone," he said.

"You are the chaperone today. No. Early meeting and I'm in demand. Le roi le veut."

"I know it's French, but that is it."

"The king wills it."

"Who is the king?"

She sipped her coffee, finished chewing and said, "The vice president of operations, Carlos Ferracco. His English isn't too bad, but at times he gets lost in the translation. So, I understand you went to visit with Ramona. How is she?"

"Her hand is much better. I felt obliged to follow up, and it's only an hour away and a pleasant drive. I wanted to see her before I took in the show tonight. How did you know?"

"I spoke with Rowie. She'd make a good catch for you. What do you think of her?"

Piearce saw it coming and was prepared. He was sure Rowie and Marla spoke on entirely different subjects than him.

"She has a great personality and is intelligent and easy on the eyes. Were I not already involved, I certainly would seriously entertain pursuing her as a prospective companion. But I am sure there are many men who would better fulfill her expectations. My wealth certainly can't compare with her family and their means."

"That is where you are wrong. Rowie can adjust or adapt to any situation. She has had many opportunities and her current escort, shall we say, is below her status and intelligence. You, on the other hand, would fit in much better in her world."

"Thanks for the vote of confidence. So how did you meet?"

"Her grandmother brought her here and I tripped and fell on her, literally on the grand staircase. Had she not grabbed me, I may have tumbled all the way down. Very few people witnessed the event, but those who did tell me that she just grabbed me with one hand and held the hand rail with the other preventing me from going over the rail and taking a twenty foot free fall."

"A heroine to boot. Why do I get the feeling that you are not disclosing the entire story? Did you know her prior to the rescue?"

"You are shrewd, and direct. I like that. I met her once in Paris. When she was younger but forgot about it. She was with her grandfather while he was on a business trip. I also had dealings with him on other occasions in Rome. That is how we learned of the Buick and tried to get him to donate it to the Cartel. He was a retired priest. It's a long story, but when she came here with her grandmother I recognized her and the rest is history. We have a lot in common."

Marla indicated that she was going to take a trip for the company in preparation for the conference next month. "Have you decided to invest in The Resort?"

"Not really. There is plenty of time. Super said he didn't get a commission for finding investors but I wondered if you might?"

"I wish! No, we think it's a good deal. And I noticed that you are a friend of Ramona, so I thought you might join her ranks."

"Actually, I'm not a close friend of hers. It is a newly acquired friendship. I find her company pleasant and intellectual, plus her daughter and granddaughter are equally interesting. I was wondering, what kind of work you do here that causes you to travel to Paris and Rome and who knows where else in the world?"

"Oh . . . I guess you could say I am a jack-of all trades and master of none. I'm called a Director of Personnel and am on the board of directors for investments, foreign primarily. Also, I do acquisition of special needs."

"Such as the Buick?"

"Yes, but that was an unfortunate incident. We doubt we'll ever discover what really happened. By the way, do you happen to own any oil stock?"

"Don't tell me you are an investment broker also."

"No. Super mentioned buying an investment, so I was just inquiring. Looking for knowledgeable people. I like to see investment property firsthand, so I go to look over the sites or properties."

"Oil companies often don't want the land, just the rights. Minerals, gas, oil and whatever else they put into their lease agreements. I'm not the one to give answers to such specific investments."

"I understand there are many lesser fields in existence that we seldom hear about. Those are the ones that should be valuable in the near future. Even now there are old land tracts about which the ownership is disputed."

"Really! I thought something like that would be a done deal."

"Quite a few are in review from what I understand. That's why I was wondering about investments. They are going to be valuable in the future."

"How is it you gathered all this information? The stock market?"

"Yes and no. Some guests in the past were heavy into debating investments, dropping tid-bits and by listening carefully to those conversations, I gleaned sufficient knowledge to know that land purchasing pays better than oil producing for the oil companies. Fifty years ago, not the case! But as time went on, land speculation in suspected oil producing areas could control the market, or ruin it."

"You'll have to be more specific."

"Suppose you or your family owned or controlled land parcels that were oil-rich and didn't know it. And someone offered you a 'fair price' for the property, even though it was in a desolate region, especially if the place was thought of as desert or wasteland. Almost anything they offered would be a plus. Now let us assume you know nothing of the sale and assume you or the family, still own the land but find out that someone else presumably has a notation indicating a land transfer fifty years ago. Now, what would you offer for that land and what would you do if they couldn't locate the title or documentation? Another scenario: The land was sold fifty years ago and is adjacent to an oil productive pool. A diagonal well would tap into the reserve and the oil field couldn't prevent the piracy."

"Sounds like you have stumbled onto something pretty big. But how does that get into the hands of the investors?"

"Apparently there are such stands of oil reserves with disputes as to who owns the property. Now, would you invest in a market that could possibly increase your returns by a thousand or possibly ten thousand percent? Of course you would!"

"Perhaps. I'd need to know the ways and wherefores first. How would you know the deeds to such lands are not forgeries or stolen?"

"Good question. The deed would have to be verified, of course. Several of the large oil concerns are currently trying to buy up adjacent land to their current holding or leases. There are several extremely valuable holding companies that are claiming ownership of these land masses that are claimed by a multitude of people who can't produce the deeds. Quite a controversy. Anyway, there are diplomatic road blocks in some areas and the 'King' has asked me to accompany an investigative group. So I am examining all possible means of investments, especially if I am privy to such facts before they hit the market."

"Wow! Sounds unbelievable. What happens if the cartel or other investors hear about it first?"

"That's the chance we take. You interested now?"

"Got to think about it. What time are you leaving and when are you going to return?"

"When Le Roi says. I don't know the exact return date but it will be before next month's mega conference."

"I'll need more information and a minimum investment spread."

"So you are interested?"

"Up to a point. This why you wanted to corner me this morning?"

"No. Actually I wanted your feelings about Rowie."

"She ask you?"

"No, but she mentioned that you piqued the interest of her grandmother and if she was so interested, then perhaps she should take a closer look."

"Do all women work in teams to entrap an available man?"

"Only the ones that are too good to be true."

His mind was racing with questions about the oil documents. Did she know about them or did she have her own source? Was she to be trusted? Was she searching for confirmation about the documents' location? Did she still have ties with the Vatican or their agents?

Suddenly she visibly stiffened while looking past him, then glanced at her coffee saying, "Oh, look at the time. Think I'd better go see if Le Roi is ready to put the agenda together. See you, and let me or my husband know about any investments."

He rose as she stood and walked out of the breakfast area. He sat and asked for more coffee as the table was being cleared of her dishes. Shortly thereafter, the two secretaries of the priests came in for breakfast. He wondered if she had seen them and if that was the reason she left so suddenly; if so, was she fearful of them seeing her with him? He also experienced a slight twinge recalling the dream. Perhaps this was an omen to leave. They didn't appear to notice him, but appearances are deceiving. While walking toward the waterfront he wondered about the oil speculation to which Marla referred and if Rowie had mentioned the documents. Maybe, just maybe he should alert Lavinia.

# Chapter XV

Lavinia needn't have been concerned about locating the home with her GPS. Rowena and Rowie flagged her down three miles outside the town limits and led her to the estate via a seldom used back road to the garage where she parked her car inside. She recognized them from their resort visits. There were polite hugs and the concealed walk to the house via the garage, greenhouse and arched walk to the patio where breakfast was waiting. She sipped her coffee and politely said, "Before we start, you must realize I am compelled to report any illegal subversive activities. Understand that although I am not a federal agent, I am still sworn to uphold the law, so I am telling you this now, as an unofficial breakfast guest visiting you. There will be a point when I'll inform you that I am acting officially and anything said after that I'll record if it is illegal. Fair enough?"

"More than fair. We found out last night that there were campers on the adjacent property and then early this morning the grounds man and chauffeur reported that there has been some wandering observed, and located their concealment along the drive. He sent a pair of men to check the back properties and that is why you were led into the estate in concealment. We hope you were not noticed, for your own safety. Also my investment people have indicated a deplorable number of inquiries about our accounts by unknown sources."

"I doubt it is the government. But who knows."

"To start out, we'll say that my daughter and my granddaughter are writing a book, and would like you to listen to the scenario, an international intrigue story with a plot that will not be divulged completely until late in the story," said Ramona. "It concerns a priest, an ex-priest and some secret papers and artifacts with which he was entrusted. These papers were forgotten for many years and until recently were insignificant. However, in light of today's economy and certain countries' need for special resources, these papers may become very important, even effecting security of some nations."

"Are these papers or documents concerned with any one country more than another?"

"No. They refer to a number of countries."

"Evidently these papers are valuable. Are these papers that can be negotiated by a higher bidder to create a bidding war thereby increasing their value?"

"Yes."

Ramona then laid out the plot of the story and how different countries might even become adamant enough to have conflicts ensue. She mentioned the safety deposit boxes and the movement of the papers and artifacts, the possible church involvement, that the papers were currently in another new location, and that the cartel and other agencies were currently searching for the documents. She spoke for half an hour giving details but no definite disclosure.

"Sounds as though you have a monetary value of an immense nature and I may have to involve more learned sources. There may be diplomatic ways of handling the security, especially if there is a danger of retaliation Can you enlighten me?"

"The documents are deeds to properties of immense size in several countries."

"International. I see the flags flying now."

Breakfast over, they retired to the office above and the safe room.

"This is a beautiful view," said Lavinia.

"Yes, my husband loved this view and this room. Here are a few of the documents. They are deeds to tracts of land that give access to oil fields."

"Oh, oh. And you mentioned that many people are interested even though they are dated over fifty years ago. Someone will have to determine the legality and verify ownership."

"That's just it. Two major groups currently are claiming rights to the lands. Originally the lands were thought to be worthless, but now they are found to be near or abut oil and mineral reserves or deposits."

Lavinia's phone rang. It was Piearce. She said, "Hello Piearce," so everyone knew to whom she was speaking. They indicated with a thumbs-up acknowledgement. She listened to him carefully, then handed the phone to Ramona. Piearce updated Ramona so she would understand that if Rowie hadn't mentioned anything, then there was another possibility operating on the same frequency. Lavinia has been updated and could divulge what is necessary, but do not trust their phones. They hung up.

Lavinia went to work looking over the documents. She spent an hour going over the documents, not the religious artifacts. She estimated that if these documents were accurate, the money involved could be in the billions. This was not a job for her. It was too vast. This was an extraordinary international exposé.

While she did this, Ramona took Rowie to get coffee and to get some exercise, then returned with coffee for all.

"These deeds could be claimed by the governments of these nations if, and I say if, there is any public disclosure of any sort," Lavinia said.

Ramona responded with, "That is why we need you to either be an intermediary or find a way of disposing of these deeds as soon as possible. The cartel is quite interested as is the Vatican, plus another group with Mafioso connections that called and are on their way here to discuss possible knowledge of lost merchandise. Somehow they obtained information that Father Tom was the keeper of these documents and they want to inspect his papers. Fortunately we have a set of his diaries that do not divulge consequential information as the secret diaries do, so we can give them those. As we mentioned, two groups have been here and appear to be satisfied, but that is not proven by the surveillance groups currently encamped. This third group we strongly suspect are a combination of Russian, Taliban, Chinese, and who knows who else. My advisors have stalled them, but to little or no avail."

Ramona was tired and looked it. Amazing how she had seemed to age in just a few days.

"From these papers and from what I know, the gas reserves in Mexico are one of the largest and most productive in the world. Thailand, I can't recall, Russia we know has one of the largest oil reserves. Canada has a monstrous one north of Hudson Bay. We can't decipher some of the material, since it is written in Arabic or a similar language, but that is another issue. I'll call the office on a high-security line and discuss this with the powers-to-be. If you'll let me be alone in the office, I'll call now. This is very sensitive material.

"It might be best if you go to the garage or leave because we don't know when the other group will be here. Lock the safe and secure the room. Leave the outer door open to the conference room so anyone can see the floor safe in the corner. Good luck. Oh, and if you see Piearce, tell him I checked and all is well here," said Ramona while Rowie, Rowena, and, Lavinia left for their cars.

In the garage, Lavinia went to the cupola and called her office on a secured line on her backup phone. The phone battery began to pulse, giving her warning that that she had been on the line for a very long time. She returned to her hosts, indicating that a subcommittee of the highest security had been alerted and would very covertly contact them. She would take the few copies they had given her and send them to-the-powers to be and send them an identifying code for the contacts in the near future.

"You mentioned there were other artifacts and documents of a controversial nature. Care to enlighten me?

The women looked at each other and Ramona said,

"It involves the Vatican, we think. We can't decipher it, but from what we can gather by the notes, they may be even more detrimental to the national welfare than the oil fields. We were going to request some neutral group, but if this entourage is that high a level of government representatives, we could include a copy of the notes left in Tomas' diary, supporting these artifacts and books, or manuscripts. Possibly a Nag Hammadi connection."

"Mom, there is a green light on the board."

"What does that mean?" asked Lavinia.

"That is a board of the property. See the dim red lights? That is apparently where the observers are supposedly hiding. The area that we came in on is the green, so it is clear. We can leave now." At that moment a young man entered the garage and opened the door so they could leave. Rowie left with Lavinia after Rowena hugged her good bye.

*　　　*　　　*　　　*　　　*　　　*

　　*　　　*　　　*　　　*　　　*　　　*

## VATICAN CONNECTION

It was a dismal day for such a momentous meeting. Grave circumstances swung in the balance of its decision. The cold rain spattered against the windows, creating an ominous setting. Had the meeting been in a log cabin with a roaring fire in the fireplace, it still wouldn't have been considered cozy. In the large official office, a frosty atmosphere prevailed. The group was solemn, their decisions could alter the world: dire consequences rode the black stallion of disaster.

His Grace was agitated. How did this happen? How were all those documents signed without the approval of the College of Cardinals? Who initiated the sales arrangement for the drilling and mineral rights? And this priest who resigned and married his housekeeper, where are they? Is it possible to reclaim those properties without jeopardizing the Vatican?

The Cardinals replied that the priest was dead and that his wife knew nothing. The report was quite thorough. Their envoys were quite certain of that. The wife had been under surveillance for a number of days and had opened her records and his diaries for the Vatican's inspection. The two Novices that were sent out earlier as spies were both dead. They died in an automobile accident. Investigations all prove that it was an accident they had while driving a vintage car to The Resort. There were never any unusual activities reported prior to their demise. They were just victims of circumstances. No evidence was disclosed indicating that the priest himself had ever possessed any of the mining papers or deeds.

As to the artifacts, there was only the word of a couple of workmen who claimed there were fifteen codices instead of thirteen. Two codices were supposedly destroyed, but some feel they were actually secreted away and the scrolls and books were supposedly translated. It all happened years ago and was only a supposition.

His Grace indicated that the search should go on and asked, "We do not know for certain that there were fifteen codices instead of thirteen, do we? Are the two or three persons who divulged this information available for questioning?"

"No, Your Grace. The information came from an archivist who spoke with an archeologist who mentioned that the workmen had inadvertently destroyed two other artifacts; and, that the remains were deposited as trash in the fill for a highway roadbed. His reference was to the workers. He never said he saw the artifacts or any fragments."

"Is it possible they never existed?" asked his Grace.

"Anything is possible, Your Grace. It is the feeling of the search committee that there is a strong possibility that they may exist, as well as papers containing the drilling and mining rights documents that have recently been challenged."

"But there is no real connection between the two. Deeds and biblical artifacts are not really related," his Grace responded.

"We can pursue the deeds but it is beginning to look less profitable to continue the search for questionable material for which we never had any proof of existence, other than hearsay. Look into the property sales and their transfer when you are at the conference, but under no circumstance release anything to the public. No press at all! And find out about this Marla."

"Yes, Your Grace. We understand. We are leaving in a few days, but so far there has been no issue presented for evidence of the deeds or codices."

"If evidence is produced, do not contradict if it involves the church. Find a scapegoat."

"Yes, Your Grace."

"As I understand it, only a few individuals know of this possible fiasco."

"Yes, Your Grace."

"Keep it that way. You say it all happened in the late nineteen forties and early nineteen fifties. What a shame we only recently found out about this. And the priest died over three years ago? Too bad, too bad."

"When should we inform the Committee? Now?"

"No. Well, yes. Probably. But only about the possible, and I repeat, possible disbursement or sale of some properties. They know about the conference, but not of any repercussions that could develop. Under no circumstance should anyone challenge the illegality of the sales or transfers. We suspect that at the time it was done, it was to unload worthless holdings. Unfortunately, no one knows who authorized it or what the true value was at the time. If no papers are in evidence, then we'll claim the properties. It would help to have copies or maybe the original documents. The evidence of our other concern has even more disastrous consequences if an existence can be proven."

*    *    *    *    *    *

  *    *    *    *    *    *

Rowie said she was going to take a nap. She and her mother and grandmother had been up most of the night going over the papers and making some copies. Once off the property and on the highway she promptly fell asleep, after telling Lavinia that she wanted to rent a car from the airport and come into The Resort alone. Lavinia agreed with the idea. An hour and a half later they parted; twenty minutes after that Lavinia parked her car. What the trio didn't know is that she taped the entire conversation for her partner's benefit and the agency's top brass if necessary. This was bigger than anything she had ever experienced and there was no room for errors.

Ursula saw her come in and acknowledged her with a slight nod as Lavinia continued to their room. She wondered where Piearce might be and remembered she was supposed to be on duty that evening. It was going to be a long day. Tomorrow, either she or Ursula would take a few documents to the airport for special handling after they contacted the upper echelon for further instruction.

# Chapter XVI

They arrived at the house at different hours over a period of two days by a variety of transportation modes. Shipments containing computers and scientific equipment needed for analysis arrived by Fed-Ex and UPS. One pair arrived as hikers with knapsacks, another as bikers with saddle bags, asking directions, then presenting their passwords. They were all shown in and their only request was for showers, and, of course, the transition was miraculous, from slovenly ill speaking individuals, to well-mannered intellects. After a brief explanation they were shown the papers and documents and artifacts. An elderly gentleman and his assistant immediately gazed at the artifacts and books and manuscripts in disbelief. They paid no heed to the oil documents and maps. Those they left to the legal experts and that entourage. They were lost in their own world. They were the only two who had come through the main drive and front doors. The others were aware of the secret entrance through the garage. At the end of four hours of examining the manuscripts and oil deed and maps, the legal international analysis had decided on their value and authenticity and were on their radios and high tech phones making contacts.

The two scholars had one of the interpretations and partial interpretations translated. They said they'd need at least another day to finish their preliminary examination. It was tedious work and much discussion ensued as to the meaning and possible interpretations.

It was a story. They worked deep into the night before retiring and were up early. Before coffee was made, they were at it again. Their laptops should have been smoking. They printed out copies for Ramona and Rowena to read saying that it was a preliminary of the story on one of the parchments that had been previously analyzed.

> *Praised be to the Creator! Survival has been miraculous. My injuries were not as serious as were originally determined. When they found me, I was unconscious and thankful for that. My so-called criminal days are now behind me as I re-travel to distant lands of my youth. My wife and children have encouraged me to record the events leading up to my withdrawal from my original homeland. It is better this way.*
>
> *I was an Essene and dabbled in Zoroastrianism for a while, investigated Buddhism, Brahmanism: all influenced my life. Let me go back and start at an earlier time of my life. I am now fifty-eight and it has been twenty-five years since they found me and nursed me back to good health.*
>
> *In my youth, I was a very precocious child, full of questions, seeing only the good and seeking to help find a way to help others. My parents thought that by joining a camel caravan, I would learn more and might even become wealthy. I could read and write: which gave me an advantage; very unusual for boys my age. Being devoutly religious has its advantages, but not in a world where you pass through religious regions that varied significantly enough to cause condemnation if you voiced your opinion.*
>
> *During the first week we travelled many leagues, set up trading our wares, picked up provisions and continued to our next destination. Ten days of travel took us three hundred leagues east. I learned directions using the stars at night and the sun by day. Two of the owners were reasonably intelligent and took an interest in and liking to me, so I began keeping their records and began discussing religion mostly through asking questions about their beliefs. In the next village I was introduced to the Essene and Zoroastrian ideas. Each of*

*them had close ties to a belief that I was to eventually know through people I met further east, in India; eventually became Brahmanism and Buddhism. It was two years before we arrived at a mountainous region of aesthetic monks who introduced me to a new feeling of dedication and language.*

*In China, another confusing religion was studied while the caravan left me to run their outpost there. I spent a year as their representative before they returned. By this time, I was considered a student monk and a teacher. I loved enlightening people and found audiences wherever I went. Rejoining the caravan, I travelled to an island to trade and discovered Taoism. It differed little from Buddhism, Brahmanism, Confucianism, Hinduism, Judaism. Many of the tribes we encountered had variations on many of these beliefs, none of which really contradicted the other if you carefully analyzed their basic dominant ideas; they were based on three significant points; love, forgiveness and faith. Actually they were all the same. Faith is based on love and forgiveness. Doing good is a combination of all three. Just do good deeds and people will love you, forgive you for any errors and have faith in you. Three in one!*

*I spent many years travelling. I sent messages to my home but received only one or two responses. My father died and my mother sent me a message. It was a long time getting to me. I was older now and still unwed. I returned via Adiabene in hopes of glimpsing Queen Heleni HaMalka, but that was not to be, so then southwest to home. I spent some time teaching. The money I had acquired I had given to the needy, helping the poor. My mother was ecstatic over my return as were my brothers. I continued to teach and travel short distances teaching those who were interested in a better way of life. There are always those who feel jealous and envious because they are misinformed. So an insurrection against me ended with an attack on me, leaving me for dead. My mother and my wife found me, took me to a safe hiding place and nursed me back to good health. There was no question about my not staying with these people, so it was best to go east again, to a familiar place where my teaching was appreciated. I also knew the trade route and profited by trading in a nomadic life. As I mentioned, we left that area 25 years ago and now live humbly, but are better off than many, but give to the poor and love doing it. I forgave those who attacked me, for they knew not what they were doing. They were influenced by governmental powers who were interested in their own welfare, not the welfare of the whole. I have written all this down and left it with some of my old friends who are becoming well known back west. Their names are . . .*

(At this point the writing was worn away)

Ramona put the unfinished article down and glanced at Rowena, then toward two people still hunched over the table, deliberately debating and discussing the several meanings of a phrase. One then glanced at Ramona and said, "That is just a rough draft. We'll have to re-read and transcribe again to be positive, and go to the original to compare. This is just the one that was previously translated and it looks like 'ben' something was the author, not an uncommon name for that time frame."

"How much truth is there in this?"

"We don't know but it certainly is going to create some controversy if it ever goes public."

"Does it have to go public?" asked Rowena.

"That's not for us to say. If it is what we think, we'd be better off destroying it but it will depend on what it turns out to be. This is preliminary and it's just the introduction." He continued, "This scroll looks like the ones at Nag Hammadi. Someone said there were one or two that were unintentionally destroyed; these could be the ones. The 'Book of Thomas' and the 'Book of Mary Magdalene' created quite a stir, I wonder what these might do."

"Do you think they are authentic?"

"We think so."

"When will you remove them?"

"Are you donating them to us?" The scholars were astounded.

"You will give me an itemized receipt properly signed with a letter of intent and they are yours," Ramona said.

"Madam, you could have a fortune here!"

"Yes, but I have a fortune. I would rather my children and grandchildren live in peace during their lifetime."

"We'll be discreet and at this moment I'd say these will not see the light of day for years. A believable story will be devised as to the discovery of these papers and manuscripts when the time comes."

"Leaving us out of it?"

"If you so desire."

"So be it!"

The other team had maps and deed, all over a conference table, discussing the possible meaning and possible repercussions of world powers should a public announcement be made. The only solution was to set up a special committee to study these controversial papers that, if lawful, could start an all-out conflict in certain areas.

'Here is the rest of the introduction. These untouched documents, books, and manuscripts should have special handling in a secure lab, security being of the utmost."

Rowena again indicated the possibility of intruders lurking in the surrounding area and not only a possibility, but a known fact. She went to a panel, slid it back revealing a map of pinpoint lights in various colors indicating an elaborate security system. "Each red dot is a possible person. Sometimes a deer or animal is large enough to set off the intruder alarm, but in these cases, we verified through our staff that these are camouflaged 'hunters' shall we say. As you can see the south is a green board; the way most of you came in and the way you'll leave, with the exception of the two who arrived via car. The limo is in the garage and it'll serve as your 'getaway' vehicle. The driver is trustworthy and well paid"

"What about the Vatican connection? You indicated last night that they were here and will probably return. Can you enlighten us?"

"There is a mega conference next month at The Resort. I suspect now, that a lot of this meeting may concern the existence of these documents and their location. Another reason to have them removed from these premises."

"I don't know if your father was wise in not telling me about this. I suspect we are being interviewed because he secretly worked with someone else, possibly the Southern Sudan, consequently the sudden interest because of someone revealing the possible connection. Had it not been for the Buick, we'd have known nothing about this."

"And if Piearce didn't have such integrity . . ."

The phone rang its special ringtone and Rowena picked it up while Ramona moved closer to listen also. It was Rowie updating them about the activities at The Resort, and that Lavinia had known of the special group, having been alerted. Apparently quite some time ago they had been informed of the possible existence of secret scrolls and were ready to move on a moment's notice, hence the speedy response. "This is evidently a major operation with possible immense repercussions. Tell Granma I love her and appreciate her now more than ever."

"I'm here Rowie, thank you. Be careful. How is Piearce?"

"I was talking to Lavinia and Ursula and they indicated they are quite certain he has committed himself to a childhood sweetheart, so I doubt anything I could do would alter his interest. I wonder if he has a brother?"

"You are beginning to sound desperate."

"Bye Gram. Bye mom."

# Chapter XVII

It had been three days since Rowie had left her grandmother's house and the limo had come to pick her up. It was good cover for anyone watching to have the limo waiting for her. Finally she ordered the limo for the return trip. Outside the town she had the driver stop and she climbed into the front seat. His speech was professional, courteous and reserved. Rowie said, "Carl, don't be so formal. Let it all hang out. Mom and Grandmother are not present."

"They would not be pleased to have you sitting here. I like my job. Your grandfather hired me and swore me to a strict code of conduct after sending me to school, for which I am very grateful."

"I promise not to jeopardize your position. I know of your training and schooling, although I don't know all of the particulars, such as your major. One of your areas I know is forensic science and one is philosophy. Quite a contrast. What was your major?"

"International business. I was originally supposed to work for your grandfather's company, but he felt I'd be more useful as a personal protector and trusted advisor. We were always discreet in our discussions and no one knew. I promised I'd work and take care of your grandmother. I have been well paid and will need no income after I leave. This is all in writing, locked in a safety deposit box complete with all the necessary letters."

"Wow, Carl, I'm impressed. Who else knows?"

"Your Grandmother, of course, and you."

"Have you been keeping tabs on me also?"

"I'd rather not answer that."

"Come on, Carl. I take that as a yes. I always wondered about how Granma would always say, 'I surmise you have done such and such' and inevitably she'd be correct. I never suspected. You are something."

"Just doing what I was hired and promised to do."

"So are you really under contract?"

"In a manner of speaking."

"Does Mom know?"

"She may suspect. I've never mentioned it. Up until last month I was sworn to secrecy. However, your grandmother said that should you inquire I was to be honest."

"All this time, Carl, And I never suspected. What kind of plans do you have for the future?"

"As you know I have travelled with the family over the years, and I still like to travel, but perhaps I'll start a small business or go to work for a corporation or, maybe be a gentleman farmer. My references will get me a position anywhere they need my professional expertise."

"How about settling down and getting married. Have any plans in that social institution?"

"I thought about it."

"Anyone in particular?"

"There was a girl that I was interested in, but she is above my station and my income would never be able to support her lifestyle."

"Carl, you are a nice looking physically fit person. You needn't be concerned about a girl thinking she is above your station. You've got a lot to offer. Go tell her or rather send her a bunch of roses or even a pansy, but if you love her and she likes you or even better loves you, tell her. Give me her name and I'll help you set up a meeting. Does she know how you feel?"

"No. I've never told her. She probably will never know how I feel."

'How long has this been going on?"

"Since the first time I saw her, years ago."

"And you've never asked her out?"

"No. Someday soon I'll be free of this job and will be available to discuss my feeling without being concerned about fulfilling my obligations to a wife."

"Carl, I am amazed. In all the years I've known you I never even thought about you leaving the employment of our family. I understand now. You going in the back way or the front?"

"Front. If anyone is watching then I'll drive in properly. I think I'll pull over in a couple of miles to allow you to get into the back."

"Roll the divider window down and I'll climb over."

The window slowly descended and she agilely hopped over, not in the most lady-like manner, earning a comment from Carl, "Your Mother and grandmother wouldn't like you displaying that sort of behavior before a chauffeur, young lady."

"Carl, if you've been keeping your eyes on me all these years then I suspect you've seen me in worse conditions than climbing over a seat."

Carl chuckled and started to roll up the window when she said, "Leave it down."

"We are coming to the area of possible concealment so I'll put it up."

"Not all the way, leave a space for talk."

They arrived at the house and he parked, got out and opened the door for Miss Rowie, then took her bags and carried them inside. A maid came, took her bag and carried it upstairs to her room. She turned to Carl and said, "I'm serious about helping you, Carl. Let me know and I'll set up a rendezvous for you. Does she have a name?"

"Of course, but I have my own name for her. I call her Euphaosyne."

"Euphaosyne? Does she know you call her that?

"Not yet."

"What does it mean?"

"You really want to know?"

At that moment they heard his name called. It was Ramona.

"Oh Carl, is the car out front? I'd like to run down to the village for a few moments."

"Yes. Madam." He left to take his station at the car while hugs were exchanged, both hello's and so-long's. Rowie updated them on the festivities at The Resort and was informed that all the paraphernalia had been transported to the laboratories where government official, were beginning their investigations.

Outside the sun was just past its zenith as Carl held the door for Ramona. The usual rule applied when he and she were driving. The separator window was down.

"Okay, Carl, report."

Carl gave a rundown on the locations of the 'campers' and also the activities of the priests and their comings and goings at The Resort. Also the activities of Rowie and the fact that on the return trip she insisted on riding in the front again and of their conversation, especially the part of his contract and employment conditions.

"Carl, are you ready to start your own life? I've told you before, you are free to go anytime you wish, especially now that this fiasco with the relocating of the merchandise has been resolved. I think we did the best thing by handling it this way."

"I fully concur, Madam."

"Carl, what do you really think of Rowie's boyfriend?"

"Please madam, I'd rather not get involved with family matters."

"Carl, you are family. Since the day you saved Tomas' life, you have been more than family and you know it. We have put up a good front and my time is rapidly coming to an end so let's not pussyfoot around. By the way, take me to the church."

"Truthfully, he is not the one I'd choose for her. He does have the wealth, but I doubt that he could love her unconditionally as a husband should love a wife."

"What type would you choose for her? We mentioned this once before and you said you'd have to think on it. Have you?"

"Yes. I have thought on it, but haven't yet come to a positive conclusion. It depends on her outlook. She has always had everything, and I wonder if she would be able to do without if she had no financial backing. I've watched her in the kitchen preparing her own luncheon and she seems to have it together, but what about running a household? And really, what kind of man does she really want?

"What were you talking about when I interrupted you in the foyer?"

"She had been asking me if she could help fix me up with a date. I had told her that I was interested in a particular woman, but the woman doesn't know of my interest in her, so she wanted the name of the woman. I told her my name for the woman but not the real name."

"And that would be?"

"I call her Euphaosyne."

"Good Cheer. A nice description, but not what I asked."

"She is beyond my station, madam, uh, Ramona, so we'll leave it at that. We are at the church." He stopped and got out to hold the door and escort her to the priest's office.

"Hang around, Carl, I won't be long." *She looks very tired,* thought Carl.

While Carl waited in the car for Ramona to finish her visit with the priest, he thought about what Ramona had said about moving on, to pursue a life. He also thought about Euphaosyne and whether she had any feeling for him as he had for her. Should he heed the advice of Rowie, confront the woman or rather express his feeling for her and ask her if any relationship would be possible? Even a plutonic affair would be better than his present situation. He had been loyal to the family for what they had done for him. He was exceptionally well paid for looking after Ramona and Tomas. Tomas was like a father or grandfather. Despite his possible involvement with the syndicate, he was caring and protective of his family. No one would ever know of his involvement in the many schemes he developed for making money. Ramona was now trying to justify and keep his name clean even though she didn't have much faith in the church and its control. Yes, maybe he would enlist Rowie's help in his dilemma, or perhaps Ramona's.

*          *          *          *          *          *
     *          *          *          *          *          *

Meanwhile, Ramona was having her rendezvous with the Bishop, leaving last minute instructions in addition to the ones he had from previous meetings. These concerned instructions for her ultimate demise and how her funeral should be conducted. She was only doing this to satisfy the church's view of an ex-priest and his wife. No one would ever know the truth except her immediate family and Piearce and his trusted cohorts. The will had been recorded and all technicalities had been in place for years.

"I have just a few final arrangements to make and then you can wait for me to expire."

"You have sacrificed and created meaningful experiences for many and will continue through your graciousness. God will welcome you and his Son will personally escort you to the throne of God."

"Oh, cut the sycophantic obsequiousness and get on with it. You know how I feel up to a point, and meeting God with a grand escort is not in my eventual plans and you don't know of the 'sins' I've committed and never will."

"Confess now and be forgiven."

"I've confessed to myself and a few others; that's all that's necessary. Just like the man in the glass."

"The man in the glass?"

"Yes. Look it up. The second verse says,

> *For it isn't your father or mother or wife*
> *Whose judgment upon you must pass;*
> *The fellow whose verdict counts most in your life,*
> *Is the one staring back from the glass.*

"Bye. See you Sunday."

Carl was waiting and immediately got out of the car and opened the door for her, acting the obedient, dutiful chauffeur, "I pray everything went well."

"Yes, thank you, Carl. Drive the scenic route. I want to talk." Carl closed her door, got into the driver's seat, started the car, and headed for the high trail.

"Anything in particular?" he called through the open partition.

"I have just given certain papers and made finishing touches for my funeral and don't say anything yet." She continued, "You probably know more about the family history and Tomas' business dealings than anyone else. You can still have a job with the company if you wish, or you can go off on your own. I've watched you grow over the years and have always admired your demeanor and honesty and loyalty. You deserve to have a life of your own. I've thanked you previously for your care for the family, especially Rowena and Rowie. Even putting up with my son and saving his fannie on two occasions."

"Ramona, you and Tomas took me in, gave me an education and Tomas has amply provided for me. We've been through this before, so where are you heading with this? Are you telling me to leave?"

"Not really. We love you too much and actually need you but the time is getting close for my eventual departure. Today you admitted that you have a woman you think you love. I always wondered and am glad you have those aims. You are thirty-five and not getting any younger. I'm over eighty and on my last leg, but I'd like to go to a few more weddings before I depart, yours being one."

"As you know, I have no parents. You and Tomas were there for me as parents or grandparents and you'd be the first ones I'd want at my wedding. I'm sorry that Tomas couldn't have been here, but I still have you."

She interrupted, "But that won't be for long. Who is this girl for whom you have these feelings, this Euphaosyne, this 'Good Cheer', as you call her, and why hasn't she ever been introduced to me? I suspect it is someone I may have met or seen; is she?"

"Yes. You've seen her and met her."

"Let's not pussy-foot around, Carl. If you have those feelings, let her know. I'll even go with you if you need moral support. Her station isn't above yours. You are just as good as anyone. No better, no worse, just as good."

"How do you propose I tell her? Just blurt out, 'I love you,' and see her response?"

"Not really. Does she have any idea of your feelings?"

"I don't know. I've been in close conversations with her on several occasions, but just as passing friends."

"No such thing. She has probably told you and as a male you missed the clue."

"Thanks. I needed that. Yes, you're probably correct. I kept my distance and probably should have been more aggressive. Too late now. She has a man in her life and I'm too late."

"Is she married?"

"No, not yet."

"You mentioned Rowie offered to help you. Do you want her help? Especially if I talk with her and we both help. Interested?"

"Oh, yes. That would be an interesting development."

"Okay. Take me home. On the way, fill me in on what intrigues you most about this girl and if she's engaged, what you think of her fiancé."

Ten minutes later they pulled into the driveway. He had phoned ahead that they were approaching the house so someone would be at the door waiting.

As Ramona was getting out of the car, Rowie opened the house door and greeted her grandmother. She called a jovial hello to Carl who was carrying a few packages.

"Rowie, I'm glad you're here. Come into the study. Carl, bring my briefcase and package into the study, please."

They entered the study. Carl placed the package and briefcase on her desk and started to leave.

"Just a moment, Carl. Rowie, Carl mentioned to me that you offered to help him break down a barrier between himself and a woman he'd like to court."

Carl just stood there, petrified.

"Yes, Gram. Did he tell you I rode in the front seat?"

"I've known about that activity for a long time. But I told him that between the both of us, perhaps we can come up with a solution."

"I don't see why not. That okay, Carl?"

"You two don't give a man much of a choice."

"Okay. First of all, tell Grannie and me who it is so we can develop a plan of action or plan of attack."

Ramona said, "He may have to tell you, but I think I know who it is."

Rowie said, "Wow! Did he tell you?"

"No. I've been suspecting it was this person for a few years."

"Who?" Echoed Rowie, with an apprehensive, almost fearful look. "And when did you first suspect all this?"

"When I saw the expression on his face two years ago when you indicated you were considering accepting an engagement ring from your boyfriend."

Rowie stared at her grandmother, dazed. She quickly looked at Carl. He lowered his eyes, then looked at her as she brought both hands up to her lips. Looked back at her smiling grandmother, looked back to Carl as her grandmother said, "Am I correct, Carl?"

Carl said nothing. Just stood in place and finally said, "I always knew you were shrewd and analytical and clever."

"Call it a blessing."

Rowie looked at her grandmother as she was blinking back tears and asked, "A blessing?"

"An Apostolic one at that."

With that response Rowie ran to Carl, jumped into his arms, wrapping her arms and legs around him, "Oh God. Thank you, thank you. Oh Carl, why didn't you tell me? Oh God, I've loved you for years!"

She kissed him. Again and again, as he held her. She finally lowered her legs to the floor, releasing him. She went to her grandmother and hugged her and said, "Oh, Grannie. How can I thank you, you conniving darling . . ."

"Number one, get rid of that boyfriend. He's useless. Number two, elope. We don't have time for a large wedding. Number three, be back here next year with a great grandchild. Now I have something to live for . . ."

*     *     *     *     *     *

*     *     *     *     *     *

The next morning as she sat on the patio overlooking her husband's favorite garden and his resting place, she reflected on the previous evening. Even with the early morning mist rising off the lake, and a slight chill, she had a warm, girlish giggling feeling about the departure of Carl and Rowie and started a conversation with Tomas.

"Maybe there is a power of goodness, Tomas. Maybe we did do the right thing after all. Just maybe this is your sign that you are waiting. But I think I'll try to wait for next year or even two. I love you so much, Tomas. It's been so hard without you, but now it's tolerable."

# Chapter XVIII

Piearce felt he had accomplished his mission after talking to Rowie about the 'merchandise' being secretly removed to a secure governmental facility. He didn't know where nor did he really need or want to know. However he did wonder about the welfare of Ramona. Her daughter could take care of herself, as could Rowie. They were independently wealthy. He did wonder about the oil maps and decided it would be fun to watch for future developments, knowing he had inside information. He toyed with the idea of investments. If he were a betting man he thought he could set up some outlandish schemes and possibly make a fortune.

Ursula and Lavinia were at breakfast and indicated that they wanted to talk, so he invited himself to join them. They mentioned his priestly company had left; they were flying to Mexico, then to Italy. After that it was anyone's guess. Both women indicated they were going to be transferred to another location, possibly within the month, to be out of the way should anything radical evolve.

"It is quite possible nothing will transpire, since the government has the sensitive documents under lock and key. Most likely they'll manage to let the various countries involved be informed on the highest and most secret levels, so nothing radical will be take place. It seems the higher echelon usually knows more than they let on and have indicators of whom they can trust."

"That's pretty complex. Glad I'm not needed to follow up. It's been nice knowing you two girls and I sincerely hope you do well and stay safe. I'll be leaving soon, but if you ever get the chance to stop by, please don't stand on formality, stop in. But don't expect the same service as you receive here."

"Don't worry. We weren't brought up in this environment either. It isn't realistic. Fun yes, but not of the real world. Good luck, and if you need a job, let us know. You have our numbers. Besides, we'll be here for a few more weeks anyway after giving our notices. Then a vacation and back to a new investigative operation. We think you are intelligent enough to know that should you see us somewhere, you don't speak to us unless we speak to you first."

"I fully understand. I'd hug you both now but in lieu of the circumstances a rain check is in order."

"Sounds like an acceptable offer. What time are you leaving?" asked Ursula.

"I'm waiting for a call from McCracken then I'll probably check out. I've paid until the weekend and there is no refund. Not that it makes any difference. Why?"

"Because there is a hugging place on a trail down by the boathouse at ten," replied Lavinia, as they left.

*      *      *      *      *      *

*      *      *      *      *      *

The next morning Piearce was awakened by the phone. It was late. He overslept. It was McCracken who reported some recent inquiries about the Buick and what happened to it. "The garage owner, Cornelius, became suspicious and called me because he knew you had hired me to find the original owners. *I told those men I didn't keep records on all old junks. I had a trucker who comes in periodically and takes away junk cars and pays for the scrap. The salvageable ones I keep records on. All others eventually get loaded for the scrap value.* So the men asking left but didn't seem satisfied and would probably eventually find that Piearce was the recipient of the Buick. Then again, maybe they were just discouraged that their hopes had ended up in scrap. I mentioned that the government representatives had informed me that I was to cease and desist any further inquiries, and that if I did continue it would be considered to be in violation of federal laws. So I had now fulfilled my obligations and was, off the case officially. But that doesn't mean I can't keep you informed about what tales I hear if he'd possibly like to have them repeated."

After his shower Piearce dressed, and was about to go to breakfast when the phone rang again. It was Ramona.

"I'm sitting on the patio and felt I needed to tell you of an important happening. Rowie and Carl eloped last night."

"What? Does her mother know?"

"No. I've been suspicious of a possible relationship for some time, but Carl was too loyal and Rowie didn't really love her boyfriend."

Ramona explained the situation to Piearce and when she finished, Piearce said, "I'll come to the christening."

"Come anytime. You are family now. Bye."

Piearce went to breakfast with a grin and lifted spirits. *Maybe he and Aggie could marry on Ramona's patio.*

# Chapter XIX

Aggie spent three agonizing days wondering what conspiracy Piearce was caught up in and if he was safe. The house was finished and they had left it spotless! A new house with an old frame. As much as she wanted to sit and relax, she kept thinking about the papers and manuscripts and the potential of what the scrolls would reveal. Also, the potential danger. Especially for Piearce. She shuddered; after their initial meeting at the cave, she realized how much she actually loved him and wanted him in her life. The question was, did he feel the same about her? She made out a list of the advantages and disadvantages based on the results from their discussions on feelings, especially the revelation of God and the conflicting meanings. The advantages considerably out-weighed the disadvantages.

Returning to the papers, she drew a genealogy or rather an outline based on the findings of some of the interpretations he had sent. She had just finished reading the overnight email and was amazed at the questionable essay, wondering if it could have been the impetus for someone to write that translated paper. It didn't alter her belief very much, more of a confirmation of what she suspected, a question any intelligent questioning or searching person would ask. Most people accept religion without question because they need or want confirmation of an afterlife. She went along with the flow because it was easier, less argumentative. Now she reread the thesis, trying to trace the possible location on a map. She figured he had been away for seventeen years before getting home again. If the translation was reasonably accurate, it made him twelve or thirteen when he left to start his travels, give or take a year. At age thirty he returned and commenced his teaching again. At thirty-three he was the subject of ridicule and supposedly executed. Then, miraculously he was literally raised from the supposedly dead and secretly whisked away to live a life in a more approving or accepting environment.

The notation indicated where he had located himself and at age fifty-eight he was a successful businessman and sought after teacher or intellect. The notation also mentioned the author had signed the document; seemingly *Yeshua ben* at the bottom edge of the document but it had been torn away where the seal or signature would have appeared. The leading edge of the manuscript was ragged and broken off so any closing statement was lost, according to the interpreters.

Aggie started to make comparative notes on a map where she traced his original trip. There was some deviation as he and his wife travelled to China, then back to the Northern India area, south of what is now Tibet. It was a good location for trading and reasonably comfortable climate year round. On the trade route he was updated on all-inclusive news from the Mediterranean Sea area to China, Singapore area, and places in between.

Aglaea was finished. *Would this ever be divulged? Ever be released to the public. Think of the debacle if it did hit the press. No wonder they were so actively looking for what they suspected might exist.* The more she thought about the repercussions the more far flung would be the consequences. She made notes:

1. What would be the immediate and long range consequences?

    - Disbelief: Argue that this is a conspiracy . . . Disgruntled sects maligning churches
    - Belief:

        • Possible rampant mischievous behavior

- Possible disrespect for the law (In God We Trust)
- Possible promiscuous behavior
- Possible 'what's the use of living? Increase in suicides?'
- Possible retaliation to churches

2. How would people face a life style change?
3. Would respect and tolerance suffer?
4. The medical field might benefit; doctors would become the answer to prayers, which would no longer be a viable avenue to a higher being.
5. Death? That would continue? Any sorrow or more sorrow?
6. Would there be a need for cemeteries?

   Eventually, no tomb stones
   Eventually use tomb stones for buildings as happened in old Rome?

7. What would be the reaction of other religious groups towards Christians and Jews? Especially Jews and Christians and their sects!
8. Destruction? More suicides, bombing to annihilate them, Increased violence? More 'cells' of secrecy throughout the world
9. - Just a better way of life through kindness
   - Just a better way of life through love
   - Just a better way of life through forgiveness

Aglaea realized she was going too far, worrying about possible repercussions when at that moment she and a handful of extremely concerned people were the only ones involved. Piearce said everything was in the hands of the most secret of secret people. But how do you know for sure? Trust. Trust that these people realize the devastation that could result if the information were ever released? No. Aglaea realized she would probably go to her grave carrying one of the world's greatest secrets with her. She didn't know whether to be thankful to Piearce or not. Well, at least this way she'd have someone with whom to commiserate and trust.

She put her pen down and started to tear up her notes, thought about Piearce and decided to share her ideas with him. Living a life devoted to helping people was a good enough outlook on life based on the premise of looking to satisfy a God; after all, look at all the agnostics and atheists in the world who have made some of the greatest of contributions and lived long happy lives without the need of a crutch.

She wished Piearce was there. Instead, why not go to visit his mother, Isabelle, and get invited to dinner?

# Chapter XX

She arrived with her mother, Juline, as prearranged, for Dora's wedding. She hadn't told her mother about Piearce possibly being there, only that they had met. They had made their pact; she would fly to Dora's for a family reunion, then meet him as a total stranger. After a reasonably pleasant family reunion, Dora and Aglaea secluded themselves in Dora's room with Dora's mother Madeline, still trying to run the show, and in tow.

"So you finally convinced your parents to accept Paul."

"Yes. Well, that was a fortuitous break for us. I recall telling you that I didn't know how we were going to accomplish it, both parents being so obstinate about whom we should marry, and claiming we were too young and inexperienced to make intelligent choices on our own. It's like your parents and grandparents being ostracized because they didn't agree with the old life styles. I always felt a twinge of sorrow after I met you and reestablished a familial relationship with you. Remember how we kept it a secret for years?"

Aglaea said, "And how ritzy I thought you were, but I was never jealous. Always thought how lucky you were at first."

"And after a while I thought the same about you. Fortunately it was a good thing we went to the same college and that your family moved."

"I wish you had included me in your circle," uttered Madeline.

Dora then proceeded to tell Aggie about the planning she and Paul evolved and how well it went; that one man was really responsible for the success of the whole deal. She detailed the events, especially the night of the proposal.

"Yeah; a night to remember, alright," chimed Madeline.

"Just thrilling! I could see it coming and was gripped with excitement but also fear. Then he popped the question and I said yes! Mom was shocked and Dad was in disbelief, all thanks to Piearce."

"Piearce? An odd name. His surname?"

"No, given. Aggie, I want you to meet him. He's nice looking, physically fit, unassuming, intelligent and I think you might like him." She continued to shower accolades on him. That he must be wealthy being at The Resort.

"Does he have all his own teeth? Appendix? Hair? Is he susceptible to any diseases?"

"Oh, stop with the doctor bit and look at the practical side of it. He'd make a great husband and he's in the medical field, although he said he wanted to become a teacher in a college."

"I have to admit, I think he is personable and has a nice tush," said Madeline.

"Mom!"

"Well he does, doesn't he?"

"Yes, but there is more to him than that."

"You girls do your thing, I'll be back in a while. Aglaea, would you like a drink? Coffee? Never mind, I'll send the maid with a tray. I'm checking the garden and patio again."

"Thanks, Mom."

"See you, Mrs. H.," Aggie called to her aunt.

Madeline left to see about arrangements, and mingle with the guests.

"Here's my dress. Like it?"

"It's adorable. Great choice."

"Mom and Dad almost had a fit when we limited the wedding to the two families and total guests to less than a hundred, and that was a compromise. Paul and I were adamant. At first there was anger or maybe it was disappointment on the part of both

Paul's mother and mine. You don't mind being a bridesmaid, do you?"

"What?"

"Well, I thought I'd pair you up with Piearce as an usher, then you could get to know him and make your decisions about him."

"What'll I wear?"

"This isn't a formal wedding. I'm wearing the dress mostly to satisfy my mother and Paul's. We are the only two dressed formally."

"Does this Piearce guy know he's an usher?"

Dora looked at her and said, "I never thought of that. I just assumed Paul asked him."

"Well you didn't ask me until now," Aggie said laughingly, thinking that Piearce was in for another surprise but would adjust without batting an eyelash.

Just then three young women entered; the other bride's maids and the maid of honor. Aggie knew the maid of honor from school and a jubilant atmosphere ensued that men might not understand or comprehend.

The wedding was scheduled for one o'clock. Piearce arrived at noon, the height of last minute preparations. It was then he discovered he was an usher and was promptly given a tour of the premises with Paul and the best man; of the toilet locations, parking, bar set-up, and the garden seating arrangement. The good thing was that he had worn a suit. His intro to Paul's parents was short and to the point, terminating with, "We'll see you later."

He joined the other ushers seating people and silently prepared himself for the introduction to his 'escort'. Paul and the best man were waiting at the altar or patio steps. It was said that the Priest was not comfortable with the arrangement; it was not a church. But when you are wealthy, waivers are easily obtained. Besides, the bishop was a close family friend.

Piearce was summoned to the hedgerow where the ladies were gathered, and the other grooms men, all of whom had been prepared about the fix-them-up-date, stood smiling all-knowing smiles.

"Piearce, this is my cousin Aglaea whom I mentioned to you; Aggie, this is Piearce."

Piearce took her extended hand, brought it to his lips, kissed it, held it while making eye contact and smilingly asked, "Will you marry me?" Silence. A shocked surprise and then laughter from everyone. Aglaea equally surprised everyone with her answer, "I'll let you know after the ceremony," she answered with a smile, while the rest of the wedding party looked on with amazement Aglaea continued, "And it depends on what kind of kisser you are." At that, he slowly took her in his arms, she embracing him, and a lingering kiss ensued to the stunned disbelief of the group, but not a disapproving shock amidst the oohs and aahs and laughter.

"Yes, I'll consider your proposal. Do you have a ring?" With that he produced a ring and placed it on her finger. They kissed again. Dead silence. Aglaea looked at Dora and winked. She took Piearce's hand before the open mouths and questioning stares as they lined up. A cloud had momentarily dimmed the sun but now passed; it was as though the heavens had opened and spotlighted the pair. The music started.

"By the way, how did you get here?" Aglaea asked.

He nodded to an opening in the garden hedgerow behind some flowers, to a 1932 Buick, that he had dubbed 'Arabella'.

# PART TWO

# CHAPTER I

The wedding kiss completed the official phase of the nuptials. Following the wedding party on the short walk back through the guests, Piearce nodded to several of the guests, especially Harriet who seemed overwhelmed to see him, winking and blowing a kiss. At seeing her, he immediately surveyed the crowd for Ramona, wondering if she had been invited. Aglaea waved to several, especially her mother who mouthed the words, 'Is that him?' which prompted Aglaea to say to Piearce, "Wave to Mom."

Piearce crossed in front of Aglaea and hugged her mother and said, "It's good to see you again, Juline," then continued with Aglaea to the reception line up. Aglaea held up her left hand and the ring to show her mother who gave a slight squeal of delight.

As they approached Dora and Paul, Dora stood laughing and shaking her finger at Aglaea saying, "You devil! We have to talk." She hugged Aglaea while Paul just smiled and looked a little dumbfounded, so Dora quickly explained the incident prior to the playing of the wedding march. The maid of honor and best man also offered congratulations as did the rest of the wedding party.

Later, as they walked through the garden, Piearce noticed a catering truck parked behind the tent and two girls holding trays of hors d'oeuvres. One girl had auburn hair and the other had sandy hair. He stopped and squeezed Aglaea's hand.

Aglaea gazed up at him with a smile and was about to give him a kiss, when she noticed his gaze and asked, "Are you hungry or enjoying the view?"

"They must be on another case," remarked Piearce

Aglaea looked again and asked, "Sandy and Auburn?"

"I think so. It looks as though they are going to be serving the hors d'oeuvres."

*　　　*　　　*　　　*　　　*　　　*

*　　　*　　　*　　　*　　　*　　　*

Within moments guests were being served in the garden, although most were heading to the tent. As the servers approached Piearce and Aglaea, one said in a heavy French accent, "Madam, Monsieur. Hors d'oeuvres? Theez ones are bay-cone and lea-ver, and these ones ur stuff-ed muush-rooomza." The other said, "Unt Vee haf heeya, lee-mon deeped enchova unt chi eece." A hint of smiles and an eye twinkle was all the recognition offered as they moved on with the trays.

"One of them nodded slightly to me," said Aglaea. "Are you sure it's them?" "Without question. They must be checking someone locally or even someone here," he said as he popped a morsel into his mouth. They continued their stroll with the others, admiring the flowers and impeccably manicured hedges. The garden wasn't huge, but it was impressive.

"Are you going to call them?" asked Aglaea.

"Absolutely not! If they had their phones on them and it rang or vibrated at the inappropriate time it might blow their cover."

"I didn't mean now."

"No. Better that they call us."

"Us?"

"Of course. I'm sure they want to meet you."

Suddenly some of the girls from the wedding party called to them.

"You two stole the show! You knew each other before, didn't you? What a great idea! All Dora can say is 'Wait until I get Piearce and Aggie'. Let us see the ring. Oh it's so exciting! Do you have a date yet?"

Piearce might as well have not been there. He just stood back and waited when a familiar voice said, "Hors d'oeuvres?" It was Auburn.

"Do you have a name?" he asked.

"Pleeze. My Eengleesh iz not goood."

"Your name, how are you called?"

Oh, my nom eez Pa-trishe, or Pa-tea."

"And what is your friend's nom?"

"I do not know her well, but shee eez called Truss."

"Thank you Pa-tea."

"Monsieur, you leeve here?"

Several people stopped and cleaned the tray off so 'Pa-tea' turned to get it refilled as Piearce said, "No, I'm not local, just here for the wedding." Patie nodded and turned away. Piearce decided he would be hearing from them soon. The loud laughter brought him back to reality as Aggie called and said, "They want us at our tables so they can start the festivities. Are you prepared for the onslaught?"

"Not really. Never thought of the aftermath when the idea hit me. Just of you and your reactions of yes, no or maybe," said Piearce.

The tent was tastefully decorated easily rendering protection for the hundred guests. Ten tables plus the head table was not at the end of the tent, but in the middle on a raised platform with a table set for the bride and groom and their parents. The rest of the wedding party had a table but not on the platform, which really didn't matter because after the initial proceeding most people would visit other tables and change places. It was a different setup to say the least, but it was what Dora and Paul wanted. This was not a traditional type wedding.

"Piearce, where are you staying tonight?" asked a familiar voice. Piearce turned to see Harriet's glowing face. They hugged and he said, "I passed a motel a few miles away, so I made arrangements."

"That's not necessary. We'll find a place for you here. And how have you been? Staying out of mischief?"

"Never. Mischief is my middle name. Harriet, may present my fiancée, Aglaea?"

"Aglaea. So nice to meet you. What a wonderful name. Greek?"

"Thank you. Yes, it is Greek in origin. And Piearce has told me all about you in grand accolades. It's so nice to finally meet you."

"How long have you been engaged, Aglaea?" Harriet asked, as the girls from the wedding party gathered around.

"About forty-five minutes. I think you know my mother, Dora's mother's sister." At that moment the girls arrived and went into a gushing explanation of what had happened, with each person embellishing the story a little more. It was then that Dora stepped toward Aggie saying,

"You! You! How many years have you kept this secret?" Then the real truth had to be told and no one in the tent talked except for a "Shhh" or a "Quiet." Then voices called, "Louder" so a portable mic was brought and Aggie was introduced while standing on the platform with Dora. She entertained the group with early history and recent meetings. Then Dora took the mic and told of the recent hopes and plans of introducing them, never realizing they knew each other and how at the first moment they were supposedly introduced Piearce asked her to marry him, and to the shocking amazement of all present, she said yes then turned and marched to the alter as though nothing had happened. The applause was thundering. Aggie and Dora hugged. Harriet held Piearce's hand. Then the servers came to serve the meal.

Harriet sat with Piearce and Aggie during dinner and was delighted with Aggie, especially the fact that Aggie was a physician. That led to Harriet asking Aggie if she wanted to work at any particular hospital or institution. If so, she'd attend to arrangements, indicating that she had enough influence to help her relocate if Aggie desired. During dinner the servers brought coffee and Piearce noticed the doily under his cup had markings, UK#121/2. He glanced up while the coffee server, Lavinia, was serving the person to his right. As she turned to go to the next table she smiled at him and he gave her a slight nod. "You know the number. Call them at twelve-thirty."

While dancing with Aggie he mentioned a potential contact at 12:30.

"Are you sure these girls are legal?" was Aggie's reply.

At four o'clock a helicopter hovered over them and landed. Dora and Paul ran toward it while everyone shouted and yelled and followed with bags of confetti and rice. They laughingly escaped. A well-organized plan well executed while the party continued. By six o'clock the caterers were packing up and beginning to strike the tent. With exceptions of close family and immediate friends, most of the other guests were departing. Harriet, Aggie, Paul and Dora's parents, and Aggie's mother, Juline, were sitting in an alcove together. It was family make-up time, especially when they discovered Aggie was an MD! Rooms had been assigned to Aggie and Juline, and Piearce had one in the guest house above the garage. Actually, it was more of an apartment.

Piearce meandered out and saw the caterers packing the last of the equipment into one of the trucks. Lavinia and Ursula were getting into a van and turned, glanced around as though checking for anything else. Lavinia put her hand to her head with pinky and thumb extended indicating a phone call. She entered the van and it drove away while Piearce smiled at the suave manner of her maneuver.

At midnight Piearce was wondering what and who the target of the two girls might be. Someone in the house? Local? Authorities? The catering agency? Who? What? Then he recalled the monastic group and school in the area. That could very well be the connection in view of what had been found in the Buick. No! No way! It must be something else. One thing for sure, it wasn't a bank overdraft. And why the false accents. One French accent and one Dutch or German. And they supposedly pretend not to know each other. They must have applied for the jobs with the catering service. Was it happenstance that both were hired so quickly? Was the catering service also an undercover operation?

He called. On the first ring, they picked up. "Hi Piearce. Good to see you and your lovely fiancée. Looks like a good choice now we know why we didn't have a chance or get a tumble. Thanks for playing along at the wedding."

"It was good to see you two, also. Why the charade? And can we help in any way?"

"Your friends are big supporters of the Monastery. Do you know anyone there? The Archbishop, Bishop, etcetera?"

"Don't tell me you are continuing on the other case? In answer to your question, no. Neither Aggie nor myself are familiar with activities here. But I'll ask Aggie. She knows you are here. Sorry, when I recognized you, I mentioned it to her. She knows about all the other happenings because she assisted me in copying and transporting the documents."

"We know her background and she passes our limited scrutiny. We suspect the monastery may be duped into being used in illegal human trafficking of some sort. It also involves possible transport of illegal documents but we don't know how. It is best if you don't get involved, but we needed to know if we could make a contact. We won't be working here long. Once we make a contact, we'll find other work."

"I'll check with Aggie and listen very carefully to what she says but at the moment I'd say we can't help. I will update you before we leave in the next day or two. What's the best time to call?"

"Eleven PM is usually good. You can always leave a message. By the way, your friend Ramona indicated that she could always use good directors on one of her boards. Thanks for the introduction."

"Great! Now you have places to go when you want to settle down. Good luck. Stay healthy. Bye."

"Bye, Piearce, stay well."

# CHAPTER II

A light tapping woke him. Sunlight was beginning to illuminate the window sills. He rose and went to the door. "Well, hello," he said as he opened the door.

"Hi sleepyhead," was Aggie's answer. "Did you brush your teeth yet? Oh, never mind," she said as she gave him a good morning kiss.

There was a second knock on the door. Opening it revealed a maid with coffee and breakfast for two! They sat at the table eating, with Piearce listening to Aggie lay out the day's activities. They were going to attend a brunch at the monastery because of a new school program being introduced and sponsored by the Hornben's. Apparently the school had new groups coming in periodically that needed to be schooled until the children are adopted or sent to live with sponsors.

"We are invited to see the new group arrive and we will be assigned to their classes and dormitories. By the way, Dora and Paul left a note saying they will, and will was underlined twice, will be out to see us when they return from their honeymoon."

"Do I get a chance to shower and dress?"

"I'll help you shower . . ."

"And have your mother drop in?"

"Okay . . . but then . . ." as she undid the top button of his pajamas.

# Chapter III

The monastery was set on a ten degree slope; a stone building with octagonal bell towers built into the stonework from the ground to the third story, then two free standing octagonal structures towering above by an additional two stories of the main building. The entrance was between those two towers; the inner courtyard was an impeccably kept lawn lined by flowers behind low, flat-stoned walls, adjacent to a road that lead to another gate and parking area. The stone buildings were apparently classrooms, different buildings for pre-school, elementary and high school. This was a boarding school and monastic theological training school. A much larger operation than one would have thought.

They were led to a large assembly room in which twenty or so individuals were gathered. The bishop and archbishop came over immediately and shook hands with the Hornbens, profusely thanking them for their support. It was a second thought to say hello to Piearce and Aggie; a bunch of would be name droppers. They started to speak to the group saying how grateful they felt being the recipients of this new group of refuges from other countries, explaining that through their sponsorship, these waifs would gain in knowledge and eventually be adopted into new homes and families. Some had already been spoken for, but the entourage would stay here for up to six months at least before moving out. Some would spend their high school years here before pursuing their future dreams.

"How many will spend their years here through high school?" asked one attendee.

"Ten to fifteen percent is the estimate. Don't forget, this particular endeavor has not been tried here at this establishment before, so we only have estimates. The idea is to find all of them homes while giving them shelter. As mentioned, some are only in transit, having already been spoken for via the agencies."

"Oh, the bus has arrived," said one of the group.

At that statement everyone's eyes turned to the door where a monk led a group of 22 children into the room, each child grasping or clutching their meager belongings to their chests. Their ages seemed to run from eight to sixteen. All were girls except two boys who were about thirteen. No one was well dressed and all were wide eyed and suspicious looking.

The administrators introduced the people who had sponsored the children and who had made it possible for them to be here. There was polite applause and some smiles from the children. A map of the school and grounds was on a flip chart and the monks went through the repertoire showing the locations of dorms, cafeteria, and class rooms. Then nuns appeared and took the age groups assigned to them and spoke with them and welcomed them. The children's English was limited. Several girls gravitated to Aggie who was able to speak to them. Most spoke an old French dialect. The interesting part was that most looked more Hindu, Asian, Middle Eastern, or Thai in appearance and their French speech was not Parisian French.

Two or three were reasonably quiet, whispering only to each other, until a person addressed them directly. Only a few words of English and French were spoken, but that was it. Then a Chinese dialect was heard. This was strange. Hornben immediately got onto his phone and requested that someone bring a Chinese speaking person to the Monastery. They sent for one of the monks who had been to China. Before he arrived in ten minutes, Aggie went to the children and was there with them when he arrived. He had limited knowledge in that dialect, but he was able to make them feel more comfortable and became their hero. He was also able to make them understand that

Aggie was a physician. The three girls actually smiled, and tried more diligently to communicate. One half hour later, two local restaurateurs arrived and went to Hornben, and he in turn brought them to the girls. Suddenly there was a squeal, as girls started jabbering away almost in unison. One of the local people spoke their dialect!

The girls were divided into groups, mostly 13 and 14 year olds and were told that they would be here until adoption or transfer could take place.

Several people had commented on the Buick belonging to Aggie and Piearce. They had great admiration of the time it took to recondition it and be able to drive it such distances. When Piearce and Aggie approached the car, there was someone sitting in the driver's seat with their hands on the wheel, looking at the dash and shifting lever, but with tears in her eyes, running partly down her cheek.

"Memories?" Piearce asked as he stood near the open door shocking her back into reality. She was attractive and obviously flushed and embarrassed saying, "I'm so sorry . . ."

Piearce interrupted her saying, "No! Don't apologize. I'm flattered that you were able to re-live an old experience! Please! Do you want to drive it?"

"Oh, gracious! May I? It's been so long . . . if I can remember . . ."

Introducing themselves, Aggie got into the back seat while Piearce got into the front passenger seat. The nun folded her cape and placed it on the seat to give her a little elevation and put her closer to the pedals. She appeared to be very excited. Piearce gave her the keys and briefly went over the basics. Aggie gave her a tissue to wipe her tears. The car was put into neutral and the emergency brake was set. The nun inserted the key into the dash, turned it to on and then stepped on the starter. Instantly the engine was alive. A smiling nun looked at Piearce and grinned like a teenager.

She depressed the clutch, put the shifting lever into first gear, found the friction point and released the hand brake. The car rolled ahead as she let the clutch out. At ten miles per hour, she attempted to shift into second as she verbally talked her way through the procedure. Approaching the tower she applied the brakes and as the car shuttered, she said, "Oh, down shift, down shift, clutch in." She coasted through the arch, then turned to follow the road while shifting again into second gear. At twenty miles per hour she put it into third and drove toward the main highway amidst "oohs" and "aahs." "This is so much fun, but I really must return."

"When do you have time in the next day or so, Sister Rose?" asked Piearce. "Perhaps we could return and let you drive to town and back or around the countryside."

"Oh, Holy Mercy. I'm free at three today for two hours, but that is an imposition–"

"Not at all; meet you here at three."

A rosy faced nun left with a glow that would light up a dark room or corridor.

"Piearce, you really made her day. She must have been a beautiful woman in her youth. She certainly has kept herself reasonably fit. Did she say she was going to be fifty?" commented Aggie.

*    *    *    *    *    *

*    *    *    *    *    *

## SISTER ROSE

Sister Rose was waiting, with three other nuns, one the Mother Superior, who wanted to see her off on her excursion.

"We have room for you all if you'd like to go," was Piearce's comment. Without hesitation, they all climbed into the back seat and pulled down the jump-seats. It was like having a bunch of teenagers going on a picnic. The dialogue was constant throughout the trip into the countryside. Apparently they had never ridden into the back country since they had been assigned to the monastery.

"Oh, look at that old hay stack. We had those when we were young," commented one.

"And that tractor with the cleats on the wheels; it is ancient." And someone remarked,

"Just like you. Telling your age!"

Sister Rose asked if someone else wanted to drive, but no one had ever tried to drive a car of this vintage. Then the question was asked of Sister Rose how it was that she was so proficient with this type of car.

"Promise never to discuss it or tell anyone?" was her answer. Of course the solemn vows were uttered and she began her story. It seems she was very fond of a young gentleman in her high school years and his parents had a car of this make and model. They would go parking and he eventually taught her to drive. She was very much in love with him, but the inevitable happened when he went off to college. His family did not like the arrangement anyway. He apparently met someone else and his family moved to a new community and that squelched the relationship. Eventually there was no communication and she gave up trying to locate him. He was her only true love and no one measured up to his standard, so when the nuns and priests asked her to join the order she said yes, she indicated she's had a marvelous life serving God and helping the needy. She sometimes wonders whatever happened to him. They had even shared the same birth date.

Everyone was silent for a few moments, then the Mother Superior said, "I think all of us have had some sort of similar activity in our past. Thank you for sharing that story with us. Maybe we should have another meeting like this and share confessions."

It was not surprising that everyone thought it was a great idea. Two hours went by very quickly and when they were dropped off at the Monastery, they said that anytime Aggie and Piearce wanted to visit, that they were not to stand on formalities. They were welcomed anytime.

Piearce thought, "Great! A possible in for Lavinia and Ursula."

*        *        *        *        *        *
    *        *        *        *        *        *

A monsignor was coming to visit and interview some of the children for a family who was seeking to adopt. He had spent two days going over the records and conversing with the nuns involved with the children. During his discussion, one of the nuns discovered his birth date was coming up and decided to have a little informal celebration for him. While planning the activity one of the other nuns mentioned that it was also Sister Rose's birth date and that they should include her in the arrangement. Suddenly everyone was involved and the little celebration was beginning to include twenty or twenty five people. What can you give a nun and a Monsignor at that age? Perhaps a trip or . . . Hey! How about driving in a 1932 Buick! Sister Rose was ecstatic for a few days afterward. Perhaps the Monsignor would enjoy that also. Quicker than quick, they called the only owner of a 1932 Buick they knew, explained the situation and, of course, Piearce and Aggie said they'd be delighted to drive up. It was only a day away. Maybe they'd trailer the car to save the wear and tear.

The party night was in two days because the Monsignor had to leave. At three o'clock, the car arrived and they unloaded it at Paul and Dora's who were now in on the party and were actually going to pick up the tab of any expenditures.

Six o'clock. Everyone was sitting in the dining room expecting the usual dinner, when suddenly caterers appeared and began serving an elaborate dinner. It was then that the Mother Superior took a microphone and said that this was a celebration of someone's birth and would the good Monsignor please come forward to receive his gift, a driving session in a 1932 Buick. AND, she continued, it just so happens that one of our own is also celebrating a birthday today. Would our birthday girl be so kind as to come up for a similar gift? They approached from opposite ends meeting in the middle with Mother Superior holding the mike. They stood looking at each other. Suddenly Sister Rose put both hands to her mouth and gasped! The monsignor, looked at her and uttered, "Rosie? Rosie? My God, Rosie!" With tears streaming down her face Sister Rose grabbed the Monsignor and hugged him and he reciprocated.

The Monsignor said, "My parents told me you had run off and married!

Sister Rose shook her head and said, "Only to the church. Didn't you ever get any of my letters?" Still holding her by her shoulders, he slowly shook his head no. The nuns who knew the story cheered while the Mother Superior said, "Oh Mercy, I should have known. I'm so sorry."

Sister Rose shook her head no and said, "Oh no! This is a birthday to remember and it answers all my unanswered questions." She looked out and saw Piearce and Aggie holding up the keys to the car. With that she turned and took the monsignor's hand and said, "Come with me. I want to show you something." She walked straight to Piearce and took the keys while Piearce said, "At the front steps," and Sister Rose continued without breaking stride. Pierce and Aggie followed and stood at the top of the steps and watched while Monsignor David took the keys, opened the door for nun Rosie and off they drove.

The car was returned two days later by two people dressed in new clothes and looking vibrant. Each held an envelope in their hands; one was for Mother Superior and the other was for the Archbishop. It seemed David had ample sums from his inheritance so they didn't need to worry about finances. Aggie, Piearce, Paul and Dora were invited to the wedding. They asked to use Dora and Paul's address to get a license and use a local J.P., to which Dora and Paul immediately agreed, but Dora said, "You aren't going to use the church?"

"No, we've already spent enough time with the church, a lifetime. And there isn't much of that left!"

So there was no argument, no debate, just a loading of cars and a drive to the town hall. It was done quickly, because Aggie's flight was in two hours to get her back for duty.

# CHAPTER IV

Lavinia called Piearce when the wedding was over to update him on the proceedings since they last met, and asked why he didn't say hello to her the other day. Piearce replied, "Where were you? I'm sorry I didn't see you! I looked at the caterers to see if you were serving."

"Well, I was right there dressed in Black and White! You couldn't miss me."

"Funny, funny. So now you are a nun. You must be Sister Rose's replacement. By the way you are on speaker phone with Aggie present."

"Hi Aggie, that's ok. Yeah . . . wasn't that a sight to behold?" She then started a monologue about their escapades during the past month's events. She said that Ursula was working in the kitchen and house cleaning department, while she had been doing a little relief teaching and some library duties. It allowed her a fair amount of freedom. She had supposedly just finished her novice status and was in a new role. Several of the older girls had been assigned to homes in a larger city and were given a special phone number in case they were abused or misused. There were three girls who didn't speak English or French well from the Thailand area. They were all picked up a couple days ago in a limousine with out of state plates which in itself is not unusual for a limousine. Two younger ones were weeping when they were picked up. What is strange is that they were supposed to be here from three to six months with the exception of four of the youngest and now they were gone. While at The Resort, we suspected that there were some 'escort' services offered to some of the guests. Ursula thought she recognized one of the drivers, but wasn't positive. That's where you come in. Would it be possible for you, on your return, to take another weekend at The Resort, seeing you're familiar and know some of the staff? We'll give the names of a couple who can be trusted. We have the number of the limo and even the VIN number, in case the plates have been changed.

"Don't forget that I am enrolled in classes in preparation for teaching at the junior college."

"We'll pay!"

"That isn't the issue. I have to," Piearce was interrupted by Aggie saying, "We'll do it. I want to see this place!"

Lavinia laughed and said, "That's what I like, teamwork!"

"I'll check the schedule when we return, which should be today. The Buick is already loaded on the trailer and we'll be off."

"Oh, by the way, Ursula and I received an invitation for Christmas at a most magnificent home in the mountains to celebrate a pregnancy. You'll have to guess who. Bye. Call you in a day or so. Thanks, Aggie."

They decided to fly to The Resort to have maximum time. With a rental car, they drove straight to The Resort. It was cold with a light dusting of snow causing Piearce to say, "It's as though the entire world has changed. Spectacular!" Several workers nodded to them when they approached the reception desk.

"Oh, it's you Piearce. Welcome back. You reserved two rooms; they are adjacent to each other. Will you be dining formally or informally? We have an extra-large gathering this weekend, so we are taking reservations for the formal dining. Also, do you desire a tour or are you familiar enough with the area?"

"I think I can find my way around," answered Piearce. Their bags were taken to their rooms while Piearce said to Aggie, "Come on. I'll show you around outside before the sun gets too low." Forty five minutes later, bundled in heavy coats, they approached the waterfront. All the boats were stacked or lined up waiting for spring. Ice had formed on the protected area. A few people were ice skating. Several fire pits were lit and people were standing around them warming their hands. The repair shop was occupied by a skeleton crew as Piearce looked for the Super. The few people nodded to him in acknowledgment of recognition. Winter time. Few college kids.

They passed the garage area where the limousines were lined up. None of the registration tags were of the correct number, so they slowly meandered and casually walked around admiring the vehicles. There was one that had a similar VIN number to the one Lavinia had mentioned. Could she have been off by a number or two? They walked back to The Resort on the workers path.

"This weekend is going to be our Christmas. I had no trouble getting coverage because I said I'd do the Christmas weekend," said Aglaea. "Is there a show tonight?"

She was enthralled with the spirit of activities and the phenomenal expansiveness of The Resort. She was excited and Piearce thought she looked as she did when her family moved away so many years ago. He stopped and kissed her, telling her how beautiful she was and how lucky he was. She reciprocated. They continued walking to finish the outside tour. Tomorrow they'd drive to the bridge and if the trail was passable, they'd go to the cave. Aggie wanted to see everything Piearce had told her about.

"Let's go for a swim before dinner." So back to their rooms to change, then to the pool for a swim. Aglaea proved to be reasonably adept on the diving board while Piearce was mediocre. The pool was beginning to attract more individuals, so draped in white robes furnished by The Resort; they had a cup of tea.

"Oh, look! They are doing 'The Marriage of Figaro' tonight at seven. Let's go," exclaimed Aggie as she looked at the program board posted on the wall.

"From now on my adventurous lover, no meandering philandering excursions, those diversions are done with and over, Cherubino, my young cavalier. Tum tum tum tum, Tum tum tum tum . . ." Piearce sang softly with a smile.

"I didn't know you liked opera," grinned Aggie

"Li Nozze di Figaro. Wolfgang Amadeus Mozart. First preformed May 1, 1786 at Burgtheater, Vienna."

"Wow! Is that part of your Art History pursuit?"

"Kind of. I only know a little about a few operas, and I only like the ones with happy endings."

"Come on, let's change and go to the early sitting for dinner and to the opera."

They stopped at the desk on the way and Piearce picked up an envelope left in his box. He had previously called and left a message for Lavinia He thought it might be from her but it turned out to be from one of the bureau directors indicating that one of the suites was possibly occupied by escorts. If so, it was very hush-hush and controlled by the higher echelon. Piearce relayed this to Aggie.

On the way down to dinner Piearce said, "You look ravishing."

"That's my hope," retorted Aggie.

They were being led to their table when a waiter stopped them and handed Piearce a paper folded several times. Aggie looked on as he unfolded the note that had one word lettered boldly. SNOB! Aggie looked at him as his smile broadened into a grin and began looking around. Ramona and contingency were all seated looking in their direction. They waved and beckoned to him and Aggie. They walked over to the table amidst hellos, welcomes, and a variety of comments, especially jibing Jacqueline and Irene as to how their chances are now gone. Good humor prevailed and every one welcomed Aggie as though she was one of their own daughters. Piearce hugged Ramona and said, "I understand congratulations are in order."

"Yes! I suspect you have been in communications with two young ladies. I invited them for Christmas, and you are of course invited anytime."

"I think my parents would be a little upset if I went elsewhere."

"And you Aglaea, are indeed a charming and attractive woman. I'm so glad to finally meet you. Piearce, you are a very fortunate man."

The group had almost completed their dinners but they slid around making room for the new comers. Of course, Ramona insisted they sit on each side of her.

"You here for the opera or the stage show?"

"The opera, of course. And you?"

"The opera, it's one of my favorites," answered Aglaea

"Aglaea, I love your name, it's a 'splendid' name.' "

"Nice play on words, you are one of the few so knowledgeable."

That comment alone cemented the bond that had started at first glimpse of Piearce and Aggie.

"This is fascinating, going back in time! And I love the different salons, rinky tinky tunes as you pass the speakeasies. The different music, the dress, the decor; I have to admire these people who dare to dress the part. There is so much to experience," expressed Aggie.

"Then return in the spring and summer; this is geared to the thirties holidays, whereas in the spring and summer flowers enhance the atmosphere."

Jacqueline and Irene excused themselves saying to Aglaea, "Now we know why we didn't have a chance attracting Piearce. It was a real pleasure to meet you, and we hope we can see you again."

Just then Piearce noticed an Asian group enter the dining room, they were seated in a secluded alcove. They were dressed in their native dress, kimonos and sashes, possibly of the thirties era. Ramona asked Aglaea if she had set a date for her wedding, but Aglaea replied that she thought that with Piearce's studies, it might be better to wait a year or two until he was settled in a job. "He is currently finishing up his first semester of grad school and the junior college has made a tentative offer to hire him when he finishes. Actually, he is teaching a one credit course there two days a week which just so happens to be a similar course he took as an undergrad. He is currently enrolled in the advance course, so very little prep time is required." Aglaea indicated that she was getting an education in an area in which she was limited. "I may be benefiting more than he is from the course," she concluded.

"It just so happens I know of a collection of art that is quite creditable, according to some people," said Ramona and continued, "Anytime you want to see it, stop by and visit." This caught Piearce's attention and he immediately replied, "I guess I didn't get to see that display."

"You wouldn't have unless you were taken into the cellar vaults," was Ramona's answer as she patted his hand.

The meal was completed with time to spare for getting to the theater. While they were adjourning, a commotion at the alcove caught Piearce's attention and it looked and sounded as though someone had slapped one of the light faced ladies, while her wrist was being grasped across the table by her companion. But the theater called.

The performance, according to Aglaea and Ramona was superb. Jacqueline and girls agreed. Then the discussion continued as to which part they liked the best and which aria was done to perfection. Nobody agreed on which was the best. Each had their own rendition and reason.

"We are staying the night, and would be delighted to have you join us for breakfast," said one of the 'girls'.

"I usually get up about six or earlier," uttered Piearce.

"No, Piearce. If you do you eat alone because I'm going to sleep in," was Aglaea's firm comment. "So don't knock on my door."

"Come on. Piearce. If you get up early, just have coffee and meet us in the breakfast cafe." He was out-voted and acquiesced to their requests.

# CHAPTER V

$\mathbf{A}$s Piearce was having his coffee at six-thirty, he noticed a limo pull up in the area reserved for such vehicles and thought, *Is someone going to the airport or on a tour?* He had taken a Danish to make the coffee go down easier. He looked at the waterfront from his window table; it was a diminishing white mist in the open water area surrounded by a border of ice and he saw a hint of the sun reflecting on the open lake.

"May I join you?" said a familiar voice. He turned to look and then rose with outstretched hand to clasp an offered handshake. "Carl! Good to see you! Was that you I just saw driving up? Are you picking up The Girls?"

"Yes. I left about five; the roads were clear in this area but partially covered in the mountains in the estate area. So how are you doing? Understand you are engaged."

"Finally, according to my mother. And you and Rowie are expecting. Congratulations. Still acting the family guardian, I see. Are you living with Ramona?"

"Rowie wouldn't have it any other way. She loves her grandmother more than she does me. So what is the occasion that brings you to these parts? And yes, I still act the obedient servant part. Very few know I'm family. It's more fun and the gleaning of tid-bits from other drivers is interesting and revealing."

"My fiancée wanted to see this resort, so here we are. The entire weekend free! We had planned to drive to the estate, but after having dinner and going to the opera with the ladies, we might just see more shows and watch the nineteen thirties parade."

"I think you should follow us to the estate and visit a few hours or longer. I'm sure Rowie would be delighted to see you and your fiancée."

"We'll see what Aglaea has to say. It's really her time off. It is her Christmas weekend because she traded this weekend for working on Christmas weekend."

At that moment, a smiling Aglaea appeared looking radiant. Both men rose and after a good morning kiss, Carl was introduced.

"Oh, Carl! It is so nice to finally meet you. And how is your wife? Is she feeling well or are mornings a time of 'don't bother me'?"

"Ah, yes. You are a physician. Rowie is adjusting and is quite active and yet restricted. Of course the guardian great-grandmother is ever present to oversee to her great-grandchild's welfare. No! Really, Ramona is marvelous and not overbearing. Her comment is, "If you need something, call. I'm here and not an interfering busy-body."

Aggie remarked, "I hope 'someone's' mother is like that, but I'm wondering how she'll react when we marry and produce an offspring. I don't think we'll have a problem getting a baby sitter; two in fact."

Piearce and Carl just smiled, and asked, "Coffee?"

"Yes, please," answered Aggie as they moved to a larger table.

# CHAPTER VI

An Oriental group were getting off the elevator and heading to the formal dining room. They looked like the group from the night before. They were in oriental garb, but not with painted faces. The young woman had her eyes downcast in a subservient attitude as usual but glanced at Piearce as he stood waiting with Aglaea. She quickly glanced down again but almost immediately glanced back while continuing with her escort. Piearce squeezed Aggie's hand and she looked quickly at him, then as the party moving to the dining room. She looked quizzically at Piearce. After entering the elevator, Piearce said,

"Did you see that girl? She looked like the eldest of The Girls at the Monastery, the three who spoke that odd dialect."

"Are you sure?"

"No, but she looked a second time and that is very unusual for a girl like that to be so forward. Would you mind if we delayed our activities for a few minutes? Do you have a handkerchief?"

"Yes, why?"

"Drop it on the floor so I can pick it up. I'm going to use it as a ruse to see her again. I'll take it to them truthfully saying I picked it up on the elevator floor. Maybe you could present it?"

"Hey, I'm with you. That's why we came here, isn't it?"

They approached the table. Not many were in the dining room, so it was easy to spot them. Piearce approached the man and asked if one of the ladies had dropped the handkerchief they had found on the elevator as they got on. The man asked but no one had lost the item. It gave everyone an opportunity to see each other. The girl only glanced up for a fraction of a second and as Aglaea mentioned later, there was a flash of recognition when they made eye contact. These were The Girls, or at least one of The Girls that had been picked up in the limo. The VIN number must have been off by a few characters. Piearce and Aggie called Lavinia and left a message to that effect.

"Piearce, that means that there is a human trafficking activity connected with the Monastery. I don't think they are involved, but it is going on."

The conversation continued as they drove to the estate. Fortunately they were able to put that aside and enjoy the scenery. On approaching the house, Aggie indicated that she could easily get used to this kind of living. "Wow!" was her utterly amazing comment as they approached the house.

"This is only the beginning," injected Piearce.

The limo was parked in front facing them as they parked by it. Piearce glanced at the VIN number out of curiosity and did a double take. It was the VIN number Lavinia had given them! My God! Could these people, Carl and Rowie and family be involved in this sordid business? Piearce wanted to tell Aggie, but she was already being greeted by Rowie and the family and of course, Rowie came over and gave Piearce a hug and kiss on the cheek.

"What a pleasant surprise. Are you staying for the weekend? Oh great! Come on Aglaea, I'll show you the house, Piearce has already seen most of it."

"He hasn't seen the Gallery," commented Ramona, "So leave that for last." As she approached Piearce, she took his hand and led him into the room overlooking the patio, leading him to the sliding door, where there was a grand view of the garden, the lake and the solitary stone pillar marking Tomas' resting place.

"If it wasn't for Rowie and Carl and their forthcoming child, I'd be tempted to join him," said Ramona.

"You still have too much to offer. If you were a doddering old fool of a woman, I wouldn't blame you, but you are sharper that most women half your age. With all the funds you support and charities you advocate, you are carrying on with him as though he were here."

"My son Duane should be like you, but he isn't. His sister is and was a bit of a rebel in her younger years, but has mellowed out since her marriage and now that she is going to be a grandmother, she is one of my best friends. By the way, she is on her way and will be here in a few hours, so please wait until she gets here before you depart. Duane did not take to the idea of his heritage very well, but he might be coming around. He has visited several times since the grand exposé. He and his wife were quite aloof for years before Tomas had the house built. They became more settled when we stated we were planning to retire. That was fifteen or twenty years ago. He has children, but I've only seen them three or four times up until a few months ago. One son is an adventurer, shall we say? Now. Tell me why you have really come to visit the area. Doctors don't take time off in their first year of employment very often. Don't be coy."

"You are fifty percent correct, however, we are not sure yet so anything I say will most likely be hypothetical. As soon as I am positive, I'll give you the facts."

"Fair enough. One question; the cartel?"

"Don't really know, possibly."

"I told you, that you were in the wrong business. Well, I ordered lunch for one o'clock. Will that satisfy you and Aglaea? By the way, she is a marvelous woman. Intelligent, personable, and apparently loves you very much. Treat her well. Tell me about how you met," she said as they sat on a divan. Piearce spent the next half hour telling Ramona the whole story from years ago to the present. When he finished she said, "That is one very nice story, and did you really look for me at the wedding?"

"Yes, especially when I saw Harriet. It immediately took me back to my time here and you were the first one I thought about."

"Sweet. Thank you Piearce." At that moment a commotion of laughter and giggling like a couple of school girls broke into their conversation as the sightseers arrived with Carl in tow.

Aggie was animated as she said, "What an impressive house. And so livable, yet spacious. Oh this room is lovely, and what an impressive view. It must be spectacular during the growing season. I love that single stone pillar way out there in that middle of that garden. It lends just the right touch. It reminds me of the heel stone at Stonehenge."

"That's my husband's marker."

"Oh, I'm sorry."

"No. Don't be. I'm flattered that you like it and when I go, another will be placed next to it. You are very astute. No one knows this, but now is as good a time to mention it as any. When I go, a second stone will be placed next to it with a lintel so that you will have a Stonehenge like marker and also the shape of a Tori, a touch of the Oriental; covering all the bases. And so, Aglaea, with your insight you have brought out the truth."

"Oh, Grandmother. What a grand idea. Tori. Isn't that also a girl's name?

"Oh? Are we having a girl?"

"We don't know yet and don't want to. Just thinking ahead."

"Well, let's show them the gallery," said Ramona. "I haven't been down there for months."


*              *              *              *              *              *
     *              *              *              *              *              *


The view was spectacular! The first statue cast was of one of the nine muses, Klio, with her scroll spread and highlighted with special lights, as thought she was taking attendance of those entering. To the right was Menander, a Roman copy of an early Greek Bronze. Menander was an early play-write who wrote approximately a hundred plays of comedy about everyday conditions in Athens.

To the left stood a cast of Aphrodite from Melos, or Venus de Milo, the original is housed in the Louvre, Paris. Stretched behind this welcoming committee were dozens of equally rare forms and paintings. It would take an hour or more to just briefly view their splendor. There was Nike of Samothrace and Venus of Capua with her partially robe-clad form and arms stretched to her left as though trying to pluck a base viola, oblivious that her robe had fallen exposing her torso from her hips up.

Rowena arrived just at the end of lunch and immediately went to her mother to give her a hug. Then to Rowie, saying hello to Carl and finally to Piearce to give him a kiss and hug saying that he hadn't changed a bit and if anything, looked even better. When introduced to Aglaea, her comment was, "You lucky dog! No, really it is so good to meet you. I always tried to envision what you might look like when he said he had found his true love, and you exceed what I had formulated."

"That's very flattering. Thank you."

"See! What did I tell you on our tour?" injected Rowie.

Everyone chuckled knowing how Rowie would describe her mother's ability to cling to adolescence even though middle aged, and were not surprised when Aggie said, "Keep up the good work. We need more frivolity and festive atmospheres."

At that moment Piearce's phone vibrated. He looked, excused himself and walked to the foyer to answer Lavinia's call.

"We just got your message a little while ago. For God's sake, don't approach them whatever you do. The network has been alerted so sit tight. Where are you?"

"At Ramona's."

"We're to be there next week. Does she know what you are really there for?"

"No." Piearce then relayed what had transpired plus the VIN number of the limo.

"Are you sure? There must be a mistake!"

"I'll check again and get back to you, but on first glance, I'm pretty sure the number is the same. I'll ask Carl if he does all the maintenance of the vehicles as a way of getting to see the vehicle again. We are leaving within the hour so I don't know how successful I'll be. Anything else?"

"No. Just be careful. You have accomplished the mission as far as we are concerned. A contingency is on the way as we speak, but won't get there until Tuesday. Enjoy your vacation. Bye."

Piearce returned to the luncheon group.

"Well, was it the president or the Queen? We were discussing whether we should keep you here over night or let you return without Aggie. I've offered her a full time job as my personal physician and we are waiting for her acceptance. Besides, we haven't finished our private discussion yet," was the welcoming back comment by Ramona as Piearce smiled and looked at Aggie saying, "I can only imagine what would have taken place if I'd been a little longer."

"Well, Piearce," asked Rowena, "what do you think of my daughter marrying a chauffeur?"

"I couldn't have made a better choice if I'd chosen him myself, Granny," was his casual remark.

"We decided to go for a swim. Are you interested? Carl has declined. He's got a couple of things to do."

"We haven't much time. I'd like to leave by four, but Aggie, you go ahead and swim. I'll give Carl a hand with whatever he is doing. Need help, Carl?"

It was his opportunity to be alone with Carl and check the limo. They all hustled off except Ramona, who indicated she'd finish a project. She also wanted to rest after her night out with the girls. Carl said he wanted to clean the garage and wash the salt and snow off the stretch. They hopped into the vehicle and drove to the wash stall in the garage. Piearce said he'd vacuum the interior if it needed it while Carl washed.

"No, going to do that first; the Shop Vac is right here." He opened the doors and mentioned that the girls must have gotten rambunctious.

"It look as though they put their shoes on the back of the seats and door panels. Usually it's just a quick vac and a rinse of the mats. Need the spray and small brush."

"Looks like scuff marks. A bit high on the doors though," mentioned Piearce whose mind could only think of the marks as being caused by struggling girls.

"I haven't driven this since we returned. We usually use the smaller limo instead of the stretch."

"When did you use it last?"

"Come to think of it, just after our wedding. I took Ramona to The Resort, oh, I know! Rowie and I took a trip and one of the grandsons was visiting and took it to be greased and oiled at The Resort. Usually I do it, but he was here visiting a few times the last few months. Perhaps he had a few friends and went partying."

Piearce wanted to leave the marks as evidence, so he did the next best thing. He photographed the inside with his phone while Carl went to get the spray soap and small brush. Piearce also photographed the license plate and their fasteners and decided that Carl wasn't involved. He recalled his conversation with Ramona especially about one of her grandson's visits. Which grandson was it?

They met the girls at the pool house after cleaning the car.

"Come on in, guys," they called. A maid approached asking if they desired coffee, tea or cocktails. Both declined with Carl saying, "No, thank you, Olga."

"While you people shower and dress, I'll visit with Ramona," said Piearce.

"Find your way?" asked Carl

"I think so. I still have my phone and GPS."

He found Ramona sitting and reading in her favorite chair and in her favorite room overlooking the patio.

"Did you say you have two grandsons? Any granddaughter's beside Rowie?"

"No. No others. My son is into investments and management, similar to his father, running one of the bigger branches of the company. One grandson, Bruce, runs it with him and is getting groomed to take over. The other grandson, Albert, is spoiled and shiftless and has recently been cut off from all funds by his father, but has recently made an occasional visit. As a matter of fact, he even borrowed the stretch to take his friends on a little trip a few weeks ago. They visited The Resort and also took the car for a check-up. It was last month I think."

Confirmation! Not Carl! What a relief that is. But was he involved or did someone else take the limo, change plates, and do the transfer via one of the other drivers? That would be for Ursula and Lavinia to solve.

They spoke for twenty minutes when the swimmers came in with Rowena escorting Aglaea; Carl and Rowie trailed with their arms wrapped around their backs, looking at each other and smiling.

It was four o'clock. Aggie wanted to get back to The Resort for another night of fun before returning to work tomorrow, so goodbyes and hugs were exchanged. In the dwindling daylight the car headed for The Resort.

Once on the way, Piearce updated Aggie on the VIN number episode and the possibility of a grandson being involved.

"No! Oh Piearce! No! There must be some mistake!"

"Isn't it probable someone took the car without anyone knowing? Maybe one of the drivers just got into the wrong limo while it was parked there."

"Quite possible and I hope that is the scenario, but what about the plates being changed? That indicates a planned event. It could very well be that that is the story and the driver changed the plates thinking he had a resort stretch. By changing the plates the car wouldn't be traced to The Resort."

"Also, it would protect The Resort by using the fictitious registration tag. No, I'm voting for someone purposely detaining, or even switching identical limos to protect The Resort and also accomplish their goal."

"And the grandson? What's his name, Albert? What was his goal? What was he doing? Why didn't he notice the car being missing? Why wasn't it cleaned?"

"It could be that they took longer to make the two day trip and didn't have time, if it was taken without knowledge. Of course, they could have made it in one and a half days if they drove continuously and never stopped except for gas, maybe even over a twenty-four hour time frame."

"Good thinking. We'll present these possibilities to Lavinia and Ursula when we get to The Resort."

"By the way, I really enjoyed Rowie and her family. If we hadn't needed to leave tomorrow, I would have stayed and I loved that room overlooking the patio and garden."

"Wait till you see it in bloom. I saw it in the summer but not in the spring, and I can imagine the fall must have been spectacular."

"Nice setting for a wedding."

"You read my mind, again!"

The discussion continued. At The Resort they decided to phone Lavinia immediately and leave a message, only to be surprised by Ursula answering, "Hi. This is the Black and White answering service; the nun is getting out of her habit of answering her own phone. I'll be glad to relay a message."

"Very clever, Ursula. How are you?"

"Tired but looking forward to a Christmas vacation and visiting The Resort. We are going to be the guests of Ramona, using her suite. She informed them that we are her guests because of all the help we rendered while we worked there. Couldn't have worked out better."

Piearce then updated her on their findings and their partial interpretation and analysis.

"You and Aggie be careful. No more active snooping for your own safety. One more item. Can you confirm the suite number or floor number for us? We think they are allowing the one girl to accompany the client to avoid suspicion and she won't attempt anything due to jeopardizing the lives of the other girls. These guys are ruthless business people."

"We are going to dinner in a few minutes after a brief tour of a few of the 1930's events, so we'll keep our eyes open."

"Seen them all, but not at Christmas time. That's next week. Enjoy and thanks. Bye."

When exiting the elevator, two Asian looking men entered and Piearce noticed they pushed button nine. Were they part of that group? Aggie thought one looked familiar, but wasn't sure. "After all, we only saw them for a few moments and in subdued light."

They loitered near the elevator looking at wall displays and a photo by Ansell Adams of the wilderness, but keeping an eye on the elevator stops. The ninth floor. Possible confirmation.

Aggie said, "Oh . . . I forgot to tell you that I can possibly have a full time job here as a house physician plus attending to a wealthy household in the mountains. So what do you think of that?"

"Is there a college near-by? Does that include living quarters? And what would you do about your current position? I think you made a very big impression on a very wealthy lady."

"No. I like what I am doing too much and want to stick with it at least for a few more years. It is the greatest of experiences for any doctor as far as I am concerned."

They stopped in one of the speak-easies and listened to some honky-tonk and corny stilted entertainment of the period. It was fun to make the comparisons to current bizarre almost embarrassing displays that one sees on almost a daily basis. They decided that it would be more fun to revert back to previous times as far as certain behaviors are concerned. They dined in the informal dining room after seeing people acting the part formally. It was fun to see, but decided it was more relaxing in the informal room. The hostesses who were on the desk and who had made their room arrangements, stopped by their table to see if everything was satisfactory. As they were leaving, they murmured, "Is your phone off?"

Piearce looked at Aggie and reached into his pocket for is phone and turned it on, but put it on silent mode. There was a text message that just said "call." Piearce noticed long ago that Ursula and Lavinia's phones had blocks and when they didn't want to chance notice, they used that mode. They ordered and told the waitress that they were going to look at the displays. They called and Lavinia said, "Marla and Super are on their way back. Don't trust Marla! Or Super for that matter. And one of the agents mentioned that the grandson was not too clean, so be alert. They might get there by tomorrow. Give you details later."

"We looked for them but didn't see them, now I know why. Off on another safari. Okay, we'll avoid them if we can. Bye"

"What is that all about?" asked Aggie.

"Rowie and Marla were close at one time and I don't know if there is still an active relationship. I assumed there was not, but . . ."

"I doubt it, but then who really knows?"

They returned to their table and the waiter brought their first course. Aggie was extremely impressed with the service, the décor and the finesse with which chiefs artistically presented the food.

"I really liked dining here," Aggie exclaimed. "It's such a pleasure."

# Chapter VII

Piearce was at breakfast, waiting for Aglaea who was luxuriously coddling herself in a hot bath and just enjoying herself. Piearce noticed that it had warmed up a few degrees, possibly enough to allow them to drive to the bridge and to the cave trail. He wished he had rented a four wheel drive or similar vehicle.

He had finished breakfast when Aggie appeared.

"Breakfast?"

"No. Just coffee; I want to get out and enjoy the next three hours before we leave."

They drove to the bridge, stopped while Piearce relived the episode of the canoe trip; they drove to the trail leading to the cave, parked and climbed the slippery path to the cave where they explored part of the cave that Piearce had only viewed from his place of concealment. He used his flashlight to illuminate the opening for Aggie to see where he stood to witness the episode between Rolando and Marla.

The return trip was a slipping and sliding event part of which the downhill return was on their gluteus maximus. Joyous laughter and whoops and catching each other, completed the trip.

"We should have brought cardboard to slide down on, like when we were kids," was Aggie's response to their experience.

"Now I'll need to dry these slacks and take another bath or shower."

They proceeded to their rooms to change, bathe, dry and pack. Then it was off to lunch. During lunch a solemn looking group arrived for a late brunch and among them was a different, a little younger girl with the Asian tour group. She was very made up and looked as if she had been weeping. Her eyes remained downcast and obedient. When food was served, she ate very little but glanced at Aglaea with recognition. She glanced again at Aglaea for a fleeting moment and Aggie place her index finger to her lips signaling to keep silent. Aggie also winked. The girl had a slight hint of a smile and brightened for a split second. Contact had been made. It would give her hope. When they exited from the dining area, they nodded their good days and waved to the man they had met yesterday as a mere formality. He smiled and bowed his head in acknowledgement.

On the way to get their bags, Aggie and Piearce highlighted their findings and Aggie wanted to act. But Piearce said, "We aren't positive and we can't prove a thing. We know the girls only speak a few words of English and French. Although during the past month they must have learned numbers and more English."

After getting their bags and while waiting for the elevator, Aggie said, "Give me your pen." She hastily wrote on the palm of her hand: 3 Jour and 3 days.

"Just in case," she said as they got out of the elevator, the group had finished lunch and were getting back on the elevator. Aglaea said,

"Oh, wait, I forgot my tooth brush," giving Piearce her bag and saying, "You get the car, I'll be right down."

Aglaea stood in front of the girl who was against the rear wall of the elevator. She slipped her hand behind her and touched the girl, gave a little squeeze, flexed her hand open and closed a few times. She suddenly felt fingers put pressure on her hand and let go. Aggie exited at her floor feeling lifted at the acknowledgement, still feeling the fingertip pressure, still trying to fight back tears at the response.

The flight home was without issue and they drove to Aggie's house only to find her mother had arrived, let herself in and had been cooking, preparing dinner. Piearce excused himself, kissed Aggie and headed home. It was getting cold.

The Buick called to him, at least that's what he told himself. He was tempted to take it for a run, but decided he needed to get back into the house and study. He looked at the stack of crumpled plastic sheathing and other paraphernalia he had removed from the underside and recalled the removing of the welded spots. He disliked the idea of taking it all to the dump: it was part of the Buick but it was a little unsightly. He moved the tin metal sheath to place it near the pile of debris he was planning to toss. While resting the metal on edge to remove a broom that was in the way, he lost his grip and it fell with the undercoated side down. He moved the broom and reached for the sheath when he noticed writing or lettering on one corner. It was a group of number and letter combinations, one would find from the marketing company or manufacturer used as nomenclature identification. He stood it up and placed it against the trash to be taken to the dump. He'd go to the dump later in the week. He glanced once more at the Buick and wondered if he should present it to Ramona to use while she was living. Maybe. After all, she had made him a wealthy man.

At 3 AM he went to bed after having completed the reading assignment. He was tired and dreaded having to rise early. At seven his cell phone made a single soft ring indicating a text message. *Hope you finished your reading. They called at 0530 for work. Mom here for a week. Miss you. Good luck, kiwugs, Aggie.* Maybe he'd call Ramona and arrange a wedding at her garden patio area for Easter. No. Her mother and his mother might object, besides, it was really her choice.

Breakfast was ready. He ate and left for a nine o'clock class, telling his mother that he may not be back for a couple of days. He would probably stay at his dorm room to catch up on his teaching prep and exams. This weekend he would spend some time with her. His mother had a dozen questions for him, half of which he answered. He said he would be back in a few days and give her a complete rundown on the recent trip. Plus, he'd be home for Christmas.

# Chapter VIII

Lavinia and Ursula were able to obtain copies of the adoption papers for the three oriental girls. Lavinia said, "These papers indicated the girls were from Thailand but they don't speak the language! They speak a dialect of Chinese. Their passports are stamped Bangkok, through an agency there, but there was no indication of where they had been born. It just says 'unknown'!"

Ursula continued, "Who checks these papers and passports? There is no I.D number from the immigration department; the addresses and names of the adoptive people are false. There is no such address. According to headquarters, the photo is of a house on the property of a lot adjacent to the address given."

Ursula was designated to go to The Resort disguised as a brunette to guide the undercover agents and give support. She'd be able to positively I.D. The Girls, and possibly get DNA and finger prints from glasses for confirmation. She had already put in for a vacation to go to Ramona's, so she'd just leave a week early. Besides, many of the children would be going home for the holidays. Lavinia was to remain for another week and then join her at Ramona's.

"Did Doctor Wright stay on or did he leave after the summer?" asked Lavinia. Dr. Wright had paid a lot of attention to Ursula on a number of occasions. No date, but a goodly number of coffee chats and accidental 'bumps into'. It was obvious that he was trying to cultivate a relationship. Ursula indicated that had she not been on duty she may have dated or at least gone to dinner with him. He was three years out of medical school.

"He was looking into starting a practice but he had a two year contract with The Resort and I have no idea when that expires. Perhaps he is still there. Why? Want to put your name in?"

*        *        *        *        *        *
    *        *        *        *        *        *

Ursula arrived on the 4:30 PM flight. The limo was there to pick up an unkempt, longhaired brunette with bangs, a dowdy dress padded to give her a matronly looking figure, and with horn rimmed glasses and flat shoes. She didn't look impressive but rather like an old maid school teacher with dyed hair. The limo driver didn't recognize her and gave his spiel about The Resort, introducing the patrons to the resort theme to which they could become a part of if they so desired. The rest of the passengers were genuinely enthused about acting the part. Ursula, aka Rosette A. Stone, sat prim and proper smiling to herself. Her half price room was on the same floor as the help; a basement dwelling with no view. Had she not known of the room's existence, she would have been charged 4 to 5 times the price.

After checking in, she went to her room and tidied up, returning in time for the tour and lecture, which she knew by heart. She then visited several 1930's boutiques. Again, no one recognized her. She attended dinner informally, quickly spotting the Asian tour group. They were to leave Friday, so she had heard, but what of The Girls? They had started to call the three Chinese girls with this appellation as if they were the only three girls of any importance left in the world. She had found the suite number and was hoping to somehow gain an introduction to The Girls. Aggie's approach seemed foolproof and if she had the opportunity she'd implement it.

Seated at a table with two couples, she was drawn into the conversation and she gave them a canned response. She was a semi-retired teacher who currently worked for a private company who represented international concerns and their products. No one questioned her. No one really cared. How you made your millions wasn't important. They assumed you were wealthy if you were at that resort.

As Ursula was waiting for the elevator to descend to her basement room, she noticed the four men and two girls. The girls looked familiar from the dining room at the Monastery even with their traditionally painted faces. How to be sure? Aglaea's technique? Time to implement. She took out her pen and wrote on her palm: 2 Jour – 2 days. She hustled to the elevator and got on, wedged herself against The Girls who were standing next to each other. She put her hand behind her and touched one of The Girls and flexed her hand several times. After a second attempt she felt two hands squeeze hers at the same time. Mission accomplished. They knew what she looked like. She got off at the sixth floor and walked down the corridor towards the stairs as the doors closed.

Who leases or rents or occupies the suite? The hotel or someone else? Is the headquarters somewhere else and were The Girls pressed into service from another location? With their white faces, who would know if they were the same girls or different ones? An unusual arrangement. Concubines? Still approved in the orient? Ursula planned to slip into the computer room to download as much data as possible. She hoped she remembered the codes.

The suite was leased by an international conglomerate catering to very wealthy clients for their exclusive patronage. Was it possible The Resort knew nothing about their activities, or were a part of the conglomerate? She thought about all the workers there and knew most were honorable but who would be the most trustworthy? Was Marla knowledgeable about this? Or Super? Did they support this, or condone it? Would they disavow such practice? And who were her contacts? They had only given her one vital bit of identifying information. They would contact her by using a number. She wished they'd make themselves known soon. Christmas was next week; this coming weekend would be the last before Santa arrives. As she packed her computer she thought of Dr. Wright and wondered if he was part of the establishment or a trusted coworker.

At midnight there was a tapping on her door. She hastened to put on her wig and her oversized bathrobe. Without putting on the overhead light, she cracked the door and said yes and a voice said, "Do you know where I can find a 1932 Buick?" She closed the door and undid the safety lock, and let the person in.

"Ursula, it is good to see you again," said a good looking young doctor. "Now I know why I didn't get any response from my poor attempts to get to know you better. You can take off the wig. It doesn't become you."

"How did you become involved with this?"

"My father works for the CIA and a special investigative group is coming to do undercover work here and he knew about it and gave them my name. That's when they gave him your name as the contact to show them around never realizing I worked here. They will be at breakfast tomorrow morning in the breakfast nook, so look your worst. Now that I know the truth about you, would you consider going to dinner with me sometime in the future? I figure if I didn't ask you now, I'd regret it the rest of my life."

"Probably, but not soon and you know the reason. Do you want a breakdown on this investigation or are you fully informed?"

"I really only got the information about the time you arrived. There are two other people that we can trust and there are several secret agents coming in the next day or so. I'm meeting the two agents in a few minutes in my office. She has supposedly become ill, so I must leave in a minute or two."

Ursula gave him as much information as she could in the allotted time, checked the passageway and let him out. God! Dr. Wright! Is he right? She wanted to call Lavinia and tell her what had just happened. She slipped into bed and just lay there with wild fantasies then finally put it out of her mind and rolled over on her side and went to sleep with a smile. A more pleasant contact couldn't have been made.

She awoke trying to recall her dream. She remembered Dr. Wright and had pleasant thoughts but they were quickly put aside when she tried to recall the dream she had. If The Girls suddenly became ill, they'd need a doctor. How could one accomplish that? Food poisoning? But they are never together at the same time: tainted food delivered, so that the entire suite became ill? What of the cleaning crew? Can they be of assistance or are they part of the illegal activities? Is this just a part of a very lucrative business that may have spread to hundreds of high class slavery acts or kidnapping? It is most likely a business based on greed, unfeeling, disregard for life at the expense of others.

She couldn't let go. With such a hush-hush activity, it must be wide spread. How many other homes, institutes, salvation groups are unwittingly a part of this empire? Each group of *'do gooders'* has within their establishment at least one, if not two unsavory individuals who would take advantage of others if they thought they wouldn't be caught. What personality trait exists that would inadvertently expose them? Some quirk, some tell-tale habit that is a common denominator running through their system; a figure of speech, an eye movement, a squint, a hand or finger flick? What imperceptible clue is there that would label them as a possible villain?

Her next call was to Lavinia. "Hello," said a sleepy voice. Ursula said, "Guess who the contact here is!"

"Do I know her or him?"

"Yes!"

"Really? Who?"

"Dr. Wright!"

"OOHH . . . MYYY . . . GODDD!"

"And I have a tentative date when this fiasco is over. He asked me outright. See you in a few days."

"Wait!"

She hung up laughing loudly, kicking her feet in the air and slapping the bed with her hands.

<br>

*      *      *      *      *      *

   *      *      *      *      *      *

<br>

Aglaea spent the day in the Emergency Department. It was one of those days when things that went right went very right and those things that went wrong went very wrong; MVA (Motor Vehicle Accidents) victims are so unpredictable. One minute they are listless, the next they are posturing, the next, gone! One can't get emotionally involved, but when you feverishly work on a 16 year old girl who had gone on her first date, with everything to live for, it is heart rendering. The driver, her date, and the back seat couple had minor injuries and were devastated over the accident and her death. They had been going to a church youth function when it happened. Black ice!

After fishing her computer work, she called Piearce to see if he was available for dinner, then she recalled her mother was preparing dinner for her, so she continued her call and asked him if he had time to come to dinner. He indicated that he had to prep a lecture and had to catch up from their weekend. He sensed a little urgency in her voice and said, "Tell you what. I'll drive out for dinner but I have to get back to study."

"Deal. See you in an hour."

*      *      *      *      *      *
   *      *      *      *      *      *

It was a joyful passionate meeting as Piearce entered, hugged and kissed a clinging Aglaea, put down his briefcase, removed his coat, and again kissed and hugged her. While holding her, he said in her ear, "Bad day?"

"A sixteen year old girl. I recognized her from the church. You know how it is, you've been there."

Her mother, Juline, arrived and announced her presence with, "Don't I get a hug from my future son-in-law?'

The evening turned into one of joviality when they discussed humorous incidents of the past week and weekend. At 10 PM Aggie snuggled up next to him as Juline went to bed. 11 PM was suddenly upon them, so Piearce reluctantly said his goodbyes and drove to the dorm room. He checked his email and set his alarm for 5 AM. He'd do much better studying after a good night sleep. His first thought was of how comforting it felt to have Aglaea snuggling up next to him while he read last night.

*      *      *      *      *      *
   *      *      *      *      *      *

One of his courses was on biblical art and another on archaeological history. He was so absorbed in reading about the 'James Ossuary' that he didn't hear the first ring of his phone. It was indicating a message was being left when he looked at the icon he had for Lavinia.

"Hi, sorry, I was reading and actually didn't hear the phone ringing. What's up? What is so important that I should be honored in this way?"

"I knew you were an early riser, so I figured I'd update you. Ursula made contact. Believe it or not, it is Dr. Wright. Can you imagine? She just called. Also she made contact with two of the girls. We figure that Ramona's grandson was having a party with his girlfriends and didn't know the limo was used and abused. Apparently one of the limo drivers is often sent off on trips; don't know why we never thought of this type of activity while we were there. It's beginning to look as though there are organizations within the conglomerate acting independently. At least that's what the higher ups are hinting. By the way, what are you doing New Year's Eve?"

"I'll check with Aggie.'

"They are having quite a bash at The Resort, think about it."

"Okay. After exams I'll be able to think better."

"Also, one of the workers we figured we could trust called on my regular phone and mentioned that there was an investigation into your presence over the weekend and they have been questioning the help as to your actions especially about having two separate rooms. They figured one of you could have been off doing the undercover work while the other was asleep. But the cleaning girls said it wasn't possible because Aggies' room had not been used. Just thought I'd mention that your secret is out, and it also eliminated you as being a possible suspect."

"I wonder if the average person knows how much intrigue continues throughout the night every night. Thanks for keeping us informed and I'll check with Aggie about New Year's Eve."

"Oh! Did you find any more papers or any written messages in the Buick? One of the researchers has apparently uncovered some possible indications that there are other clues or data, perhaps still in the Buick."

"Not really, but I'll scour it once again."

"Okay, bye."

"See you." He packed his briefcase and left for his exams and lecture.

# Chapter IX

As she waddled along on her way to breakfast, Ursula suddenly had a brilliant idea. Although The Girls were seldom seen at breakfast, this morning the youngest, about 14, was with two men. She in her Kimono and with a powdered face which did not hide the puffiness around the eyes. If one didn't know her, no one would consider that she had been crying. Ursula got her food and set her tray down at a table near them. She glanced and saw Dr. Wright with two people at the window table. They must be the agents that he had mentioned. Sitting and facing the girl, she took out her pen and wrote a note on a small pad. One of the two men had his back toward her. The other sat next to the girl but his view was obstructed by the man with his back to her. Lavinia had mentioned that the youngest was the most affluent in English. She wrote the words in large letters. FAINT – BE SICK –. She held the notepad up against her chest so no one else could see it. The girl glanced up at her. She squinted for a second, looked back down at her plate, then back again at the note. She looked directly into Ursula's eyes. After a few moments, the girl spoke to her escorts and rose. She took a step or two and fell to the floor knocking over a chair and grabbing the tablecloth causing a glass to crash to the floor.

Dr. Wright immediately went to her aid, telling her escorts he was a doctor and called for a stretcher. The men said they'd take her back to the room but Dr. Wright said no, he'd take her to the infirmary to examine her. Within two minutes the stretcher arrived with attendants, who removed the child to the clinic. One of the agents with Dr. Wright stopped and whispered in her ear, "We were watching you. Nice going!"

She very smugly finished her breakfast, then took a doddering walk to visit the displays that were open. Wondering how or what the crew was doing in the doctor's office, and chiding herself for not accompanying them she fretted. But wait! There was no reason she couldn't visit to see how the poor little child was doing. So off she went to the doctor's office. The nurse didn't recognize her and said the girl was to have no visitors. Then Rosette A. Stone asked to see the doctor. The nurse politely said to wait one moment and went to tell the doctor. On his arrival he was very serious, then his eyes lightened and a bit of a smile quickly replaced his reserved face when he recognized who it was and he asked, "How may I help you? Oh, yes. You are the woman who assisted at the breakfast incident. Miss Rosette A. Stone, is it not?"

"Yes. I was concerned for the poor girl and came to inquire about her condition and welfare. Did she hurt her head or anything?"

"I'm afraid we will have to keep her a little while to run some more tests. I'm sure that her guardians wouldn't mind if you visited for a moment. Nurse, hold all my calls for a few minutes. Thank you."

They entered a closed room after knocking. The girl was in bed wide-eyed with one agent beside her. When the door closed and clicked, she jumped out of bed and hugged Ursula and began sobbing.

"We told her it would be at least a day or two before she would be free and that she could go back to the other girls and tell them what happened. The gentleman will come to pick her up in a few minutes."

The girl said, "Other woman, she here?"

"Which one?"

"Sunday woman."

"No. She has left but I will stay," said Ursula as she removed her wig. The girl's eyes opened wide and a smile of delight and recognition blossomed as the girl said, "The kitchen! Sister's friend, she come?"

"Yes. Later! Now be careful. No talk about this. Other woman may be back also." She felt compelled to say that; she was sure that if Aglaea knew how much of an impression she had made, she'd come if she could.

Dr. Wright said, "Time to go." Rosette replaced her wig. As she left the office, two men appeared and entered the room to take the girl to the suite. Ursula was tempted to say "so long" to Edna, the nurse, in her natural voice to see the reaction, but training prevented her from doing so.

"Miss Rosette A. Stone, thank you for your help. May I buy you a drink or coffee?" The corridors were filling up and music of various types was faintly heard. Walking in her dowdy fashion aside the good doctor, he laughingly said, "Boy, you take the cake in that outfit. And how you impressed these agents with your strategy is wonderful. It saved all sorts of time, eliminating delays. Several other agents are due this afternoon who have been working on this for months. Apparently they have pretty well figured out the entire operation and have several key persons under surveillance. Even as early as tomorrow or by Thursday at the latest, they'll close this whole operation down and no one will know they were here. The girls have been abused, but fully realize what is going on. Ordinarily I'd call the authorities, but under the existing circumstances, the government is in charge."

"Well, if you need anything, call. What are they going to do with The Girls?"

"I don't really know. Back to the school, I suspect. They'll need counseling and possibly medical attention. The church can supply that. Why? Do you want to take charge of them?"

"Not really, I think that I know someone who impressed them so that it's possible they might be able to consider befriending them for a period of time, until permanent arrangements can be made. I'll let you know later. Phone calls first." They stopped at the café.

Ursula called Lavinia, reported and then called Aglaea. She explained the situation and Aggie's reply was that Piearce was finishing his exams Thursday morning, and perhaps they could be there by late afternoon. It will take a great deal of juggling to accomplish this. Perhaps we could take the families there for Christmas weekend. "I'll call Pierce. I'll have to be back here by Saturday. Oh, gosh, what a dilemma!"

Piearce's reasoning was that if Aggie wanted to consider taking them for a while, the authorities could release The Girls to them for a week or two. Then they could bring them back to her house for adjustment and rehabilitation. During that time, decisions could be formulated and feelings analyzed. They'd talk it out later. Aggie said, "Do you think you could entertain them at The Resort over the Christmas weekend? I promised I'd take duty so I am committed. Can we afford this?"

Pierce finally said, "Aggie, we have money. I was planning to give it back or give it to some nonprofit group. Basically this is the same sort of activity. Plane tickets are inconsequential and I'll pay for your tickets to and from The Resort. It's only a short flight time, so order the tickets and leave the rest to me. We'll meet with your mother and my folks this afternoon or evening and solve the dilemma in one way or another."

"Done. I love you! I'll attend to the preliminaries for you over the phone. I am doing a double shift today. Bye.

# CHAPTER X

Wednesday morning and afternoon he had exams. His graduate chairman saw him coming from his afternoon exam said, "Piearce, as you know I was going to give the exam tomorrow but if you and the rest are ready I'll give it this afternoon or this evening and you will be free tomorrow. Truth is, I can catch an earlier flight for the holidays."

Piearce said, "I'd like more time to review, but I'll check with the crew and see you at 4:30 to let you know."

"I've seen Snyder and Rundane; they said okay and will meet the others to get their feelings."

"Okay. I'm on my way for the study group to see them now."

Everyone was in accord, giving them an earlier departure time also. At seven-thirty they had all completed their exams and were joyously on their way wishing everyone happy holidays. Piearce's exams were a snap according to him. Of course, taking the courses and teaching the same one certainly gives one an advantage.

Piearce stopped by the Emergency Department to see Aggie. Everyone showered happy holidays to him and welcomed him back. Some of the guys kidded him about being too late and that he shouldn't have gone to college because now the doctor wears an engagement ring. They loved to tease Piearce. Aggie was standing at the board checking reports and smiling at the razzing. An instant decision! She was going to announce her engagement in a very special way. As far as the ER people were concerned, she was engaged, and persistent questioning did not divulge the ring giver. She put down the clipboard, walked with determination toward the group, who saw her coming and instantly stopped the joking and said hello. She responded with, "Oh, you are Piearce! Tell me, was it you who sent me this ring?"

Everyone stopped. The entire emergency room became silent as Pierce said, "No. I just sent you a box of Cracker Jacks. That must be the prize that came inside!" Aggie put her arms around him. They kissed. There was loud clapping of hands amidst the "Oh, no! No!" "Yeah team," "You kidding?" "Best-kept secret" "How long have you known each other?"

Aggie said, "Since I was 14. Maybe even earlier."

"But you just came here a few months ago."

"Yes, but I went to school here and lived at the farm I bought. This is really my home. Now you know the truth."

"Congratulations to you both. Piearce, you lucky dog. What sly ones you are."

"Got a minute?" Piearce asked Aggie.

He mentioned the exam change and that he was free Thursday morning. She indicated she'd be done by 11 PM or before that evening. It was a slow night, so she might be able to leave early if the relief came in sooner. It was 8 PM. He went into the staff room while Aggie finished up. As he entered, he was bombarded with questions including how he was doing at school.

"I'm really enjoying it, and didn't realize how much I'd seen in my travels and how much I had read about art and history before taking the courses. Travel does marvelous things toward your knowledge of art and history providing you take advantage of the museums and the lectures instead of night clubs.

At 9:15 they drove their separate cars to Aggie's home. Juline was in bed, but rose when she heard them come in. She greeted Piearce with a hug and asked if he was hungry. She said she was intrigued with the idea of Christmas at The Resort but didn't want to impose. It was no imposition, they said. Piearce asked if his parents gave any indications of their feelings about the subject. They said they'd think about it.

Aggie said, "I think they will want to talk it over with you. By the way, what did you find out about that request from the higher ups about any other findings?"

"Nothing yet, but I'll check tomorrow morning now that exams are over. What time does our flight leave?"

"One fifteen. I reserved a suite and we pick up tickets at the counter."

"Do you realize how much money this is costing you?"

"Can't take it with me and you and family are worth it."

"I can hardly wait to see those girls! It must have been terrifying for them!"

"You really connected with them and impressed them after only seeing them four times. It is amazing. After all they've been through, they asked Ursula about you."

"I remember how they smiled at us when we made eye contact at the monastery. They probably appreciated our concern. I really tried to talk to them for a few minutes on each occasion."

*     *     *     *     *     *<br>*     *     *     *     *     *

At seven he was up enjoying coffee with his parents, discussing the weekend, the three girls and their situation. It sounded like a rescue mission to his parents and they suddenly became intrigued with the idea and went off to pack. Piearce had packed before he had come down for breakfast. He went out to the 1932 Buick.

He carefully looked in every crevice, sliding under the car again to examine the entire undercarriage. Sliding out, he looked at the pile of debris, thinking that he'd better get that out of the way as soon as possible. He started walking to the back of the car wondering if the trunk space had anything in it that he missed, when he suddenly stopped. Retracing his steps, he went to the disposal pile and picked up the metal sheathing and turned it over to examine the printing that he assumed was nomenclature stencil from the manufacturing company. It looked like ordinary stamping, but more extensive now that he viewed it again. Could this be it? Could it be in code? He needed a pencil and paper to copy it. Also, he should photograph it. But he'd continue his perusal of the Buick just in case. He wondered if the lining of the roof hid anything of interest. The spare tire covers? The hood? No, that had been repainted.

Painstakingly he copied the nomenclature and photographed it. Perhaps he would go to the lumber yard and see if their aluminum sheets had similar stamping. If not, then to the sheet metal shop and to make a comparison.

# CHAPTER XI

Lavinia's plane landed at 11 AM and she was picked up by limo and went directly to Ramona's suite as arranged. Lunch was being served and she had had little breakfast. Her previous co-workers welcomed her with open arms, asking where her cohort was. She'll be around shortly was her comment, and went to lunch after going to the suite with her luggage and to freshen up.

As she walked into the informal dining room she turned around and left immediately, trying to choke back laughter. She had seen Ursula sitting alone at a table in her black wig and dowdy dress and she couldn't control herself. She exited, rounded a corner and started laughing and coughing to cover up her laughter. Leaning against the wall, she took a tissue and blew her nose, dabbed her eyes and reentered the dining room. She asked to be seated near Ursula. As she sat she said, "Gosh, you are a hysterical sight." Ursula replied, "I noticed the quick cover up. I think I know what my Halloween costume will be next year. The raid is going on as we speak, or at least the preliminaries are underway. They are really waiting for another group of agents who have been detained and will come in on the next flight."

"That must be the same flight that Aggie and Piearce are coming in on. Boy, old home week," answered Lavinia. "How are The Girls?"

"Dr. Wright says they'll be okay but will examine them more fully when they are freed. It's a waiting game now."

"When are you coming out of hiding?"

"As soon as they signal us. My question is: how do I make the transformation? In the open or go change and return?"

"Go to my room and change, then wait for the limo from the airport to arrive. Wait, better yet, we'll call Carl to bring the limo, you check out, go to the airport via the limo service, Carl can pick you up and bring you here to check into the suite with me. You'll only be gone for an hour or so."

"Sounds like a plan. We'll play it by ear," Ursula answered as Lavinia got on her cell phone to call Carl.

At four o'clock, the limousines were approaching the lake area to The Resort carrying Piearce, Aglaea and family. The limo driver was going through his introductory speech and pointing out areas of interest or historical importance, even the area where it was suspected that Sundance Kid and his partner lived with their girlfriends, none of which was true.

Lavinia met the group as they were checking in and went with them to their suite, where she updated them on the current status. As soon as The Girls were freed, they would go to the doctor for examination and then probably be assigned to their suite. Then the option, if the authorities acquiesced, was to remain there or be taken to Aglaea's home.

"We don't know if they will complete the raid today or tomorrow, so enjoy yourselves and leave the rest to us. Ursula is on top of it and in communication with the authorities constantly. You know that if you recognize her, don't speak to her."

"One other item," said Piearce as he handed an envelope to her, "This may not be what you are looking for, but it is all that I could discover that might be meaningful concerning the other question you asked."

Lavinia opened the envelope disclosing photographs and copies of the stenciled nomenclature from the Buick.

Suddenly there was a disturbance as an Asian looking man ran past them pursued by another man who nearly knocked them over. Ursula, in a split second decision, squatted down before the first runner, sending him flying into a hallway lounge chair and continuing off balance into a corner, which caused a nasty cut on his forehead, allowing the pursuer to pounce on him and take him into custody. Ursula didn't get up. She was unconscious and had suddenly regained her original hair color as her wig was partly under the chair. Apparently the knee of the pursued had hit her in the head rendering her in need of medical attention. Within seconds the stretcher arrived and she was delivered to the doctor's office while the raid was finishing up. Within a few minutes she had been examined and no severe injuries could be determined, but Dr. Wright wasted no time getting x-rays for her. She regained consciousness while he was checking her pupils, to which Ursula said, "Hmmm, we could make this a routine if you behave yourself and even if you didn't."

To which Lavinia replied, "She's normal. I guess I'll call Carl and tell him of the change of plans and to come directly to The Resort." The nurses were quite confused when they recognized Ursula, and more confused when the agents started treating her with the utmost respect and admiration. The Agent-In-Charge said, "Ladies, you have just witnessed an event that will remain just an occurrence and you will not mention it to anyone, not even your closest kin. It was just a mishap at which you rendered assistance. Never say any names. Thank you."

Edna just put her hands on her hips and said, "Rosette A. Stone, huh." Then she went and hugged Ursula saying, "I thought Dr. Wright spent extra time in there for a reason. Are you back to work? No, I didn't think so."

"Hi, Edna, tell you all about it in a few days."

As Lavinia was dialing, agents brought three young teary-eyed girls into the doctor's office. They burst into joyful laughter and sobs on seeing Ursula and Lavinia. The doctors and nurses declared Ursula fit, and they began taking The Girls into the examining room, but they spied Aglaea and ran to her, practically knocking her over. Piearce was the next recipient and smiles and nervous laughter prevailed. Dr. Wright indicated he was waiting to examine them, but The Girls literally dragged Aglaea with them. Now they had two doctors with them to examine them and explain in detail that they were now free of any of the men. They were to try and forget the past while Piearce, Ursula and Lavinia spoke with the agents. In the corridor, everything appeared to be calm and peaceful. There was no evidence that a disturbance had occurred a few moments before. The question was, that as orphans, should The Girls be returned to the Monastery or remain with the local authorities. Piearce interrupted and indicated that Aglaea had mentioned an interest in furnishing a possible home for them, at least temporarily. It was a long wait, longer than seemed necessary. Suddenly the examining doors opened and smiling giggling girls appeared, the youngest clinging to Aglaea as a child would to a mother.

The agents indicated they were ready to transport them when Aglaea interceded saying, "I believe Dr. Wright, as the medical authority, has a say in this, am I correct?" An agent said, "Only in an advisory capacity if he deemed the victims were at risk to travel." Dr. Wright said, "In that case, you can see these girls are in need of rest and individual attention so that complete recovery will be insured. It will probably be a month before we can review the case and pronounce their return to normal activities, so I'm putting them into the care of Dr. Aglaea until further notice."

Aglaea said, "Thank you, Dr. Wright, I'll see that they spend the weekend here with my mother and Piearce's parents while your agents also tend to them and protect them." The smiling agents nodded their heads in consent saying, "We'll be around for a few days until legal documents for custody are forthcoming. The immigration agents will tend to that aspect and approve the matter." The smiling Agent-In-Charge looked at Lavinia rather than at Aglaea to whom he was speaking.

"Girls, go with Lavinia to the suite. We'll be there in a few minutes."

"We no go to room with men again?"

"No. As we mentioned in the examining room, you are free to go anywhere you wish as long as you tell us where you are going," answered Dr. Wright.

"Better yet, let's go buy some clothes," said Aggie as she paraded past with the entourage in tow, including Ursula and Lavinia.

# Chapter XII

Carl entered The Resort and went directly to Ramona's suite, rang and a maid opened the door saying, "Oh, Carl. How good to see you. Come in, come in. You have arrived at a most opportune time. Don't tell me that Ramona is here because we have no space left, but we are having a grand gathering and celebration."

"Hello, Clair. Yes, I know a little about it. You look well and sparkling. Do I see a hint of tears in your eyes?"

"Yes! Tears of joy! Tears of joy that I can be a part of this highly unusual activity. I've seen these girls going to and from the dining room but never suspected they were . . . ." she broke into a sob but quickly recovered, as she announced Carl's arrival to the jabbering living room occupants. The result was a grand applause and calls of welcome to Carl. Carl shook hands and was introduced to those who didn't know him. He then proceeded with a statement saying, "As you know, the holidays are here and if you'd rather, you are invited to Ramona's home for the weekend. Or you can continue to enjoy yourselves here at her expense. All I must do, other than act as chauffeur, is to phone how many would be attending, including the care givers if they are not needed here. Hear that, Clair?" Clair answered, "Already have received the phone call alerting us, Carl. You know Ramona, no stone left unturned. The suite next door has been reserved also, if needed. And, I believe that includes a few agents, if necessary."

Aglaea shook her head and said, "I've got to return and take duty at the hospital this weekend, but that doesn't mean The Girls can't go if you want that responsibility." For the next half hour the pros and cons were debated and suddenly the door chime sounded and Clair went to open the door to admit Piearce. Aglaea said, "Where did you disappear to? Hate to say it, but I didn't notice that you had left."

"Took advantage of the lull and called a couple of the boys to wish them happy holidays. I went outside where there is less confusion and a little more quietness."

"Well, I think they have decided not to put Ramona to any more trouble and perhaps just drive out for a visit and return. Oops! My phone; it's the hospital. I've got to answer this. Come on, I'll take it in the bedroom." In the bedroom she closed the door while Piearce stood by her.

"Hello. What's up?"

"Hello, Dr. Aglaea? This is Dr. Rathbourne, retired. One of the paramedics called me and indicated that you were going to leave your resort vacation and take duty this weekend and he prevailed upon me to intercede and cover for you for the weekend. Are you at The Resort now?"

"Yes. Yes I am and I was getting ready to confirm my flight back."

"Well don't bother. I'll cover for you. I'm alone and need something to do this weekend. Call it a fulfillment of an overdue favor. Just a minute, the charge doctor wishes to confirm this."

"Hi, Aglaea. This is Freedrick. Enjoy the weekend. It's nice to have friends. One of the paramedics called Dr. Rathbourne, who I might mention is an old hand at this. See you next week. Bye."

She put her phone away, put her arms around Piearce's neck kissed him and said, "Just called a few friends to wish them happy holidays, huh?" She kissed him again and the door burst open and young girls, Chu Li, Man Dhi, Uh Lay stopped, put their hands over their mouths and giggled. Then Aglaea put her hands out to them and they asked her if they could go to the amusement area to look around. Piearce laughed and said, "The future revealed. Timing is everything."

"Do you feel comfortable going alone? If not, I'll go with you."

"No. That alright. We go in new dresses, thanks you."

"Wait! I have something for you," said Piearce, as he reached into his pocket and retrieved cell phones, saying, "These two icons have my name here and Aglaea's name on this one. Just push them and our phones will ring. Do it now." One pushed the button with Aglaea's name and Aggie's phone began to ring. She answered to the glee of Chu Li saying hello, and giggling. Then Man Dhi pushed Piearce's button and his phone rang, to the delight of the girl. They were ecstatic as they walked out dressed in their new attires speaking in their native tongue. They had had introductions to the phone system through the more wealthy girls at the monastery.

"That's what I love about you, full of surprises, and still very practical."

"I'm amazed at how quickly they reverted to almost normalcy after such a harrowing experience."

"Different culture, different age, different needs, and do you think I'd really let them go without supervision? Lavinia and Ursula have alerted the staff and the agents will keep them under surveillance," she said as she resumed her position prior to the interruption.

He was about to kiss her when his phone rang. It was the youngest girl's icon. Piearce said, "Hello Uh Lay," A voice said, "Thank you for my phone. Bye"

"You are welcome. Bye," Aggie laughingly said, "Timing is everything."

# Chapter XIII

The girls entered the room with a noisy enthusiasm accompanied by Juline and Matt and Isabelle, whose hands the girls were holding. Two were holding Piearce's mother's hands and one looped her arm through Aggies mother's arm. They were followed by Matt, who was beaming as though he was a kid again. Seeing Aggie, they rushed to her and they all started speaking at the same time telling her about their tour. It was Grandmother this and Grandmother that and Grandfather bought this and that they were allowed to go for a swim. It was an endless, incessant chatter and Uncle Carl came and showed them this and that, and Aunt Lavinia and Aunt Ursula bought this and that. They then carried their treasures to their room while Aggie sat down with tears of joy flowing as she repeated, "Grandmother, Grandfather, Uncles and Aunts? Now there is no question that I have done the correct thing by keeping them for the next few months until the hearing and trial. Oh, Piearce."

"Aggie, I think I see a longer range commitment than just a few months." The group chimed in saying that the girls were delightful considering what they had been through recently.

"We have room at the farm," was a smiling remark made by a want-to-be grandmother, while the other want-to-be grandmother smilingly indicated that they could share. Carl stopped in and said that the resort limo would be at their disposal for the next few days and that he was heading back with Ursula and Lavinia in tow.

"Merry Christmas to all. See you in a few days or sooner. See ya, Doc," said Carl as he made a two finger salute on his departure. Just as he reached the door, the girls came flying out and ran to him hugging him and wishing him safe travel. Uncle Carl meandered to his limo where Ursula and Lavinia were waiting, "You come back soon?"

"Yes, in a few days."

Carl mused out loud, "Wait till I tell Rowie what she missed. From a day of possible cataclysmic beginnings, to a joyous blessing of a real holiday with the ultimate gifts."

His drive back with Ursula and Lavinia was interesting, especially when Ursula said the Agent-In-Charge had a unique mannerism; a habit of not looking at the person to whom he is speaking. "He reminds me of that bearded nuisance at the catering service, and also the janitor at the monastery. Both were unusually attentive to you and your needs, Lavinia, if I recall correctly."

"Yup. One had a squeaky voice, the other was gruff and he smelled."

"Let us not forget the stable driver here at The Resort that almost always showed up to take you for a ride in the cart. What was his name? Ira? I'm surprised they kept him here for so long with his long hair and slovenly look."

"Yup. But he always had a kind word and was well mannered. Just a little weird."

"I think the agent has an interest in you," said Carl. "I watched him at the meeting and it seemed like he was looking at you while talking to the others. He was invited to Ramona's for the Christmas Day gathering along with any other agent who wanted to attend."

"And he's fifteen to twenty years older than I am. That scar on his face must have an interesting story. It's not obnoxious but a good conversational starting point. His hair is getting white indicating he might be aging rapidly. Or prematurely," mentioned Lavinia.

"Maybe he's ready for retirement and wants to travel; there's your chance," laughed Ursula.

"That's easy for you to say with "Mr. Right" waiting in the shadows."

"I'm not qualified to judge, but he looks like he is in good physical condition. Probably has a degree in criminal justice or law. Ira you say. Like in investments?" asked Carl.

"Funny, funny, Carl."

The subject returned to The Girls and Aglaea's taking them home with her, and the expense that she'd incur. The question of Piearce having sufficient funds came up, indicating that he then perhaps would pay for their welfare. It was observed that if he didn't, the grandparent's would come to the rescue.

"Is Dr. Wright going to come to Ramona's?" asked Lavinia.

"He said he called his father and indicated that he was planning to spend Christmas in this area. I really do like him. And I like this area more than I realized. We'll see what the next week brings forth."

"I'm glad for you, Ursula. You deserve the best."

"It is amazing how, in just a short period of time, we have become so close, as though we've known each other for a lifetime," said Ursula. Carl interrupted, saying, "We are almost to the house."

As they rounded a turn, they saw that the house was ablaze with Christmas decorations, very tastefully done. It took their breaths away.

The welcoming committee was in full regalia, as though the queen herself had arrived. Rowie hugged and kissed them and clung to her husband as they ushered the guests into the patio room, Ramona's room, while their bags were taken to the guest rooms.

"Ramona, the tree in the foyer is beautiful, but this one is exotic!" claimed Ursula as she went to examine the tree more closely. Lavinia followed her while Ramona explained the decorations and their history.

"Some of them belonged to Tomas, and I don't know all the significance for two of them. This ornamental cylinder, with its intricate design he brought back from one of his trips. I thought it was a bird feeder at first because of the rod running through the bottom that looks like a perch. Then Tomas removed the rod and tapped the cylinder and it emitted a lovely and unique sound, a haunting tone," Ramona said as she demonstrated for them.

"It has an oriental tone, like the old prayer calls. Perhaps it is an old prayer wheel," said Lavinia.

"That's an interesting thought. That would tie in with the 'Tori' and other artifacts from around the world. We call this our international tree. All the decorations are from around the world; just about every conceivable replica or representation from every religious group is displayed, so that no one visiting would feel left out due to their religious orientation. There is no star or angel on top, but a replica of a specially designed oriental temple as an example of neutrality. Keep looking, but tell me now about what happened at The Resort."

"We can't tell you everything, but . . ."

Both Ursula and Lavinia gave renditions of what basically was discovered and how it was theorized that trafficking of young people was actively an ongoing service at The Resort. Several staff people ranging from an assistant CEO to the chauffeurs, to oriental political *'big shot'* were involved. "Fortunately only two injuries were sustained in the whole operation. One person was rendered unconscious in an attempt to stop an escaping villain and the villain sustained a head injury and lacerations. But other than that the operation was successfully accomplished and no one knows it happened. As far as we know, publicity will be nil thus allowing for future raids and arrests without giving the villains a chance to be alerted."

"Would you girls enjoy a glass of wine or a cocktail or other refreshment of any sort?" asked Ramona.

"A nice glass of wine would be delightful," replied Ursula and Lavinia agreed.

Ramona rang for the maid while asking Ursula and Lavinia to continue with their stories. They continued by saying it was quite evident that other parties were involved and one person they were tracing came from a very wealthy family will be devastated when they learn of his possible involvement.

"Does this person have a very wealthy great-grandmother living in the area?"

"We are not allowed to divulge that until all the facts are in, but we can say that your astuteness is remarkable."

"As is your declaration. If his great-grandmother can persuade him to share information might that reduce his penalty?"

"That remains to be seen."

"Oh, let's get to you two. I know about Dr. Wright. How about you, Lavinia? Any pursuers?"

At that moment the wine arrived and the subject changed from seriousness to gaiety and frivolity, as Lavinia said, "The only men interested in me are bearded long haired men although articulate and in most cases mannerly, such as the cart driver at The Resort, the janitor at the monastery and the chef or dishwasher at the catering service. All have their good points, but also . . ."

Ursula interrupted and said she had a new admirer, "scar face", another Ira.

"He really is nice . . . but getting grey and older," interrupted Lavinia.

Next morning Ursula asked Lavinia if she remembered going to bed, or the conversation leading up to going to bed, "Not really. Did we have a good time?"

"I think we forgot that you haven't had a vacation in quite some time and tried to catch up in one sitting. I didn't realize what an impression the lead agent made on you. And such a lot of gobbly-gook on how he reminded you of the other guy at the caterer's and the new janitor at the monastery."

"Oh, God! What else did I divulge?" questioned Lavinia.

"That his scar didn't really interfere with his looks so much, it was what kind of person he was inside that counts. And Ira, the stable man came into the picture, the one who only worked part time and kept disappearing."

"Boy, I must have been a lot of fun. Know what? I really don't have much of a hangover: course I haven't gotten up yet. I see you are dressed. Wait! I'll take a fast shower and go to breakfast with you. You said they have a workout room here. Know where it is?"

Ursula answered, "We could jog, but it's cold and the roads sides are piled with snow. Yup, I guess we'll locate the workout room."

"Yeah, Ira was grungy, but intelligent. Actually they all had a great deal of similarities. Height, weight, although their statures were slouchy in one case, and 'hunchy' in another and all had beards except scar face. I can only recall Ira's name," her voice trailed off as she entered the shower.

Everyone was up early after having attended mid-night mass with Ramona. Only the help who volunteered to work were on hand to tend to the needs of the Christmas guests. All guests were asked to pitch in where they saw a need. It was a big family affair. A chef and a skeleton crew tended to the buffet style breakfast. It was a help yourselves meal.

At noon, guests began to arrive. Aggie, her mom, Piearce, his parents and the three wide-eyed girls arrived. Ramona welcomed them all and was delighted with the young girls and took them through her alcove to her garden room. Suddenly the girls shrieked! Everyone turned to the room in alarm only to view the girls hugging Ramona and literally jumping up and down, still hugging and jabbering in their native tongue. Everyone migrated to the garden room to watch and listen. The girls were pointing to the Stella in the garden, and pointing to the tree. Apparently Ramona had spent a year in their country when Father Tomas was assigned as a relief priest there because of his language skills. The next few minutes were filled with Ramona trying to recall the language and basking in the glory of attention showered upon her by three appreciative young ladies, as the entourage watched in amazement.

Ramona turned to Aggie saying, "They mentioned going to live with you for a month or so. Should you need financial assistance, do not hesitate to call me." Then she turned back to the girls and spoke to them briefly in their native tongue and then to them in English for the benefit of the rest of the gathering.

"English only except when occasionally needed. Girls?"

"Chu Li?"

"Yes, Grandmother."

"Man Dhi?"

"Yes, Grandmother."

"Uh Lay?"

"Yes, Grandmother."

Everyone applauded.

After half an hour of mingling with the family and other guests, a tour was organized. The girls had taken Aggie by the hand and dragged her to the tree to ask questions about the different ornaments, then saying they recognized prayer wheels, but not terminology depicted. They joined the tour with a dinner time set for four o'clock. Buffet style again.

Returning from the tour, almost everyone gathered in the banquet room amidst the tantalizing aromas. At four, they began serving with Rowena's husband and Carl and Rowena's brother doing the honors, each displaying a white chef's hat which added to their official status. Piearce wondered about the brother who took the car to The Resort. At that moment the chimes rang so Ramona was summoned to greet the new guests. As the last person was served and seated, Rowena and Ramona accompanied two gentlemen into the dining area and announced to the gathering, "This is agent Ross Rankin, and this is agent Jeffery Slant, whom I met on previous occasions. Gentlemen, help yourselves and the rest of you introduce yourselves. I see a few empty chairs over at that table." Ramona pointed toward Lavinia and Ursula's table.

Ursula poked Lavinia and said, "Looks like the head agent but he has wrong colored hair and no scar!" Lavinia just squinted and shook her head slightly, while Ursula rose and along with Rowie, served the two men. While Ursula was serving Ross, she held the spoon of mashed potatoes in mid-air and stared at him; he waited, but then grinned and winked at her. Then he spoke, saying, "I heard about you and Doctor Wright. Congratulations, he's on his way as we speak and should be here momentarily."

"Thank you."

"Where is she?"

"I was hoping you'd ask. Third table to your right. Take my seat, I'll slide over one." Ursula almost couldn't contain her exuberance for her friend. This guy was nicer looking without the scar and graying hair. He stopped and sat at Lavinia's left, while Ursula slid her plate over. He said with a smile, "Lavinia, may I join you?" to which Lavinia replied, "I see you've been to a surgeon and hair stylist. Very nice modification."

"Thank you. I just told Ursula that Dr. Wright was on his way."

"So, do you always go around masquerading or altering your appearance? And is this the real you?"

"Yes, this is the real me."

"Tell me about yourself." Suddenly everyone at the table was asking him questions. He answered one only to be deluged with other questions. Lavinia kept thinking she had seen him somewhere before.

"What other jobs have you had or should I say, played at?"

"Well, that's hard to say, there have been so many. I've recently worked as a janitor at one place doing undercover work," he answered as he continued explaining how in his role as a janitor he was privy to a lot of information while people passed him by heedless of his actual function. Suddenly Lavinia and Ursula leaned forward and looked, one left, the other right, at each other while he was seated between them and smiled and one of them said, "Stop! Stop right there!"

"Ira?" They said to him. He smiled.

"The catering service." He smiled. They continued on questioning him, suddenly Lavinia said, "Not fair. You know all about me and I know nothing of you!"

"Sure you do. You've seen me and worked with me for over a year."

"Not fair. You play all those roles, how do I know you're not currently playing a role right now?" Lavinia asked, "Look at it this way, he's studied you at different phases of your life and he's still here. Must have liked what he saw!" At that moment the chime sounded again. Ursula rose and said, "Sit. That's probably my doctor. I'll get it.'

"No smooching, just bring him here," shouted Lavinia. Aggie and Piearce smiled their approval as Ramona said, "Perhaps I'll host several weddings here in the garden,"

Matt said, "I'll supply the beef and pork."

Lavinia smiled and chided by saying, "Whoa! We just met and already you are planning weddings."

Jeffery laughed and said, "Before saying no to his attention, you should know that ever since we started looking into the Buick and he first saw you, he set his sights on the girl of his dreams. Sorry, Ross, but I had to say it, so, Merry Christmas to you both."

Ursula returned with Dr. Wright as Ross and Jeffery rose to greet them like long lost buddies.

"You sure you don't want to be addressed as Ira or some other name?" Dr. Wright asked Ross.

"Funny, funny, Doc."

"Quite a transformation from a few days ago. I admire your make-up artistry and acting abilities. Do you do Sherlock Holmes also?"

"Actually, Sir Arthur Conan Doyle is one of my favorite authors. And it is quite possible he influenced my decision to choose this field of endeavor. Time is taking its toll however, and a desk job is in order."

"Why would you trade an active career for inactivity?"

"Diversity. Move up in the system and train others and coordinate. Jeffery can replace me in the field, maybe."

"We work better together. Solo work is only used in extreme circumstances."

"Okay. No more business talk. The case is basically over and it is time for intermingling," said Ursula. Olga, the house manager, came in to see to Ramona's needs. At that moment Jeffery said, "Think I'll get a little salad," and left.

Ross remarked, "Salad my eye!" as he gestured toward Olga, asking, "What's her name and who is she? She apparently made an impact on Jeff." All eyes were trained on Jeffery's trip to the salad plates, but he wasn't looking at the salads. He picked up a dessert dish and strolled over to say something to Ramona. Everyone smiled and Lavinia's laughter started a chain reaction with Ursula and Aggie. Dr. Wright said, "I'll bet his blood pressure is not normal at the moment," as Olga, Ramona and her table glanced up at the sudden outburst of laughter that had erupted.

"They are probably wondering what was so funny," said Ross.

"Well, your alertness and comment started it all. The funniest part was his picking up the dessert instead of the salad. Wait till he discovers that!" Everyone ate, but kept glancing at Ramona's table. Olga was apparently introduced to Jeff and as Olga left, Jeff trailed after her with dessert in hand. Ramona glanced at the table and smiled, holding up four fingers on her left hand, then twisted her ring, indicating another wedding with questioning gestures.

Small talk continued until the three girls came to Aggie and said, "Swimming inside house. Kaylette and brother Kwang take us with friends." Aggie glanced at the table where the young people had congregated; all were anxiously looking at her for a reply.

"Don't you want dessert?"

"No. Swimming inside house more fun." Aggie glanced at Rowena and Ramona, as both gave a thumbs up indicating it was safe.

"Be careful. Have fun."

"You come watch?"

"Yes, in about a half hour. We are going to leave at six-thirty or seven, so enjoy your swim." Piearce winked and smiled as the girls gleefully returned to their table and the entire group left with laughter. It seemed as though there would be some language lessons taking place as the girls paired off and the youngest skipped as they left the room. No one would ever have suspected their recent ordeals. Aggie was misty-eyed which caused Ursula and Lavinia to do like-wise. Ross said, "I can't believe their readjustment. Is it an oriental inbred trait? Something not really done well here in this country?"

"It's possible they were introduced to this way of life early and expected to be treated in this manner because it was a way of life. Who knows?"

Ross spoke to Piearce saying, "Where is the Buick now?"

"At my parent's home safely protected in the workshop garage."

"They think the nomenclature may be a code and the team wishes to see the Buick and the metal sheets you removed and photographed. They inferred there may be a microchip somewhere."

"Fine. When would they like to come?"

"Within the week. When do you return?"

"In two days. The garage is semi-heated and insulated so your crew won't be working in the cold," smiled Piearce.

"I'll call and tell them."

"What do they think the code is referring to?" asked Lavinia, "And why is all this so secretive? What can be so important to create all hush-hush-ness? We were privy to the partial translation of some possibly devastating revelations. Could this be any worse?"

"Enough speculation! Where has everyone gone?"

"To the pool area to watch the kids."

"Let's go; may I offer my arm Miz Lavinia?" said Ross with an obvious smile of admiration. "I'm trying to make a good impression," to which Lavinia replied, "You've done a good job so far."

Ursula chimed in with, "Don't worry about that, Ross, I heard all about you through her own lips last night."

"Like what?" asked Ross.

"Enough! I'll tell my own story in my own way and time," injected Lavinia. Ursula laughed, then whispered to Dr. Wright who also laughed as they walked arm-in-arm toward the pool. She had evidently mentioned Lavinia's 'too much wine' night.

The girls and other children were having a blast, with Chu Li following Kwang to the low diving board preparing to dive into the water. Apparently she had made several botched attempts prior to the group's arrival.

"Lean a little more," said Kwang as he held her waist while standing behind her.

"Okay, now when I release you, just push a little with your feet and fall letting your hands part the water. Ready, go!" and he released her. Her hands parted the water and she entered with very little splash. As she surfaced everyone was applauding and yelling hoorah! Chu Li was all smiles and immediately climbed up and tried again. This time she pushed Kwang away indicating she could do it herself. And she did!

After another half hour, it was time to change and prepare to depart. The new found friends were reluctant to say goodbyes. Rowena claimed she had never seen children achieve such a strong bond in such a short time frame. Amazing! Ramona thought that perhaps she'd start giving lessons to the children in the special Chinese dialect for possible future meetings and even closer bonding. Yes, these orphans would not return to the Monastery if she had anything to say about it.

The three girls hugged Ramona and spoke to her in their own language, then two of the girls took Aglaea's hands and one took Piearce's hand and walked to the limo. Two snuggled to Aggie and dozed on the way as the rest discussed the memorable Christmas in a remarkable atmosphere. Aglaea looked at Piearce, smiled and whispered exaggeratingly mouthing the words, "May or July, NOT June."

Piearce said, "May. The alpine flowers will be grand then."

It was 8 PM when they arrived at The Resort and to Piearce and Aglaea's surprise, Rose and David were standing at the desk!

"What a small world," exclaimed Rose as she hugged them both. "Is the Buick here?"

"No. Not this time."

"How long are you staying?" asked David.

"We leave in two days," answered Piearce.

The girls hugged Rose and were now wide awake, asking to go to the arcade. Piearce held up his cell phone and each of them reached into their pockets and produced their phones and smiled as Aggie said, "Nine o'clock in the suite."

Chu Li gave a thumbs up, initiating a similar response from her comrades, a newly acquired response. They were adjusting rapidly. An attendant, whom Piearce and Aglaea recognized, nodded and followed The Girls. It was one of Ross' crew, an undercover agent. The girls were in no danger.

Rose reacted with a surprised look, asking, "Are these really the girls from the monastery? What a transformation! Are you the ones who are adopting them?"

"Most likely," answered Aglaea. "As soon as we complete the paper work. What have you two been up to?"

"We just returned from Tibet and wanted to be in an especially memorable Christmas atmosphere. Something different than a church experience. They did a fantastic job here at The Resort. How long have you been here? Just a few days? A week? Well, we'd love to have dinner with you."

"Fine. By the way, these are Piearce's parents." Introductions were made and Rose discovered that Piearce's mother, Isabelle, came from the same region as Rose's mother, so a delightful reunion began as they walked to the cocktail lounge while David and Matt trailed the two women. Aglaea and Piearce just shook their heads in disbelief and smiled, mentioning that they wouldn't be surprised to see visitors at the farm in the future.

As they started to the suite, they were approached by an elderly gentleman and a younger man who was in good physical condition. Aggie whispered, "CIA or FBI?"

"Excuse us, we are from the International Defense Agency," said the older man as they presented their credentials, "and would like a few minutes of your time. Would now be convenient?" Piearce turned to Aggie and whispered, *"Neither department."* He turned to the agents and said, "We have a few moments. How may we help?"

"That message you gave to Ross and Jeffery has been partially decoded and we need to know if we may gain access to the Buick immediately."

"I suppose we could leave tomorrow," said Piearce.

"No. We have men ready to enter the premises. We just need permission to do so. We tried to call your cell, but there was no answer."

"Of course. The garage is not locked and everything that I removed from the car is in the two bays." Piearce gave them the names of the foreman and some of the resident workers. They thanked him and were on their phones as they walked away.

"What is so important that they have a crew working on Christmas? More lost or hidden artifacts that might end up in the wrong hands?" wondered Piearce

"Probably a misinterpretation, but can't take the chance," answered Aglaea

"We realize that's a possibility in view of the previous findings. Perhaps I should never have purchased this vehicle. But then I would not have been exposed to such a variety of adventures, nor have contacted the persons or had the experiences, not to mention the excitement in your eyes and face during these episodes, or the financial benefits."

"Please! Remember the location of a desirable wedding site," declared Aglaea. They were about to enter the elevator when they were again hailed by the agents.

"One more detail. Were either of you ever in any of the Arabic countries in the past few years? Iraq, Iran, Turkey, Egypt, or even India? We have information that indicates those countries are possible origins of data applicable to our search or may hold locations of data desirable for answering questions that have arisen from our current analysis."

"Just what are you looking for? I looked over the car several times."

"We are not sure. It could be something as small as a microchip or dot, which makes it even more difficult. Supposedly information leading to a possible stash of ancient documents or controversial information that may have grave political and possible international repercussions if allowed to get into the wrong hands."

"Good luck with your search. Try to keep the Buick in one piece."

The next morning the girls were getting ready for breakfast when Aggie tapped on their door and entered. The girls all grabbed her enthusiastically. Chu Li winced when she brushed her hair and Aggie said, "Chu Li, I noticed you rubbing your head periodically and now you've reacted to the brushing of your hair. Let me take a look at your head." Then the girls indicated that Chu Li had bumped her head and had a stitch put in several month ago. Aggie examined her and felt a knot which she and Dr. Wright assumed might be a node. Now she wasn't so sure. She examined it with a magnifying glass again. Then she had a recollection of the agents mentioning a microchip, and wondered if it was possible that Chu Li was really the target of all the activities. If the villains didn't know who, but suspected that one of these girls unknowingly carried information, it spelled trouble.

"Chu Li, I think I'd like Dr. Wright to look at this also and perhaps have an x-ray taken. Would that be alright with you? We'll go to breakfast first, then have that tiny bump examined again."

"Okay."

Aglaea called to Piearce and mentioned her suspicions to him. He responded by calling Dr. Wright, then the agents from last night. They went to Dr. Wright's office immediately after breakfast. The x-ray showed an implant. Aggie and Dr. Wright immediately talked to the girls and Chu Li, saying they would make the bump better. It took three minutes to prepare freezing the area and removing the chip, cleaning the wound and putting in two stitches. In three days, Chu Li would hardly feel anything and in a week, the bump would be gone.

The agency called again after examining the chip indicating that it referred to other possible data sources.

*      *      *      *      *      *
   *      *      *      *      *      *

Aggie asked Piearce where they might find such an important document, or if, he thought any of the other girls might have been subjected to some sort of deployment technique like tattoos or artifacts to carry. But such intricate developments would have undoubtedly been created long before the chip and would probably be of a different design. Was it possible that there was something in Tomas' regalia that was done for him or given to him that would lead to the discovery and the location of the additional data? What she couldn't understand, was why or how he became the *"keeper of the keys."*

# Chapter XIV

It was time to return home and work. The girls mentioned that Grandmother said they were invited to "undress the tree" if they so desired. Aggie said, "I'm a doctor and must return to the hospital and the E.R., but if Piearce wishes to take you to Ramona's, then I'm sure we can make some arrangements." They called Ramona and Olga answered, saying the tree would be dismantled after New Year's Day. Probably the seventh or tenth of January. That was the usual procedure. She indicated she'd mention it to Ramona and was glad the girls wanted to help "undress the tree".

"Well, girls, we have over a week to wait and I don't know if Piearce wishes to return with you or not. Let's ask him." Piearce said he'd make reservations and plan accordingly. They left the next morning returning to Aglaea's home where the girls retired to their room with their new paraphernalia, chatting in their native tongue to the shout of *"English"!*

It was suppertime and Aggie had called ahead to have food prepared so she could eliminate the preparation. Everyone sat at the table and Juline claimed it was the easiest meal she had ever prepared. During dinner, she informed the girls that she had to rise early, and sometimes wouldn't be there when they arose, so they would need to start rising early because they were to start school next week on Wednesday the fifth.

"We go to school? We stay here forever?"

"I hope so, but at least for the next three months. By that time, we'll have more knowledge of your legal status."

"And I have tickets for the seventh which is Friday afternoon, so we'll spend the weekend at Gramma Ramona's house," said Piearce who had entered and was removing his mackinaw.

A squeal of delight erupted, except for Uh Lay, who, being the youngest, had developed a special attachment to Aggie and her mother. They were interrupted by a phone call. It was Lavinia and Ursula.

"Are you people doing anything for New Year's Eve?"

Aggie said, "Not yet. Haven't seen the schedule."

"Well, if you have a vacant floor space, we'd like to invite ourselves."

"No problem. Are you coming alone?"

"No. But the guys' are staying at Piearce's, however he doesn't know it yet. His mother invited them."

"Oh, that's funny. It's a good thing I had the attic done over as a dormitory and The Girls are there. And I'll tell Piearce; he just arrived. You two can have the other two rooms."

"Uhh . . . That's three of us. Olga was going to be fired by Ramona if she didn't take a vacation. God! It must be nice to have extra cash."

"Great. See you in a week. And there is a small bunkhouse in the barn. It has a woodstove for heat if you prefer that," Aglaea laughingly hung up.

The rest of the evening involved the girls, and Aggie and Piearce's mother making lists of duties. They were duties that the girls would take on as responsibilities; not unusual for these girls. They learned new words, had chores, and thought everything was great. Aglaea had gone to shower and to bed so she could rise early and assume her doctoral duties. As she slipped into bed she thought of the contact she had made with the Commissioner of Education and the request for guidance in placing the girls into the appropriate grade levels and the need for special English education classes. She said she'd have someone contact her on the twenty-ninth or thirtieth. Tomorrow! She rose and scribbled a note as a reminder for her mother in the morning, then slipped into bed again for a luxurious sleep.

Piearce had mentioned he'd return in the mid-morning to take the girls to show them the town, schools, churches and the hospital, and of course, where he lived because his Isabelle expected them to be home for dinner. The girls smiled and clapped their hands.

"Grandmother come too?"

"Of course."

Piearce left to go home, take a shower and get some rest.

# Chapter XV

$P$iearce woke early and stretched as he looked out the window but stopped and dropped his arms quickly as he saw a light in the workshop. He stared. Someone was in there with the Buick. He quickly dressed and went to the shop. Opening the door, he confronted two men who were on their knees and shinning lights while looking carefully at the underside of the car.

"Hi Piearce," said one of the men. "I thought you'd be up early. Did you find anything else in this vehicle? Anything at all? Oh, and this is Franklyn," He walked over to shake Piearce's hand, and Franklyn offered his, also.

"Don't you ever sleep?" asked Piearce.

"Only when we're tired. The crew has been over this area a dozen times, but there is definite reference here to something spinning away from the normal. Something turning away or rotating in the opposite direction. It is almost illogical; nothing seems to fit. The higher-ups are passionate over finding the answer. Time is of the essence, according to them."

"Well, time can't be that important if they used this car to transport information and such. What about the people you picked up at The Resort? Are any of them cooperating?"

"No idea. We aren't privy to their problems. I doubt they'll confess to anything other than being involved with the sex trade.

We have to be careful how we ask a question without divulging too much about another independent case."

"Good luck, guys. I'll tell mom there are two more for breakfast. I've got an appointment at ten."

When he arrived to get the girls, there was a car in the drive, and people were coming off the porch who waved to Piearce as he parked. They were from the school department and were all smiles when they saw him. One who knew him, greeted him saying, "Well, Piearce, how does it feel to become a father before you even get married? Oops, that didn't come out right, did it?"

"So far, it is a miraculous experience. I never knew there were so many variations on a theme. A world of Why, How, Who and What is simply amazing."

"We gave a list to the doctor of the needs and grades and classrooms to which the girls will be assigned. See you next week, and Happy New Year."

The girls were more than excited. They could hardly contain themselves when they visited the school. Each wanted to stay and explore, even though the buildings were closed to students. The cleaning staff recognized Piearce and let them into the buildings and gave them a tour. Otto, the building superintendent, (Chief custodian, as he put it) made himself known to Uh Lay, who would be assigned to that school building, and told her to see him if she needed anything, or if anyone bothered her.

"What's bothered?"

"Never mind. I'll explain it later." Otto called the high school and made arrangements for the staff to give them a tour of the facilities. All were thrilled about the tours and talked about them all the way to the hospital, where they stopped to see Aglaea. They waited in the waiting room until Aglaea was done. Finally one of the EMT's saw Piearce and said, "Why are you waiting here? Come on back."

"No. I have to teach them proper protocol and the girls are not cleared."

"So, are these the girls she's been bragging about?"

He turned and reentered the E.R. proper. In one minute, six people were bursting through the double doors saying 'Hi' to Piearce, and introducing themselves to the three girls. They sat and spoke slowly and engagingly to them. One of the oriental nurses spoke to them in a Chinese dialect that was very close to theirs, so they were enthusiastically involved and a new friend was made as well as a positive connection to the hospital. Then a few more people came out of the E.R., engaged the girls in conversation, took them by their hand and led them into the E.R. for a tour. Aglaea was just coming out to see them, when one the girls ran to her, shouting *'Ma'am ma Aggie'* and hugged her while laughing joyous. Everyone looked at each other and smiled and mouthed the words, *'Ma'am ma Aggie.'* They all agreed that it was the best Holiday Greeting they had experienced that year, *'Ma'am ma Aggie.'* It wouldn't be long before the entire hospital staff would be referring to the doctor as *'Ma'am ma Aggie,'* at least behind her back, if not to her face.

Two of the girls rode with Aglaea to her house where they picked up her mother and drove to Piearce's home for a tour and dinner. The agents were still there, hoping to be invited to another meal after having had breakfast and lunch there. It was getting dark, and Piearce's mother said, "It's too dark and too late to drive these dangerous roads, you'd better stay for the night and for dinner." There was no argument. The girls roamed with Piearce and Aglaea through the barns and found the trail to Piearce's hide-away and asked where it went.

Aglaea said, "To a very special place where heaven meets the meadows, and moonbeams reflect from the streams and diamonds shine at night and angels sing to nature's music, especially in the summer, and where you feel inspired by a warm embrace from Nature. This spring, we'll take you to that special place. Personally, if it wasn't so cold, I'd go tonight." Aggie slipped her arm through Piearce's. Piearce whispered to her, "There is a fire pit and wood and I've got matches." She just squeezed his arm and smiled.

At eight-thirty the girls were starting to nod so Aglaea and her mother packed up and left, telling everyone they'd see them in two days. "Oh, did I tell you that Lavinia and Ursula are coming for New Year's Eve, Piearce?" asked Aggie. His mother said, "I'll tell him all about it. You go home and get some sleep. I love you all."

"What's all that about?" asked Piearce.

"We have house guests for the weekend. Lavinia and Ursula are staying at Aggie's, and their gentlemen friends are staying here."

"What? Who?"

"Ross and Jeff and the doctor, and maybe one more. I made up the spare rooms with my house assistant that you insisted I hire. For once, I see that it was a great idea," replied Isabelle.

"This should be quite a New Year's party."

# Chapter XVI

The girls were excited to see Grandmother Ramona again and to start "undressing" the tree. Each item was carefully removed, wrapped in tissue paper and placed into a box. Ramona explained each decoration in detail and why they were special. The girls were very enthusiastic about everything and Ramona was in her glory. Aggie was on a tight schedule. She had to leave on the early morning flight, which only gave her the rest of this day and evening. Carl said not to worry, he'd have her at the airport in plenty of time. Piearce and the girls would follow in two days. But for now, they stood looking out the window at the snow covered Tori area with their arms around each other's backs. The snow was a magnificent diamond-sparkly white.

"Yes. I'd like to get married here. It's perfect. I love you," said Aggie as she kissed him. They turned and saw Ramona and Olga were looking at them smiling as the girls found another decoration different from the rest. They rushed to Ramona and began speaking in their native tongue for an explanation. After a little talk and demonstration, the girls returned to the tree. Aggie said to Ramona, "Perhaps you should write down about each gift from all those people and the meanings of the gift. No one will be able to interpret them after you've left."

Suddenly a squeal of delight. The girls had gotten to the prayer wheels. As they carefully removed them, they assumed an attitude of quietness and prayer. Then Man Dhi said, "Not real. Wrong signs. Theses numbers no good."

"They were given to Father Tomas long ago. I found them locked in the vault and put them on the tree. What is wrong with them, Man Dhi?" asked Ramona.

Then Chu Li said, "This one not right. Not prayer!"

"What does it say?" Piearce asked.

"Don't know. Make no sense."

All family members and visitors gathered around to look at the wheels. They made no sense to any of them anyway. But Aggie looked at Piearce. Piearce nodded his head in affirmation saying, "Maybe this is what they are looking for." He left the room and phoned Ross, explaining what they discovered and suspected. Ross mentioned that there were two agents at The Resort and that they could be there in an hour or two if Piearce was going to be there. He explained that Piearce would recognize one of the agents and he would know Piearce so no mistakes would be made and a safe exchange could be made. Piearce relayed the message saying to Aggie, "They are sending two agents from The Resort. They will be here within two hours. Do you think you'd like to ride a few miles on a snowmobile, while they finish the tree?"

"Only if we can go for a swim on our return," smiled Aggie.

"I knew we wore the correct clothing for a good reason. You can always take off, but you cannot put on what you don't have."

"I'm going to leave that statement alone."

They rode for an hour exploring trails. When they returned everyone was at the pool area, according to Olga. They went to the changing rooms, donned suits, and met at the hot tub, languishing there as two thawing logs. Then, they went for a swim. In the middle of their frolicking, Carl appeared with a middle aged man, smiling broadly, saying that two men had arrived to see Piearce. He introduced him to Piearce who immediately climbed from the pool, shook hands and started to go to change, but they asked where the other agent was, to which Carl responded, "He is interrogating Miss Olga and probably Ramona in the garden room. He claims to know you, so I felt safe to leave them." Carl had an odd smile and gleam in his eyes. Aggie was at the edge of the pool studying the exchange.

Then she began to laugh and climbed out of the pool to go and change.

When they entered the garden room, Ramona was sitting alone and Piearce asked, "Where is the agent?"

"Oh, Olga took him to the kitchen to get a coffee," Ramona answered with a smile.

Piearce looked at the coffee pot and cups on the coffee table, looked at Ramona questioningly and Aggie finally said, "You don't get it do you?" to Piearce. He looked at her, to Carl with his smile, and the other agent. Aggie continued, "They said you'd recognize the agent. Someone must have had to return for additional duty. Special agent, Olga is missing, Coffee on the table, able to get here in record time."

"Okay, Jeff is the agent. I should have known." At that moment Olga and Jeff returned with a tray and with laughter preceding their entry.

After greeting the group and joking about Piearce's reaction, they showed the prayer wheels to the agents and explained what the girls had said. From what the girls said and what the other agents indicated about being in an Asian country, this find made sense. Jeffrey said, "The information about spinning the wheels in opposite directions is in the chips, among other statements that I am not privy to divulge, so when we saw these and heard the girls responses we came to the conclusion that these may shed some light on the possible answers to the problem."

Ramona commented, "Tomas always said ornaments are the key to everything, especially life and religion."

The agents had to return immediately, so Jeffery said to Olga, "Miss Olga, Ursula told me about an inexpensive room at The Resort, and I have a month off in a few weeks, and may take a week of that time in the area. Would you be free to attend a few dances with me or go to a show or two with me during that week? If you are free, that is."

"If she wants to go, she will be free and have a car available. If she doesn't want to go then she'll be working here," said Ramona with a chuckle. Everyone laughed as the contingency left.

Aggie turned as the group left to see the men off, then sat next to Ramona and asked, "Did you really mean it when you said you'd host a wedding here in the Spring?"

A gleam and smile was the obvious answer without the need of a word as Ramona clapped her hands.

"I've been waiting for your decision. Do you have a date? May is a desirable time here."

"We decided on May or July. Piearce is leaning toward May. He claims all the mountain flowers are in bloom then. I'd rather it not be an elaborate affair"

"Have you told anyone about your plans yet?"

"No. Not even Piearce knows I'm asking you. We'll pay all the cost. I just love the setting and you and your family. My mother was impressed with your outgoing nature and no nonsense manner but your loving attitude and your devotion to your husband."

"Has Piearce confided anything to you about my husband? If he has, it is perfectly alright, I just wondered."

"Only that he was once a priest and that you were his housekeeper. Your first husband was killed in an accident of some sort. Automobile, I believe. Then you became a housekeeper, which I never understood, because he indicated that you had money of your own."

"That is true. Clever man. Here comes the send-off crew, we'll talk again. Let me know the date so we can plan, and the number of attendees. You know, May the nineteenth is someone's birth date, if it's not too early in the month or in the middle of the week." Aggie took out her phone and, checked the date. Saturday. The bargain was sealed.

"When are you going to tell Piearce?"

"Think I'll keep it between us for a while. Should be more fun."

"Agreed. Enjoy."

While driving to the airport, Piearce and Aglaea were reviewing their activities, especially trying to interpret the prayer wheels and whether there was a possible connection or code to the Buick. Aggie said, "Ramona said that Tomas indicated ornaments held the key to everything, even life and religion, or the origin of religion."

Once home, Piearce said he had some unfinished business that needed his immediate attention, and he left Aggie with the girls and Aggie's mother. He went home, changed clothes, loaded his pickup with a wheelbarrow and headed to the cave. The burning question of a cavern or tunnel possibly being attached to the cave had been praying on his mind for quite some time, and maybe this would be revealed in a few hours. He had allowed himself four hours. He carried several wheelbarrow loads out before he cleaned up the hide-a-way-honeymoon suite. Now he was convinced that there was a passageway after five feet. The rocks were not tightly packed, but there was definitely passages that animals had use before it was blocked by Piearce. He decided to stop and return at another time. It would be an adventure they'd continue after their marriage, tempting as it was to continue, he put the wheelbarrow outside and hung a drape over the opening, cleaned up, replaced an old bed for the cot/bunks and placed a vase on the table to put flowers into when they moved into their honeymoon suite. It was Aggie's idea; a complete escape into their own world of hiking and remembering old times and how dreams do come true.

Piearce had done as much as he dared without Aggie and he was close to being late for a second appointment so he rushed off.

*     *     *     *     *     *
    *     *     *     *     *     *

Aglaea arranged a meeting with her mother and Piearce's mother after Valentine's Day about her upcoming marriage and disclosed the date to the delight of both ladies. She mentioned May 19th as the date and that she had reserved an establishment for her wedding, not a local establishment.

"You are going to have it at Ramona's, aren't you?" stated Isabelle.

"That doesn't surprise me. Will Piearce be finished teaching and taking courses by then?" asked Juline. The celebration and planning had begun with Aglaea emphasizing that it would be a simple affair. "Too much money is spent foolishly on dresses, elaborate dinners, expensive honeymoon suites and I have planned a location for years and have made tentative reservations."

"Where?"

"Oh, No! You two would figure out a way to drop in unexpectedly or some other 'teenage' activity just for the humor and enjoyment it would give you. No way, will I divulge the location!"

"But what if someone is ill or dies?" asked Juline, her future mother-in-law.

"Call a doctor or a mortician."

"How hard hearted and cruel."

"Look at it this way. I'm saving you all and myself peace of mind," laughed Aggie.

"Probably, The Resort," claimed her Juline.

"Yes. Or one of the cottages," said Isabelle.

"You two have a good time wondering."

"Yup. Probably, The Resort; we'll be there anyway."

"Or Ramona's; the house and grounds are large enough so we'd have to search all night to find them."

"Would you two really do that?" Aggie questioned.

"No, but it is fun thinking about it."

"Besides, most weddings are duplications. If you've been to one you've been to them all. It's just a big party."

Aggie grinned but didn't agree.

# Chapter XVII

A few days later Piearce was looking at the Buick and decided to take the girls and Aglaea for a ride. When he arrived, the girls were delighted and scrambled into the rear seat, trying each position including the fold downs. He took them to the Alpine village and Cornelius' garage for a hot chocolate and to say hello to Cornelius. As they were returning, Aggie asked, "Did all the old cars have ornamental radiator caps? And did all Buicks, Oldsmobiles, Nashs or Fords have their own styles or were they all the same?"

"I understand you could buy aftermarket designs if you so desired, something more fancy." They were almost to Aggie's driveway when Piearce suddenly slowed and stopped on the edge of the road, looking at Aggie he said, "Tomas said ornaments held the key . . ." he hesitated, and Aggie said as she stared at the radiator ornament, "Do you think . . . ?"

The girls thanked him for their ride as they entered the house he and Aggie went to examine the radiator cap. They twisted it in order to release pressure, then unscrewed the cap and examined it. There was a slight seam between the cap and the ornament. They'd need a wrench to separate them.

"I'll go back to the house and garage to see if I can loosen this," Piearce decided.

"Wait, I'll ask mother to watch the girls and go with you."

He backed the car into its stall, closed the door and proceeded to remove the cap, placing it into a vice after placing a protective cloth around the cap and on the ornament. He took his vice-grips and with considerable effort twisted the top and unscrewed the ornament from the cap revealing a very small waterproof packet with a key sealed in a plastic protective covering.

"More microchips?" asked Aglaea. The Buick had done it again, revealed secrets to the past, and perhaps predicting the future. Reassembling and replacing the cap and ornament, they called the agency number that was given to them. They also called Lavinia and Ursula who were still at Ramona's and claimed this could easily become a permanent residence. He updated them on the radiator cap ornament, and especially about Tomas' commenting on "ornaments hold the key".

"That Buick is still productive and full of surprises," they exclaimed.

*   *   *   *   *   *<br>*   *   *   *   *   *

The helicopter hovered at fifty feet, looking over the touchdown area, did a 360 degree turn and then descended, landing without a bounce behind the barn. Three men including the pilot approached the garage door as though they knew where they were going. Franklyn introduced the men to Piearce and said, "I can't believe we didn't notice the seam in the ornament on this radiator cap. Never thought of it." He attempted to separate the ornament from the cap. With increased exertion, he disconnected the two revealing the prize. One of the men was videotaping so that key activities were recorded. They carefully removed the key and packet.

"This key looks similar to the ones they have in some Switzerland security vaults if my memory serves me," said Franklyn. "Another international activity, we'd better not attempt opening the packet here. We'll take it to the lab."

Each man carefully examined the cap and ornament. One of the men took a cap from his pocket, placed it on the radiator and it fit, so they took the original cap and ornament saying they'd return them later. They placed the cap and ornament and contents into a container and sealed it. The helicopter crew started to leave when Piearce's mother shouted that she had lunch all prepared. Franklyn smiled and said, "I told you so."

*　　　*　　　*　　　*　　　*　　　*

*　　　*　　　*　　　*　　　*　　　*

A few months later, the agents returned and presented Piearce and Aggie with this scenario. "In the recent microchips, there are two renditions. The historical, which is difficult to decipher and is very extensive and then there is what we consider to be a diary or log that was started and never finished. These translations are in no way complete. This report is for your edification. Call it a wedding present. The report was put into a small satchel to be read on your honeymoon."

A small wedding activity took place at Ramona's whose face glowed as though they were her own children being married. The wedding went off without a hitch and everyone was trying to figure out where the couple were going for their honeymoon. The mothers were still questioning the honeymoon location, which spilled over into the wedding party. Suddenly the limo pulled up to the front door and Piearce and Aglaea jumped in and off they sped. By the time the rest of the crew were able to get their cars to give chase, they were several minutes underway. Carl, the masterful driver, had parked another car for them half way to The Resort at an intersection on a road that led to the airport. The transfer was made and Carl drove on to The Resort. As he approached The Resort, he kept glancing in his mirror. He pulled up and unloaded bags and sent them to the rooms that had been reserved. Then he drove out, waving to the contingency who were arriving to harass the newlyweds. Carl was grinning from ear to ear. Aggie and Piearce by this time were airborne as the crew was being led to the reserved rooms where they decided to tie clothes into knots or take them all away only to find the suitcases empty and a note inside in extra-large letters saying, "HA, HA! ENJOY YOUR WEEKEND!"

While flying, Aggie said, "I can't wait. I've got to look at the documents and at least start to read them." Piearce said, "Read them in the car while we drive to our suite. Speaking of our suite, do you have any idea how many times I've envisioned this over the years since we were kids?"

Aggie started reading as soon as they were in the car. (*A hand written note was scribbled across the side of the document indicating that Hornben, Super and his wife had been picked up on suspicion.*) The agents had summarized the findings as follows.

> This is a very controversial document at the moment. It would be impossible to imagine and divulge all the Buick has to offer. We refer to them as the 'Buick's Secrets' but you realize it's in reference to the chips. In one aspect, it involves the disclosure of a direct correlation between two cities, one at Sanliurfa, Turkey (Urfa) at around 9500 B.C., Göbekli Tepe, and the other at Nag Hammadi, Egypt and indicates the origins of religions, especially in reference to the Dead Sea Scrolls. Currently, it is thought that organized religion started about ten thousand B.C., but this evidence indicates or hints at possibly fifteen thousand B.C. These seem to be the documents ordered to be destroyed by the Nicene Creed Committee, a Gnosis of sacredness. Many claimed that a book of Gnosticism existed and was missing or hidden. This may shed some light on that location. It'll be a few years, but this addition to what was disclosed previously, may revolutionize religions.

Aggie stopped reading and said, "Didn't they mention that Göbekli Tepe manuscripts indicated the origins of religions, the Gospel of Thomas, or was that the Nag Hammadi documents? Somewhere, someone mentioned the Sacred Union, or whatever. I'll have to check it out."

Piearce, "It's out of our hands now and into the hands of the special committee."

The report continued:

> In some records, there are indications of Pre-Christian groups existing and the books are hidden

or missing. There is evidence of the existence of temple-like structures 6,000 years before Stonehenge, in Turkey and these hinted to thoughts or ideas were supposedly recorded in the missing books, which this information might lead to. In the fourth century meetings were held to reject Marcion and his teachings. Some of the literature indicates that the development of the Nicene Creed established the idea of a physical resurrection, whereas prior to this time it was a concept of the misinformed. There are indications that some people mentioned that the candles of incense that burned during the meetings were made of the same hallucinogens that Oracles breathed at Delphi when the priests ignited so called aromatics that rose through the openings in the seats of the Oracle, sending them into a euphoric state resulting in a babbling that was interpreted by priests to predict the future, become wealthy and controlling.

A reference to Marcion, who was a person that started a movement in the 2nd century called Marcionism, dealt with the Gnostic idea that rejected the Old Testament and this prevailed during the 2$^{nd}$ and 3$^{rd}$ centuries. Then the popes became powerful. Gnosticism was once widely believed as a spiritual viewpoint dealing with the knowledge of the heart. In some minds, it raised the question to who started religion or started believing in God.

Aggie and Piearce finished reading the document, knowing that there was much to discuss. They'd come back to it later. Then they continued reading the rest of the agency's report:

As far as the Log (which follows) is concerned, it is much more interesting than the actual descriptions previously mentioned. At first the agency thought it was a personal diary, but it is more than that. You understand that you can never divulge anything you read. You can take these papers and study them.

*This is a description of our wakeup call because our energy source is so low. Actually almost depleted. We probably have enough to last out the year, but whether we have enough for another suspended animation remains to be seen. My son woke after our twenty-year sleep saying, "Mommy. Mommy, where did we come from?" Although I had programmed myself and my son for the identical wake-up stimulus, he had apparently preceded me by a minute or so. His faster metabolism was more likely the reason. Also it may have been his last thought before the suspended animation and automatic learning transmitter programmed his brain and mine. What a delightful instrument! Update and learning while sleeping, getting nourishment and excrement automatically removed. Twenty years in one night and updating of major events delicately recorded in the brain.*

*The bed rollers rippled and vibrated under my back; the exercisers had automatically disconnected and the feeding units and excrement units had been retracted. My body had been maintained through the past 20 years as though I had been asleep one night. I looked at my son and thought he might have aged slightly: his sparkling eyes and inquisitive demure caused me to smile and say,*

*"That is a difficult question to answer. You have been updated in physics, math, medical history, and major happenings while we've been asleep, but not the history of us prior to living on this planet. I'll tend to that after we adjust for this next year."*

*"I'm a little hungry for some real food. Can we go out and get some of that fruit for breakfast?"*

*"If the tree is still there!"*

*"Oh yes, I forgot! And the children I knew will be unrecognizable."*

*"We'll check the updated and the surveillance screens before venturing out for a stroll and food. It will take a few days to check the data, but if it is clear, we'll go out and return to finalize the update and attempt contacts with the others."*

*The area had changed little. The road to the South had been improved and many of the trees were gone, but new ones had replaced the missing ones. The fruit tree was gone, but nearby several others had grown and their branches were bending with fruit. Evidently someone was there gathering the first harvest. He wanted to go and mingle with the children. The last time he lived with them for a year before disappearing. How immature and ignorant the last group had been, but I said we should guide them and help them and definitely not let them know who we really are . . . which brings us back to where we came from. One beneficial factor was the built in warning device that would alert us to anyone digging or tampering with our habitat.*

*I began to explain that we were the last of an advanced civilization. Through time and interbreeding, a diminished intellect developed. We cannot infer that we are the intelligentsia; that's one reason certain marriages were arranged in early times, in the past, to ensure preservation of the intellect was paramount, love could not stand in the way. This was misinterpreted during what they called 'the middle ages,' religion became a misconception of tales.*

*Unfortunately we are without sufficient power to constantly monitor other groups and their inability to send prolonged signals for droid guidance. That is why the construction of visual signals are needed to serve as guidance systems for the rescue pods. The locals call the structures Naxca in some areas. Voyagers who left as we did, after lack of communication from our group, may send out search pods. Should they do that, they would be able to see this planet as habitable through the presence of the monolithic structures. We took that calculated risk to cut through this galaxy and solar system but one malfunction caused severe ship damage in the asteroid belt and life saving pods were jettisoned with maximum survival equipment. The Pods all landed in different locations and set up communication beacons. This was not our original destination. Necessity ruled.*

*Years of limited communications existed, then one by one each area realized that conservation of energy was needed for survival. Training humanoids was of major importance for our continued existence. The slower supply vehicle we passed was not programmed for this shortcut. It has a self-repairing helio-piezio-electron unit with a search guidance system that needs minimal signals to engage visual scans for certain structures and areas that are likely to have life. Apparently our weak signals at the abandonment and ship destruction failed to activate the distress. When our signals failed to periodically be received after a period of time, an automatic search would be instituted of planets for existing features or structures resembling possible life forms. Till then, we need to train the earthlings in various locations to build structures large enough to attract attention of the droid ship.*

*Someday soon searchers will come looking for remainders of genetically related individuals and will return them to the eternal galaxy.*

*Virgo was a major sign, but that was years ago. The universe is in constant motion, therefore change is inevitable. Intermarriage in all areas will be used to raise the intellectual level and standard necessary to continuing gene pools. Sometimes I recognize them and there is a mutual understanding or bonding.*

*Father returned and left mapped locations of other groups/ pods/ and their progress; he mentioned that one group thought they had made a temporary contact but had lost it. However, if even a miniscule contact would give the other crews an indication of our approximate location, it would be helpful. Later I made these trips to help by continuing teaching and building of societies with diminutive tools of the locals. Then many reverted to a primitive type life style and rediscovery remained to be re-established. I have successfully been through 50 suspended animations. On this awakening, I find it may be the last according to notes and records left here. This may be our last suspended animation due to the energy level being so devastatingly low. Each time we return they think of us more as Gods.*

*The location of new crystals of piezo-electronic energy is more difficult without equipment. Crystals found are of poor quality and are used up more rapidly before disintegration.*

*From the records, several times in the past, large celestial bodies came close to the planet to alter its inclination, rotation and revolution. Floods, earthquakes, and volcanism, caused continental drift and land bridges formed and then were destroyed.*

*Now I must spend my remaining lifetime teaching all I can to preserve our kind and to lead those who are left to continue the lineage. In some cases, there will be times when you will readily identify the offspring of our people. They'll be more intelligent and have incite, compassion and physical alertness. Not that all the humanoids are not capable, but the gene development is still latent. Mating must be accomplished with the most astute. There will be a time when the great leaders in those distant areas will be in evidence, especially their mental abilities. A time may come when all that is left of our kind will be identified only as great leaders. If we can find the correct crystals to continue suspended animation, we most likely will live to be rescued or be reinforced. Some self-induced suspended animation can be accomplished for short periods without hook-ups, a week to a month in emergencies.*

*Come. It's time to continue our lessons. As you have been told, you must become adept in use of our now useless tools in case we discover new energy sources. It has been our major job to keep notes for those asleep, to ensure that guidance systems are functional for the Supply Pod when it visits this solar system, for it will search out each planet in each solar system looking for signs or several signs. Let's review the maps and charts, Father made on his last venture. I hope he was successful in his endeavors.*

*Some of the people are cooperative and learned trigonometric functions important to our needs. Many groups need to be coerced into constructing astronomical observatories through superstition or belief in a superior being which seems to be the best approach. Some people are suspicious but most submit to the idea that we are what they call a savior or priest or king. Different climates and temperatures seem to have an influence on the mental abilities and reception of such learning.*

*People have changed slightly over the past 20,000 years and have taken on characteristics of environmental niches and genetic inheritances of mixed marriages. Eyes change due to sun reflections and snow glare. Eyes change due to the sun of the tropics, due to high elevations, and to squinting. According to our automatic recorders and warning devices that are solar powered, the ionization layers have increased during the last 100 years and seismic records show volcanism increased proportionately. This planet pulsates, but weather and cosmic energies initiates certain chains of events that initiate some of this atmospheric activity. Prolonged interference of upper levels of the troposphere effects pressure and solar energy on the planet's surface resulting in temperature differences causing a period of glaciation, trapping water, amassing it on the continents thus reducing the sea level. Our outposts in various locations are currently experiencing a variety of weather and climatic conditions of unique degrees. We are at the edge of a tropical zone, whereas clan 12 is practically encased in ice and is limited to periodic transmissions. They must time their rejuvenation period to coincide with weather allowing freedom to dismantle some of their pods to construct mobile land or water vehicles thereby repairing parts to enhance reconstruction of their spacecraft from all the remaining vehicles. Clan 9 and 8 are close enough to 12 to allow the best chances of contact. However, Clan 9 is on an island and Clan 8 is inland, near a large river. We have the best receiving and recording units so we are the relay for all the twelve Clans. That is why we must cycle more frequently and for longer periods to keep contacts, but at the same time build a community in our respective locations. (pyramids and the great wall). Until we lost the two flight pods that survived the initial landing, we had a much better chance of getting the jobs done sooner, but now we are in that state of late glaciations and no pods. There were land bridges where land connected the major continents due to the low sea levels, and were excellent by-ways for transportation via hovercraft.*

*A number of our groups have cohabitated with the locals, resulting in some very intelligent individuals, capable of being trained to the highest degree for their abilities. His mother was very attractive and one of our crew was smitten and succumbed, resulting in a miracle as far as the locals were concerned; I'll locate the electron transfer book for you to read about all the native's traits that will indicate the result of genetic transfer by interbreeding. They, in most cases, will be declared geniuses: brilliant by their standards and unacceptable ideas in the beginning. We have had no communications with any of the clans and I fear for the worse. We may just be the last ones, so*

*we must plan accordingly and decide where would be the best
location to dwell to insure a continuing of some recording for
the possibility of a rescue in years hence. You'll have to be very
strong after I go.*

It was the end of the document!

"My gosh! And that's the end? When will they have the rest
of it translated?" asked Piearce. "According to the information
verbally given by the agents, the rest of the documents are hidden
somewhere else, waiting to be found. Notes by the translators of
this indicates they are so fragile that it may never be possible."

"What of the possibility of finding the space pod they were
using as a dwelling and safe house during their waiting. And they
must have used other buildings while they so-called materialized
for a few years as they acted as Gods or whatever. I'll bet that is
why all the Mayans, Aztec, Stonehenge, and other worldwide
structures exist. Wow!"

"You know what excites me a little? The fact that they mention
the 12 clans. Could they be the twelve lost tribes?"

They exited their honeymoon cave and looked at the stars
with a new meaning, then to the Buick that was parked in the
field below. Aggie snuggled up to him while looking at it saying,
"All this wonderful story and beautiful night because of you, our
marvelous 1932 Buick."

The sky seemed to brighten and they looked up to the peak
above the cave, their honeymoon suite, and she exclaimed, "That
old tree that's been there since we were kids seems to have move
slightly, doesn't it? Or is it the angle at which we are looking at it?"

"In this light, anything is possible, but it sure does look
as though it has turned or we are seeing everything from a
honeymoon point of view." They kissed and entered their
dwelling place. They had left the lights on and the gas lamps were
illuminating the room so that there were no shadows. Piearce
stopped and stared at the drapery he had placed over the tunnel-
like entrance. Aggie looked at him and then gazed in the direction
of drapery.

"What?" There seemed to be a movement and on the floor
was a single sheet of paper, one of the pages of the report. Piearce

turned to Aggie and whispered, "I opened the cavern except for a few feet as a surprise for you. A few animals have used it in the past before I blocked their hole. I'm wondering if they have returned or . . ." as he reached over to retrieve the page of the report, "or if I'm seeing things in lieu of reading this and my creative, wild imagination." She smiled and picked up a flashlight and taking his hand proceeded to the entrance, slid the drapery aside and screamed!

"I mean no harm, do not be alarmed. I have read your report and it is quite accurate. You are not the usual earthlings. Please! Your work clearing the tunnel tripped our safety devices and woke us. Only a few years sooner than expected. You know what this means. It's the beginning of a new era. Our periscope recorder has been tracking you for the past few days. It is located in the old tree atop the crest of this peak. We would be Clan 2 in reference to your report. Someone has done some fine searching and translations. I am very old and do not have more than a year or so left. Perhaps you will consider being my contact to continue the wait?"

They looked at each other with an intensity never before experienced, then to the old figure with a staff in his hand. At that moment another figure appeared behind him saying, "We have made many contacts over the years, but never such an intimate and revealing one as this. Never has anyone been this close to locating our refuge. We have reviewed the past few years of this locale and you are obviously familiar to the area. We mean you no harm. You are intelligent and capable and with a little training will be able to carry on for us." The older man said, "You are thinking that if you don't, we could kill you. Not necessarily so. We could incapacitate you temporarily until we move to another location, but that will not serve our needs. We need you more that you realize. Your team knows that someone like us exists, so why not work to the benefit of all and save many lives and the future."

"No, you are not dreaming," said the second figure in response to Aggies thoughts. "Come with us into the cavern and see our command post and inner workings. In just a few days, we can program you so that your understanding will be like that of Plato, Einstein or others we have previous met."

They ventured into the cavern and into a tunnel just a few feet in length to what looked like a solid stone wall that suddenly slid open and revealed a well-lit room with more gadgets than a museum. It was a spaceship pod. This would be a honeymoon to remember. It was a new beginning. They hoped that if their brains were altered, they wouldn't wipe out the memory of a sister, brother and a 1932 Buick. They also wondered, was Tomas indirectly one of their offspring? They were off to a new beginning.